THE FINAL DEFENSE

THE WAR ON TERROR FOLLOWED HIM HOME

Kenneth Wash

THE FINAL DEFENSE

THE WAR ON TERROR FOLLOWED HIM HOME

BY
KENNETH WASH

Kenneth Wash

WASHBOARD PRODUCTIONS

Copyright © 2010 Kenneth Wash

All rights reserved, including the right to reproduce this book or portions thereof in any form whatsoever. For information, address Washboard Productions, 1041 Trelane Ave. St. Louis, Mo. 63126

Washboard Productions is a non-registered name of a fictitious company and symbol used to denote the personalized video, audio, graphics and writings of Kenneth Wash. Any similarity to any other real or otherwise made up company or logo is strictly coincidental.

Certain names and modifying characteristics have been changed.

This book is a work of fiction. Names, characters, places, and incidents are the product of the author's imagination or are used fictitiously. Any resemblance to actual events, locales, or persons, living or dead, is coincidental.

Cover Design by Washboard Productions/Kenneth Wash.

ISBN-13: 978-0-9851076-2-8

ISBN-10: 0985107626

Revision Three

DEDICATION

In memory of my best friend, Bob.
"The hardest part about any task is just getting started."

Prologue

June 2007, Operation Phantom Thunder
Arasani Apartment Complex, Sadr City, Iraq

Staff Sergeant Villacruze, known by his team as
Sergeant Vee, pulled up the map overlay on his Blue Force Tracker
monitor. He located his platoon less than 100 meters away and
scanned outward toward the town. The Walled City, as it had
become known due to the thousands of barriers that had been
erected, surrounding the city with concrete, had at one time been a
haven for insurgency and terrorism. There were still some pockets
of resistance: out of work Iraqi citizens in need of a quick buck or
small bands of foreign terrorists that had found a place to hole up
to train and rearm.

But this group was different. If the intelligence was correct,
inside this apartment complex was the terrorist cell responsible for
the deaths of hundreds, if not thousands of people. The recent

explosions in Pakistan were just the latest attacks from this group of special criminals.

Like bin Ladin himself, Hamza al-Muhajeer and Leaja bin Masri, the leaders of the Al-Sadr terrorist cell, had proven extremely elusive to capture. Villacruze read the orders again to verify the shoot to kill instructions. As much as his team would like to capture and interrogate these men, the new Iraqi governing council had given strict orders to eliminate them if given the chance. After many false leads and near misses by the Iraqi Army and police, the opportunity had been given to the last of the remaining American forces to finish the job and tonight, Villacruze thought, would be the end of it.

As he rolled the scroll-ball to the right the targets came into view. The red squares, satellite-fed infrared images transposed onto the screen, shuffled about between the two rooms. He changed views to verify that it was the second floor and noted the location of the sentries posted at either stairwell. The latest recon came back with the information that there was no rear exit to worry about and no rear guards, so all of the team members could be used for the assault. He quickly summarized the information and downloaded it to his Portable Battle Story Board. The PBSB refreshed the menu showing that the entry had been stored and gave it a number that referenced the time and location.

Staff Sergeant Villacruze grabbed his weapon, secured his helmet, and sprinted from the commander's mine resistant, ambush protected FPI Cougar toward the location of the teams, calling back to the drivers who were now manning the crew operated remote weapon or CROW.

"You bitches better have these MRAP's ready to roll when we get back. And don't be fallin' asleep or I'll kick your asses while you're dreaming about your mommas." He smiled to himself as he silently ducked around the corner of the brick structure.

"It's me, asshole," he said as he pushed aside the awaiting muzzle of Sergeant Marks' M-4.

Marks dropped his guard, but scanned behind his team leader to ensure that he wasn't being followed. "You could have waited for the challenge, Vee."

Villacruze spoke quietly as he passed by, "Not my fault you're so slow, old man." He stepped over the rubble of the building as Marks pulled in his weapon and fell in behind him.

"You know, I'm only three years older than you. I can still kick your ass," Marks replied.

Vee was quick to answer, nearly whispering his reply, "Yeah, but you have to be able to catch me first. Don't you have arthritis or something?" Villacruze again smiled to himself, feeling smug that he'd bested Marks in another round of bantering. The two men fell silent as they entered the staging area and approached the assault team's commander, Captain Ramsey.

Villacruze held out the PBSB for Ramsey to view. "Sorry it took so long, Sir. I was overlaying the second floor map. I added a door to connect the rooms together here because of the movement between the two." He extended the secondary monitor. The image automatically displayed on both seven-inch LCD screens. "It appears that the rooms are interconnected," Staff Sergeant Villacruze said as he touched the screen with the stylus and the image displayed both ends of the hallway simultaneously. "There are spotters here and here. Looks like small arms. Possibly some frag grenades."

Captain Ramsey took the PBSB from him and studied it for a moment. He looked up, motioning to his teams to form around him for the final brief.

"Listen up, fellas." The two assault teams gathered in a little closer around the six-foot-two, two hundred and fifteen pound commander.

"The mission here is fairly straight forward. We want to go in black, take out the guards and gain surprise. Starks, you're team two. You take the west stairwell. Vincent, you're team three. You have the east side. My team will come up from the middle here."

Ramsey pointed to the locations on the device and held it out for the team leaders to see.

"Intel says that the Arasani Apartment Complex is a safe-house for Hamza al-Muhajeer and Leaja bin Masri, two accomplished terrorist insurgents who escaped a black ops mission in Pakistan. Both are directly linked to, and trained by, Musaq al-Zukar, the leader of the al-Qaeda factions in Iraq. It's believed that the building houses the leaders as well as the bulk of their specialized bomb teams and bomb making equipment." Captain Ramsey shifted his weight to his other foot and looked around at his teams before continuing.

"Our orders, if we make contact with al-Muhajeer or Leaja bin Masri, are 'shoot to kill'. Those orders come from the Iraqi Council, but you and I know that if those two are eliminated we stand to lose tons of information. That's why I would prefer to capture them if possible. Besides, there are civilians within the targeted areas of the complex, so I want you to use your escalation of force procedures. Be discretionary, but use common sense, too. Don't risk the mission. If something doesn't feel right, go in hot. Are there any questions?" With that he held out the PBSB for anyone who wasn't sure of the plan and wanted another look. There were no takers.

Villacruze took the device from his commander and slid the secondary screen back in. He docked the stylus and brought up the touch screen keyboard and typed in the date and time in the entry log. He slipped the unit into his backpack and turned back towards the teams. "The rally point is the Cougars. I'll call the drivers when we're good to go. If everything goes to hell hit your panic buttons and those guys will cover us back to the trucks so we can haul ass."

Captain Ramsey motioned for his men to move out. The teams slipped on their night vision goggles and after a few quick maneuvers, were in a stacked formation against the side of the apartment building. Starks led his squad to the far end of the building, while Staff Sergeant Vincent formed his men up at the opposite corner. Ramsey tapped Villacruze's shoulder telling him to move the team forward and then fell in behind the last squad member. Once the men reached the center of the building Villacruze sent ready messages to the other teams. "Lead team ready."

"Roger. Team two good," Starks replied.

Vincent had moved to the bottom of the stairwell and was ready to move up. "Team three in position."

Inside one of the second floor rooms Hamza al-Muhajeer was discussing the success of their most recent mission. One of their key bomb makers, Makim Jeribi, had just completed training in Iran and was now proficient with explosively formed penetrators or EFPs. Jeribi was explaining to al-Muhajeer the process for aiming the coffee can sized canisters using an off the shelf laser pointer when al-Muhajeer raised a hand, interrupting his bomb maker in mid sentence.

"Excuse me, what you are telling me is very interesting, but I must have a word with Leaja before his son comes back from his mother. It is hard to hold a conversation with him when he is rolling on the floor with his son. Please, forgive me."

The man nodded his head and placed his hand to his heart accepting al-Muhajeer's apology. "Inshallah," he said as al-Muhajeer turned to leave.

Al-Muhajeer responded, "Yes, thank you. Salaam."

He walked across the room and met with Leaja bin Masri. "Leaja, I need to speak with you. Do you think you could take a moment from your family so that we can discuss our mission?"

Leaja bin Masri was tall and thin with wiry hair that mostly remained unkempt. His beard was scruffy and mottled giving him a wild appearance. He was not always serious and it was hard to relate to him at times, but Leaja bin Masri was fearless, very cunning and highly respected as a leader.

"We have plenty of time to discuss work, my brother," Leaja began. "Tonight is for celebration. We must praise Allah for the fine soldiers he has delivered to us." Leaja raised a glass of chai tea to make a toast. "Allah be praised. Death to the aggressors!" Hamza al-Muhajeer raised his cup and waited for the others in the room to do the same. He looked back at Leaja bin Masri who was now holding his younger son in one arm. The boy raised his arms palms upward and responded with the rest of the room, "Praise Allah. Death to the aggressors!" Leaja bin Masri smiled proudly at his youngest son's remark, but Hamza al-Muhajeer saw bin Masri's smile fade suddenly, only to be replaced by a scowl. He looked to where bin Masri was staring so intently across the room when bin Masri put down his son, set his cup of chai aside, and stepped off quickly in the direction of the front door.

Al-Muhajeer called after him, "Leaja, where are you going? We need to talk."

Leaja bin Masri ignored al-Muhajeer and rushed over to a man who was standing at the door talking with one of the other soldiers. He moved quickly toward the soldier, drew his knife, and then pressed himself against the man, pushing him hard against the door. Bin Masri grabbed the man's hair and yanked his head back and to the side, pushing the blade of the knife hard against his throat.

"Why are you standing here? You are supposed to be out there watching out for your brothers," he seethed, putting a little more pressure on the blade and causing a slight cut through the man's skin. "You risk the lives of your fellow soldiers for what, to have chai and tell jokes?"

The guard, startled by bin Masri's sudden action, stuttered as he tried to explain, "I am sorry, Leaja, I only came to use the bathroom. I was only going to be a minute, but, when you began to speak, I stopped to listen. Please forgive me. It will not happen again."

In the darkness outside the apartment, the assault teams moved up the staircase to the second floor. Staff Sergeant Vincent reached the top step and lowered himself to the floor to take a quick look around the staircase wall. The sentry was leaning with his left shoulder against the wall and his back to the stairs, his weapon slung loosely at his side. The smoke from his cigarette drifted around the corner and dissipated near Vincent and his team. Vincent stood, pressed his body flat against the wall, and motioned for his men to wait, then disappeared around the corner out of sight of his team.

Vincent looked through his NVGs, beyond his target toward Starks at the other stairwell. Sergeant Starks used an infrared beacon to signal to Vincent from the end of the long balcony that he was tracking him and that there was no sentry at his end of the building. The thought that the mission was going too smoothly crossed Vincent's mind as he crept up behind his target and quietly swung his arm around his neck and applied pressure to the carotid arteries. The sentry died silently as Vincent pulled him back around the corner and lowered him to the floor, careful not to let the dead man's weapon clatter against the concrete. Vincent keyed his headset and spoke quietly into the microphone, "East sentry down. Team Three ready to move."

Captain Ramsey replied with a simple, "Roger."

Starks again verified that the west sentry was nowhere to be found. He transmitted that there was no contact at the west end of the building and, as best he could tell, the hall was clear.

"Team Two ready," he said quietly.

Ramsey moved his team toward the center of the hall about ten feet from the targeted doorway. The other two assault teams stacked against the wall and continued to move in towards Ramsey.

Suddenly the door opened and light from inside the room splayed out into the hall casting the shadow of a man with a weapon. Ramsey and his men pulled up tight and ready as the guard stepped out and closed the door behind him. He paused for a moment, one hand rubbing on the cut on his neck, waiting for his eyes to readjust to the darkness of the covered balcony.

Villacruze reached out, grabbed the man, and pulled him against the wall. He grabbed the insurgent's free hand and pulled it behind him, then pushed it up hard into his back while holding his other arm tight against his nose and mouth. Starks stepped in front of the closed door and plunged his Ka-Bar upward into the man's chest. The guard's eyes opened wide in surprise. Villacruze quietly lowered the guard's body to the floor as Starks removed his knife, wiped it across the dead man's shirt, and placed it back in the scabbard on his tactical vest.

The noise of the scuffle outside the door drew the attention of Leaja bin Masri. He raised his hand to stop the noise in the room and then called out to the guards stationed outside. He got no answer. He signaled to two of the armed men inside the room and had them stand near the door, then motioned to his family to move into the adjoining room where there were more men armed with Kalashnikov rifles to protect them. Leaja bin Masri tossed an AK-47 to his leader, Hamza al-Muhajeer, and then grabbed his own weapon.

Outside the apartment Captain Ramsey noticed that the voices behind the wall had fallen silent. The door to the apartment to his left opened slightly. Ramsey signaled to his men to cover down.

Vee kicked the door open as one of the terrorists raised his weapon to fire. Sergeant Vincent pulled a grenade from his utility vest and threw it down behind the door and shouted "Grenade out!" to warn his teammates. The grenade bounced to a stop near Makim Jeribi, the bomb maker. Jeribi tried desperately to grab the grenade and throw it back to his attackers, but wasn't fast enough. The grenade blew off his hand as dozens of steel shards tore through his chest and face, the force of the blast hurling him against the wall. He died in seconds not knowing that his actions had saved the lives of his fellow insurgents, at least for the moment.

Vincent's squad entered the room with weapons at the ready, eyes searching for targets, ready to draw aim through the close combat optic sights mounted on their weapons.

The second team moved into the adjoining apartment through the opposite door. Ramsey crouched next to the door as it was forced open. Bullets blasted through the doorway from the inside, striking Sergeant Marks in the chest plate of his I.B.A. His improved battle armor managed to absorb the impact of the rounds, but he had to fall back to recover. As Marks stepped backward into the hallway, the apartment door was slammed shut and the outside walls suddenly exploded into splinters and plaster as a volley of rounds from the AKs inside the apartment was concentrated on the doorway in an attempt to cut off the attacker's point of entry. Ramsey nearly fell backward, tripping over himself as he scrambled away from the opening.

Inside the apartment one of al-Muhajeer's men grabbed him by the arm and forced him toward the back of the room. "Yalla, Yalla!" he yelled, pleading for him to hurry, then motioned for one of the others to get Leaja bin Masri. He knew that al-Muhajeer and bin Masri must escape. He moved his leader to an open window at the back of the room.

Al-Muhajeer surveyed the outside, but saw only the back of a huge fabric banner, a poster of one of the local clerics that covered nearly the entire back of the building. He slung his weapon and yelled for Leaja bin Masri to follow him. Bin Masri signaled for his men to cover his exit and then fell back toward the window. Hamza al-Muhajeer lunged for the fabric hoping that it wouldn't tear under his weight. The fabric held fast, allowing him to grab one of the nylon ropes securing the two-story poster. The rope burned the skin on his hands and fingers causing him to let go, landing hard, but unhurt. He ducked in between two parked vehicles and then moved into the alley behind the apartment complex.

Leaja bin Masri looked around for his wife and sons. He saw his wife briefly through the door of the adjoining apartment as he moved back towards the opened window. His younger son was clinging tightly to her legs screaming violently, his eyes closed. Bin Masri could not see his older son and assumed that he was assisting with the struggle to defend against the aggressors. His wife turned to look at him, her brown eyes wide with fear. She motioned for him to go, knowing that he must survive for the sake of the Jihad.

Suddenly, several grenades and flash-bangs exploded and the room next to his was filled with flames, noise, smoke and debris. Bin Masri turned away from the blast debris and dust coming through the door. He managed to look back one more time as he moved toward the window. He could no longer see his wife or child and assumed the worst. The sound of automatic gunfire filled the apartment as the words "room clear" were broadcast for the sake of the American team that had just entered into the other side of the apartment, defeating those who resisted their entry, and made their way carefully, scanning for booby traps or other explosives, to the adjoining doorway.

Captain Ramsey and Starks' squads were still trying to enter the apartment. They exchanged small arms gunfire and then had to fall back to regroup. Ramsey leaped over his men to where his SAW Gunner was crouched with his back to the wall, waiting to get through the door and get into the fight. He pulled at the gunner's tactical vest and began yelling for him to move. "What the hell are you doing, Mac, waiting for an invitation? Get your ass in that doorway and give us some cover!"

Specialist McClain jumped up and ran around the squad, then, without hesitation, threw himself to the floor. The muzzle of his squad assault weapon forced the bullet-riddled door open as the

SAW belched out a steady stream of tracer rounds that tore through flesh and bone, leaving a phosphorescent trail as the bullets tumbled and spun through the air to their targets.

Ramsey and his team entered the room between the machine gun bursts, fighting their way through the doorway. The terrorists dropped to the floor or pitched backward as Ramsey and his well-trained assault team selected their targets and fired with deadly accuracy, aiming through their close combat optical sights.

Through the intense battle bin Masri moved back against the wall near the window, but could not manage to get out. The terrorist leader screamed for the lone soldier aiding his escape to cover him and pushed the man toward the tactical team that was descending upon him. In a last ditch effort to ensure bin Masri's escape the man pulled his weapon up and began to fire blindly from behind the protection of the wall. He pleaded to his God for strength, yelling loudly as he stepped out into the open and began to spray the attackers with rounds from his assault rifle.

The plaster on the wall next to Ramsey exploded as the burst of rounds from the AK-47 zipped past their target, missing him by inches. Ramsey dropped to one knee and raised his weapon, placing the red holographic dot in his optic sight at center mass of his target. He fired a three round burst into the chest and neck of his attacker, dropping the last obstacle between his team and Leaja bin Masri.

As his last man fell to the floor in front of him, bin Masri trained his weapon on the looming figure of Captain Ramsey, who was now rushing toward him at full speed.

Ramsey grabbed the muzzle of bin Masri's weapon and forced it upward with his left hand. He let his M-4 hang low on the combat sling and advanced around the corner to face his enemy. Ramsey grabbed bin Masri by the throat and forced his back against the splintered wooden frame of the window. Bin Masri struggled, but could not break free from the American's vise-like grip on his throat.

Sergeant Villacruze moved in to help his team leader, who was now locked in close quarters combat. Leaja bin Masri detected the movement to his right and fired his weapon. The burst caused Villacruze to back down and Ramsey to loosen his grip on the hot AK-47's barrel.

Regaining control of his weapon, bin Masri yanked the barrel of the AK down and fired at near point blank range at Ramsey. The first of the seven-point-six-two-millimeter rounds shattered the lowest ceramic and kevlar hybrid "sappy" plate of Ramsey's improved battle armor. The successive rounds followed the path through the penetrated I.B.A side plate and tore through Ramsey's left side causing sudden, incredible, searing pain. Ramsey fell hard against the wall in a spray of blood and tissue. In the brief reprieve, bin Masri lunged through the open window.

The terrorist managed to grab the tapestry, but the force of his downward momentum caused the twenty-foot long fabric to rip away from its mountings. Bin Masri fell hard and landed on top of a vehicle nearly two stories below. He rolled through a cloud of dust and broken glass, off the car and onto the gravel and asphalt of the road and painfully maneuvered between the parked cars, trying to catch his breath after having the wind knocked out of him.

Despite the intense pain, Ramsey got to his feet and struggled to the window. He groaned loudly as he leaned against the crumbling plaster and wood frame and scanned the shadows of the pre-dawn darkness below. He had lost his night vision optics sometime during the struggle and cursed when he couldn't see either of the two terrorists.

Ramsey turned to Staff Sergeant Villacruze. He was pissed. It showed through his obvious pain. "What the hell, Vee? You said there was no rear exit!"

He unsnapped his chinstrap and threw his helmet to the floor. Grimacing and bending over he growled at Villacruze, "Go! Get down there and find that son of a bitch!"

Villacruze pushed Marks toward the door and disappeared, sprinting out of the apartment and down the stairs with Marks directly behind him.

Ramsey grasped the velcro fasteners of his I.B.A, pulled it open and shook the heavy vest, along with any gear attached to it, off of his shoulders. He instantly felt lighter as the weight of the vest fell away, but the weight of the I.B.A was replaced with the weight of concern when he placed first three, then all four fingers through the hole in his blood soaked combat shirt and felt the damaged, lacerated skin and muscle of his wound.

Sergeant Vincent stepped out of the grey-white smoke and plaster dust of the adjacent apartment, waving the particles of dust out of his face, coughing and wiping at his eyes. He saw the look of pain and lack of color on Captain Ramsey's face and was just about to ask if he was ok when Ramsey's knees buckled and he collapsed to the floor.

Bin Masri scrambled to his feet. He was shaken and bleeding from the broken glass, but surprisingly not seriously injured. He looked around for his weapon and found it close to one of the parked vehicles. As he reached down to pick it up he noticed the nametag from Ramsey's I.B.A. It was stuck between the barrel and handgrip. He must have pulled the velcro tag from Ramsey's armor during the struggle. He read the name, thinking about his murdered wife and children.

Al-Muhajeer called out from the extreme darkness of the alley for bin Masri to move. Leaja bin Masri took a quick look around and then rushed toward al-Muhajeer. Bullets hit the parked cars and the dirt at their feet as the two men made their escape while exchanging gunfire with the Americans.

Al-Muhajeer was the first to make it to the next corner where the alley ended at one of the dimly lit solar streetlights installed by the infidels. He ran into the street and fired his AK-47 in the air halting a small sedan and yelled for the driver to get out of the vehicle. Bin Masri moved to the opposite side of the vehicle and screamed at the woman in the passenger seat to move out of the way.

Villacruze and Sergeant Marks heard the gunfire erupt as they scrambled down the two flights of stairs and around the building in an attempt to catch the fleeing insurgents. After reaching the end of the sewage filled alley, Villacruze slammed against a metal trash dumpster and took aim at al-Muhajeer, but lost his shot when the owner of the hijacked car got in the way.

Marks fell into position next to Villacruze. He yelled for bin Masri to stop and fired a three round burst from his M-4. The rounds sped toward his target barely missing the man, shattering the back glass and right rear side glass out of the door. The gunfire and flying glass startled bin Masri who fired blindly back toward the two soldiers striking only the metal dumpster. He yanked the screaming woman from the car, pushed her to the road, and jumped into her seat as al-Muhajeer smashed the accelerator to the floor and sped off with bin Masri still half out of the car.

The two soldiers pulled back their weapons and scanned the area to ensure that the bursts from Marks' weapon that had shattered the windows of the vehicle hadn't caused any other damage to anything or, more importantly, hurt any civilians in the area. The man who had been driving the car helped the woman back to her feet. Both appeared to be unhurt.

Satisfied, Marks and Villacruze placed their weapons on safe and quietly disappeared back into the alley. With Sergeant Marks guarding the rear, they headed back to the two-story building that was now bathed in the reddish haze of a new morning. The warriors picked up their pace when they saw their captain outside the apartment complex being treated by the medic.

"We lost our shot, Sir. You ok?" Sergeant Villacruze asked. He looked at the medic trying to gauge the severity of the injury.

Sergeant Simmons, the medic, looked concerned. She shook her head indicating that it didn't look good.

"I'll be fine. My side hurts like hell and I can't stand without falling over, but I'll be ok. Doc's looking after me." Ramsey winced noticeably as the medic literally pinned his skin out of the way so she could look at the wound more closely.

Simmons cleaned inside the wound, flushing out bits of plaster and bone with saline, then began closing the skin to apply a temporary bandage. "We need to get you out of here, Sir. You have severe damage to muscle, tendons and tissue on your left side. I've ordered a medevac. They're inbound and will be here in a few minutes."

Ramsey was polite as usual thanking the medic for her time and expertise. He then turned his attention to his lead sergeant.

"Vee, get the others and then get back to the base. We need to get on these guys and get them under control."

Ramsey tried to turn toward the building, but stopped about half way due to the intense pain. Instead, he motioned with a nod of his head.

"Looks like there's a lot of stuff up there. Let me know the numbers after you do the count. Tell the guys that I'm proud of them and I'll see them back at the base."

"You got it, Sir." Staff Sergeant Villacruze turned to Marks. "C'mon Numb-nuts, we got an inventory to do."

Sergeant Marks just shook his head. "You hear what I've got to put up with, Sir?" Marks pointedly asked the Commander.

"What can I say, Marks? You're the only guy he will trust with his back. Must mean something." Ramsey grimaced as he replied.

Marks gave a quick salute and smiled, "Yes, Sir. Take care, Sir." He ran off to join Villacruze as the sound of the medevac helicopter became loud enough that they could make out its direction. Captain Ramsey watched his men as they entered the building. They were good troops. They would be all right until he got back.

Several miles away the sedan carrying the two insurgents sped down the dirt and gravel road passing every vehicle it came up behind. Al-Muhajeer recklessly rounded the next curve and slammed the accelerator to the floor again. He nervously watched the sky for any sign of helicopters, or worse, the unmanned aerial drones that were now being controlled by the Americans at their company levels.

He looked at the man bent over in the seat next to him as he had been since they had escaped. His head was buried in his hands; one hand clenched tightly, a piece of material protruding from his fist. "What is that you are holding?" al-Muhajeer asked finally.

Bin Masri raised his head enough to look at al-Muhajeer. He stared at him as he rested his head on his right hand and allowed his left to fall across his leg, opening his clenched fist to expose the full length of the fabric.

"What is that Leaja?" al-Muhajeer asked again.

Bin Masri sat upright, picked the nametag from his left hand and held it out to read the name on the tag. "Ramsey" he said with a scowl. He held it out for al-Muhajeer to see.

"It is the nametag from the man I was fighting. The one who is responsible for the death of my wife and of my two sons." He crumpled the tag and stuck it into his pocket. "It is the name of the man I am going to kill."

CHAPTER 1

MISTRUST
MOSCOW, RUSSIA, PRESENT DAY

THE older of the two men leaned across the table and lifted the candle to light his smoke. The glow from the candle lent an odd look to the man's face. He was rugged and ancient looking, much like the inn where the transaction was taking place. Bin Masri had not been in Russia before. In fact, he thought to himself, he had never been out of his own country of Iraq until now. Except, he remembered, as a child soldier in the war fought against Iran.

"Trust me, Leaja, as I told your friend Ahmed, you are getting what is advertised. Your money has been well spent on a quality product."

Leaja bin Masri glared at the man who sat across from him. He had a hard time trusting the ex-Soviet patriot and studied the man for a brief moment.

"For your sake, General, it better work," bin Masri threatened. "I can remember that the quality of your equipment was very poor.

When the Americans supported our cause against Iran your vehicles were broken and rusted. Hamza al-Muhajeer does not like pissing away his money."

"Ah, yes, the forgotten war. Our leaders were broken and rusted as well then. Besides, the Iranians are better suited for camels than mechanized equipment. The camels can take care of themselves. There is no dipstick or batteries to check." Dmitri Gregorov smiled broadly showing his crooked yellow teeth.

"You need not worry. It was removed from one of the newer arsenals near Iskeive. The warhead has never been attached to a rocket." Gregorov fell back against the padded booth exhaling a cloud of smoke. He thought for a moment, then asked blatantly, "How are you going to get it into the United States?"

"That is none of your concern," bin Masri snapped, and with that began to stand. Gregorov leaned across the table and grabbed his arm, keeping him from rising. Leaja bin Masri's men moved forward, followed by Gregorov's.

"Please, sit back down." The Russian motioned with his cigarette for the man to sit down again, and then to his men, waving them back into a less tense posture. Leaja bin Masri shook off the ex-Soviet's hold and relaxed back into his seat.

Gregorov took the last drag from his smoke and smashed it out in the thick glass ashtray at the center of the table. "I am sorry, but I disagree. It is my concern." He exhaled the smoke before continuing, "It is my concern that you do not get caught and that the components are not traced back to my organization, here or in the United States."

Gregorov downed the last of his drink and spun the glass as he set it onto the table. With his head down he looked through his eyebrows at bin Masri and then raised his head, leaned forward and spoke quietly, "I can help you get the warhead into the country, undetected, for a fee of course."

Gregorov motioned to his palm with his index finger. "For two million additional dollars, I can get the warhead into Texas, U.S.A.

Then, it will be up to you to get your prize where you want it and do whatever it is you will be doing. As you said, that is none of my concern." He waved his hand in a gesture that gave the appearance of indifference.

"And if I agree to your offer, when will the warhead arrive? Our mission begins in less than one month." Leaja opened the calendar application and poked at the screen of his smart phone to mark the date.

"Today is the sixth," Gregorov began, "Your package will arrive in Mexico by the tenth. From there the device can be transported by helicopter to a town just inside Texas, a small town very close to the border of Mexico. If everything goes well you will have your device by the thirteenth."

Gregorov sounded like a salesman closing a deal. "You can not get that kind of service even from the UPS. What a deal you are getting." His large smile came back and then disappeared. "What is wrong, Leaja? Where is your sense of humor?"

This time bin Masri stood without interruption. "Believe me, I will be smiling when the delivery is made. You will have one million of the money in a few days. Then, when the bomb is delivered, you will get the rest. Until then, I will be worried that you have only stolen our money."

General Gregorov slapped the table with his hands and laughed loudly. "I am a business man, not a thief. This is business." His grin faded as he pulled away his glasses. "You will have your bomb on the thirteenth. Now, go back to your boss like a good boy and tell him what a great bargain you got today. Hamza al-Muhajeer will be happy. Trust me." Gregorov's grin returned.

Leaja bin Masri turned his back on the man, motioning for his men to follow, and then walked out into the cold Russian night.

Gregorov looked at the time on his phone and swiped a finger across its glass surface to scroll through his contacts, stopping on the appropriate entry and touching the icon to begin the call. The phone played through part of a musical ring-tone, and then abruptly quit playing when a female voice spoke quietly. "Hello?"

Six thousand miles away Nikki Sidorova pulled the phone away from her ear, grimacing, as she heard Gregorov's too loud, too early in the morning voice.

"Hello, Nikki, or maybe, I should say good morning. It is early there, isn't it?"

Nikki looked at her clock. "Yes, too early. Why are you calling me at five o'clock in the morning?"

"Perhaps I just wanted to hear your voice. It is like a bird singing." She couldn't see the smile on Dmitri's face.

"Not funny, Dmitri." She searched her memory. "You are the one who said my voice was too soft. Not the voice of a leader. Remember? Now, what is it you want? I would like to get back to sleep."

Gregorov became serious again. "Tell your, ah, boyfriend, that I am still waiting for him to fulfill his end of our transaction. Explain to him that I am not a patient man and that I have already given him more time and money than was agreed upon. Tell him he has two days. Make sure he understands. Good night, Nikki."

With that the phone went dead. "Good night, Dmitri," Nikki said to nobody as she threw her phone to the floor and headed for the shower.

CHAPTER 2
SALVAGE

MARK BEIRMAN'S phone buzzed in his pocket. He set down his toolbox and fumbled to retrieve it before the buzzing stopped. He looked at the name of the caller as he flipped open the phone, wishing instead that he had ignored it.

"Hello, Marcus, how are you today?" The voice was soft and alluring.

The airman looked around nervously. "What do you want, Nikki? I'm at the Air Base. You're not supposed to call me here."

"Dmitri is asking about what you promised to deliver over a week ago. He wants to be sure that you haven't changed your mind." The woman's voice was still as seductive as it had been the first time they'd spoken.

"I don't see that I have much of a choice. Most of the money is gone, and I still have more debt than I care to think about, so I need to finish the job. There has been a lot of concern about the Black Hawk and the fact that it has been down for such a long time. The maintenance inspectors were reviewing the paperwork yesterday and are just now deciding to classify the bird as a total loss. We should be able to start removing the classified components today."

"What about the transponder, will you have it today as well?" Nikki's voice was soft and sexy.

"Look, Nikki, you are getting too specific over the phone. I will deliver it tonight. I'm hanging up now." Mark Beirman closed his cell and threw it in his pocket. He walked into the hanger that housed his "hanger-queen" and set his toolbox on a crate near the front of the bird.

The Kevlar Armored Helicopter was a marvel. It had been hit twice by surface to air missiles and taken enough fire to kill all of the civilian contractors on board. The pilot and copilot, both skilled Warrant Officers, had been hit several times, but had managed to bring the aircraft back to the base with the smallest section of a rear rotor that Beirman had ever seen. The bird was a total loss but had been the subject of investigations by the Department of Defense, the FAA, and the manufacturer due to its ability to remain airborne and controllable with such extensive damage. The fact that the two Army pilots worked their asses off and kept their heads never seemed to be part of the equation. If it weren't for the quality of the pilots, the bird would have been just another pile of debris in the middle of Baghdad.

He opened his toolbox and got out the required tools to remove the lower panel of the communications equipment compartment. He carefully removed the panel hoping that the equipment behind it was not damaged from the gunfire or the near direct missile strikes. He found the Blue Force tracking array and removed the yellow oval shaped antennae. He followed the wires around and found the communications control module and removed it also. Within a few moments he had the two components that he intended to sell to Nikki's boss, Dmitri, or the highest bidder. The Blue Force Tracker was recent technology that was not included in their agreement. Mark Beirman figured it would be worth enough money to someone that he could easily retire. Both pieces would fit into his toolbox without a problem. The transponder would be a different story.

The Airman knew that what he was doing was wrong and really didn't care. His only concern was with getting caught. What his buyer did with the merchandise was none of his business, and he intended to stay as far away from that information as possible. He did wonder why anyone would need a transponder from a Black Hawk. Even if the folks working the radar thought, for instance, that a Cessna 380 was a Black Hawk, the transponder identification number would probably flag the image as a retired or destroyed vehicle. He figured that by the time Dmitri, Nikki, or whoever, figured that out, he'd have his money and be long gone, end of story.

Airman Beirman reinstalled the panel and snugged down the retainers. He closed his toolbox and headed toward the service door. As he opened the door, Sergeant Atkins, his immediate supervisor, came in.

"Hey, there you are, Mark. I figured I would find you here. You really need to think about doing something other than working on these birds. There is more to life than turning wrenches and testing electronics you know."

Mark tried not to appear nervous. "Yeah, well I wanted to check the tail shaft bolts on Alpha Six-One. We replaced the carrier support bearings yesterday, and I woke up this morning not sure that I had tightened them." He paused for a second to think. "You ever do that, Sarge? You ever dream about not tightening something down or leaving out a cotter pin and wake up in a sweat wondering about it?"

Atkins smiled as he replied, "Oh yeah, too many times, but I found out a long time ago that the way to cure that was to step away from your toolbox for awhile. You know, take a break." Atkins smiled again. "Oh, but today's not that day. I just got word to strip down Four-Ten. It's going to the yard as scrap. Salvage what you can and turn it in. Otherwise, tag it for destruction. Either way we need documents."

This time it was the airman's turn to smile. "Finally, we can free up that hole. But, I have a full plate today with two other birds that are going out on mission for a couple days. We'll have to tear in to Four-Ten afterward. You mind if I get an early start tonight? I'll catch dinner and come back to get things started. I may be able to get all the secure shit out, get it tagged and secured. Jenkins and Peters can rip into the mechanicals tomorrow. I told them to save the rotor links. We just replaced those before this happened. It took us weeks to get them."

Mark Beirman was one of Sergeant Atkins' best workers and he was worried that the man worked too much. Atkins suddenly felt guilty for taking advantage of Beirman's strong work ethic. Atkins stared at the airman for a moment before answering, "Alright, do that, but once you get the sensitive items secured or prepped for destruction I want you to stop and take a few days off. Those other guys can handle the rest of the dismantling. Are we in agreement?"

"You got it, Sarge. When I get finished tonight I'll jump on my bike and you won't see me again for quite a while. Hell, you never know, I might just keep on going." Beirman thought to himself that at least he wasn't lying to the guy.

Daryl Atkins laughed. "Hell, if I didn't know you as well as I do I might be worried, Mark. You just make sure you don't kill yourself on that motorcycle. You'd be a hard one to replace. I might even miss you." The Sergeant looked around and then in a quiet voice said, "I'll tell you what, Mark. I'll go fill out your four day pass request, get the old man to sign off on it, grab some beer and meet you back down here later. We can shoot the shit and remove nuts and bolts till the cows come home. I got nothing going on tomorrow. Masterson has the duty shift."

Mark Beirman didn't need his boss hanging around while he tried to remove and store the transponder. He planned to swap it with one from a crash that should have been destroyed, but was still sitting in a pile of junk mechanicals. "That's pretty tempting, but if I get to talking and drinking a beer or two I won't get everything I want done and will have to be back here to finish tomorrow. Besides, I like working late alone. It gives me my quiet time."

Atkins feigned a look of discontent, but then smiled and said, "All right then, Mark, I'll just go find some other poor soul to talk to death. You work your fingers to the bone if you want. I'll leave your pass paperwork with the Duty Officer. If something changes I'll give you a call." With that the Sergeant turned to leave, but stopped just short of the door.

"One more thing, Mark. Make sure you sign out when you take off tomorrow morning. And, give them a number and an address so I can find you just in case you do fall off the face of the earth like you threatened." He smiled at the airman as he closed the door behind him.

Mark Beirman stared at the closed door then muttered to himself, "That wasn't a threat, asshole".

CHAPTER 3

DELIVERY

THE Harley rounded the last corner and stopped at the traffic light about a half block away from the hotel. Mark Beirman thought about what he was going to do. The payoff was excellent, but he couldn't help thinking about how this would make him a traitor to his country.

Nikki would be waiting for him with the money. He had tried to get two million out of the deal, but her boss, Dmitri, refused to exceed one and a half million. Given the fact that the original deal was only for five hundred thousand and the fact that he had already been paid and had spent the first two hundred and fifty thousand he looked at the deal as a good one. He knew that it would set him up for the rest of his life if he didn't get stupid and blow it all.

He thought about Nikki and wondered if the excitement she'd displayed over the phone was genuine. He had asked her to leave the country with him and she'd agreed. He asked if she was really interested in him or if it was all part of the plan to get him under control. She said she was. Maybe now they could get their relationship together. He told himself that with the money he could make a good life with her.

The light turned green and the airman pulled down the street and into the parking lot. He passed the office and drove around to the back of the building. He parked his bike, opened the compartments on either side of the rear wheel and removed the canvas bags that held the merchandise. He looked up to the second floor and saw Nikki looking back at him through the raised venetian blinds. She was wearing a short business skirt and a blouse that looked perfect on her tall, slender body. She unfastened the first of the buttons on the blouse and smiled wickedly as she lowered the blinds to the sill.

Beirman walked up the steps and found the door to the hotel room. He opened the door to find the room dark with the exception of the light streaming through the slats of the lowered blinds. He set down the bags as Nikki walked out of the shadows. The light from the blinds created horizontal bars of light that contoured to the bare upper torso of the Russian agent.

The airman's eyes searched through the darkness putting together the full picture of her near naked body. The lowest beam of light started just below the bottom of the frilled edging on her panties and reappeared in intermittent bars of light illuminating only parts of her body. He raised his gaze, starting at the "v" cut waist of her panties and began taking in each bit of her nearly six foot tall body. He followed the contoured bands of light around her flat stomach and her perfect belly button. He moved upward where the next source of light revealed her breasts. They were small, but perfectly formed. His gaze moved on to shoulders that were wide and strong supporting a slender neck that was highlighted by short-cropped auburn hair.

Nikki walked towards him and took his hands in hers. Silently, she leaned forward and kissed him, drawing down on his lower lip with a gentle suction. She led him toward her, slowly backing over to a large chair, and sat on the edge of the cushion pulling him down as she reclined against the chair back. She guided his hands to her breasts and gently squeezed her hand over his causing him to massage her and rub her erect nipples. She gently maneuvered him down for his performance. He slid his hands down from her breasts and struggled to remove his shirt as she wrapped her legs over his shoulders and slid even further down into the softness of the chair watching the man as he moved his arms around and behind her to bring her closer to him.

For more than an hour the two bodies entwined themselves with passion until both were satisfied more than once. Nikki sat up from his chest, her green eyes falling perfectly into the lowest band of light. He stared at her, taking in the sight of her body and studying the depth of her eyes and thought how these moments of passion were only just beginning.

For the moment all thoughts of his treasonous actions escaped him. There was no guilt, no frustration of right and wrong. He remained on the floor as the woman rose and walked away to the other room. He watched her disappear and then got up and pulled his clothing from the pile they were in, drew on his briefs and trousers and waited for Nikki's return. He was anxious to see the money, the reward for his disservice to his homeland.

When she appeared again she was standing close to the door opening. "You are a very good lover, Airman Beirman." She smiled playfully. "I am not sure that I will ever again be able to find someone with your...special skills. You truly know how to satisfy me. It is a shame that we will not be able to live the life you suggested."

Mark Beirman looked quizzically at the woman. "Why? What are you talking about? I thought we were going to leave the country together." His voice trailed off when the silenced pistol came into view.

"I am afraid that I cannot do that, Airman Beirman. Unlike you, I am not a traitor to my country."

She pulled the trigger twice and watched the man fall backward to the floor. She gathered her things and quickly dressed. After a quick clean up, she picked up the canvas bags and walked out the door, locking it behind her.

CHAPTER 4

TRANSPORT

THE Mi24E HIND helicopter flew low over the Gulf. The pilot, Mikael Yolokov, was skilled in evasive maneuvering and pulled in closer to the Texas shoreline as he neared the Mexican border. He leaned over to the console of the blue force tracker and flipped the power switch on. The touchscreen LCD monitor instantly came to life and the system began to perform its self-test and calibration.

Yolokov pulled back on the collective and twisted the throttle bringing the bird up from the close proximity of the water. He looked to his right to verify that he was close to the Coast Guard base and upon seeing the communications tower in the distance settled in at a cruising altitude of two thousand feet. The Blue Force tracker suddenly chimed and the words "Signal Acquired" were displayed in the menu bar at the top. A graphical representation of the Coast Guard building and the icon for the tower showed on the center of the display. A translucent rectangular box appeared on the screen and the identifying role name for the newly installed transponder populated the fill.

The radio suddenly came to life after several hours of total silence. "November Delta One Five One Zero, this is Coast Guard Base Tango two three. Over."

"Coast Guard Base this is November Delta One Five One Zero. Go ahead. Over." The pilot mentally crossed his fingers and hoped that what he thought was near perfect English, was good enough for the tower.

"Five One Zero, be advised. I do not have a track for you. Where did your flight originate? Over." The operator scanned his identifier and waited for his answer. His system showed the aircraft hangared at PCN, Pensacola Naval Air Station.

"Roger Base, departure from Papa Charlie November. Destination is Homeland Seven. Over."

The operator knew the abbreviation for the Homeland Defense Base Station and took the information as correct. "Good copy Five One Zero. You shake out all the cobwebs yet?"

The Russian wasn't sure about what he had just heard. He was fluent in English, but the slang could catch him off guard. "Say again last transmission, your message was weak and garbled. Over."

"I'm just sayin' that your bird's been hangared so long you must have a lot of cobwebs to blow out. You know, how's she flying?" The tower operator found his coffee cup and took a drink waiting for the response.

"Yeah, copy that, Base, flying straight and true. Just had a complete overhaul, so I'm keeping it kind of low just in case the maintenance guys screwed up. I don't want to splash too hard." He tried to sound like a good ol' boy.

"Ha, right. Not likely. It's hard to do anything wrong on a Black Hawk. They are pretty easy to maintain." The operator paused for a moment for another sip looking over the information for the helicopter he was tracking. "Don't you Border Patrol folks buy anything new? Seems like everything you got is fifteen to twenty years old."

The Russian was tired of talking. He didn't like the way the Americans wanted to banter back and forth over the radio. He wanted to end the conversation. "We like to think of them as battle hardened. Base, be advised, I will be switching radio frequencies now. It's been nice talking to you."

"Roger, Five Zero, I'll keep watch to the next tower, then you're on your own. Good luck with your bird. Hope you know how to swim just in case. Coast Guard Base, Out."

The pilot turned his COM set to internal, dropped his American accent, and spoke into his microphone. "We are about twenty minutes out. We should arrive right at zero two three zero. I will drop you and your cargo and then I must leave before the Coast Guard figures out that we are not who they think we are."

Hamza al-Muhajeer flipped the lever on his set. "Yes, that is good news." He twisted around to look out the window. He could no longer see the reflection of the moon on the water and assumed that they must be flying over Texas. This was the first time he had been assigned a mission in the country of the infidels. He was proud to be selected to lead such a mission. He wondered how the Americans would react to such a large attack. The bomb that they would build with the Soviet era warhead would kill ten times more than the attack on the towers. Still, the attack on the World Trade Center was hailed as the most successful operation in the existence of al-Qaeda.

So far, everything was going smoothly. If the helicopter could make it to its destination without being detected, all they would have to do was load the warhead in the truck and move it to the warehouse in Missouri. The final assembly would take place in St. Louis. Then, depending on his final orders, he would move the bomb one more time to Washington D.C. He thought about Allah's soldiers and vowed once again that he would complete the mission that had left his brothers dead on the field in Pennsylvania. He would make their deaths worth something after all.

Hamza al-Muhajeer felt his ears pop. They were descending. It would not be much longer. The landing gear being lowered from the belly of the HIND helicopter made a loud screech and then clunked to a stop. Hamza looked to the ground and could see only desert below. The shadows cast by the moon were long, exaggerating the height of the hills and cacti that littered the desert floor.

The helicopter dropped quickly then hovered above the ground blowing sand and debris in a circle marking a target for the bird to settle onto. Outside, men who were to unload the warhead waited, covering their faces with bandanas and shirtsleeves to avoid breathing the sand and dust from the rotor wash.

Lieutenant Harrison reviewed the transcripts of the last conversation. He still wasn't sure why that helicopter was not there one minute and then suddenly showed up the next. The Coast Guard Base had recently been outfitted with millions of dollars worth of new equipment. Some of it sat unused waiting for another program, the T2T Program, or whatever they were calling it, to ramp up. In the meantime the Department of Homeland Security and the CIA had been swarming over the small coastal base training the Coast Guard on the equipment they would be using.

His partner, Sergeant Dan Thompson, had had some training on the new systems, so Harrison turned to him for assistance. "Hey, Thompson, back up your RADAR and play it back from, let's say, zero-one-thirty-five and zero-one-fifty. Let me know if you have anything unusual."

Thompson rolled over to the panel and typed a few key commands. The large wall mounted LCD screen came to life showing a picture nearly identical to the live screen to its right.

"What exactly are we looking for? I've been tracking this all night and didn't see anything unusual."

Harrison watched. "Look real closely at about zero-one-forty and fifteen. I made contact with an aircraft on the Blue Force Tracker at that time, but it was odd that we didn't see it before that. Like he just turned the system on or something." He looked at the time track. Zero-one-thirty-eight, thirty-nine. "Slow it down some."

Sergeant Thompson changed the playback speed. "What kind of aircraft was it?"

"A Black Hawk. I punched in the numbers. I'm waiting on the response. According to our info it has been out of service for over a year and was in OIF Service before that. Wait, what was that?"

Thompson was sitting forward. "I saw it too. Hang on." He stopped the track and rolled it backward slowly. A nearly undetectable blip showed up at about nine hundred feet.

"Can you go lower on the height?" Harrison asked, now standing in front of the monitor.

"Give me a second. I'm not too sure how this thing works other than straight up monitoring." Thompson zoomed in and then found that by moving the trackball downward, he could get a view down to five hundred feet above sea level. The blip became an image, but lasted only a couple seconds.

"There must be better terrain clearance in that area. You can't see that low anywhere else. Just here between zero-one- thirty-nine-ten and zero-one-thirty-nine-thirteen."

"What is that?" Thompson asked, scrunching up his face and lifting away his glasses for a closer look. "It's not a Black Hawk. Look at the rotor signature and the fuselage reflection." Thompson traced the image with his now folded glasses, "It's bigger than a Black Hawk, fatter or something."

The Lieutenant grimaced. "Damn, I didn't catch that, even at two thousand."

Thompson scrolled forward until the aircraft's image was clear and then slowed the recording down even further, scrolling it forward one frame at a time. "Hold on, I'm gonna see what happens when I copy it and paste it into the search program."

He cropped the image and copied it to the desktop. Once the search program opened, he placed the image on the right of a split screen and pressed "Find Match from Library." The system flashed through images and stopped within two seconds.

"Shit! That was fast," Thompson marveled. The two men stared at the screen in disbelief.

The Lieutenant spoke first. "An Mi24 Hind? What the hell is that thing doing in our airspace?"

Thompson split the screen to overlap the images. "Uh, and that ain't all. Look here. See the difference between this wing or aileron and that one?" He put down his glasses and circled the area with his paint pen.

"Yeah, it's different. What is it?" Harrison asked.

Thompson made another circle around the image and sat back deep into his chair. "Sir, that is some bad shit right there. Those are missiles. That helicopter is armed with missiles."

Lieutenant Harrison stood upright. "Shit! Wake Gomez. We need to get Homeland Security on the phone now."

Hamza al-Muhajeer jumped down from the helicopter squinting to see through the dust and blown sand. He reached back to grab his duffel and holster when the helicopter's radio suddenly screamed to life. Al-Muhajeer could not make out what was being transmitted, but knew it couldn't be good. The radio was drowned out by the sound of the aircraft's engine and spinning rotor.

Yolokov, the pilot, listened through his headset. "November-Delta-five-one-zero, come in over." The pilot looked at the display of the Blue Force Tracker. Two aircraft were moving in his direction. The radio repeated the call for the pilot to answer, but the pilot ignored the caller.

"Muhajeer, you must hurry. There are aircraft heading this direction! Unload the warhead. Hurry!"

Hamza al-Muhajeer ran to the cargo door and opened both doors motioning for his men, who, for some reason, were not moving. "Come now! Help me! Hurry!" Four men ran forward while a jeep backed up to the helicopter. Once al-Muhajeer saw that the men had the device in the jeep, he shut the cargo doors. The pilot took that as the sign that they were clear and gunned the engine for takeoff.

The turbulent winds were incredible. The huge five-blade rotor caused the desert sand to swirl and shoot through the air like a swarm of bees stinging at the flesh of the terrorists. Al-Muhajeer ducked behind the jeep to avoid the blasting sand and pulled his jacket over his head to protect his face. He could not protect his hands from being pelted with the granules of sand. They stung fiercely as if they were on fire. He pulled his arms tight against his ears in an attempt to stop the horrible noise of the Russian built aircraft as it rose from the desert. Eventually the aircraft was up and heading southeast toward the Gulf of Mexico.

The pilot pushed the aircraft for all it was worth dropping low into the Rio Grande Valley. The Blue Force Tracker showed that the two American aircraft were hot on his tail. The radio spat orders telling the pilot that he was in violation of the border agreement and that he should comply with all directions and head to the closest airfield to land his craft. He had air-to-air missiles but did not want to light them up unless he was sure he would not escape. He needed to lure the Americans as far away from the landing zone as possible.

The lead pilot of the two Border Protection Patrol Black Hawks, CW4 Robert Hunt, closed in quickly. He pulled up and to the left putting his bird between the fleeing aircraft and his wingman's bird. The hills surrounding them suddenly disappeared and the ocean came into full view. The Mi24 banked hard right and headed south. Hunt estimated they were about eight miles out over the gulf, far enough that he could take a shot at the fleeing Russian helicopter. With no collateral targets to worry about, he fired what would be the first and last of the warning shots given to the pilot of the Russian helicopter.

The twenty-millimeter rounds punctured the left aileron extension just behind the pilot's hatch and the helicopter shuddered sideways as the aluminum frame of the wing extension came loose, clattering against the body of the helicopter.

Yolokov pushed hard on the collective and throttled down to put the bird into a dive toward the surface of the water. He was almost to the point that the Americans would have to call off the chase, the convergence of the territorial waters, a twelve-mile stretch of water that was made up of the outlying boundaries of each nation's borders. This was the most dangerous time for a running pilot as the American "cowboys" always fired their air-to-air missiles if they felt a fleeing aircraft was going to get away.

The first Black Hawk was directly behind him after coming out of the dive. The second seemed to fall back as if giving up. He must have made it, he thought, the American must know that to proceed further would be to enter into the territorial waters and airspace of Mexico. Yolokov was wondering about why the second aircraft had not done the same when suddenly the missile radar warning light came on. The American had fired up the weapon control panel, arming his missiles.

Yolokov swerved hard to one side and then up. He quickly slammed the throttle closed, causing the American pilot to drop low to avoid colliding with the Soviet-era bird. The Russian quickly armed his own system and set the firing system to "Auto Two." The missiles went hot detecting the Black Hawk's super-heated exhaust. The Weapon Tracker had already acquired the target and only needed activation to fire. The two heat seeking air-to-air missiles jumped from their mounts and moved rapidly toward the Black Hawk.

Hunt saw the missile detection and simultaneous launch and reactively fired off the chaff flares, dropping decoy, super-heated, phosphorous flares in streams from the launchers located near the Black Hawk's exhaust stacks. The flares shot downward looking like fountains of bright white fire. The missiles chased the flares down and away from the Black Hawk and exploded at nearly the same time causing a huge fireball in airspace directly in front of Yolokov's helicopter. The Russian had not anticipated the wall of smoke and flame and did not see the Black Hawk circling to the right until the "lock/launch" missile indicator showed that CW4 Hunt had just fired his own missiles at Yolokov's aircraft.

The first missile struck the aft section, destroying the rear tail section and rear rotor shaft of the Hind Helicopter. Yolokov only had a brief second to see the cause of his death, riding an orange plume, as it curved from the Black Hawk and shot toward his cockpit.

Hunt squinted as the second rocket found its target, blowing the remainder of the Russian helicopter to pieces. The debris spattered across the water and then quickly sank below the surface. The pilot called in his kill to his wingman and headed back to join him. They would have to collaborate a little on the location of the helicopter's demise. Hunt was too far south into Mexican airspace to have splashed another aircraft. By rights, he should have stopped when his wingman did, but he wasn't the kind to give up the chase. He did consider himself a cowboy and to him that was a good thing. He was sure he would have to answer to his commander, but he knew that what he had done was right. He circled around the crash area looking for any signs of a survivor. After a few minutes, he assumed that if there had been both a pilot and a copilot, neither survived. Chief Hunt maneuvered his Black Hawk to fall into line with his partner and headed back to base. He needed fuel, food and a couple more missiles. He would have to remember to tell the weapons guys to ramp up his flare load. He had used all of his flares in one maneuver. Had the pilot of the Russian aircraft recovered it would have been his own helicopter sinking in the ocean below.

"Oh well," he thought, he would have to cover all that in his report. He knew it was going to be a long day and probably a long night for the folks who would get the information about the border incursion. There would be a whole lot of people trying to figure out what exactly an Mi24E HIND troop-carrying attack helicopter loaded for bear was doing near the southern border.

CHAPTER 5

DESERT WAR

MATT FRANKLIN'S Hummer bounced across the washed out shoulder and came to an abrupt halt in a wide ravine just off the gravel surveillance road. He reached over, rotated the ignition switch to the left to kill the engine. His partner began to complain about the sudden maneuver, but Franklin quickly put a finger up to his mouth and motioned across the road. "Call in and get Gary up here. It looks like there's something serious goin' on over there."

"Golf Hotel One, this is Romeo Sierra One. Over." The radio hissed loudly before Rauelle Sanchez could turn down the squelch. He looked over at Matt Franklin and winced. Franklin did not look happy.

"Golf Hotel One, this is Romeo Sierra One, Come in. Over."

"This is Golf Hotel One. Go ahead." Gary Hendricks was the Senior Border Patrol Officer on duty.

"Golf Hotel be advised that we have activity to our ten o' clock, in sector Three-Two-Alpha. I say again, Sector Three-Two-Alpha is hot."

"Roger, that's a good copy." Sanchez's location was not far from Hendricks and his team. "Stay put. Keep visual only. Do not engage until my team is at your location." Gary Hendricks had learned the hard way that one can never have too much back up.

"Roger. Romeo Sierra One. Out."

Franklin and Sanchez could see several people with flashlights from their current position. They were approximately two hundred meters away and on the opposite side of an ancient desert dune. Sanchez wondered how Matt Franklin had spotted them at night, while driving with blackout drive lights only, from so far up the road. "Man you must have eyes like an eagle," Sanchez quipped.

"Actually, I heard something. It didn't register at first. I thought something was going on with the Hummer, like the exhaust was real loud all of a sudden. That's when I killed the engine. Then I saw the flashlights."

Matt Franklin moved up the dune some and peered into the darkness with his night vision binoculars. "Look to the left of that group of people. How many vehicles do you see over there?"

Sanchez scanned the near horizon. "Looks like a Jimmy or a Blazer and maybe a Jeep." He looked again. "Wait, there's a big truck down there too. Not sure what kind, but it's a cargo truck. I can only see the back."

Franklin was struggling to regain his night vision, when he glimpsed the blackout drive lights of the convoy's lead vehicle rounding the last curve before their position.

Gary Hendricks motioned ahead of his vehicle. "There's Franklin's Hummer. Pull in behind it, but be sure to leave room to maneuver out in a hurry." His driver placed his vehicle at an angle facing the road and shut it off. Hendricks bounded out of the Humvee. He moved in next to Matt Franklin and positioned himself so that he could see over the dune. "I brought Stanley, Johns, Marcus, Benedict and Mason. What have you got?"

Matt Franklin gave a quick update. "Sanchez sees two vehicles. Both are four wheelers. There may be more, but can't tell from here. Possibly a big truck of some sort there, too. There are at least six people milling about."

Hendricks pulled his radio up close. "Stanley, send Benedict over here. Take Mason, Johns and Marcus to circle around the back of the group to your left. Call me once you're in position." The radio cackled a low "Roger".

Jerry Stanley motioned for his men to move out. They made their way around the back of a dilapidated cedar fence and down through the ravine to where the vehicles were parked. In total there were three SUVs and a cargo truck parked along the fence line.

Stanley could hear a conversation near the truck. The language was not Spanish. It sounded more like Arabic or some other Middle-Eastern language. "Golf Hotel this is Juliet Sierra. Over."

Hendricks's radio suddenly came to life. "Go ahead Juliet Sierra."

Stanley reported quietly. "Be advised we are in position. There are three four wheelers and a Ford box truck parked down here near the ravine. Everyone is gathered behind the box truck. These guys aren't Mexican. They're Mid Eastern. I can hear them talking. Sounds like there's a bunch of them inside the back of the box truck. Could be that they're smuggling in illegals, I guess."

Hendricks radioed back, "We need to know how many there are. Can you get around to where you can take a look in the truck?"

"Good copy. We'll move to the left and swing around to get a better view. Stanley out."

Hamza al-Muhajeer watched as the others loaded the crate into the back of the box truck. "Make sure to strap it down securely, Leaja. The terrain here is rough and the roads are worse."

"You worry too much, al-Muhajeer. I have gotten you and the package this far. Have I not? It will make it to its destination without incident." Leaja bin Masri took a long draw on his cigarette. He exhaled the large cloud of smoke forcefully, attempting to blow it beyond the proximity of his boss, while examining the straps to ensure they were indeed secure. He looked back at al-Muhajeer and feigned a look of concern. "You act as if you don't trust me. That, my brother, pains my heart." He stood up and grasped his heart with both hands looking as if he was about to cry.

"You are a fool, Leaja. And you are right to ask if I trust you." Hamza al-Muhajeer stood to face Leaja bin Masri and placed both hands on his shoulders to get his full attention. "How can I trust someone who knows only jokes and laughter? Don't you ever worry about living up to the laws of the Quran? I do worry too much...about you and your life with Allah."

The two stood for a moment face to face. Leaja bin Masri leaned in close to al-Muhajeer and forced the smoke from the last drag of his cigarette through his nicotine stained teeth. He tossed down what remained of the cigarette and scowled.

"I have given everything to Allah. Everything! Do not preach to me about faith. My children are dead. My wife is dead, and how many of our fine soldiers have died under my direction and under the watchful eye of the great Allah?" He reached in and pulled the nametag from his front pocket. He slapped it down on the crate so that the name RAMSEY in all block letters could be plainly seen as he slid his hand away.

Bin Masri walked around the crate and pointed to the tag. Then, as if trying to drive his finger through it, forcefully hammered down against it.

"This is now my motivation. This man and all he stands for. His army, his country, his government, his humanity, everything he believes in, is my enemy. I want to destroy all of it and take from him what he took from me." He grabbed the nametag and quickly put it back in his pocket.

Hamza al-Muhajeer stepped forward. Bin Masri would not look into his eyes. "This is not about personal vengeance, my brother. It is not our will, but Allah's, that we continue on our path."

"I am sorry al-Muhajeer," bin Masri cut him off, "but it is about vengeance. It is about justice. It is about an eye for an eye!" Leaja looked away and ran his fingers through his hair trying to regain his composure.

Hamza al-Muhajeer turned his back on him and moved to the open cargo door. He turned back to bin Masri. "You must get serious about this mission. Put it in perspective. We are in America now, and we are here to do Allah's bidding. We are not here to avenge the death of your family or to hunt down one man. We can have no mistakes or distractions. What we do here has far greater ramifications, far greater glory. The sooner you wrap your mind around that concept the better off we will all be and the better for you in the eyes of Allah."

Hamza al-Muhajeer jumped down from the height of the cargo bed and lost his footing. He crashed loudly against the wooden fence, but quickly recovered, standing fully upright. Bin Masri stepped off the truck, landing next to al-Muhajeer with his weapon drawn. He held up a finger to silence his boss. "Shhhh! There is someone out there."

Agent Stanley held up his hand to tell his team to stop. There was silence at the back of the truck, and he could see both men quietly standing near the fence. The taller of the two held a pistol out in plain view scanning it along the fence-line. Stanley keyed the mike three times in short burst, waited a few seconds then repeated the action.

"They've got weapons. We need to move in." Hendricks, Franklin and Benedict drew their weapons and moved quietly to the right of the parked vehicles. The key code that Stanley had transmitted set a series of events in motion that Franklin knew there was no stopping. Jerry Stanley had relayed in the short radio burst that the suspects were armed and that he and his men could be in jeopardy.

Franklin's radio squelched another burst of eight squawks, was silent for a few seconds, and then repeated the same number of squawks followed by two sets of three. At least now the teams knew what they were up against and the match was even. Eight of them, eight Border Agents and all were armed. Matt Franklin only hoped his teams had the better weapons.

Leaja bin Masri called out into the darkness, "Who is there? Ahmed? Is that you?" When he got no reply, he called again in Spanish, "quién está allí?" The response was silence. He tried several times to no avail.

"Enough of this!" Hamza al-Muhajeer demanded. "Move to the vehicles. Get the truck ready to go. We are leaving now!"

"There is someone there. I heard them," protested bin Masri.

"All the more reason to move. Let them chase us then, but we must get the truck going. Now, get in." Muhajeer jumped up on the back of the truck, pulled the door down and threw the latch to lock it in place. He slammed his hand against the truck cargo box to signal bin Masri to start the engine.

The sound of the engines starting covered Stanley's transmission. "The trucks are moving out! We need to move in. I need authorization to move in to stop the trucks from leaving!"

Hendricks wanted to call in helicopter support, but knew there was no time. He cued the mike and shot back the order to go. "Move! Move! Move!"

Hamza al-Muhajeer opened the right side door of the cargo truck and stepped up on the running board just as Agent Stanley brought his weapon up and ordered him to stop. "Halt, Federal Border Patrol!"

Bin Masri saw what was happening and revved the engine indicating that he had no interest in obeying the orders of the Border Patrol Agent. The Ford's 460 cubic inch motor gasped for fuel and backfired loudly before the truck lurched forward. Hamza al-Muhajeer lost his grip on the door handle and stumbled backward off the running board.

Agent Aaron Mason's weapon followed al-Muhajeer to the ground. Mason yelled for al-Muhajeer to put down his weapon as the flash of the exhaust and the sound of the backfire punctured the night. Instinctively Mason fired his weapon thinking that he had been fired upon. The bullet raced to its destination impacting just to the left of Hamza al-Muhajeer's forehead. Al-Muhajeer's head pitched backward as the round passed through his brain and shattered the back of his skull, killing him instantly.

Stanley ran to the open door of the truck and jumped onto the running board, his weapon drawn on bin Masri. He yelled for bin Masri to stop, but did not complete his demands when bin Masri fired his weapon hitting him in the chest. The round smashed through Stanley's sternum and severed the Superior Vena Cava, one of the two large veins providing return blood flow to his heart. Stanley felt the impact and knew that he was badly hurt. He looked at the damage to his chest instinctively as he began to lose his grasp on the door, and then looked up one more time as bin Masri fired a second time. That bullet smashed into Stanley's right shoulder shattering his clavicle and proceeded on to shatter his right shoulder blade. The impact forced the agent backward and to the ground.

As the truck pulled away Aaron Mason, Edward Johns and Scott Marcus all found themselves unprotected. The Jeep that was parked near the box truck was circling around to follow the truck out. Mason fired several shots through the passenger side windshield killing the gunman on the right, while Johns and Marcus both trained their weapons on the driver. The jeep maneuvered abruptly to the left as the corpse of the driver slumped over, forcing the steering wheel into a left turn. The Jeep rolled over on its side and stopped in a cloud of dust and smoke.

Bin Masri floored the accelerator of the box truck and steered the truck around the fencing and onto the road nearly running over Franklin, Sanchez and Benedict. Gary Hendricks jumped out in front of the truck firing rounds into the windshield, narrowly missing the driver. Bin Masri turned the steering wheel hard to avoid the eight bullets just fired in his direction barely missing the opportunity to run over the Senior Border Patrol Agent. The truck careened into the dry ravine smashing into Franklin's Hummer and rolling up and over Greg Hendricks's Humvee smashing the fiberglass hood and destroying the radiator.

The four agents fired at the truck attempting to take out the rear tires as bin Masri recovered from his collision and sped away. Sanchez ran to the last Hummer and pulled it out into the gravel roadway as a blockade knowing that the other SUVs would be attempting to escape using the same route. Just as the Hummer was in place the Chevrolet Blazer came out of the darkness, full throttle, and slammed into Sanchez's vehicle. Sanchez was hit hard by the impact of the steering wheel slamming into his chest, shattering his rib cage, as his vehicle was being forced from under him. He continued to move forward from the momentum of the impact. His head collided with the metal frame of the windshield as his body crumpled around him, forcing his neck into a position too contorted for his bone structure to accommodate, snapping his neck just below the base of his skull.

The passenger in the Blazer was ejected from the vehicle through the windshield and slammed hard against the upright "A" pillar of Sanchez's hummer, smashing his skull, and killing him instantly. The driver amazingly was shaken from the impact and the successive deployment of the air bag, but managed to escape from the vehicle.

Hendricks yelled for the driver to stop and fired a round hitting him in the thigh when he didn't. The driver struggled to his feet.

He raised his weapon, pointed it at Hendricks, and began yelling, "Allah Akbar! Allah Akbar!" The three agents all ordered him to drop his weapon then let loose a volley of rounds dropping him where he stood.

The final vehicle never moved. The remaining driver and passenger both got out of their vehicle and began firing on Mason, Johns and Marcus. Mason took charge and maneuvered his people safely into position, then ordered the last of the suspects to drop their weapons. After several failed attempts were made to take them into custody, Johns and Marcus rushed the gunmen's positions from the side while Mason came in head on.

Marcus took out the first of the two and, as Mason moved in, the final gunman stood and moved toward Marcus, shooting him low in the torso. The bullet passed through Marcus' body without inflicting much damage and, in the intense activity, almost went unnoticed by Marcus. Mason fired the last round of the day into the skull of the lone gunman. The man stood for a moment and then crumpled, lifeless, to the desert ground.

CHAPTER 6

JUST ANOTHER DAY

ALAN RAMSEY pulled through the security gate and drove toward his parking place. The CIA headquarters was a large facility and the parking for non-tenured residents was near what Ramsey fondly referred to as the Lower North Forty. He grabbed his laptop bag and jacket and began the early morning trek to the security station.

It had been a little over four years since he had been medically retired from the Special Forces. The injuries he had suffered in Iraq were more severe than he had first thought and had ended his career. Ramsey had put everything into his job as a special operations officer and had been devastated when he'd gotten the news from the Medical Review Board that he would not be retained for future service in the military.

Ramsey had shown an uncanny ability to predict where and when the al-Qaeda-in-Iraq and other groups that supported the AQI, known as special criminals, would attack next. It was this understanding of intelligence and the ability to develop patterns of terrorist activity, out of the ordinary for a young captain that helped him secure a job at Langley only a few months after his medical discharge.

His Commander had seen the unmistakable signs of a good Intelligence Officer and had tried to convince Ramsey, long before his injury, that he should be poring over intelligence estimates and building patterned surveillance models, not leading teams of SPECOPS troops that acted on that information. The problem for COL Lester was that Ramsey was really good at what he did. He could conform to almost any situation and master any task he was assigned. That made it hard for his Colonel to rationalize the argument to bring in from the field.

After he'd been wounded and unable to perform his duties Lester had gladly helped him put together an Officer Record Brief and resume that could not be overlooked. Ramsey landed the job with the CIA at Langley, where he implemented the Terrorism Tracking, Surveillance and Counter-Intelligence Division. The T2SCI, or T2T for short, fell between the CIA's Terrorist Strike Force and the still young Department of Homeland Security. He was thankful for the faith that his Lieutenant Colonel had shown in him. They emailed or talked routinely and, after a few months battling the politics of his position at Langley, Ramsey would jokingly blame his Colonel for his newfound problems. The response from his former boss was always the same. "You're a good troop. You can handle it I'm sure," he would say in his choppy, east coast dialect. Ramsey thought about how many years had passed already since he'd last worn a uniform as he fell into line at the security station.

The threat level was yellow today, so the security scans were less intrusive, but still necessary. In the years since he had arrived he had met hundreds of people and built a reputation as a team player and an indispensable commodity for the CIA and Homeland Security. Once again, his instincts had led him to success. Although his parking privileges had yet to catch up, he had otherwise moved up in the agency, and as the head of the T2T, was one of its most successful agents. He was doing well. He had his own office and his own page. And when he asked for it, he had the run of the research teams.

Alan Ramsey slowly made his way to the head of the line. He listened as the head of the ground floor security team greeted the incoming personnel. "Good morning" or "How's it going?" seemed to be the typical generic greeting. No names, just a simple, "How do you do?" However, some greetings did come with a name. Alan Ramsey's was one of them.

"Good morning, Mr. Ramsey. I see you're early again this morning. You've really been raking in the O.T. lately. Your wife must just be loving you." Paul Jackson smiled as he gave Ramsey the once over and ushered him toward the other security team members who were waving him toward the newly installed Upright Imaging Scanner, commonly referred to as "the tunnel".

"Morning, Paul. I told you I don't get overtime pay. I do this for God and country, and yes, my wife loves me, not for my money, but for my good looks." Alan Ramsey liked Paul Jackson. He was a retired Sergeant Major of the Mechanized Infantry and was courteous to everyone. He was also friendly, and the man knew his name.

"I also remember telling you that my name is Alan. Remember, Mr. Ramsey was my father," he said as he stepped into the scanner and turned to face a large numeral one that was painted on the inside wall of the scanner.

"Mm mm, that might be so, Mr. Ramsey, but there is such a thing as protocol, and I ain't one to break protocol." Paul Jackson feigned a look of innocence, looking upward while rubbing his chin as if contemplating some past transgression and leaving

Ramsey with the impression that following protocol wasn't really one of his better traits.

Alan Ramsey completed the four position scanning procedure, lowered his arms and exited the scanner to collect his laptop and bag. "You just keep thinking that and I'll just keep telling you to call me by my first name." He began to walk away, but stopped to ask the man a question he'd wanted to ask for a long time, but had not had the nerve.

Alan turned back to face the hulking figure. "Paul, have you ever thought about doing something other than standing here, watching people walk through the tunnel, waiting for the buzzer to go off because they forgot to drop their keys in the basket?"

Paul Jackson dropped his clipboard down to his side and faced Ramsey. "It's a good job, Sir, and I make some good money. It makes my old lady happy. Why would I want to do anything more than that?"

Alan read the look on Paul Jackson's face and realized he must have sounded like a presumptuous ass. "No, look, Paul, I don't mean any disrespect. What you do here is important. Don't get me wrong. I just thought that, having been prior military, you might wonder about, you know, being in a more active role."

Jackson sighed. "Look, I went in the Army in 1982. I was 17 years old, fresh out of school. I trained through the Cold War, fought in every skirmish and war since, including Afghanistan. I was one of the Army's youngest Sergeant Majors and felt that I did pretty well for myself. I pulled the plug on the military after twenty years. About six months after getting out, I joined the police academy, thought I'd become a cop. I thought it would be something worthwhile, you know, serving others and being a part of a team again. I did my job and was passed over for promotion several times. I started to complain, and when I did, I was treated like an outcast. It was very politically charged in the precinct I was in, but I put up with it, and was just starting to feel like it was worth it, when everything went to hell."

Paul glanced back at the others in his security detail and made sure there were no problems before continuing. "Anyway, I ended up arresting this punk-ass junkie who was high on crack. It was a scene straight from the TV show, COPS. The kid was belligerent and rude and pretty damned big. I manhandled this kid pretty well, but he deserved it, you know. He was spitting on me and kicking me. You know how they are, no respect. Anyway, as I was putting him in the car he tried to get away. He popped up, intentionally slamming me hard under the chin with his head. I lost a couple teeth and he split open my jaw. I was bleeding like hell. He went for my pistol and I was like, aw, hell no. I elbowed him and smashed him against the door opening. I pushed him down into the car and slammed the door closed. Just as I closed the door, the idiot tried to block it with his head. The window shattered on the guy's head, and he went down to the floorboard.

Somehow, because of the force of the door closing, or 'cause he had his head turned a certain way, I don't know, I broke his neck. The bad thing was that the little asshole didn't die, but got paralyzed from the neck down. His slick-ass lawyer sued the city and the precinct. And, because someone got a couple pictures on their cell phone of me beating on the guy, I was the one who ended up on trial. The city lost the suit. The Chief of Police was moved to another precinct, and I was relieved of my duties as a police officer. About a month later I landed this job, but only because the police department got involved. To hell with helping other people. All that did for me was waste a couple years of my life."

Alan could see that Paul was a lot like him. He was restless, wanting more, but not sure what to do about it. "Look Paul, you've got a law enforcement background and I'm sure you have an excellent military record. You had to in order to be a Sergeant Major. Why don't you try out for a job in one of the special units inside?"

Paul smiled, "I think I'm a little old to be chasing bad guys across the globe." He looked around and continued, "I'll be fifty in a couple days. I don't think there is anybody inside that facility that wants some old-ass ex Sergeant Major getting in their business."

"Well, I for one would be honored to work with you. I was always told that if you saw a good officer you would find a good Sergeant Major close by," Ramsey said.

Paul Jackson took a dig at Ramsey with that one. "Yeah, well you must not be a very good officer then, 'cause all I see is a dumb-ass, old, retired, Sergeant Major standing close by."

Ramsey smiled. "Maybe that's because I'm an old wore out, medically-retired Captain. It's a perfect match. Just think about it a little. You never know, it could get you that overtime pay you're always giving me crap about."

The bantering stopped as Paul Jackson feigned another look of contemplation. "Hmm, now you're speaking my language," he said with a smug grin. Alan Ramsey disappeared around a corner pointing his finger, and then giving a slight wave at Paul Jackson as he turned the corner.

"See ya later, MISTER RAMSEY," Paul Jackson, bound for the last word, called down the hall, then turned his attention back to the security team's efforts. Just as he did so, he heard a muffled voice come back to him from down the hall and around the corner. "The name's ALAN. Mr. Ramsey was my dad."

Paul Jackson smiled a large smile and said quietly, but out loud, "Whatever, Mr. Ramsey," and felt triumphant at getting in the last word.

CHAPTER 7

FUGITIVE

LEAJA BIN MASRI sped through the small Texas town of Harlingen, maneuvering as best he could, the beat-up Ford box truck. It was hard to see through the smashed windshield and even harder to steer given that some of the steering mechanisms had been damaged in the collision with the border patrol agents' vehicles. That, coupled with the early morning darkness, made driving exceptionally difficult.

He rounded a corner to find a small repair shop with a parking lot large enough to accommodate the box truck. He drove towards the rear of the three bay metal building and moved as far forward as he could to hide the damaged truck.

The driver's door creaked and popped as bin Masri forced it past the edge of the fender that had been shoved backward in the accident. He tucked his pistol into his waistband and stepped down from the running board.

He listened to the early morning silence of the small town and waited for the wail of sirens indicating he was being pursued. There was nothing. The sun was just coming up and the town was still asleep. He walked to the front of the building and looked up and down the two-lane highway he had just traveled. Across the road and up a bit at a small market, workers were unloading vegetables and bakery goods from two trucks, otherwise the street was empty.

He stepped to the office door, looked around cautiously, and tried the door. It was locked as he had expected. According to the sign on the door the office would not be open for another hour. bin Masri surveyed the interior through the plate glass window and spotted keys for the vehicles being repaired at the shop hanging on the "SERVICE" board. On another board were the "FINISHED" vehicle keys. He pressed his face against the window and saw that there were two sets of late model GM keys, a set of Ford keys, and what looked like Toyota and Nissan keys.

He turned to face the parking area and found a Chevrolet Trailblazer and an Oldsmobile Bravada. Next to the Olds were a Toyota Camry and a Ford Taurus.

He inspected the doors and the single window looking for any alarm sensors or tape but found none. Bin Masri pulled the weapon from his waist and smashed the barrel against the glass close to the window jamb of the door. The glass shattered just enough for bin Masri to reach in and unlock the deadbolt. He walked in, grabbed the keys to the Trailblazer from the "FINISHED" board, stepped out and closed the door behind him.

He started the truck and backed it up to the rear of the box truck. Bin Masri jumped out, opened the cargo door and climbed into the cargo box. He kicked at the crate smashing the thin wooden packaging material to reveal the teardrop shape of the two-decade-old warhead.

Bin Masri lifted it to one side, rolled the warhead up on one end, and pushed hard to roll it towards the back of the truck. Getting it into the back of the SUV by himself was not going to be easy. He looked around for a flat board or something he could use as a chute that would allow him to slide the warhead from truck to truck, but quickly realized the height difference of the two vehicles. In order to clear the rear hatch of the Trailblazer the trucks would have to be eight to ten feet away. Even if he found planking suitable in length, more than likely, it would not hold the excessive weight of the warhead.

He looked around for anything he could possibly use, but could only find the railroad ties that were being used for parking stops throughout the lot. The ties weren't long enough to act as a bridge, but if he could use one as a pedestal he might be able to lower the warhead with some control. He lifted the one closest to him, raising it up on end and found that it was about the same height as the cargo truck's bed. Bin Masri dragged the timber over and leaned it upright against the rear of the truck. He climbed back into the truck and struggled, but managed to move the warhead, scooting it off the edge of the truck bed and precariously balancing it on the end of the upright tie. Carefully, he climbed back down and stood to the side of the two vehicles. If he could control the fall of the warhead into the back of the truck by arcing it over on top of the board, he should be able to get it into the Trailblazer safely.

He pulled the post with the warhead perched on top into a fully upright position, then pushed it over the center and guided it to the truck. The warhead fell hard, landing with a loud crash on the back of the rear hatch and then spun to a stop against the back of the rear seat.

Bin Masri rolled the warhead over and inspected it quickly to make sure he hadn't cracked the bomb's casing. Satisfied, he closed the hatch and walked around to the driver's seat. He pulled around the building and out onto the two lane highway passing the market on his left. There was nobody in sight. He checked his fuel level and saw that he had a full tank and thought that maybe his luck was changing.

He thought about Hamza al-Muhajeer and the others who had died in the desert. "How did the Americans know we were there?" he thought. He wondered if they had been tracked or if it had been just dumb luck. The phones could have been monitored. He had once heard that the NSA actually monitored every phone call made in the United States. He was sure that was not true. How could they?

He picked up his cell phone to call his contact in Missouri, the first stop on his journey. Ahmed Zuqawri had secured the phones and vehicles for the mission. All of the phones had been cleaned of their electronic signal and should not have been able to be located. The call could be traced, but the position of the caller could not be pinpointed using the standard global positioning system. The authorities would have to triangulate the signal in order to trace the call. Since he had not been on his cell, it must have been one of the others. Served them right that they did not survive, if they had given away their position. "Allah forgive my thoughts, if I accuse unjustly," he thought.

Bin Masri scrolled through his contact list and found Ahmed Zuqawri's listing and placed the call.

"Hello."

"Ahmed, this is Leaja bin Masri. Do you know who I am?" Bin Masri had never talked to Zuqawri, but knew of him through al-Muhajeer. According to him, he was a great soldier who was both sly and cunning.

"I know of you. Where is al-Muhajeer?" Zuqawri asked.

"He is dead. Killed this morning at the delivery point. Leaja bin Masri continued, "They are all dead. American federal agents attacked us within minutes of loading the truck. I am the only one who escaped."

There was only silence for a few seconds. "Praise Allah for their strength and their gift of martyrdom," Zuqawri said quietly. "Do you still have the device?"

"I have it, and I am on my way to your area. We will build it and deliver it as planned. We will need more men to assist us with our mission. How many people do you have there?" Leaja bin Masri passed a police car as he turned onto the highway. He watched in his mirror making sure it did not turn around. He accelerated up the entrance ramp, brought the vehicle up to speed, and set the cruise control.

Ahmed reassured the man. "There are six men here ready at the warehouse. They are waiting for the device."

Ahmed heard a sound from the top of the stairs that led to the hallway on the first floor of his house. It was his wife, Bedalla. "Ahmed, who are you talking to?"

He rolled his eyes before answering her, "I am on the phone, woman, with a physician about one of my patients. It is no concern of yours."

Bedalla Zuqawri stepped back from the doorway and began to close the door, then suddenly opened it wide again. "Well, while you are down there could you please replace the light bulb over the washer and dryer? I can hardly see to wash the clothes."

Ahmed shot back, "Yes, yes. I will replace it. Now go back to what you were doing and leave me be."

The door closed. "My apologies, Leaja. Where was I?"

"You were telling me about the others." Bin Masri was patient of family matters. He knew what it was like to have a family and how it was to lose them as well.

Ahmed picked up where he had left off. "One of the men is a physicist. And, as Allah would have it, is very familiar with the workings of the device. It took some convincing for him to help us with our cause."

Leaja bin Masri was concerned. "You are holding his family?"

"It was the only way he would cooperate with us. He is Russian and shares no love of the infidels, but we had to convince him that it was the right path to follow. He is Muslim after all."

Leaja thought about what he had just been told. "I want no harm to come to this man or his family. Reward him well when his task is complete. Is that understood?"

Zuqawri protested. "Our funds are nearly depleted. We have left only what we owe Dmitri for the delivery. If we do not pay him it may jeopardize the operation. We must still transport and deploy the device. I do not trust Dmitri or his organization. They are greedy, godless criminals that act only for money. They cannot be..."

Leaja cut him off. "Enough! I will make arrangements for more funding. Al-Muhajeer is dead. It is my responsibility. If Dmitri contacts you, send him to me. I am in charge now."

Zuqawri regained his focus. "The building is nearly set up for the mission. We have temporary structures in place that will be used to disassemble and prepare the device for the final assembly. Once the enclosure arrives we will have the casing and the means to transport it. We will avenge the deaths of our brothers in the Pennsylvanian field and those who now lie lifeless under the desert sand. We must retaliate for our dead brothers."

Bin Masri grimaced on the other end of the call. "Yes, yes. Calm down, Ahmed. They will have died for a noble cause in the end. But first, I must get to the warehouse. We must concentrate on what has happened today. The Americans will be looking for me. They will have tested for traces of explosives and will know what is in store for them. The trucks and the phones are tied to your location. Too much has gone wrong. I must not be stopped. There is too much at stake."

"I will fix it," Ahmed said. "It is my responsibility. I will lure them from you by creating a diversion. They will think that the bomb has been deployed. It should tie up their investigators and police so that you can arrive with the device. By the time they figure out what has happened or who is responsible, the mission here will be over and you will be on your way to the east coast."

Bin Masri knew what this meant for Ahmed. "You do understand that you will become the target of their investigations? That all roads will lead to you? Are you willing to make such a sacrifice for yourself and, more importantly, for your family?"

Ahmed answered reassuringly, "My family is already involved. Their place is with me and I am willing to do this. They do not have a choice in the matter." Ahmed quickly changed the subject. "How long will it take for you to get to St. Louis?"

Leaja looked at his map and made some quick calculations. "Twelve to fourteen hours."

Ahmed Zuqawri felt that they had spoken much too long, but still, he wanted to reassure his new leader that he was in control. "I will have everything ready tomorrow. You will see then that your path will be clear and that Allah will be pleased." He ended the conversation.

Ahmed looked at his watch. It was still early enough to get the ball rolling. He had been waiting for such an opportunity to show his willingness to sacrifice to his God and show also that he was dedicated to his cause. Yes, tomorrow was that day.

On bin Masri's end the phone fell silent. He leaned back and tossed the phone onto the passenger seat. He pushed in the lighter and fumbled for his smokes. It was a long drive to St. Louis. He might as well get comfortable. He lit his cigarette, inhaled deeply and contemplated his fate.

Kenneth Wash

CHAPTER 8

THE OFFICE

"GOOD MORNING, Mr. Ramsey," Jennifer Wilkins said as she made her way to the office kitchenette with the coffee carafe. The room smelled of fresh grounds.

"Morning, Jenny. Preparing the morning's rations? I may need an extra cup today. Kind of slow getting started." Alan let the door close behind him as he made his way to his desk.

"I filled it to the 12 cup mark." She carried the coffee carafe back to the coffee maker, poured the water in and closed the lid. "There seems to be a lot of activity this morning. The phone has been lit up across the board. Not sure what it means, but my guess is that you will be invited to an unusual amount of 'emergency meetings' this morning." As a first year page, Jennifer seemed to have a keen sense for what was going on. She was a little overzealous at times, but that was ok, Alan thought, because his office always benefited from her eagerness.

"I put this morning's updates on your desk. You might want to check your email first thing. Mine was overflowing." She flipped the switch on the front of the black plastic machine and made sure the light on the coffee maker lit up, indicating that the process had started, before heading back to her desk.

"What kind of correspondence are you talking about?" Alan pulled his laptop from its case for the second time that morning, this time mounting it in the dock on his desk and pressing the start button before continuing, "I got a couple things on the issue with the Syrian embassy, but that was early last night. Looks like Rashir Allad's people are getting tired of the sanctions that were imposed. Didn't see anything surprising though." He inserted his CAC card into the keyboard's card reader and logged into the system.

The coffee maker came to life, sizzling and bubbling, as Jennifer motioned toward her monitor. "I got three emails this morning from Beth Sanders in Gabe Anderson's office asking for any info you may have on file about a group called the Brotherhood of the Quran and one of their insurgents, a guy named al-Muhajeer."

Ramsey stopped her, looking up suddenly. "Whoa, whoa, did you say al-Muhajeer, as in, Hamza al-Muhajeer?"

"Yes, sir. Do you know of him?"

Ramsey picked up his empty coffee cup and rolled it in his hands. "Oh yeah, I'm very familiar with al-Muhajeer, and his buddies." Alan thought about the one who had nearly killed him, Leaja bin Masri. He thought about how close they had been to catching them four years before.

His page continued, "Oh and that guy down in Image Control, Rick Something, you know, the kind of creepy one, well he wrote me at, like, four this morning asking for anything you can give him about an organization called JTJ. Stands for Jama al-Tawil Jihad, I think."

Alan peered into his empty coffee cup thinking about what his page was telling him. Al-Muhajeer. Why would they be dragging him up from the depths, he wondered almost out loud.

Ramsey reached down and grabbed his left side. He squeezed just enough to feel the deformities in his muscle tissue. He pushed a little more firmly and felt the pain that he had lived with since that day four years ago.

Jennifer Wilkins reeled him back in from his thoughts. "I'm not sure why they are looking for this stuff, Mr. Ramsey, but the information search is a new development as of really early this morning."

Ramsey mulled over the last time he had opened a file on the terrorist leader. Al-Muhajeer had taken over after Musab al-Awari had been killed. It wasn't a year later that the "Surge" began and both the JTJ and the original Brotherhood of Iraq fell apart. Without al-Awari's leadership they could no longer exist separately. Both groups were absorbed by al-Qaeda in Iraq and controlled by a local Shiite cleric, but the groups lost public support as the American engineering efforts began to bring water, sewage and infrastructure repairs to aging cities and towns. The population was tired of the violence and chaos. All of that led to his mission in Sadr City, the last mission for Captain Alan Ramsey and the last reported sighting of Hamza al-Muhajeer.

"Well, send them everything they need, but I would like some explanation as to all the sudden interest in a guy who never really made it to the top ten of terrorist leaders."

Alan fired up his mail program. "Holy cow, you're not kidding about overflowing mail. I must have thirty or more new messages since last night." The list of new emails scrolled off the screen as Alan surveyed the names of the senders and the urgency tags. Gabe Anderson appeared to be the winner for the most new mailings and was also the most demanding of a reply as every one of his correspondences was tagged as urgent. "But, that's what one should expect from the T2T Director," Ramsey thought.

The cursor highlighted the first of the string of emails sent by G. Anderson. Alan read over the information regarding the border intrusion and subsequent firefight several times, and then fell back into his chair, not believing what he had just read. He held out his coffee cup to Jennifer Wilkins who was waiting with the coffee. "Fill it to the top, please."

Down the hall, the Director of the T2SCI, Gabriel Anderson, looked at the information that had been sent to him from the U.S Customs and Border Protection Agency's special operations teams. Although the agency was an "open-file agency" they ran "black ops" under the jurisdiction of Anderson and the direction of Ramsey's T2SCI.

There were several photographs of two men of Middle Eastern origin. Neither of the men had any identification. Both of the men were dead. The assistant to the director picked up his phone. "Beth, get Alan Ramsey on the line. Tell him it's important."

Alan's phone chimed. He looked up to see that the call was from Gabe Anderson's office. "Speak of the devil," he thought as he picked up.

"Morning, Gabe. Got your emails. Sounds like you're having a busy morning".

Gabe Anderson got right to it. "Looks like you might be right about the migration of the al-Qaeda in Iraq's leadership, Alan."

Ramsey had long theorized that the al-Qaeda groups were playing an "out of sight, out of mind" game, pulling all of their leaders in to plan for one major attack. Between the CIA, and the T2T, as well as Britain's "M" units, there were hundreds of agents working in at least ten countries trying to find some of the lost souls of al-Qaeda, but none had generated any substantial leads. It was as if all the major players had been eliminated, which was a very real possibility given the failures they had suffered during the surge.

"Yeah, this is a first, an actual firefight with the Border agents, and al-Muhajeer in the middle of it all. We haven't had a track on him for nearly four years. Hell, I thought he was dead. I figured he'd been tortured and killed by the Sons of Iraq. Remember, they liked to do that near the end of the insurgency."

Alan Ramsey reflected on his Special Operations assignments. The Iraqi intelligence agents, once members of the Sons of Iraq, used the threat of dismemberment to coerce the captured extremists to cooperate during interrogations. It was believed by some that the Muslim body, the temple of Allah, must be in one piece at the time of death in order to ascend into heaven to be greeted by Allah and the virgins. In the case of the suicide bombers who routinely destroyed the markets, businesses, and those who shopped there, the clerics made exceptions. They allowed that the martyrs would die a fraction of a second before the explosives they wore shredded their bodies, thus meeting the requirements to enter heaven.

Just to be on the safe side, the clerics sent the bombers on their way with a special prayer that hopefully would convince their God that what they did was done in his name. This would prove useful when the explosive vests detonated incompletely, a dud, so to speak. It was better to have a plan to gain martyrdom in full, in case things just didn't work out as planned.

By the close of the war the Iraqi interrogators spitefully cut off the fingers and hands of the captured insurgents before killing them, sometimes allowing families of the victims to stone them, even if they cooperated. They felt that it was a just ending for the foreign extremists and traitor conspirators that had killed the citizens of their country by the hundreds. They felt there simply should be no mercy for those who misrepresented the will of Allah.

Gabe Anderson continued, "We'll be absolutely certain once the FBI labs in Houston are finished processing the prints and DNA and bounce them against what the CIA in Baghdad has on file for al-Muhajeer. Still, based on the photographs we have, and the Border Patrol's report, I'd have to say that the son of a bitch was getting ready to set up shop here in the states."

Alan read through some of the Customs and T2T Border Patrol report. "The Border Agents that were assigned to the Harlingen, Texas station were really on the ball with this one. I'm sure their supervisors will be putting them in for awards. Unfortunately, it looks like two of the agents will receive theirs posthumously."

"There's more to this," Gabe interjected. "Last night while the border patrol was working their end, the Coast Guard sent out an "all points" to the surrounding bases that a helicopter had come into their airspace. It was tagged as American, but the technician working the tower got suspicious when he figured out that the last known flight of the bird had been in Iraq and that the helo had been a hanger queen for more than a year. After contact with the pilot he called the Pensacola Naval Air Station and found out that the helicopter was slated for destruction within a few days and that all of its electronics had been gutted."

"So they think the equipment went into a different Black Hawk?" Ramsey stated more than asked.

"Actually, Alan, it appears that the equipment was put into a Russian Mi24 Hind E helicopter." Gabe explained the contact and eventual kill of the Russian aircraft.

Alan whistled and sat back in his chair. "How did the equipment get in the Hind? Jesus, Blue Force Tracking is some of our newest equipment."

Gabe continued, "Well, we don't have to worry about that. The Black Hawk team splashed it all over the Gulf. There will be teams looking for it, but you can bet that it will never be found. Luckily for us the Mexican Air Corps was asleep at the radar. No incident report at all."

Alan ran the whole picture through his brain. "Are there any leads on the one that escaped? Seems like it wouldn't be too hard to find a man of Middle-Eastern descent driving around Small Town, USA in a box truck riddled with bullet holes."

Gabe Anderson pulled another document from his desk. "Actually, they are looking for a Chevrolet Trailblazer. The Harlingen sheriff's department reported finding a truck that matches the description of the box truck, complete with bullet holes and front end damage, behind a small automotive repair shop just outside of Corpus Christi, about a hundred and twenty-five miles from Harlingen. There wasn't any cargo in the back. The shop had been broken into and one of the customer's vehicles, a Chevy Trailblazer, was taken with the key."

Alan Ramsey asked for Anderson to send him a copy of the report. "We should get a team down right away. Have them check for trace radiation. I have a very bad feeling about what was in that truck." Alan Ramsey had been worried that there would be a major attack on American soil for years and felt strongly that it would include nuclear weaponry.

"Dan Burns has his men headed that way now. I told Burns to interview everyone and photograph everything. He will head up the whole thing start to finish."

Burns was old school. Alan knew he would get all the information available and not miss a thing. Still he wanted to be on the ground picking through the Texas desert dirt himself.

"Maybe I should head down there, Gabe. I'd sure like to get hands on with this."

Anderson thought about Ramsey's request for a second or two. "No, Alan. I'm gonna need your expertise here. If the driver of that truck is carrying around a nuke and starts getting crazy I want you to be available to work it." He attempted to ease his colleague's concerns. "Besides, Burns is one heck of an investigator. He's been doing this a long time. He'll get the job done down there and won't miss anything. I think you should be following that gut feeling you have and start looking for the al-Qaeda folks who have been dropping off the radar in the Mid-East. If your theory is correct we could be in for one hell of a summer."

Kenneth Wash

CHAPTER 9

REST STOP

BIN MASRI had driven only two hours when he began to feel the weight of his fatigue. He had been up and very active all night long. He was also tired from wrestling the steering wheel on the box truck for the few hours it had taken him to find an adequate replacement. He presumed that he had lost the power steering right away, as the truck whined and complained the whole way from the landing zone to Corpus Christi.

He spotted a truck stop with a diner and decided it was time to take a break. He wanted to make it out of Texas before stopping, but he was suddenly feeling exhausted. Looking at the fuel gauge he guessed he could drive another two hours before he would have to refill. As much as bin-Masri hated to stop he needed the break.

Top off the tank; have some coffee and maybe a little something to eat. Twenty minutes, he told himself, no longer.

The Trailblazer pulled off the highway and slowed to a stop at the end of the exit ramp. Bin Masri directed the vehicle onto the rural highway and down the road to the Truck Stop entrance. He pulled up to the pump and read the directions for paying with a credit card, something he had never done. He swiped the card and waited, hoping that the card would work properly. Within a few seconds the pump was ready and he filled the tank. With the fuel topped off he pulled the SUV around to the side and parked where he would be able to see the truck from inside the diner. As he walked around the parked vehicles he noticed two trucks nearly identical to the one he was driving. He was glad to see that the type of vehicle he was driving was so popular. It would be easy to blend in with traffic. The license plates were a problem though. By now the repair shop had surely opened its doors and noticed the missing truck as well as the addition of the box truck on their lot. That meant that the license number and the description of his stolen truck would be broadcast to all local police stations.

He eyed the plates on one of the other trucks and then removed the Multi-Tool from its pouch on his belt. He stooped down as if to tie his shoe and removed the front plate from the front bumper, then, after making sure he was not being watched, removed the rear plate and moved back to his truck to swap out the tags. He was installing one of his Texas plates on the front of the identical SUV when he heard people talking close by.

The voices belonged to a couple of over-the-road drivers. Bin Masri tossed the second plate face down under the truck and folded up his tool. He waited for the two truckers to walk by, stood and moved towards the door of the restaurant. One tag would have to be sufficient. The driver probably wouldn't notice that the front plate was missing as there was a vehicle parked directly in front of his. Hopefully the owner of the plates would be back in his home state of Illinois before noticing that his plates were gone.

Bin Masri pulled the door open, stepped into the restaurant and waited for the hostess to seat him. He would have to be careful that what he ordered did not contain any ham or pork. These Americans were swine eaters. Pork was in everything. The hostess came and led him to a small table where he took his seat and immediately asked for a cup of coffee.

The woman smiled and nodded, handing him a menu. "You just take a look at this while I go git your coffee. I'll be right back to take your order." Her southern drawl exposed her as a local.

For the moment Leaja bin Masri was relaxed. He pulled a smoke from his pack and lit it. The smoke drifted away and up to the powerful nicotine stained vent fan in the ceiling above him. He inhaled deeply and sat back in his chair and looked around the room. Nobody paid him any attention at the moment. He knew that was about to change. Soon, like after the World Trade Center victory, all people of Middle-Eastern origin would again become suspect. He would no doubt be interrogated after the attack. Yet, the American laws would protect him. He found the American justice system amusing in that the infidels could arrest someone, charge them with a crime, provide them with someone who would attempt to prove to a jury that they were the perpetrator of a crime, and then, use the same system of laws to protect them and fight for their freedom. He could not understand how it could possibly work.

Hamza al-Muhajeer believed that the attack he was planning would end America's meddlesome relationship with the world. Bin Masri was sure that al Muhajeer was right. That once an attack of the scale that they had planned was successfully carried out, America would close the door to the world. Al-Muhajeer theorized that such an attack would be the catalyst of change for the United States. America would then close and guard its borders. They would build walls to keep out evil, listen to every phone conversation, arrest and interrogate the innocent and trust no one. In doing so America would transform from an open democratic and free country to a closed, protected society with limited rights and freedoms not unlike China or the failed Soviet Union. America would become the very entity that its own constitution was designed to protect against.

Al-Muhajeer would say on occasion that America was like a Goliath and that it was the will of Allah that he was put in a position to challenge the giant. Only the weapon they would use to bring down this Goliath would not be a simple slingshot. If they were victorious, the country of the infidels would be reduced to the equivalent of a scared little child. Good, he thought. Maybe then others on the planet could live without the meddling interference of the infidels.

The waitress came back with his coffee and set it down on the table. She pulled out a notepad and pen and asked if he was ready to order. "Perhaps some toast with fruit jam," he stated rather quietly.

"Are you sure that's all? Doesn't seem like much to eat." The waitress waited, her pen at the ready.

"Just the toast, please and some jam, and more coffee upon your return," he insisted. The waitress flipped the book closed and shoved it back into her apron pocket. "Ok, I'll be back in a minute." She turned on her heel and headed back to place the order. As she neared the register a young couple and their two children smiled to her and thanked her for the service she had provided them. She smiled a big smile and thanked them. "Why, thank you so much. You all have a safe trip back to...Chicago, right?" They nodded and smiled as they backed towards the door and then walked out.

Bin Masri watched them as they stopped at the Blue Trailblazer. The parents helped to strap in their children and then got in the front seat and pulled the seat belts around themselves. "So that is the family from Illinois," he thought.

The waitress returned with his toast, a selection of butter and jelly and a refill for his coffee. He opened the packages and spread the contents on his toast as he watched the Trailblazer drive away.

His own children would be so big now. His elder son would be a man and would be working or helping with the mission and his younger would be about eleven. He tried to remember what they looked like but could only remember the haunting image of his younger child screaming in fear, holding so tightly to his mother. He remembered the explosions and the flashes, and after that, his fight with the tall American captain, and running to escape the Americans, bullets whizzing past him.

In retrospect, it seemed like there should have been no escape. But now, here he was in the country of the aggressors. He was sure that Allah had spared him for this mission. A mission given to him partly so that he could avenge the death of his family and because Hamza al-Muhajeer had great faith in him and knew that he would be compelled to complete the mission. He was right.

His waitress came back once more holding the coffee. "You doin' ok over here?" she asked as she began to top off Bin-Masri's coffee.

He motioned that he had enough coffee and thanked the woman for her service. He downed what remained in his cup, stood and walked to the register. The waitress met him at the register, smiled and told him to have a nice day.

Bin Masri stepped out into the mid-morning Texas heat from the air conditioned restaurant and headed to the Trailblazer, stopping only to pick up the license plate lying on the pavement and toss it into the trash. He checked the time. It was nearly eleven-thirty. He had to get moving. He still had at least twelve hours of driving ahead of him.

Kenneth Wash

CHAPTER 10

PREPARATION

AHMED ZUQAWRI rolled out the plastic explosive onto the waxed paper covered cardboard stock. He used a rolling pin to make the clay-like explosive paste a consistent six millimeters thick then laid the plastic thermos bottle on its side to measure the length against the explosive material and marked it to be trimmed to the length of the inside of the canister. It did not have to be exact, but he was somewhat of a perfectionist and believed in quality work, no matter what the task.

Ahmed began to place the first of hundreds of eight-millimeter stainless steel ball bearings into the face of the material, slightly pressing each one into the explosive's permeable membrane. Once the entire length of the "dough" was covered with the metal spheres, he covered the C4 and its embedded projectiles with another piece of scrap cardboard, creating a C4 and cardboard sandwich, and carefully lifted the explosive paste up, then flipped it over. He removed the cardboard and began the process to fill the exposed surface with more stainless steel projectiles.

Eventually nearly 300 steel balls were placed into the explosive material. Ahmed slowly and carefully rolled the material over itself. His calculations were nearly perfect. The roll of composition four, high energy RDX explosive material embedded with the projectiles fit snugly into the hollowed out shell of the plastic thermos.

Ahmed secured the top of the thermos back in place using a hot glue gun. All that was left now was to drive the blasting cap into the C4 and then apply the nine-volt battery and the triggering mechanism. The cap would serve as both the trigger and the storage for the nine-volt battery. Ahmed placed a piece of smooth plastic down through the opening and carefully pulled the wires to the detonator through a small hole in the center of the disk. He twisted the wires in a counter-clockwise manner and attached them to the contacts on the bottom inside of the lower portion of the cap. With the battery removed Ahmed tested the resistance of the circuit. The contacts were closed. Perfect, he thought. If the battery had been connected the electrical energy would have been able to travel from the battery, through the switch to ignite the model rocket engine. That would have set off the blasting cap, in turn detonating the C4. He wondered how many of Allah's soldiers had died due to mistakes they made making such explosive devices. Even in their carelessness they were martyrs in the eyes of Allah.

Ahmed studied the web page on his laptop and then turned his attention back to the final assembly. He lifted the thermos lid and carefully placed it on the threads of the bottle and began to slowly screw the lid down. As the cap turned clockwise, the wires within unwound and the contact pin contacted the plate and pushed upward on the bimetallic steel contact shoe separating the two pieces of metal causing the circuit inside to open. Once the lid was snug, he tested the resistance of the switch. The reading was infinity. The circuit was open and he could now safely install the nine-volt battery. Without wincing Ahmed fastened the clip-on connector to the top of the battery and placed it down inside the lower section of the cap. He installed a piece of foam to take up the loose area so the battery would stay in place and used the hot glue gun to secure the outer plastic of the lid to the cap and buffed away the slag from the application of the glue erasing any indication that it had been taken apart. Lastly he placed the red cone shaped lid on the thermos to cover the cap. He thought it ironic that the thermos was designed to look like a rocket.

Ahmed closed the page on his laptop that showed the plans for the bomb. He was about to close the laptop when the chime sounded, indicating he had mail. It was from his contact in Moscow.

"Dmitri is not happy. He wants to be paid. Do not jeopardize your project with unpaid debt."

Ahmed deleted the message and emptied his trash. "Damned Russians," he thought.

CHAPTER 11

DECOY

JIM WHEELER saw that his two girls were asleep as he glanced in the rearview mirror. He pushed the volume control on the steering wheel to turn the sound down.

"Hey, I was listening to that, Mister." His wife shot him a look, but then smiled. Jim pointed to the back. Linda turned to look. "That's pretty much how I feel about now," she said as she reached back to pull the blanket further up on her sleeping daughter.

"Tell me about it. I'm feeling the same way, but lucky for me your snoring keeps me from falling asleep at the wheel." His wife playfully smacked his arm. "Stop it, I do not snore."

Jim was always pretty fast with a comeback. "Yeah, you do. I almost stopped in the town where we ate to see if a muffler shop was open, but then when you woke up I realized there was nothing wrong with the car."

Linda laughed out loud then tried to quiet herself with a hand over her mouth. She suddenly stopped laughing. "Jim, are you speeding?" Her husband reactively took his foot off the gas and looked at the speedometer. "Not by much, why?"

"Because that cop pulled out of that side road as we went by and he's moving pretty fast this way." Jim looked in the mirror. "He doesn't have his lights on. He's probably just late for shift change."

Linda continued to stare as the speeding police car approached the rear of their vehicle. "Well don't stare at him. He'll think you're guilty of something if he sees that look on your face." Jim smiled broadly as his wife turned to face the front, smiling as well. "That is so bull. They don't pull you over just because you are looking at them."

Jim glanced in his rearview again. It was as if the officer in the patrol car had been waiting for him to do just that.

"Shit, he's calling us in," Jim said quietly.

Linda turned to look in her rearview mirror. "What? He is not. Why aren't the lights on then?"

"I don't know." Jim checked his speed again. He wasn't speeding, and it was daylight, so he wasn't being pulled over for having a light out. He was baffled at the interest the cop seemed to be taking in his car.

The Trailblazer moved along at the speed limit as the state patrol vehicle held steady at about a 100-meter distance. The two vehicles came upon a median crossover where two more patrol cars were facing their lanes. The Wheeler's truck sped past the two sitting cars. Both officers were on their mikes.

"Jim, they are staring at us. This is eerie," Linda blurted out.

Jim had to agree. "I know. I feel like I'm a kid out cruising who just ran a stop sign. What the hell?"

"What?" Linda saw Jim looking in his mirror and turned again to see what her husband saw. Both of the patrol cars had pulled out of the center median crossover and were now taking up both lanes behind their vehicle. The lead patrol car had moved forward and was closing in on the bumper of the truck.

Linda and Jim both jumped when the lights came on and the siren whooped to life.

Jim slowed the vehicle and pulled to the side of the road and then onto the shoulder. He began to roll the window down when the voice of the officer behind him came over the loudspeaker. "Place your hands on the steering wheel and remain facing forward. Have your passenger place his hands on the dashboard in front of him."

Linda looked at her husband. "What did you do while I was asleep? Rob a liquor store?"

Jim smiled nervously. "I swear I didn't do anything. I'm sure I paid for the gas at that station." He tried to remember swiping the card at the pump.

"Jim Wheeler, are you telling me you are a drive off?"

Her husband laughed. "No I didn't drive off, I paid with the card." But he looked a little unsure.

"Jim?"

"Well, it was late and I was tired. I'm trying to remember. Shhh! Here he comes." Jim looked in his outside mirror and could see the highway patrolman walking towards the car. He noted that he unclipped his holster and held his right hand close to the weapon. Jim focused on the vehicle behind him and couldn't believe his eyes. The officer from one of the cars behind them was outside his vehicle, gun drawn and taking cover behind the open door of the car. Jim switched views to the center mirror. The officer from the other vehicle was also out, weapon drawn, at the front of his vehicle.

"What is it, Jim?" Linda looked worried now. Her husband shushed her again as the sound of the approaching officer came through the partially open window.

Sergeant Randal Schaffer carefully moved towards the driver's door. He glanced at the license plate and confirmed that it was indeed the one that he had committed to memory. He paused for a second to look quickly again at the plate. He noticed that the top right fastener was not screwed down all the way and immediately got the feeling that this was not the right vehicle. Still he moved cautiously forward. The windows were tinted and Sergeant Schaffer could not see the two children inside. He stepped back towards the traffic lanes away from the side glass just in case.

Jim looked intently from the slightly lowered glass. "Can I help you officer?" he asked, feeling a bit rehearsed.

The officer directed him to roll his window down a bit more. "I'll need to see your license and registration, please." The officer began to relax a little as the window lowered and he could see that the person in the passenger seat was a female. Jim could see the officer's stance change and felt more comfortable as well. He removed the license from his wallet and handed it to the officer.

"You guys were freaking us out back there," Jim began. "Can you tell me what I was doing that brought on all this attention?"

"Just relax, Sir, and stay in your car." Schaffer backed away and moved towards the front of the car. He looked for the license plate on the front of the vehicle and saw that it was missing, but obvious dirt traces indicated that it had a plate that had recently been removed.

Linda watched as the officer stood at the front of their vehicle speaking into the radio. "What do you think is going on, Jim?" she asked. Jim looked in the mirror and saw that the two officers at the rear were falling back from their positions. To his relief they holstered their weapons.

Jim thought for a moment. "My guess is they thought we were somebody else. Evidently, someone who's not a very nice person."

CHAPTER 12

CLOSE CALL

BIN MASRI pulled hard on his smoke. He breathed in deeply then exhaled the smoke out the window as he sped toward Oklahoma. He'd wanted to be out of Texas by now and at the speed he was moving it wouldn't be much longer. The road was fairly heavy with traffic. Large semi trucks and trailers blocked the lanes ahead. Bin-Masri pulled into the fast lane, but found that he had no place to go. There was nothing he could do until the trucks maneuvered out of his way. He fell back into the right lane behind a large reefer trailer as the two north bound lanes suddenly turned downward and curved to the right.

Bin Masri saw the flashing lights and didn't think much about them at first. Probably an accident, he thought. He looked around the truck ahead of him, straining to see more of what was happening, when the unmistakable image of a blue Chevy Trailblazer came into view. "It couldn't be," he thought.

He sped up, pulling closer to the semi-trailer in front of him and looked again. They were coming down a sweeping hill and he could clearly see the vehicles parked on the shoulder now. He could not see the tag on the vehicle, but could see that the police officers had their weapons drawn.

Leaja bin Masri decided that he needed to be in the left lanes, to minimize the possibility of being spotted. If the police saw him they would no doubt give chase. The traffic slowed suddenly as the truckers neared the flashing emergency lights at the bottom of the long hill. Bin Masri used the opportunity to pull into the left lane and move close behind the lead truck.

The semi in front of him suddenly braked hard. Bin Masri was following within a few feet, too close to the rear of the trailer to be seen by the driver of the truck. Startled by the sudden slow down, Bin-Masri slammed on his brakes. He looked in his rear view mirror in time to see another semi, a red Freightliner, barreling toward the back of his Trailblazer. The semi was moving way too fast to avoid ramming bin Masri's SUV.

Bin Masri suddenly and intentionally took the only course of action he could think of, and pulled hard left onto the narrow shoulder.

The driver of the truck in front of him was still on the brakes when he saw the SUV pull onto the narrow left shoulder and wondered why on earth the driver would do such a thing. Then he saw the Freightliner. He let off his brake and stepped hard on the accelerator to give himself a little room between his trailer and the bright red truck that was moving toward his ass end. He glanced through his mirror at the SUV on his left and moved over in an attempt to give bin Masri the room he needed. The right mirror struck the mirror of the semi next to his shattering the glass and causing it to crack loudly against his right door glass as the mirror folded inward, pivoting on its spring loaded mounts.

The driver of the Peterbuilt on the right turned his attention from what was happening ahead, startled by the sound of the mirrors crashing together. He instinctively yanked his wheel to the right, swerving hard trying to avoid a collision with the truck that was nearly into his door.

Bin Masri found himself in an awkward position between the median and a semi moving at a speed in excess of seventy miles an hour. When the semi suddenly moved to the right bin Masri took the opportunity to speed past it on the shoulder. He had just accelerated when the shoulder ahead of him narrowed to accommodate a small drainage abutment. Bin Masri had no choice but to move closer to the truck on his right or smash hard into the concrete ahead. The driver of the semi saw the impending disaster and had to decelerate rapidly to allow bin Masri's truck to run the remaining length of his tractor-trailer and pull ahead of him. Bin Masri was inches from the left front fender of the truck. The driver of the semi forced his truck even closer to the Peterbuilt on his right. The Peterbuilt's driver felt the wake up strips rumbling as he moved as far as possible to the right to avoid the looming semi. He was now partially on the shoulder and coming up fast on the first of the three state patrol cars. There was nothing he could do but lock up the brakes completely and hope for the best or move back to the left abruptly and force the other truck back into the left lane. The driver had no idea why he was being crowded, but he had seen the result of a multiple semi pile-up. Usually it meant death by fire. He chose to stand on the brakes.

Kenneth Wash

CHAPTER 13

SIDESWIPED

RANDY SCHAFFER had just put down the mike after telling his men to stand down when the sound of what he first thought was a propeller driven aircraft punctured the air.

Mike Phillips, the patrolman at the last patrol car heard the sound and looked over his shoulder in time to see the growing shape of the semi heading directly toward him. He spun around and ran at full speed, yelling to his partners to move, as the noise of the first of eighteen screaming tires being tortured by the asphalt struck his ears. The howl of the skidding truck was overwhelming. The officer had the sudden impulse to cover both of his ears, but fought it away as he jumped over the left corner of his patrol car and slammed into the back bumper and hatch of the Wheeler's Trailblazer.

Linda heard the tire noise and then the thud at the back of the truck. She spun around in time to see the officer careen off their truck and stumble to the opposite side of his car. Suddenly, the sound of the howling tires and the view of the out of control truck came together to form a complete and startling picture of imminent danger.

Sergeant Schaffer yelled something to the other patrolman, but it was inaudible to Jim. Linda was screaming for Jim to go, but there was no way that he could start the car and move it soon enough to escape the massive truck that was barreling in their direction. All he could do was turn and yell for his wife to get out, but there wasn't enough time for that either. Jim glanced at his children. The thought that they were sleeping and wouldn't know what hit them crossed his mind and was almost soothing.

On the other side of the highway Leaja bin Masri was struggling to maneuver back into the traffic lane from the shoulder. His SUV caught the edge of the railing that guarded the concrete form he was trying to avoid. Bin Masri pulled in front of the semi within a millisecond of full contact with the barrier. The driver of the truck thought for sure that the SUV wouldn't make it, but was relieved when he saw bin Masri's vehicle squeeze by. Realizing that he could move back to the left, he swerved sharply, nearly overcompensating, and almost put the truck into a roll.

The Peterbuilt's driver suddenly had an option.

The driver released his hold on the brakes, downshifted, accelerated and began to steer away, back into the traffic lanes to keep from colliding with the patrol car.

The sound of the tires skidding and the gurgle of the engine's jake-brake suddenly stopped as the trajectory of the truck began to change. Jim could hear the downshift and the successive scream of the Cummins turbo diesel as the driver matted the accelerator in an attempt to shift the truck away from the cars ahead.

The right front corner of the gleaming chrome bumper being pushed by eleven tons of truck narrowly missed the back bumper of the patrol car, but skimmed down its left side removing the radio antennae and the door handles and slicing off the left outside mirror and floodlight. The mirror rolled and bounced between the semi and the Wheeler's truck, careened upward over the hood, and flew toward Sergeant Schaffer like an incoming mortar round, landing within a foot of the officer before rolling to a stop twenty meters away. A wall of dust and bits of sand and gravel blasted through Jim Wheeler's lowered window. The loud roar of the truck passing and the sound of the pieces of flying police car parts combined into a noise that sounded like the passing of a tornado.

Bin Masri continued to move quickly up the highway, unseen by the police, contemplating his close brush with death and praising his God for allowing him to live. He was lucky in more than one way. Had he driven up the road any sooner he would have been the one stopped by the State Patrol. His heart was still pounding when he cleared the remaining traffic and drove into Oklahoma. It wouldn't be long before he was in Missouri, but there were several hours of driving before he made it to St. Louis. Hopefully his luck would continue to hold.

Kenneth Wash

CHAPTER 14

HOMEBODY

ALAN RAMSEY had finally given into the pangs of hunger that had been trying to get him to stop and eat for over three hours. It had been a long day spent looking for leads that would answer the questions that were filling his head.

He had been hungry since five o'clock when he'd gotten a call that the Texas State Troopers had caught up with the blue Trailblazer. He was quickly disappointed when they sent word that it was not the one they were looking for. At least the Texas authorities were putting forth a good effort.

The forensic folks had since questioned the family who'd been stopped and taken prints from the vehicle. The prints taken from the restaurant where the Illinois family had dined matched the prints taken from the license plates, the garage in Texas and the recovered box truck. The waitress had given a description and a sketch artist was at the restaurant creating the image of what

Ramsey hoped would be the key to catching the fugitive. They were definitely on his trail, but at the moment, the trail ended with the license plates.

Ramsey's thoughts were interrupted by the rattling of the cell phone on the desk in front of him. He picked up the phone and read the caller I.D. It was his Mrs. Ramsey, probably wondering if her husband was coming home or was planning on spending the night on the couch in his office.

Alan glanced at the time. Eight o'clock! How did it get so late? He pressed the button on the phone knowing that he was in trouble for not calling and expected that he was about to find out exactly how much trouble.

"T2, Ramsey speaking." Alan gave his standard line.

Instead of the sharp tone he'd expected, Kate Ramsey's voice was soft. "Hello, Man. Did you forget we had a date tonight?"

Alan grimaced as he looked at the calendar. Crap! He had promised her that he would be home by eight to spend some alone time with her. "I'm sorry, Honey. I'm walking out the door now. But I have to warn you; I'm going to need to have some calls forwarded to my cell. Our night could be cut short. It's been a rough day today."

"Just get here before the food… and your wife, get cold. You have fifteen minutes. Get ready, get set, go!" And with that she hung up the phone. Alan stood there for a couple seconds and then quickly reviewed his notes. He was good for now. At the moment all he could do was wait and it could be hours, days or even weeks before the next lead would develop. He'd promised Kate when they got married that he would always keep time for her. He had had to expand that promise with the birth of the twins. Now that they were old enough to spend the night at Grandma's, Alan and Kate Ramsey got about one or two evenings a month alone.

He grabbed his jacket, but left his laptop and case. He was sure he wouldn't need it. It was definitely not a work at home night.

That's good too, he thought. That will make it a hell of a lot easier to get through security in the morning.

Alan looked at his watch. At this hour traffic would be light. Five to ten minutes is all he needed and he would be in the door. He closed the door to the office making sure it locked behind him and headed towards the elevator. He decided that the stairs would probably be faster. Besides, he could use the exercise. He flung the door open and ran down the steps four floors to ground level and sprinted out into the parking lot and to his car at the far end of the lot.

He yanked off his tie as he threw the car in gear and sped out of the lot. He looked at his watch. One minute gone. "Let's go, Mario," he said to himself as he waited for a break in the traffic. Within seconds he was heading to the interstate.

He and Kate were lucky. Their home was only five miles away from "the complex" as Kate liked to call it. It was a four bedroom Cape Cod, story and a half that had been left to him when his parents died in a plane crash on a trip to the Florida Keys. That had been well before the war. Alan had been finishing up his degree, not yet out of college. He had been devastated. He was an only child and had had no one to turn to. That's how he met Katherine Burnett. She wasn't like the other students at school. They offered condolences, but she offered to help. She was earning a law degree and bluntly spoke about the things that Alan needed to do legally. She helped him through the processing of the will and all the related details.

After the World Trade Center and the Pentagon were attacked, Alan decided to enlist in the Army Special Forces. He chose the intelligence corps hoping that he could come back with skills that would lead to becoming a special investigator in law enforcement.

Kate knew Alan was patriotic and loved his country. When they were out with friends and talk turned to politics he always stood up in defense of the country. But the vengeance he wore on his sleeve after the attacks was disheartening to her. She often told him to check his personal feelings and not be so angry at the world.

And then he left.

He called her from Fort Benning, Georgia and told her he had enlisted. Her heart sank. Kate cried for days and was so angry with Alan that she refused to answer emails from him.

But then Kate began to worry. She knew that the images of the burning towers and the promise of revenge would call out to him. Within days of his graduation from advanced skills training Alan managed to get himself assigned to one of the first units to engage the enemy in the new war against terror.

Before shipping off to Afghanistan Alan came home and proposed to Kate. They were married in a small church and spent the next week as husband and wife. Then it was time for him to leave.

Alan proved to be an excellent soldier. He rose through the ranks to become a sergeant and a squad leader and soon was selected for direct commissioning to become an officer. By the time his unit redeployed from the theater of operations Alan was wearing the gold bar of a Second Lieutenant.

Ramsey shook away his thoughts realizing that he was almost home. He turned left onto Claris Drive and spotted his wife's BMW in the driveway. She always seemed to park in the middle of the driveway, not leaving any room for his car. Once again Alan Ramsey, man of the house, would have to park on the street.

One day he would like to get home from work without needing the light from the streetlamp to guide his way. It seemed that if he left in the darkness of the morning he should be back before dark. Sometimes in the summer he did manage to get home before the sun set.

The door was unlocked. He stepped into the dimly lit foyer and peered around the doorway leading to the dining room. Dinner was not on the table, but a chilled, open bottle of wine was. He poured himself a glass and was going to pour Kate's, but noted there was only one glass on the table. He stood quietly for a moment as he sipped the wine, staring into the flickering flame of the candle. Feeling a presence behind him he turned to see his wife as she set her glass down and reached around from behind him and hugged him.

"Hello, Man," she said in a playful voice as she rested her chin on his left shoulder. Kate breathed out a sigh that told Alan she was happy he was home. Her breath teased his ear and sent a shiver that caused him to smile and tilt his head away a bit. Kate questioned his movement. "Ticklish, Mr. Ramsey?" she asked and then leaned over to blow a bit more at his ear.

Alan felt the stirrings that were all too familiar when his wife was so close to him. "Yes, Mrs. Ramsey, and how about you? Are you ticklish?" He spun to face her and set his glass down. She leaned back against the wall, the light from the candles giving an orange glow to her auburn, shoulder length hair, and making translucent, dancing shadows on the surface behind her. Alan looked at his wife and what she was wearing. The dress was tight and short with a medium neckline and no sleeves. He couldn't tell for sure what color it was in the glow of the candles. It was dark was all he knew.

He pulled himself against her. "Well, well, you seem happy to see me," Kate said and she slid her hand between the two of them and gave a gentle squeeze. Alan reached behind her placing his hands low on her rear and slid them up under the edge of her dress. As he'd suspected, she was not wearing anything underneath. They locked into a passionate kiss as she fumbled a bit with the front of Alan's pants until she released what she was after. Her breathing quickened as she wrapped a leg around his waist and began to rock in unison with her man. They looked into each other's eyes relishing in the love that they'd found so many years before. They moved together for several more minutes until he couldn't hold back any more.

Kate began to shudder and bit down on his lip, a sign Alan had learned that she had reached a point of no return. She was his and he knew it. She gasped, as did he, and convulsed, arching backward as Alan slowed his pace.

They stood together with their foreheads touching, giggling and smiling. Alan looked deep into her brown eyes languishing in their natural beauty. "I do love you, Mrs. Ramsey," Alan said quietly.

"Not as much as I love you, Mr. Ramsey." She relaxed the hold she had on him and gave him a peck on the lips. Smiling, she said, "And if that is your way of tickling someone then yes, I am very ticklish."

Alan smiled broadly. "You definitely know how to build up a guy's appetite. Or is this just a ploy to get me to eat your cooking?"

"I'll have you know that I made something very special tonight. Spiced Cornish hens and steamed broccoli and those little red potatoes you like so much." She put on a pouting look.

"Well, then let's eat 'cause I am starved." Alan tried to put himself back together, but still had a disheveled look as they walked together into the kitchen where Ramsey could now smell the food. Kate opened the oven and pulled out the two hens. They were beautifully glazed with glistening red potatoes surrounding them on the dish. She removed the aluminum foil that covered the broccoli and handed it to Alan.

"Honey, this looks excellent. You made all of this?" His wife was not well known for her culinary skills. She looked at him again playfully and nodded, but Alan knew better. He looked at her quizzically as he placed the aluminum foil in the can. Kate heard the sound of the two paper bags as her husband fished them from the waste bin. He held them up. "So, since when do you package your cooking in deli take out bags?" Kate turned and headed to the dining room with the food. "I don't have a clue where those bags came from and if you want any more desert..." She paused and hoisted her skirt just a little. "I would think you had better thank me for the work I put into this meal I made for my man."

Alan could tell tonight was going to be another exceptional night. His wife was beautiful, sexy and funny. She was just a lousy cook. So tonight she was a liar as well.

Alan watched as she sat in the chair and pulled up to the table with the light from the candles creating a glow that was almost magical. She really was beautiful. He couldn't stop looking at her.

"Well?" Kate asked.

Alan sat next to her rather than across the table and took a small section from the Cornish hen on his plate. "Well," he began, "You did a great job on the dinner." He smiled and continued, "I hope it wasn't too much trouble."

She looked at him slyly. "Nothing is too much trouble for you, Mr. Ramsey."

The rest of the night proved to be as Ramsey expected. Much later they lay exhausted next to each other. Looking at the ceiling, Kate said, "Alan, I miss you. You need to take some time off to be with your family." There was no answer. "Alan?" She turned to face him only to find that he was fast asleep.

Kenneth Wash

CHAPTER 15

SURPRISES

JOSHI ZUQAWRI stretched for a long moment and thought about the day's planned activities. He loved the zoo and remembered that his fourth grade class would be going there today. He threw back his covers and found the clothes he had set out on the desk chair. He did not want to waste any time the morning of his field trip. He had begun to dress when he heard his father call up to him. "Joshi, are you awake? Today is a busy day."

Joshi leaned out the doorway of his room, surprised to hear his father's voice, and called down the steps in his native language. "Yes, Father." Joshi preferred to speak English, but it was a forbidden language in his home. It was his father's doing. Ahmed Zuqawri was active as a tribal elder and assistant to the Imam at the Mosque of Rahs Allah. His faith and family history were very important to him.

"What takes that boy so long to get moving?" his father asked rhetorically of his wife.

"It will be fine. He is a boy. Boys get sidetracked. Besides, it has only been a few moments since you first called to him. He's a good boy. He will be right down." Bedalla looked at her husband with feigned suspicion. "And speaking of taking too long, shouldn't you be at work already, or did you plan something that I do not know about? You are the one who is going to be late." She reached for her husband's briefcase.

"Don't bother with that. I am leaving with Joshi this morning. I know how much he likes the zoo, so I made him a special lunch and I am going to drive him to school. Sometimes it is good to talk with him, father to son, with no interruption. The car is a good place to do this."

Bedalla knew not to question too much, but was curious. She whispered so as not to let Joshi hear as he bounded down the staircase, "And what is so special about his lunch today?" She moved toward the kitchen counter where the colorful tin lunch box sat. "Maybe I should inspect this lunch to be sure you haven't overloaded it with too many snacks and not..."

"Stop, woman! You will ruin my surprise." Joshi's eyes went wide as he stepped into the room hearing only the last word of the conversation. "Surprise? What surprise?" Ahmed looked at his wife with disdain, then to his son. "Ah, yes. There is nothing wrong with your hearing is there?"

He picked up the lunchbox and held it out to his son, but stopped short of releasing it as Joshi grabbed the handle.

"I made something special for your day at the zoo. BUT, you cannot open it until it is time for lunch. No peeking before. Ok?"

He released his grasp on the box and Joshi answered with a quick "Ok" back to his father.

"Promise me that you will wait and I will let you in on another little secret."

Joshi smiled and looked quizzically at his father, "I promise" he said.

"Then I must tell you." He leaned down and whispered that he was going to drive Joshi to school instead of him riding the bus. The reaction from his son was not what he had expected.

"No, Father. I want to ride the bus. All of my friends ride the bus. They will think I am a baby if you drive me. Mother, tell him I always ride the bus."

Ahmed quickly began to show his anger. Bedalla stepped in with a hand on her husband's shoulder. "Joshi, your father has decided to spend some time with you today. He made you a special treat for lunch. So special and secret that even I don't know what it is. You should be happy that he wants to do these things for you. Praise Allah for his love for you and accept the gifts that your father bestows upon you. It is wonderful that he takes the time to plan for these moments."

Joshi turned his gaze to his father. "Sorry, Father. I am happy, but I still have to have my breakfast before we can leave for school."

"You must also have shoes on your feet. Now go finish getting dressed and then come back. We will eat quickly. Too much time has passed already this morning. You will be late if you do not hurry." Joshi ran off leaving his lunchbox on the table.

"He is a creature of habit, Ahmed. He is definitely your son," Bedalla said with a smile that Ahmed didn't see.

Ahmed Zuqawri spun to face his wife, seething, "I know my own son. You should not interfere when I am speaking to him. It is not your place." He spun slowly and gestured wildly with both arms spread and continued to rant, "You are not one of the westerners that we live among, yet I believe that when I leave the house you become one. Do you plop down on the couch and turn on Oprah? Remember who you are. You are the wife of Ahmed Zuqawri. We live our lives for Allah. We are not here to chase the self gratifying dream of the American infidels."

Bedalla Zuqawri looked surprised and hurt, but knew that she would get nowhere with any reply to her husband's harsh words. Although she would never admit it, she admired the way American women could speak freely to their husbands without reprimand. She wondered how her husband could hate America and its populace so deeply, yet make a life here that included a career, a home and a family. Her husband raised a hand and swatted the air as he sighed and turned away.

As Ahmed left the room her attention turned to the lunchbox that sat on the edge of the kitchen table. She wondered what surprise her husband had placed in the box for Joshi. It was not like him to think of small gifts that would surprise her or their son, and it intrigued her to think about what had caused such a change to take place. He was not a playful man and lately had been wrapped up with the counsel and the needs of the Imam and the Mosque.

She moved to where the lunchbox sat on the table and looked at the pictures of the astronauts and space shuttle that adorned its metal cover. Suddenly she realized that her son's name was not on the box anywhere and thought that she should write the information on the inside of the lid in the event that one of the other students happened to have the same lunchbox. This would also give her the opportunity to see what was so special inside. She would have to work quickly though before her husband returned.

Bedalla Zuqawri moved to the kitchen drawer and began to rummage through the menagerie of pencils and pens. There she found a black permanent marker and headed back to the table. She took a breath and glanced out of the room to be sure that her husband was not heading back to the kitchen. She could hear the sound of Ahmed's dresser drawer being slid open in their room above the kitchen and calculated that she had enough time to at least put her son's name on the inside of the lunchbox lid.

She spun the box so that the chrome latch was facing her and released the mechanism. The lunchbox seemed heavy. She picked it up to feel the weight. Yes, it was definitely heavier than usual.

Glancing around one last time she set the box back on the counter and opened the lid and wrote "Joshi Zuqawri, 18201 West Park, St. Louis, MO" with the Sharpie. Under that she wrote their phone number knowing that more than likely someone would call before they would mail a lunchbox to a forgetful owner.

She quickly looked through the contents of Joshi's lunchbox, but could not see anything that could be considered a surprise. She had made Joshi's lunch the night before and saw only the peanut butter and jelly sandwich in the zipper seal bag, a fruit cup of peaches and the thermos bottle that she had filled with chocolate milk, Joshi's favorite. She heard her son's footsteps as he landed on the tile floor at the bottom of the stairs. She closed the lid and latched it shut, then spun the lunchbox back into its original position on the table just as Joshi came into the room to claim it.

Joshi picked up the lunchbox and gave it a little shake near his ear, as if he could tell what was inside by the sound of it banging back and forth against its metal confines. Bedalla looked at him. "I'm trying to figure out what the surprise is," Joshi explained quietly so that his father didn't hear.

Ahmed startled them both when he walked briskly back into the room. "Well then, you must be patient." He stopped to look his son in the eyes. "A patient man is rewarded many times over. You will see the surprise as soon as you open the box; I promise."

Ahmed's wife was confused and it showed on her face. She turned away from them both so as not to give away her feelings. She gathered her thoughts and asked about the surprise that was supposed to be inside. "Are you sure you put your surprise in there, Ahmed? You have been very busy with the Imam. Sometimes you can get a little sidetracked."

Zuqawri's frown returned. "What are you saying, woman?"

Bedalla attempted to explain, but could not gather the courage to say that she had opened the box to look for the special gift being promised to her son, but had found nothing.

"I am only saying that you are a very busy man and that after promising your son something, if he were to look forward to it all morning, it would be a shame, if with your busy schedule, you had forgotten to put it in his lunchbox."

Her husband looked at her fiercely and moved very close. She was afraid for the first time since they'd been married that he was about to get physically violent. He hissed through his teeth, "Do not question me in front of our son. There is a surprise. I am not crazy. Mind your own business." He then turned to his son. "Let's go, Joshi."

Bedalla wanted to call after her husband to ask if he was going to the Mosque today. She noted that the prayer mat that he carried was not the one he normally took to his office. The one he carried was the one he used for special prayer services at the Mosque of Rahs Allah. She decided that she had asked enough questions and instead silently watched them get into the car.

Joshi opened the rear door of the Nissan Maxima and slid into the seat. Ahmed turned to ensure that his son was buckled in. He thought briefly that it was a rather pointless action given the day's planned activity. Ahmed began to pull away from the curb when the bus that normally picked up his son rumbled by. The bus slowed to a stop and deployed the stop sign and front gate. Bedalla Zuqawri waved the bus on from the front door. The warning devices retracted and the bus slowly pulled away.

The Nissan pulled out behind the bus. As the bus pulled away the child in the last row of seats raised both middle fingers and stuck out his tongue at Ahmed and his son. "That child should be punished. His insolence and disrespect for others is disgusting."

Ahmed did not hide his feelings from his son. "If I had done that when I was his age my fingers would have been cut off and my tongue removed," Ahmed exaggerated. "He should suffer no less a fate. But here, in America, we must be careful that we do not hurt the feelings of those who thrust upon us their crude and barbaric habits."

Joshi explained, "His name is Demarcus Johnson. He thinks he's funny, but he's not. He's just mean. Ahmed thought for a moment, and then spoke. "Well, maybe you should tell him that you do not appreciate his rude behavior."

Joshi questioned the logic of addressing the behavior issue with the boy on the bus. "I am worried that he will strike me, Father. He likes to fight and the ones he chooses to battle with generally do not fare very well."

Joshi's father faced straight ahead and contemplated his son's remarks. After a moment of consideration he spoke. "You must choose to make a difference my son. You must sometimes do what is needed even though it is not the popular course of action. It is your decision to make, not mine." He paused for a second and then continued, "Success and sacrifice often go hand in hand." After a short drive the bus pulled into the parking lot of North Laclede Public School.

The school was a sprawling campus of older tan brick buildings. The golden bricks of the ornate art-deco facade gave a glamorous appearance to the otherwise aged, but refurbished school.

Ahmed watched as the tall child from Joshi's bus stepped from the bus onto the curb. He pushed the child in front of him out of his way and when the child protested, Demarcus grabbed his crotch with one hand, flipped him off with the other and loudly cursed at the smaller boy. He laughed loudly, spun around and walked away. All of this took place under the watchful eye of a teacher standing nearby.

"That child, Demarcus, he is in your class?" Ahmed asked.

Joshi replied quietly, "Yes."

Ahmed continued, "Then he is going to the zoo with you today?"

Joshi opened the door and began to get out. "Unfortunately, yes. The teachers will have to watch him carefully all day."

111

Ahmed replied somewhat sarcastically, "Then, may Allah be with you today and forever."

Joshi smiled a large smile and said goodbye. Ahmed watched his son walk to the doors and into the building. He thought about whether his son would have been able to comprehend the important role he was about to play in the actions against the infidels. Even more so, he wondered about Bedalla and how she would react to the news that her son had been chosen to be a martyr as he steered his vehicle back into the traffic lanes and headed to work.

CHAPTER 16

LATE AWAKENING

THE high-pitched sound of the secure digital print/fax machine woke Alan Ramsey. He stared at the ceiling for a moment and then realized that the room was flooded with sunshine. The feeling that he was unsure of his location or what day it was crept into his consciousness and he dwelt for a moment on whether he was supposed to be at work or not.

Shit! He thought as he sprung to a sitting position. His brain was putting together the puzzle of the morning after. His mind zeroed in on the sound of the fax machine as Alan looked for his wife. The smell of coffee told him she was probably in the kitchen.

He got to his feet and looked at the clock. Seven thirty. He was two and a half hours behind his self-imposed schedule. He pulled on his briefs and walked into the den to retrieve the incoming fax. Still somewhat groggy, he turned his head sideways and looked at the image that was ratcheting out of the machine. Alan tilted his head a bit further to the left to try to make the image as close to upright as possible. The man looked familiar, but he couldn't place him. Finally the paper dropped free.

"Holy crap," was the first thing to pop from his brain and out of his mouth as the image of Leaja bin Masri connected and pulled together his memories. Alan stepped back into the bedroom to find his pants. Not there. He remembered they were downstairs in the living room. He ran down the steps, passing Kate and fumbled through his pocket for his phone. Kate entered the room looking at him quizzically as Gabe Anderson picked up on the other end.

"Gabe, Alan. I just got the fax you sent. Is this the guy that was in Texas?"

"Good Morning, Alan. Where are you? I figured you would be in early this morning," Gabe pointedly stated.

"Yes, Sir. I'm on my way in a few minutes. Do you have a name yet?" Ramsey asked impatiently.

Gabe flipped through a couple sheets of paper, but was sure he did not have the answer. "No, just the drawing at this point."

"His name is Leaja bin Masri. He was the right hand man of both Musab al-Kuwari and Hamza al-Muhajeer. I chased his ass around Afghanistan and then Iraq. I last saw him jump through a window just outside of Sadr City."

Alan paused to take a breath. "Leaja bin Masri is the guy who about killed me. He's why I am here and not back in Afghanistan with the SPECOPS right now."

Gabe didn't say anything at first and then quietly asked, "Are you sure, Alan? That's some big news. First Al-Muhajeer, and now bin Masri."

"Yes, I'm sure. Shit, I'm so sure I'm shaking." Alan looked at his hands and realized he had been affected by what was going on. He looked at his wife who was looking worriedly at him. "Gabe, these guys mean business. They are bad news. With al-Muhajeer dead we have one less evil mind to worry about, but this bin Masri is ruthless. We used to call him Darth Vader because he would kill his own people if they showed weakness or made mistakes. I don't believe he will take Hamza al-Muhajeer's death, let alone the others that were found in the desert, easy. This guy holds people accountable. He will consider his mission a vendetta to avenge their deaths."

"What about you, Alan? Didn't you say that your men..." Gabe thought how to phrase what he was about to say. "Didn't you tell me that his family was killed in the raid? Do you think he holds the same vendetta for you?"

Alan looked at Kate again and then at the picture of his two boys on the wall. Her eyes followed his gaze. "No, I wouldn't think that he would risk his mission to chase down one person from his past."

"Maybe not one Alan, but what about four? An eye for an eye, remember?" Gabe retorted.

Ramsey turned away from his wife on the pretense of putting the scanned drawing on the table behind the couch and spoke quietly, "This guy has been in business a long time. I can't believe that he would jeopardize what plans they have to hunt me down. What I'm saying is that his mission will be hard pressed to fail given his convictions, that's all. He will make it personal to make sure he kills as many Americans as possible."

"Alright Alan, but I wouldn't take any unnecessary chances. Look, we will know more soon. Dan Burns will be on the conference call from Texas that starts in less than an hour, so you need to get in here."

"Roger. I will be there as soon as I find my keys...and put some clothes on," Ramsey joked.

Kenneth Wash

CHAPTER 17

CONFERENCE CALL

"**ARE** you on, Alan?" Gabe Anderson's voice asked from the speaker on Alan's phone.

"Yes, Sir. I'm here. Sorry about being late."

Gabe turned his attention to the group. "Ok folks, I have Dan Burns on the secure line. He has spent the last eighteen hours combing through the sand down in the great state of Texas and has some interesting information."

"Good morning, gentlemen. It is now six twenty-five a.m. here in Harlingen, Texas. As you know the incident here took place around zero-three-hundred yesterday morning. A lot has happened since then, but no real leads have been generated and forensics has not yet completed ballistics or positive identification on several of the dead terrorists. We are pretty sure that Hamza Al-Muhajeer is one of the dead. Two others, Ali-Anis al-Tawid and Habbib-Anis al-Tawid have a positive I.D. as brothers and legal residents of the United States, in St. Louis, Missouri to be exact. The vehicle they were driving was their own, unlike the others that were leased or rented. All of the vehicles here, except for the box truck, were registered in Missouri. I'll cover the box truck later."

Burns continued, "First off, we are looking at several cell phones. Muhajeer's had no information stored that we could use. The others had the numbers for each other's phones, but nothing else. According to the component board serial numbers they were all purchased from a company called Brazen Technologies at a mall kiosk in St. Louis within days of each other and all of them were on the pay as you go plan, and there are no past records. The only info we gleaned from them was the purchase point, and possible credit card info. We're still working that angle.

Given the fact that al-Muhajeer had zero information stored we figured that the phones were purchased in St. Louis and transported to Texas for the initial meeting with al-Muhajeer. Prints found on the phone belong to al-Muhajeer and two other people. They don't match any of the dead guys. More than likely we'll find that one set of prints belong to the driver of the box truck. The other could be the store clerk's for all we know. The forensics gurus are looking for matches on the box truck as we speak."

Ramsey interrupted, "Dan, within the last hour we received some info on that driver. The witness' description and the artist rendering I saw is a guy named Leaja bin Masri. I can get his prints from the archives. I think you'll find that he's the driver of the box truck."

Burns thanked Alan and continued, "That sounds right. Between the phone, the truck, and the repair shop it looks like we have a positive match. Get me those print samples and we will probably put this all together. We have the National Terrorist Database working the DNA portion. They'll want to be sure. We also have a team heading to St. Louis to talk to Matt Sanders, the manager of the sales kiosk." Dan Burns took a sip of his coffee before continuing, "OK, you should all have what I'm looking at on your monitors. You can see that the fingerprints lifted from al-Muhajeer's phone and the prints from the passenger door of the box truck are identical. We should have confirmation from forensics anytime now that the dead terrorist in these pictures is Hamza al-Muhajeer.

Alan Ramsey looked at the photos that were appearing on his monitor. "I think the boys from Harlingen may have really screwed up al-Muhajeer's plans. From what you're saying, Dan, I'm getting the picture that whatever was in the back of the box truck, that for now let's say is a bomb, a big bomb, wasn't the only package being picked up from Mexico. I think al-Muhajeer himself was the other package."

Dan Burns placed another document on the HP digital sender and pressed send. "Alan is right. What you should be getting any minute is the passenger manifest from Avion Airlines out of Caracas, Venezuela. This flight originated in Caracas and flew to General Mariano Escobedo International Airport in Monterrey, Mexico night before last. There are several passengers from outside the United States that we should be concerned about, and believe me, we will be watching for, but take note of the fifth down in the first class listing."

"Got it." Gabe Anderson acknowledged the receipt of the sent document.

"Yusif al-Dardiri! That's al-Muhajeer!" Ramsey exclaimed. "Damn, I was only tracking him as al-Muhajeer. Son of a bitch!"

Dan Burns interjected, "We think Muhajeer, AKA, Dardiri *and* "the bomb" were the intended "packages". Looks like someone is looking for an organizer or a leader."

Gabe Anderson asked for some clarification. "Dardiri, al-Muhajeer, bin Masri. Ramsey, seeing how you're the insurgent expert, explain this to me and tell me how you think this guy, Dardiri slipped out of our range of vision."

Alan detected the sour note embedded in his boss' last remark as he began to explain. "Yusif al-Dardiri and Hamza al-Muhajeer are two pseudonyms of the same person according to the FBI and the U.S. State Department."

"During the war it wasn't uncommon for these guys to change their names. It seemed like every time one of them came to power we would suddenly lose track of them. At first we thought that they were being sent out of the country for specialized training. It wasn't too long before we figured out what was going on. Like some of the others, al-Muhajeer did the same thing. He was known as al-Dardiri when he was a member of the Egyptian Islamic Jihad. He was a senior aide to former leader Musab al-Awari, who was killed in a U.S. air strike. My Pentagon sources identified him as among the prime candidates to assume direction of the Iraqi Insurgency." Alan typed a few keystrokes and pulled up a picture of al-Dardiri and sent it out for everyone to view before he continued.

"Dardiri was a native Egyptian. He joined the Muslim Brotherhood, and in 1982 he joined the Egyptian Islamic Jihad, which later became part of al-Qaeda. He went to Afghanistan in 1999, where he became an explosives expert and in 2004 he was put in charge of al-Qaeda's overseas networks. Then, like magic, he disappeared from the radar. All of the intel agencies tried to relocate him. And I mean all of them. They found nothing, as if al-Dardiri just fell off the planet." Alan looked at Gabe before going on. His boss rolled his hand as if to tell him to continue.

"Then, in 2005 things took a major bad turn in Iraq. Insurgency climbed, the Shia and the Sunni began blowing each other up on a daily basis, and the use of Improvised Explosive Devices or IEDs started to take a huge toll on our soldiers and equipment. Suddenly the name Hamza al-Muhajeer began to be spoken everywhere. We assumed that he was just another new player in the conflict. But this guy was bad news. A very strategic and quick thinking insurgent whose strategy was to target the civilians and kill the soldiers who were trying to protect them. He took away the security of the people of Iraq and then removed the hope that the Americans could make it better. He was very illusive and has been wanted by Coalition and Iraqi authorities since 2005. He was one of the al-Qaeda leadership that dropped off the radar early in the 2007 Surge. The last time we had good solid information was just before the raid in Sadr city. We almost caught him and the other one, Leaja bin Masri, but both of them managed to escape."

Dan Burns spoke up, "We thought they had been recalled back to Afghanistan and never picked up another trace on either of them. It was assumed they were dead or M.I.A."

Gabe Anderson looked as if he'd gotten more information than he had bargained for. "So why weren't we tracking this al-Dardiri fellow? I mean if we knew al-Dardiri was really al-Muhajeer why didn't we have a good track on him?"

Ramsey offered the information before Dan Burns. "Well, that's the thing. We didn't really know the two were the same. I had no Idea. In fact, the name al-Dardiri didn't really come up again after his disappearance in 2004, other than in an article that was published in the Washington Post titled something like "Where Are They Now?" The writer of the piece tried to place the blame of all the missing al-Qaeda leadership on the ineptitude of our clandestine government organizations. He mentioned that an anonymous official in Washington told him that Hamza al-Muhajeer was also known by the name Yusif al-Dardiri. But, because the only reference to al-Dardiri came from the article in the Washington Post I didn't consider it factual. I tried to find confirmation of their reporting, but whomever the "Officials in Washington" were refused to step forward to take the credit for enlightening the Post. Looks like they were right. I should have followed up on this."

Gabe Anderson shuffled the information around his brain and stared at the papers in front of him briefly before continuing. "Ok. So what we have is an airline that is sanctioned by the Venezuelan government shuttling in al-Qaeda leaders." Gabe Anderson's conclusion was the same as everyone else's at the moment.

"Sir, right now we only have proof that al-Dardiri was transported on an Avion flight out of Venezuela to Mexico. There is nothing to indicate that the Venezuelan or Mexican governments had any knowledge of his background or for that matter his being wanted by the FBI. We don't exactly have a good working relationship with Chavez, so asking him to cooperate with an investigation that basically accuses his government of aiding and abetting a terrorist fugitive is a little daring to say the least. If it was me, Sir, I think I would have all available space based imagery trained on South America looking for al-Qaeda training camps and maybe a few special ops teams in place to snoop around just in case."

Gabe Anderson was deep in thought. He wondered about the time frame of the flight. "So, his flight arrives in Monterrey at eleven fifty-four, let's just say midnight, and the U.S. Customs and Border Protection Agency Harlingen teams confront him somewhere around three AM. Therefore, Dardiri or al-Muhajeer, place your favorite terrorist leader's name here, has about four hours to get to Harlingen from Monterrey. How far is Harlingen, Texas from Monterrey, Mexico?"

Alan pulled up a map on his laptop. "According to this it's about a hundred and seventy-five miles. We're pretty sure that the Hind dropped him in the desert, but it would only take twenty or thirty minutes to cover that mileage by chopper. Any ideas as to when the helicopter may have left Monterrey?"

One of the technicians at the table chimed in. "Obviously it didn't fly straight in. If it had it would have been spotted by the border patrols or the Mexican Air Corps. We think it left Monterey and tracked east over the Gulf, then turned north and finally west to fly into our airspace looking like one of our own Black-OPS Border Birds. According to the Coast Guard, what they thought was a Black Hawk popped up on radar suddenly, like maybe fifteen to twenty-five miles out. It was probably coming in low and then did a jump to confuse things. Guess it worked, at least for a while."

Those paying attention nodded in agreement. Ramsey contemplated the young technician's assessment. "It's also obvious that the man had some type of help from inside the United States. Have we gotten any info on who may have supplied the transponder and the tracker device?" Ramsey asked.

Dan Burns jumped back in. "We are near positive that an airman by the name of Mark Beirman was the supplier. He was the last guy working on the bird when it was at the Pensacola Air Naval Base Station. He took off on his motorcycle for a few days R and R. They found him half naked at a motel with two bullet holes in his forehead. The proprietor said he's seen the guy with several women over the course of a year or so, but never any other guys. Could be we need to look for a woman who has interests that lie outside those of the U.S government's. They are also reviewing phone traffic. Seems as though Beirman's boss thinks he had some kind of relationship that may have gone sour. He said he was constantly on the phone when it first started, but then he began telling the woman to stop calling him. Said he sounded angry at times."

Ramsey finished up the timeline. "So the firefight takes all of about twenty minutes and the box truck speeds away ending up in Corpus a hundred and fifty miles away. There's another two or three hours, maybe more if the damage inflicted on the truck caused it to have problems. Now, we have reports from the truck stop. Dan, have you collected the prints there?"

"Yeah, Alan. Looks like a match on the phone and the box-truck. We're sure it's the same guy."

Ramsey interjected, "And now we have a drawing and if we dig deep enough we can probably find a couple images of the guy in our shoeboxes full of photos."

The technician spoke again, "We are all over that. I have been gathering stuff all morning to sift through, and spent all night going through about ten terabytes of data in my office. She's searching right now while we are here."

Ramsey had to ask, "Who is she? Who's searching?"

The scarecrow looking young man held up his hand and smiled. "Cheri." The technician continued, "You see, I designed a program that can read the image on the sketches. It's a networking program that is controlled by a single host computer that draws information from the whole database. I call the program CHERI. It's an acronym for Controlled Hosting Enhancement and Recognition Imaging."

"Good job, uh...I'm sorry, but I didn't get your name," Alan acknowledged.

"Rick...Rick White. I work down in the ICA office,...oh, sorry, Image Control and Access office. Alan just looked at the young man who obviously lived for his work. "Very impressive, Rick. Keep us posted on the progress. In the mean time we need to get the artist's drawing of Leaja bin Masri circulating."

Gabe Anderson spoke next. "Already been sent out. We didn't do any live media outlets yet, but plan to once we have a good photograph of the man."

"We haven't talked about where this guy might be going." It was Dan Burns now. "His last known location was traveling north on I35 towards Oklahoma. And that was about sixteen hours ago. He could be anywhere now. You would think if he were heading towards the East Coast he would have taken Interstate Ten across, not gone straight up north on Thirty Five. The anniversary of the Oklahoma City Bombing is in two months. You don't suppose that has any significance do you?"

Alan had thought about that, but had dismissed it. "I can't imagine any outside terrorist organization giving a crap about Timothy McVeh, let alone, Oklahoma. That's not their fight. It's not populated enough. I think we can all agree that this next planned attack has nuclear stamped all over it. Whether it's a dirty bomb or a detonation there will be radiation and it will kill many, many people. They'll target a major metropolis and reap a large reward for their time spent. I don't think Oklahoma is the target. Since we have so many leads to Missouri we should start there, specifically St. Louis. I have no idea why they would pick out St. Louis for an attack. Sure, it has a lot of people and the Gateway Arch, but no real governmental ties."

Gabe Anderson drew the conference to close. "OK, folks, here's the homework: Let's get some potential targets given the path taken so far. Let's not rule out the East or West coasts for that matter, but look at everything. My gut feeling says they are going back to New York to finish what they started. Why they are going the direction they are going makes no sense to me, but hey, what the hell makes sense any more. Let's figure this out and head it off at the pass. I have a briefing with the Joint Chiefs at one o'clock, so see if we can get a speculative answer that is based on everything we have including any contacts or associates that may be active across all of our intelligence agencies. White, can CHERI talk to the FBI, the CIA, ATF and Homeland Security?"

"I'd have to hack..I mean patch into their system and download the program. So far they won't cooperate with me." Rick White was hopeful that this would be his moment.

Alan jumped in, "I'll talk to a couple people I know to get the door open for Rick and CHERI. If we get Homeland and ATF on board we can make it into the others through a back door I believe."

Gabe reminded everyone about his one o'clock meeting, giving them a deadline of an hour for any updates. "Alright then. Let's get to work. For God's sake let's hope we get some Intel soon.

CHAPTER 18

DAILY PRAYERS

AHMED ZUQAWRI sat at his desk contemplating his fate and that of his son. He looked at his watch and then at the clock on his desk. It was only eleven-thirty. He felt somewhat uneasy. He questioned whether what he was about to do was right. So many young lives would be taken. He rationalized that because of his duty to his God this was a necessary evil and told himself that this diversion was only a small task, but possibly the key to the success of the mission as a whole.

For those who were true believers of Allah and faithful followers of the Quran, this was a moment in which to be proud. His son would be the martyr that would show others the way and give hope to the soldiers of Allah. The death of his only son would be an example to others showing his commitment to the Jihad.

Ahmed walked over to the window of his office and looked out across the highway to the entrance of the zoo. The St. Louis Zoo was world-renowned and rated the number one zoo in the United States. It was situated in one of the largest city parks in the country and his hospital overlooked the southern edge of the thirteen hundred acres that made up the park.

From this vantage point Ahmed could see the parking lot and the yellow busses. Through the trees he could make out the upright concrete pillar that spelled out the word ZOO in a vertical stack of letters, indicating the park entrance. He saw open areas with benches and people milling about and wondered if his view from seven stories up in his hospital office would enable him to see the explosion. Then, he wondered, could he watch the death of his son, even from a distance?

Soon this hospital's emergency room would be full of the injured and the dead and his son would be among them. He must be ready when they called him to the emergency room to assist with the casualties. He glanced once again at the clock on his desk. Fifteen minutes had passed. He pulled out the rolled prayer mat and set it down in front of the window on the floor and kneeling down, he began to pray.

Back at their home Bedalla Zuqawri gathered up the laundry basket and headed down into the basement. She threw the switch for the light, but there was no change in the darkness at the bottom of the steps. Carefully she walked down the steps and made her way to the laundry room where she set the basket of dirty clothes on top of the dryer. She had asked Ahmed to replace the bulb for her, but it was obvious that he had forgotten, or worse, ignored her.

She made her way across the basement and pulled the chain for the light in the workroom. Light flooded the workbench and cabinets that the original owner of the house had installed. She wished that her husband were more the handyman type. As it was he could not or would not, she wasn't sure which, even repair a simple loose door handle. And then there was the light bulb. A simple task left for her to do instead.

Bedalla looked on the shelf above the bench where the light bulbs were stored, but there were none. She looked around the workroom and on the shelving that held tools that went mostly unused. Then she looked toward the metal cabinets hanging on the wall near the bench. Upon opening the first cabinet she found cans of spray paint, and some sandpaper. She fumbled through the cabinet's contents and found some batteries and two Sony cell phones.

She wondered why her husband would have phones in the basement. If they weren't any good he should get rid of them. She flipped open the first one and pressed the power button. The display on the phone came to life displaying the number of the cell phone before showing the name of the service provider. She did the same to the second one. She pressed the numbers to dial their home phone and she heard the phone ring upstairs. She repeated the process with the other phone with the same result. She scrolled through the contact information, but there were no names listed. Finally she navigated to the received calls menu and pressed ok. There was one call listed and an indication that there was a voice message as well. Bedalla selected play and heard her husband's voice. "Phone six, testing, testing, testing". The message ended abruptly. The same scenario played out with "Phone seven".

Bedalla could not figure out why her husband would have extra phones, working phones, in the workroom cabinets. There must be five other phones somewhere. None of this made sense to her. She began looking in earnest for more clues that might shed light on what she had found. She found boxes of small electronic boards, wire and a package containing a box of wireless doorbells. There was solder, a soldering iron and small screwdrivers in a pouch. She began to tremble when she found a small brown cardboard box hand labeled "detonators" in Ahmed's own handwriting.

Her mind was reeling. This could not be what she thought it to be. She closed the cabinet door and opened the one next to it. Her heart stopped when she saw the packaging. She knew what C4 was and the package in front of her spelled it out plainly: "CAUTION EXPLOSIVE PASTE C4". She avoided any contact with the package, closed the door carefully and backed away wondering why her husband would possibly need these items.

Bedalla leaned against the workbench knocking a small glass jar of screws off the edge, which shattered at her feet, spilling its contents across the floor. The sound of the glass jar striking the floor startled her from her thoughts. She knelt down and began to retrieve the screws looking for a container to put them in. Her eyes scanned the length of the shelf that was mounted under the bench.

For a second she stopped breathing. There on the shelf under the workbench was Joshi's lunchbox. But, how could that be? Next to it was the thermos shaped like a rocket. She looked at the box for a long time before picking it and the thermos up and placing them on top of the bench. She threw the latches on the lunchbox and opened the lid. It was empty. She looked at the underside of the lunchbox lid and saw that there was no name or address written on it. She pulled her hands through her hair and leaned against the bench trying to understand what she was seeing. This was not her son's lunchbox. Why is this here? Why is there a second, identical lunchbox?

She picked up the thermos and turned the lid to open it. She held the space-capsule shaped lid in her hand and sniffed the contents of the bottle. She could smell the chocolate milk that was inside. She poured some of the contents into her hand and realized that it was still cold. It was the drink that she had poured for her son's lunch the night before. Then this was Joshi's thermos. She thought about her husband and how he had been acting lately. She stood very still and her thoughts churned. She could only come to one conclusion. Frantically she ran upstairs to call her husband.

CHAPTER 19

ATTACK

MR. VARNER, the fourth grade teacher, rounded up his students and guided them to a large open mall where the students retrieved their lunch bags and boxes from their backpacks and began gathering at the tables. Joshi sat down at one of the green benches and placed his lunchbox on the table in front of him. He spun it around to flick both latches down to release the lid. Suddenly Demarcus Johnson reached across the table and slammed his hand down on the lid of the box with a thud.

"Hey man, whatchu got for lunch?" Demarcus turned the box around and flipped open the lid. He removed the thermos and dug through the contents of the box. "There ain't nothing in here except a soggy-ass sandwich and some pretzels. This stinks!"

Joshi grabbed the box, slid it back and glanced inside. Demarcus was right, there wasn't anything special in his lunchbox.

He lifted out the peanut butter and jelly sandwich, the fruit cup and the small zipper bag of pretzels and peered into the empty box. Nothing. His mother had been right. She had asked his father if he was sure he'd actually put the surprise in the lunchbox. He had seemed so sure.

Joshi thought about what his mother had told him about gifts. It was the thought that counted. If his father forgot to put his surprise in the box he would get it when he got home. Maybe, he thought, his father would feel so bad that he would get him something even more special to make up for it. He would just have to wait and see.

His thoughts were interrupted by his teacher's announcement. "Attention, everyone. Hello, North Laclede students." Mr. Varner made sure that he had everyone's attention.

"If you all look behind me you will see a concrete building that looks like a big red rock. That is the bathroom. I want all of you to quietly go into that big rock and wash your hands before you begin eating. Especially those of you who were holding that disgusting snake in the reptile house." Mr. Varner made a face that revealed once again to the students what he thought of the slithering creatures. The children laughed out loud at their teacher's theatrics.

"If you have to do anything else while you are visiting the big red rock bathroom then make sure you wash your hands after you do whatever it is you have to do." He made the same expression of disgust by wrinkling up his nose and squinting his eyes, garnering more laughter from the students.

Joshi turned his hands palms up and looked at them. They looked clean to him, but with a shrug of his shoulders he swung his legs over the bench seat and ran to the bathroom to wash his hands.

Mr. Varner noted that very few of his students had heeded his directive. He looked across the expanse of picnic tables and watched his good listeners as they jumped up and headed towards the restroom. That was when he spotted Demarcus Johnson casing the lunches that were left behind, looking for easy pickings. He felt somewhat sorry for the boy, but couldn't have him stealing from others.

Mr. Varner didn't have problems with any of his other students, but Demarcus was a constant challenge. The child had no respect for anyone and Varner knew that if confronted, Demarcus would get belligerent. He would have to report him if that happened even though that would lead to paperwork and statements. Then, he would have to deal with the boy's parents. Mr. Varner sighed deeply and began walking toward Demarcus who was holding a thermos that he knew belonged to Joshi Zuqawri.

Demarcus Johnson had kept his gaze on Joshi as he disappeared behind the thick red concrete wall of the bathroom. He glanced all around and, when he thought that nobody was watching, grabbed the rocket shaped thermos from the table. He wrestled with the lid for a second before it finally popped loose and began to unscrew. He took one more look to his left and right as he lifted off the lid to take a drink, not really noticing the metallic click that emanated from just under the cap as it was released.

The triggering mechanism forced the contact switch to close, completing the circuit for the battery and sending nine volts to the model rocket engine fused into the detonation cord. The voltage, traveling at the speed of light, coursed across the intentional short, into the igniter, initiating the primary ignition. This caused the blasting cap to detonate, in turn fueling the explosion of the steel embedded, high energy, RDX explosive material.

Mr. Varner sped up as Demarcus started unscrewing the cap of the thermos and, in the last seconds of his life, was met by the force of the explosive nitrogen and oxide gasses expanding at over twenty-six thousand feet per second.

The intense heat generated from the blast engulfed Demarcus Johnson as the massive ball of flame and pressure consumed the tables, the students and parents who sat there. For the briefest of milliseconds the steel tables strained at the end of the chains that secured them to the ground. The tables closest to the blast shattered the restraining chains or pulled the anchors from the asphalt and were propelled away from the center of the blast. The people sitting at the tables nearest the blast were killed instantly by the hundreds of steel ball bearings packed in the plastic explosives within the confines of the thermos bottle. Those who sat at the neighboring tables were either blown away or severely injured by the ball bearing shrapnel and benches that had become projectiles.

In a fraction of a second the eight millimeter steel balls tore through wood, metal, flesh and bone as the radius of the inferno expanded to include the exotic animals housed nearby and the starlings, sparrows and squirrels that flitted about picking up scraps of bread crust and potato chips that littered the food court.

Mr. Varner had only enough time to impulsively react to the blast by raising his hands to block the flash. The wave of heat and flame and the force of the onrushing atmosphere struck him hard, throwing his body across the food court and slamming it into the outside wall of the rough textured, red concrete bathroom. The steel projectiles that were uninhibited by flesh and bone, embedded into trees and the concrete of the rock shaped building. Others, with their energy nearly expelled, ricocheted off of the thick concrete and rolled down the gently sloping asphalt toward the sewer.

The sound of the blast moved slowly across the highway and could barely be heard through the double pane insulated office window of Dr. Ahmed Zuqawri. From his location seven floors above and nearly a quarter mile away Zuqawri felt the shockwave from the explosion and rose from his kneeling position in time to see the large plume of smoke rising from the food court at the zoo across the way. He knew that his son was dead and that Allah would see Joshi's death as a great sacrifice. He was too proud to be sad for his son.

The cell phone on his desk rumbled and danced across the veneer surface. It would be one of his colleagues downstairs calling him to tell him what had happened and that he would be needed in the emergency room. The phone vibrated a second time as he picked it up and read the number on the display. "Bedalla?" he said out loud. He thought, how coincidental it was that she should call now. Surely she couldn't know already what had just occurred. Not even the hospital would as yet have information of the damage done, that there were kids from a school involved, or how many people.

He looked at the phone as it vibrated in his hand and then fell silent. His wife would have to talk to his voicemail. He needed time before telling her what had happened. Hopefully she would see the news flash and figure it out for herself. She would then understand that he was too occupied with saving the lives of those who'd been visiting the zoo to talk to her.

He knew that she would come to the hospital to check on her son. Then he would tell her about the attack and maybe blame it on the racist infidels. As the minutes passed, the sound of rescue equipment could be heard heading away from the hospital on the way to the scene. He heard the rumble of a helicopter that buzzed over the hospital and looked out towards the zoo to see that it was the local news helicopter on its way to report on the mayhem. How fortunate for the Channel Twenty News that their office studio as well as their heliport were located across the street from the hospital and less than a quarter mile from the zoo. They would be the first to report on the attack. Their cameras would be on the scene when the dozens of children and parents of the North Laclede School were pronounced dead.

The crews would be waiting under the canopy of the emergency entrance, cameras rolling, as the first of the dead were wheeled into the hospital. And it would be their reporters that would have the opportunity to talk with police investigators first.

The speaker on the wall behind him crackled then gave the distinctive alarm that indicated emergency personnel were needed in the E.R. Ahmed put on his white jacket and took one more look out the window. It had only been ten minutes since the explosion and already there were three news helicopters hovering above the park. By now the local stations would have broken into their scheduled broadcasts to report the tragedy and speculate how many children were involved. Ahmed threw his stethoscope over his shoulder, placed his phone in his pocket and headed out of his office toward the elevator.

Other doctors and nurses were scrambling through the hallways pushing wheeled carts full of supplies. One of the nurses saw that he was not in a hurry and asked if he had heard what happened. He acted as if he knew nothing.

"There was an explosion at the zoo. We've got at least thirty casualties being sent here. Most of them are children." The nurse pushed the cart past him and looked back to see that he wasn't moving any faster than before.

"Dr. Zuqawri, did you hear what I said? We need to be ready for mass casualties."

Ahmed stopped walking and fumbled for his phone. "My son was at the zoo today. I must call his mother. Maybe she's heard something." He tried to act dazed or befuddled.

"Doctor, I'm sure your wife wouldn't have any more information than we do. The accident just happened and we are across the highway from the zoo. Come down to the E.R. I'm sure your son is ok. I was told by one of the interns that most of the casualties were...black, from one of the schools in north city."

"Joshi goes to Laclede North. It is mostly black children that go there."

The nurse could see that he was obviously shaken up. "Doctor, let's go downstairs. We'll find out about your son." She put her hand over his that was holding the phone.

"Don't call your wife just yet. Wait until you know something more. You will only upset her if she hasn't seen the news reports already. When she does she will call you. It's going to be all over the television."

Ahmed Zuqawri snapped his phone shut and placed it back in his jacket pocket. He took a deep breath and stood tall. "Perhaps you are right. Maybe there is nothing at all to worry about. We should get moving...to be ready when the casualties arrive."

He thought how easy it was to fool these people. So much time wasted with ridiculous television shows and movies that they can't tell what is real and what isn't. They are their own worst enemy.

The doors of the elevator opened in front of them. They stepped into the car and headed down to the first floor.

CHAPTER 20

BAD PUBLICITY

ALAN had just cleared the videoconference line when Jennifer buzzed in. "Sir, you need to see what's going on in St. Louis. Just happened about fifteen minutes ago."

Alan pressed the power button on his remote to bring his HD monitor to life. The reporter on camera was giving his take on what had happened a short time before.

"...What we know so far is that there was an explosion in the food court. According to authorities and witnesses here it looks like a deliberate attack, quite possibly targeting the students and teachers of the Laclede North Elementary School, which, as I reported earlier, is a public school whose student body and staff is made up primarily of African Americans." The news reporter glanced at his notes before continuing, "I spoke with one of the officers on the scene and was told that this was not an accident. He showed me this." The reporter bent down as the camera followed. He pointed to a steel ball bearing and a small numbered placard on the asphalt and moved to the side so that the cameraman could get a good shot of them.

"According to my source inside the zoo, the bomb contained hundreds of these small stainless steel ball bearings. Now keep in mind that I am standing just outside the entrance to..." The reporter's voice faded as Alan thought about what he had just heard.

He felt relieved that the bomb wasn't nuclear and didn't appear to be a dirty bomb either. Dirty bombs don't contain projectiles, just radioactive waste. Alan wondered whether this attack was even related to the missing fugitive. Chances of finding him now would be slim...as far as getting any assistance from the local authorities was concerned anyway. He paused and thought about that for a second as the talking heads on the television continued to proclaim their instant knowledge of the incident.

The anchorwoman looked into the camera. "We will have more on this story as it develops and will stay live with you throughout the day as information becomes available. To recap this late breaking story, there has been a terrible explosion today at the zoo here in St. Louis. This happened about twenty minutes ago. Police and investigators are on the scene of what is apparently a hate crime targeting the African American students and faculty of the Laclede North School..."

Hate crime! Alan couldn't believe what he had heard. How in the hell could they know in less than twenty minutes the reason for an attack like this? That type of reporting made him crazy. They couldn't possibly already know why this had happened.

"...Authorities have issued no official statements at this time, but they have assured us that an investigation is underway to determine who is responsible for this attack."

"Good," Alan thought, "They know why the zoo was attacked but have no idea who did it. Marvelous reporting."

The anchorwoman plugged the station and praised the teams on site for getting the story out so quickly. She wrapped up her report as the cut scenes rolled to the News-Channel-Twenty title sequence showing emergency vehicles, helicopters and just a glimpse of what was happening on the ground. From the air one could see the sheets and body bags on the ground below. It didn't look very promising for the families of the victims. The only parents who would not feel the pain of a broken heart today lay with their children on the asphalt of the food court.

Alan Ramsey fumed at the poor judgment of the news station to present the incident as a hate crime. As usual the media jumped to a conclusion without proof, and presented a story as fact that was based purely on speculation. But, something that they said about the authorities being on the scene and the thought that getting support for anything else when something like this was happening made him suspicious. Was this a diversion?

He wondered if there were any special CBRN teams on the way. Every National Guard and Army Reserve unit had specialists in the field of Chemical, Biological, Radiological, and Nuclear weapons. They would need to verify that there was no radiation present. He picked up the phone and dialed his boss. Gabe Anderson picked up on the first ring.

"Are you watching the news? The media has already labeled the attack as a hate crime and no one has even started an investigation to determine the motive yet. The bodies are still warm and they've got the crime all wrapped up, tied with a bow and delivered to the public."

Ramsey took a breath and continued, "I need to go to St. Louis to see if I can sort this out. And don't tell me we've got good people on it. I know we do, but I have to get some boots-on-the-ground info to help clear my head and get me tracking."

Gabe Anderson didn't argue. "You're going. Look Alan, we put out the hate crime story to buy us some time." Anderson didn't have time to continue before Alan interjected,

"What? Why would you do that?"

"I didn't make the decision, but the fact is, the plan has merit. The Director figured that if we don't give credit for the bombing to a terrorist organization they might make a statement to claim the credit. If they do we will know we are on the right track. Hell, Alan, we don't know who did this anymore than that talking head on the news, but one thing I do know is I have never seen any organization, hate crime or otherwise, use projectiles in their explosive devices here in the United States. If the preliminary reports we've received from the local authorities are correct then this bomb has a Mid-East signature all over it." He paused to collect his thoughts. I'll get you orders to get to St. Louis. A flight from DCA to Lambert, then one of our Black Hawks from there to the zoo."

Ramsey didn't feel comfortable with the cover story at all. To him it just didn't seem wise to incite a population by playing on deeply rooted suspicion and fears. He knew that he couldn't change it, but his disapproval was obvious to his boss.

"You do realize that this could escalate into a civil disturbance or even worse, a riot, if those people believe that this explosion was the act of some white asshole. I sure as hell wouldn't inject any more fiction into this storyline."

Gabe Anderson tried to reassure Ramsey. "This will be all the cover we need to get teams on the ground. We will be sending in agency support, all in the name of finding and arresting the person or group responsible. The black population of St. Louis will see that we have sent our best agents to assist their own police department with the investigation. We can work with the local African American councils and have press conferences and public releases. That should help to ease the tension. If Bin-Masri is in St. Louis watching this unfold then we'll let him think we fell for the media story. Meanwhile we'll have agents spread all over the city looking for the bomb. That is, if there is a bomb."

Alan thought about what Gabe said. "Oh you can bet your ass he's got something nasty in that truck. Since you are already stoking what could be a potential firestorm of dangerous possible reprisals I have a request. It's kind of a favor."

"Go on," Gabe said cautiously.

Alan continued, "There's a guy by the name of Paul Jackson who works downstairs. He's the lead security guy for the facility, used to be Mechanized Infantry, a Sergeant Major. I want to take him with me."

"I know who you're talking about. He's contracted through Capitol Security, not a trained agent," Gabe pointed out. "I can't *make* him do anything. All I can do is talk to Larry Stokes at the security office and see if we can get him. His background has to be clean and he will need training. That'll take weeks. One thing we don't have here is time."

Ramsey pushed the issue. "I'm not saying he needs to be indoctrinated as an agent...yet. We can change his security detail and make him a mobile asset. Hell, Gabe, make him my bodyguard if you have to. I will talk to him today before he leaves and let him know his detail has changed. He used to be military. I'm sure he's used to getting orders on short notice."

Gabe Anderson thought for a moment about Ramsey's request. "What's so special about this Paul Jackson fella that you feel the need to take him with you? There are several agents that are already trained that you could choose from. Why him?"

Alan explained. "First he has a background in community level law enforcement. We'll be working with the local police and FBI in St. Louis. Frankly, I think he may have a better inside track on how those departments work than our own agents. I think it could be real helpful to have him on site with me. Secondly, his military success tells me that he's dedicated, and has a high degree of integrity and most of all doesn't give up easily."

"Alright," Gabe said reluctantly, "If you can convince Jackson to be a part of this then get him in here to be briefed and we will get you a flight to St. Louis so you can get this rolling."

"Thanks, Gabe. You won't regret this. I promise." Alan hung up the phone and gathered his things. Ramsey knew that Jackson started his day at four o'clock every morning and, unless there was a national security alert, was off the clock at noon. Ramsey would have to catch him before he left for the day. He guessed that he would have to authorize the overtime pay for Paul Jackson after all. They would have a lot to talk about over lunch.

CHAPTER 21

ON-SITE TRIAGE

At the scene of the explosion local police and other first responders were busy evacuating the zoo. Most visitors were more than willing to leave for fear of another attack. Some wanted to stick around to see what had happened. Like passers-by after an accident on the highway, people stopped to watch the medical teams as they worked to revive the dying and treat the wounded.

Joshi sat on a bench with a few other students who had been protected from the explosion by the thick concrete walls of the bathroom. All were stunned by the carnage that had occurred in the few moments they'd been away from the class.

Praise Allah, Joshi thought, as he sat thinking about what had happened. He wondered what could have caused such an explosion. He was glad that his mother had not volunteered for the field trip. Normally she would have, but this time there were enough parents involved that she felt she could stay home for once. He thought about his father and the surprise that he was supposed to have packed in his lunch. With all that had happened he felt it best not to say anything about it. His parents would be worried about him as it was. Asking about some present seemed petty to him. His present was Allah's intervention. It was not his will that he should die today. Praise be to Allah.

Joshi looked at his fellow classmates who were crying and screaming. He had attempted to calm some of them down, but could not. The girl with the braids and colored beads was not in his class. He saw the name on her identification bracelet, but couldn't make out the hand written letters from where he was sitting. She was older, one of the middle school chaperones who was here with her own mother and brother. She sat quietly sobbing at the far end of the bench, exhausted from her hysterical outburst and after learning that both her mother and her brother had been killed in the blast. She had unintentionally eluded death's grip only because she happened to be standing near the bathroom's entrance, behind the wall, texting someone on her mother's cell phone.

Her brother had been in Joshi's class. Joshi felt sorry for her and moved over to sit by her. He noticed that she still had the cell phone in her hand and had the sudden urge to ask if he could use it to call his parents to let them know he was ok, but he wasn't sure how to approach her. He decided it was best just to be up front. Joshi looked her over quickly and decided that she was not injured and then asked if she was all right.

She began to wail, her shoulders convulsing as she gasped for air between sobs. After a few seconds she stopped crying and looked at Joshi through red eyes welled with tears, "My Mamma...and my brother...were...sitting...right...there." She was convulsing again as she pointed at one of the only benches that remained staked down. At least the bent galvanized steel legs and the steel cross braces were still there. The tabletop and bench seats were gone, torn from the mounting hardware. The bolts that had secured the missing pieces lay on the ground below the metal framework, having fallen from their recesses after the force of the blast ripped the anchored material, and anybody sitting on them, away.

Joshi looked at the remains of the bench and across the asphalt surface to the cast iron fence and the concrete walls of the bathroom looking for the missing lumber. He spotted one bench board, not necessarily a part of that particular bench, leaning against the bottom of the fence. Where the others ended up and where the people who sat on them were remained a mystery. He surveyed the grounds again noting the medical packaging and red soiled gauze that still littered the area. Though the bodies were gone, taken away by the ambulance crews, dark stains and medical trash marked where they had fallen.

There were now enough paramedics on the scene to start worrying about the less injured. One of them walked over to the small group of children, relieving a police officer to return to his duties and set his first aid kit on the ground at Joshi's feet. "You guys ok?"

Joshi and the others nodded their heads. The paramedic started rummaging through his bag grabbing the stethoscope and some bandages for the light abrasions he saw on some of his patients. He introduced himself as Roger. "You guys are some really brave people. I don't know that I could just sit here waiting after what just happened."

He began cleaning a small bleeding cut on the smallest child, one of the only bleeding injuries among the group. He noted that his patient's school nametag said Andrew J in black marker.

"Hey, Andrew, how you doing? Does your knee hurt? That's a pretty good cut you got there. Did you bump into something or fall?"

Andrew sniffled back his tears. "Naw. I was over there by the bathroom and something hit me in the leg and knocked me down. When I got up it was bleeding."

The paramedic pressed on the tissue around his knee. "Does that hurt when I do that or if you bend it does it hurt?"

Andrew started to cry again. "Uh huh, it hurts real bad when I try to move it or stand up."

Roger peeled the paper off the bandage and called to a gurney team and then applied the bandage. When the gurney team arrived the paramedic spoke so that Andrew and the team leader could hear.

"Andrew, I think that you still have something in your knee. These guys are gonna take you to have an x-ray done to see what it is and then we will get it out of there, ok?" Andrew J nodded his head in agreement and then began crying again as he was placed on the gurney and wheeled to the waiting ambulance.

When the doors of the ambulance were closed Joshi got the attention of the paramedic. "Mr. Roger, I think that boy was hit by shrappel or one of those steel balls. I don't think he really knows what happened." Joshi jumped up from the bench and showed the paramedic how the child was standing and how his leg suddenly jerked backward and how he fell down. Joshi made the sound of an explosion as best he could and imitated the other boy's movements ending up on the ground.

"Wow, that was pretty good, I don't know whether to call you a good actor or a good doctor." Roger smiled at the boy as Joshi regained his footing and sat back on the bench. "And, I think you mean shrapnel, not shrappel."

Joshi made a face, thunking his forehead with the palm of his hand. "Duh, I meant shrapnel."

Roger concentrated his efforts on Joshi, looking him over for injuries or signs of shock. "What do you know about shrapnel? You been playing war games on your computer? Look up for me please." He was looking into Joshi's eyes when Joshi surprised him with the answer.

"I used to live in Iraq. Bombs killed a lot of people that I knew. I have some relatives that still have pieces of metal from the bombs inside them. They told me it was called shrapnel."

The paramedic sat back on his heels releasing Joshi's eyelid to flop back in place, surprised by the information he had just been given by a ten-year-old veteran of war.

"Well, Sir, you appear to be unharmed. Where were you when all of this happened?" Roger started working with the girl next to him, but still continued to talk to Joshi for a moment.

"I was in the bathroom washing my hands, cause I petted the snake in the petting zoo and Mr. Varner said they were yucky, so I was lucky cause I was just coming out of the red rock bathroom."

The paramedic thought about what Joshi said as he got to his feet to look at the rest of his patients. As he stood, brushing the dirt from his knees, looked at Joshi and said, "Ok, mister, you'll be ok for sure, but just the same I'm going to send you with your buddies here to Children's Care at the hospital." He did a quick inspection of the other two who sat on the same bench and felt they were going to be ok aside from their memories.

"Well, you guys all look perfectly healthy to me." He spoke to the waiting ambulance crew next. "Let's get these guys a lift to the children's clinic and get them back with their parents who should be waiting there when they arrive. That's where they were all told to report to wait for word on their children."

The girl, Lorita, broke into the conversation. "Mister?"

Roger stopped giving directions and looked toward her. "Yes, Ma'am?"

She held back a shuddered sob and tried to speak clearly, "My...Mamma and...my brother were both here. The tears flowed down her cheeks again as she struggled to talk. I...don't think they...survived the explosion. They were right next to that boy Demarcus when the thing he was holding blew up."

"Wait a minute. Are you saying you saw the explosion happen?" Roger looked at the ambulance attendants and motioned for one of them to get one of the investigating officers.

Lorita looked up at the paramedic, tears tracked through the dirt on her face and dripped from her chin. She bit her lip trying to compose herself so she could speak and took a few choppy breaths between sobs. "I was texting a friend of mine who is home sick today." She stopped to take a couple breaths and wipe at her eyes. "As I was coming out of the girls' bathroom I stopped by that rock wall to finish up, cause my momma didn't know I had her phone and I didn't ask, so I was kind of hiding."

She thought about what she was going to say, knowing that it would probably be important to remember exactly what happened. She saw the officer walk up and waited for him to get caught up before continuing. Roger prodded her to keep going.

"Anyway, that Demarcus is always such a jerk. When I peeked through the stones in the wall to see if my mom was looking for me I saw that boy going through somebody's lunch. He didn't see me looking, but I saw him look around like he was going to be stealing something and was looking to see if he was being watched." She stopped and took a shuddered breath and collected herself. "He picked up something that looked like a rocket. And then he turned the top or something and..." Lorita looked pale as she described what she saw next. "The thing... it just...exploded him, and...and...my momma,...and my brother and everybody else. Even Mr. Varner." She began crying violently, her shoulders convulsing with every breath.

Roger had never heard anything so tragic from a child before. He fell to his knees, cradling the pigtailed girl in his arms telling her over and over that it was going to be ok.

Joshi hung on every word of the story. He knew that she was talking about his lunchbox and his thermos. How could his thermos blow up? It didn't make sense. He took a step forward to tell the officer that it was his lunchbox and thermos that she was talking about, but then thought that he would probably get in trouble for causing the whole thing to happen.

He did not want to be accused of anything. He remembered how his mother explained that because of who he was and his relationship with Allah he would always be distrusted by the

Americans. That if he did anything wrong he would be looked at by the people of this country as evil. She always ended the warnings by telling him to try extra hard to stay out of trouble. "Mind yourself carefully, Joshi. Be aware of what you do and how it effects others around you." He could hear her voice telling him that now. He decided that now was not a good time to say anything. He would wait and ask his mother. She would probably be on her way to the children's hospital anyway. He stepped backward and sat back down with the others to wait quietly for his ride.

CHAPTER 22

THE RECRUIT

"*PAUL*...wait up." Alan was somewhat out of breath from trying to reach Paul Jackson before he got to his car. Luckily for Alan Ramsey, Jackson parked in the same section of Langley's large outdoor parking area as himself.

The large man could easily be seen walking between the parked cars in his white Capitol Security shirt with the large red and blue shield on his left shoulder. Paul Jackson turned nearly completely around, almost walking backward. He spotted Alan Ramsey's raised arm moving quickly between the parked cars and stopped walking to give the man a chance to catch up.

"What's up, Mr. Ramsey? I'm thinking you must have something pretty important to tell me to be chasing me through the parking lot like that. Everything ok?"

"Yeah. Everything's fine. Look, I talked to my boss about you earlier. I asked to have you moved into a different office tomorrow to help work some issues that are going on as part of my team. That is, if you want to. Nobody's forcing you, but I could use your help. And besides, it will give you a break from that monotonous security line you control every morning. What do you think?" Ramsey was still slightly winded from his chase and leaned against one of the parked cars while he waited for a reply.

Paul Jackson looked skeptically at Ramsey. "I think you are a smart man and that scares me. I know the kind of work that you do and for you to chase my big black ass down and move me to a different job makes me think you might be trying to recruit me or something."

Ramsey looked incredulously at the man in front of him. "OK, yeah, I have a mission, an investigation. I can't really give you any real details here, but I think you would be really good and I could use your help. I was going to tell you about it tonight on the plane to St. Louis, but..."

Paul Jackson's voice raised several octaves. "St. Louis? On the plane? Tonight? What exactly are you talkin' about, Mr. Ramsey?"

Ramsey sighed, "Aw, hell, you want to get something to eat? I'll explain it over lunch."

"You buyin?" Jackson raised an eyebrow.

"I wouldn't dream of going dutch at my suggestion of discussing business over lunch. I'm talking something simple. You know, fast food," Ramsey smiled and then continued, "They haven't increased my budget enough to support you yet."

Paul Jackson agreed to the plan for a business lunch. "I will have to call the boss at home to let her know what's up. I don't think it will be a problem." He pulled his phone from his pocket. "Oh, does this mean I'll be getting a raise? The boss likes it when I get a raise."

Ramsey rolled his eyes and shook his head. "There may be some hazard and travel pay, but no real salary change just yet. It's really just a position change at the moment."

Paul Jackson feigned a scared look. "Hazard pay! What are you getting me into, Mr. Ramsey?"

Ramsey thought for a second and then answered, "Not exactly sure yet, but I'm pretty sure there will be a lot of overtime pay involved."

Paul's wife answered his call. "Hey, honey, it's me. I'm gonna be a little late getting home. I got a guy who wants to talk to me about a job that I might be interested in, so he's gonna buy me lunch. Don't want to miss out on a free meal, you know." Paul Jackson gave a thumbs-up sign and smooched the phone before hanging up, then smiled at Ramsey. "I'm kinda feeling like Chinese. How 'bout you?"

CHAPTER 23

E.R

ANOTHER ambulance pulled under the canopy turning off the warning siren mid-whoop. The doors opened and the typical scene unfolded with the legs of the gurney being locked into place and an I.V. stand turned upright with a bag hanging from the rolled metal hanger. An attendant yelled the vital signs over the words of other attendants briefing other doctors. He handed charts to the waiting emergency physician as the doctor began to inspect each casualty's wounds. About the time the doors closed on one ambulance two more arrived to drop off their human cargo. There was enough room at the curb to allow five vehicles to back into the Emergency Room drop point at once. The vehicles were beginning to back up at the entrance now. Teams rolled gurneys toward the doors of the hospital as the first ambulance peeled away, headed back in the direction of the zoo.

"Dr. Zuqawri, we need you over here."

Ahmed found the person who beckoned him standing behind the last ambulance. It was a young doctor named Jason Taylor. "We've got multiple contusions to the skull, neck and upper torso. There are second and third degree burns on the right side of the body."

Dr. Zuqawri thought highly of the young looking doctor. He looked to be around thirty, but was actually nearing forty with a wife and three children. Ahmed had wondered on many occasions why he didn't have the young appearance of Doctor Taylor.

Ahmed pulled the sheet up to see the damage that had been inflicted to the middle aged, African American woman who lay under it. There were easily fifteen different points of entry between the abdomen and the top of her head. Amazingly both eyes were undamaged and stared in shock at the doctor who hovered over her. Her eyes were wide with horror, but unresponsive to Dr. Zuqawri's penlight probe. He lifted the woman somewhat to allow a look at her back to check for exit wounds. Then he found it, a critical wound at the base of her skull. He could tell that she would not survive.

"Make her comfortable, but save our efforts for the next patient," Ahmed stated almost nonchalantly.

Jason Taylor looked incredulously at the doctor. Zuqawri saw the look and explained further, "She is not going to survive. She has holes in her back large enough to drive a truck through and she is already in shock. Look at the amount of saline and plasma that she has been given, yet we cannot control the bleeding." He flipped the empty plastic bags hanging from the stainless hook with his hand to make his point. "There will be others who will have a better chance if we do not waste our time on the already dead."

"Dr. Zuqawri, we can't just set her aside and let her die. We have the resources and the obligation to help her."

"...And you will be wasting your time when there are those who require immediate assistance and have a chance for survival.

Trust me, Doctor. This is the way to separate the living from the dead. Maybe you would understand better if you doctored in my country and had to deal with this every day." Zuqawri waved him off and pushed the cart to the side. "Put the ones like her in this hall, along the wall. We will tend to their needs last." He directed the ambulance attendants to the corridor to his left.

Dr. Taylor stepped in between Zuqawri and the cart. "You can't just park them in a hallway and not attend to their needs. It is not only against the law, but it is morally wrong."

Zuqawri was tired of arguing with the young man before him. "Dr. Taylor, I am the head of the emergency response teams here. The hospital has placed that responsibility upon me and I plan to execute the duties they have given me in a manner that will save the most lives. You must do as I say so the end result is exactly that. Do not lecture me about what is moral and what is not!"

Zuqawri pulled the sheet up and rolled the woman on her side despite any discomfort, to expose the large exit wounds to Taylor and the ambulance attendants. "If you haven't noticed, the wounds that you see here are not from an everyday car accident or house fire. These people are the victims of an attack that occurred in the middle of the day, in a public park. My own son is among the dead." He let her head roll downward and pointed out the huge wound on the back of her skull, an exit for one of the steel balls that had torn through her body. "Do you see this? Do you see how much of her brain is missing? For all practical purposes this woman is dead!" Ahmed let the patient fall back on to the gurney. "You should concentrate your medical efforts on the victims who have a chance for survival. After that, if you have the time, then you can direct your prayers on those who do not. Now, Dr. Taylor, there are more casualties that may actually have a chance at survival."

Jason Taylor seethed knowing that he would get nowhere. He turned away to help with the next person who was being lowered from the ambulance. He disagreed with the way Dr. Zuqawri was

159

working the triage, but understood what he was trying to do. It did not change the way he felt about the treatment of that last patient. Yes, this was a chaotic series of events that had to be handled in a controlled manner to save lives, but they had enough staff on call to tend to all of the wounded. It was the amount of the dead that could take up the available resources. There would not be enough pathologists on hand to perform the autopsies that would be required by the state and federal levels of government. Luckily they could figure that out later. The dead could wait.

He watched Dr. Zuqawri as he directed the next patient to be prepped for treatment. The gurney teams turned their charges over to the waiting doctors and nurses briefing them on the status of their patients. When the patients were clear of the doors the ambulance crew would load up an empty cart and speed away to retrieve another.

Jason wondered how this man could be so stoic knowing that his own son was among the dead. He asked the nurse next to him how many children had been injured in the attack.

"Not sure yet. I was just going over a list that Hope Children's just sent over," she said.

She looked down the list of names. "Looks like twenty-three. But these kids are DOA. No Zuqawri on this list. In fact, I heard from the paramedics that all of them are black...I mean, African American."

Taylor asked about Zuqawri's son. "So no Middle Eastern kids?"

"Not that I could tell, at least, not by these names. She was trying not to sound politically incorrect.

Jason wondered about the list and how they could compile one so quickly. He assumed the school must have furnished a list as soon as they found out what was going on. "Well, that tells me that maybe his son survived. That's good news. But don't say anything yet until we know for sure. No false hopes."

He looked towards Ahmed Zuqawri who was busy directing triage. Jason's expression suddenly changed.

"Wait a minute, Dr. Zuqawri just said his son died in the attack at the zoo," Jason Taylor turned to look toward the elevators, "...yet he came straight out of the elevator to the ambulances. That's weird. How would he know if you just now got the list?"

The nurse reflected on the conversation she'd had with Zuqawri in the hall before they both got in the elevator.

"When I passed him upstairs he didn't know what the emergency was until I told him. He was taking his sweet time getting down here after the All-On-Call went out, so I stopped to let him know what we were expecting." She thought for a moment.

"He can't know anything about his son for sure, other than he told me that his son was at the zoo today and that he went to Laclede North. I think he said his son's name was Josie or something. No, Joshi. He was going to call his wife to find out if she knew anything, but I told him to wait, that it would only make her worry, so he put the phone away."

"But you came down with him in the elevator and that's when I called him over." Dr. Taylor felt something in the pit of his stomach. Something wasn't right.

The nurse saw him gazing. "What? What are you thinking?"

He shook his head and waved away his thoughts. "Not sure...just weird the way he spoke about his son. It's probably nothing, but..."

Dr. Taylor noticed that Zuqawri had just backed away from the ambulance and pulled his phone out of his pocket. The doctor looked around briefly and then motioned for Jason to take over for him, calling him over with a vigorous hand gesture.

Taylor jogged over to the ambulance to help prep the patient being unloaded. This time the victim was a white male. Judging from his identification badge he was a Laclede North teacher. Ahmed spoke into the phone in a language that Jason Taylor knew to be Mid-Eastern and then held the phone to his chest.

"I must take this call. Take charge here until I return." He placed the phone back against his ear and continued his conversation.

Jason knew limited Arabic and could tell as Zuqawri walked away that whoever was on the other end had surprised the head of the hospital's emergency management team enough to shake him up a little.

Dr. Taylor turned his attention to the task at hand verifying that the man on the gurney was indeed deceased and instructed the attendants to take him to the morgue where he would be identified and autopsied.

He looked around for Zuqawri and spotted him in the shadows of the tall bushes that flanked the dumpster corral. He didn't seem at all upset, but acted suspiciously secretive. It was hard for the young doctor to shake his feeling that there was something wrong with the way Dr. Zuqawri was acting. He directed his attention to the next patient, relieved to find that she was only wounded from flying glass and debris. He took her vitals and attempted to put his suspicions on hold until he was sure there weren't more dead or wounded coming. He knew he was in for a long afternoon and vowed to call his wife at the next opportunity to let her know not to wait up for him. Chances were he would be pulling an all-nighter.

CHAPTER 24

REUNION

BEDALLA ZUQAWRI sped through the red light narrowly missing the cross traffic and disappeared into the parking garage across the street from the always growing Hope Children's Hospital. Her tires squealed loudly as she turned into a parking space and hurriedly gathered her purse and phone. She checked the display on her phone to see if Ahmed had tried to return her call, but the phone only displayed the time.

The sound of a slamming car door reverberated through the parking facility startling Bedalla. She opened her door to the sound of running footsteps and turned to see a woman sprinting toward the walk-bridge to the hospital. Bedalla followed suit, first walking at a brisk pace and then breaking into a jog as she neared the bridge. She glanced to her right as she gained on the skirted woman ahead.

The sun was high overhead and the sky was clear enough that Bedalla could see it reflected in the stainless steel of the St. Louis Gateway Arch about two miles east. It was a beautiful day. Too bad it was marred by such ugly violence. Bedalla entered the elevator, still in full stride, and stopped abruptly, causing a discomforting shake of the elevator car to those inside.

She was afraid of what she was going to find when she got off the elevator and stepped into the hospital emergency room. But her sense of dread did not stop there. She was also afraid of what she was going to find out after the trip to Hope Children's. Although she hoped she was wrong, she knew that her husband had something to do with the attack. Her mind was reeling from the thoughts of Ahmed being involved in any way and how she would deal with the truth if it came to that.

How could she support her husband if he was the one responsible for so many deaths and quite possibly the death of her own son? He would call it a sacrifice saying that she must be strong, that their son was a martyr doing the will of Allah. How can he be a martyr when he did not volunteer to die? How can Allah be so heartless as to accept the death of their son as an act of loyalty and faithfulness, when the child did not make the decision to fight the Jihad against the Americans? Only Ahmed would be in Allah's favor and, she supposed, so would she, if she accepted and supported such a violent act against a people whose only crime today was to seek the enrichment of their children's lives.

The elevator doors opened and Bedalla stepped into chaos. There before her were the families of the students who attended Laclede North. Most of them women, they huddled together, hugging, awaiting news of the conditions of their sons, daughters or grandchildren.

Following the skirted woman to the counter, Bedalla waited. The noise of grieving parents and grandparents was incredible. Some parents, having heard the fate of their children, were being restrained and given sedatives to calm them. There were clergy of all denominations on hand to help relatives cope with the grievous news.

Bedalla spun around taking it all in and felt the weight of sorrow and grief. Everywhere she saw overwhelming fear and sadness. Tears welled up in her eyes and ran down her face as the frustration and helplessness engulfed her.

"Miss, Miss...HELLO!" The voice of the nurse at the desk snapped Bedalla back from her emotions to some level of reality.

"Are you here about a child who was at the zoo today?" The nurse was nearly yelling to be heard over the surrounding noise.

Bedalla answered back loudly, "Yes. His name is Joshi Zuqawri and he was on the field trip today."

The nurse suddenly looked relieved and smiled a broad smile. She had been waiting to give out some good news. Her first inclination was to yell it out so that everyone could hear, but she couldn't do that. How would the others feel? The smile on her face waned and she once again took on a professional look.

The nurse beckoned Bedalla to come around the side of the counter and down the corridor. They walked several meters down the hall and the nurse stopped. She grabbed Bedalla's hand in hers and spoke very clearly, "Joshi is ok. He didn't get hurt at all." Bedalla nearly collapsed with relief as the nurse continued, "The paramedics and the police on site sent us a list of survivors. They spoke to him. They said he was in the bathroom when the explosion went off, so he was protected. He should be here any minute now. He was one of the last to be evacuated because he didn't require any medical care. Your son is just fine."

Bedalla wept with joy. Tears poured down her face. The nurse held Bedalla's hands in hers, her eyes also welled with tears. She shook her head to regain her composure and then stepped back. Bedalla had never felt so grateful. The shared silence ebbed away slowly as the sounds of the emergency room waiting area began to seep back into their consciousness. The two women continued to hold hands as they walked back into the waiting room from the hall. The nurse broke free and moved towards the entrance doors as she saw the paramedics heading in her direction. As the paramedics turned toward the desk, Joshi and two other children could be seen stepping through the entrance looking around for someone they would recognize. Joshi saw Bedalla and broke into a run as his mother dropped down on her knees, arms wide to accept her son.

Joshi slammed hard into his mother nearly knocking her over backwards. He crumpled into her arms as she pulled him to her, absorbing as much of her son into her heart as she could. They rocked together crying as she held him tightly. The others in the room stared, some of them crying.

The nurse stood at her station collecting information from the paramedics, but looked over at the only encouraging image she had seen that day. She was happy for the two who sat on the floor in the embrace that only a parent and child could share. She looked at the clock. It was only two-thirty. She stored the image knowing that the rest of the day would not be so promising.

CHAPTER 25

CONTACT

LEAJA BIN MASRI looked around the warehouse as he spoke on the phone. "The authorities will find you. They have the phones. They will trace them to where they were purchased and use the information to find you. They will do the same with the license plates from the captured vehicles." Bin Masri stepped into the makeshift living quarters and turned on the television. The images shown were the helicopter coverage of the scene at the E.R. Bin Masri looked closely at the screen looking for the person on the other end of the phone. "Where are you now, Ahmed?"

"I am at the hospital assisting with the injured from the zoo."

"So, you are helping to save the lives of those that you tried to kill?" Leaja bin Masri found an ironic humor in that thought. He laughed and then continued, "Yes, I understand that you are at the hospital. Where are you right now? Where are you standing?"

Ahmed wondered why he would ask that, but he responded just the same. "I am standing near the dumpsters behind the large shrubs near the emergency room entrance. Why do you ask such a question? Are you here?" Dr. Zuqawri looked around once more to see if he could see bin Masri, but only saw the ambulance crews. He noticed that Dr. Taylor was looking in his direction again and wondered if he suspected something was wrong.

Leaja bin Masri searched the television. "Step out of the shadows, so I can see you."

"What are you talking about? Are you here?" Ahmed was aggravated with the game that was being played at his expense. "Tell me, Leaja. Tell me where you are!"

"I am at the warehouse. Now, do as you are told. Step out of the shadows!" Leaja kept his eye on the television. The helicopter was circling over the ER dock. The front of the ambulances could be seen, but the patients being unloaded and treated were under a steel canopy that extended from the building out of sight of the news crews that hovered over the building.

Ahmed stepped away from the dumpster corral and into the heat of the sun, squinting in the bright sunshine. "There, I am standing in plain view for all to see, but I still do not see you." The shadow of the hovering helicopter spun across the pavement and moved over Ahmed Zuqawri for only a few seconds. He looked up at the craft that hung in the air above him eclipsing the sun, holding his free hand out to block the rays that were flaring out from above the aircraft.

"I am above you, yet I am miles away." Leaja was enjoying himself. The prospect of such a coincidence amused him greatly. It was like talking to Ahmed from the helicopter. "Put your hand down Ahmed. You are beginning to look like Adolph Hitler."

Ahmed Zuqawri dropped his hand down to his side and immediately heard bin Masri laugh out loud. "Are you in the helicopter that is flying over us? Why are you laughing? What is the joke?"

"I am watching you on the television you fool." He laughed again.

Ahmed seethed with anger as he stepped back into the shadows. "You bastard. You have just shown my face to the country and quite possibly the world." Zuqawri peered around the bushes. There were no more ambulances at the dock and he could not hear the wail of their sirens any longer. All of the dead or wounded had been delivered. He saw Dr. Taylor working just inside the doors of the E.R. He turned his attention back to Leaja bin Masri. "You have jeopardized my cover and possibly the mission with your self amusement. What is wrong with you? Do you not see that you have given the authorities a face to look for?"

Bin Masri shot back. "Do not speak to me with such insolence! You are already a dead man. You must join me here at once. You know far too much. Your obligation to the brotherhood has not ended. It has only just begun. Besides, the phones will be traced to you regardless of how well you think you "cleaned" them. Yes, Ahmed, you will be captured. You will be questioned and probably tortured. Are you prepared for that? You will have to be strong. Allah expects it. If you fail, you will fall from the protection and graces of Allah. Are you strong enough, Ahmed?" Bin Masri sounded almost cynical.

"You must leave there at once and head to the warehouse where we can make the final plans for the attack. Remove all of the money from your savings and meet me in one hour. If I do not see you in one hour I will have you killed. Do you understand?"

Ahmed was taken aback by the thought of being captured or tortured. Bin Masri was right, if he was not strong enough, did not resist enough, he would lose favor with his God. How much was enough? He was not sure what would be expected.

The prospect of giving up everything that he had worked for did not appeal to him. He had not thought that it would have come to this. He had assumed he would do his part and then leave the country with his wife and child. Now, his son was dead, used for the sake of the Jihad in a glorious martyrdom. He would not have the opportunity to console his wife and prepare for their move back home. He opted for the path of least resistance.

"I have to gather my belongings. I will call you when I am on my way." Ahmed had given in to needs of the Jihad. Again he would make the sacrifices to advance their cause. He closed the phone and turned back toward the entrance of the emergency room.

CHAPTER 26

A LATE LUNCH

PAUL JACKSON picked through the remains of his fried rice thinking about what to ask next. He had hammered through a lot of the pertinent questions that mattered as a husband and father and was satisfied, at least from a family man's perspective, that what he was about to get involved in would, at least, benefit his family financially. The job security issue was covered also. He could stay on in a special operations status for as long as there were people trying to kill the citizens of the United States. That appeared, at least by recent events, to be quite a long time to come.

The hours away from his family would be a new issue to deal with though. Working with C.I.A Spec-Ops liaisons in the military and at his current job he had watched the special operations people come and go for over twenty years. They sometimes spent weeks away from their families and sometimes they didn't come home at all for reasons he would never know. He had a security clearance level of "Secret" and had always felt that that was pretty good considering his background. Now his T2T clearance would be "Top Secret". That alone would open up doors to more possibilities for him. He enjoyed working the hours that he worked. He liked getting off around noon and going home to the honey dos, for dinner and to spend time with the kids and his wife, Ming-Lee.

The kids were actually not really "kids" anymore. The last two were in high school and his oldest was about to graduate college. Still, two more to get through college and eventually, two weddings to deal with down the road. They had robbed Peter to pay Paul many times and unfortunately, Peter was running out of money. So, financially this would be a good move, he thought.

The last piece of the puzzle for Jackson was the issue of his six years of accrued retirement points with Capitol Security. Alan assured him that because Capitol was contracted for government security and because Jackson was being recruited from within the agency his retirement benefits would transfer with no penalties. In fact, after a year probationary period, Jackson would qualify for the entire retirement package of a twenty-year employee with the agency. He could still retire as early as next year and have full benefits.

He felt that he couldn't lose unless, of course, he was killed. Even then Ming-Lee would be better off financially. Paul stopped playing with his rice and put the fork down. He was about to officially accept Ramsey's offer, but noticed that Alan Ramsey was engrossed in the images on the television in the lobby of the restaurant. CNN was on, doing a report on the St. Louis Zoo bombing.

Jackson broke the silence. "Does me suddenly working for you have anything to do with what happened at that zoo?"

Ramsey glanced away from the TV long enough to answer, "Yes and no. The bombing this morning did open up a bit of a can of worms. Not the reason that I'm asking you, really, but it will help me get you in the door. I've been mulling this around for a while. Timing is everything, I suppose."

Back on the TV a caption appeared under the suited man center screen indicating that he was Thomas Gordon, the National Director Pastor of the largest Ku Klux Klan organization still operating in the south.

Paul Jackson waved a hand in front of Ramsey. "Will I get to shoot people like him?"

"He says that his knights didn't have anything to do with the attack today." Although Ramsey knew that this was true, he continued to attack the man on the television. "I don't think that the head asshole of the largest remaining organized chapter of the Klan would lie about that. Do you?" Alan Ramsey showed his disgust for the organization in his sarcasm.

Ramsey leaned in toward Jackson as he threw the tip onto the table. "They didn't do it. They aren't responsible for today's attack. It's not a hate crime, it's a terrorist attack."

"Call it what you want, but they targeted a black school and black children. Seems a little one sided to me." Paul Jackson shot Ramsey an angry stare.

"No, Paul, what I mean is, we don't know exactly who did this or why yet, but the agency put out the hate crime story to give us time to figure out who actually planned and orchestrated the attack and get close to them without raising suspicion. We believe it has something to do with a terror suspect we've been tailing for a couple days. The bombing may be a diversionary tactic meant to throw us off their trail. The agency figured if they put out some misinformation the attackers might come forward to make a statement claiming responsibility."

As they stood to head out the door Paul Jackson looked at Ramsey with a surprised look. "Are you guys insane? Of all the stories you could make up, why a hate crime? Don't you know that the black community can get a little overzealous? You go around telling these people that whitey done killed their kids and, talk about opening a can of worms, more like a box of pythons."

"Which is part of the reason why you are coming with me to St. Louis."

Paul Jackson's sarcasm returned, "Uh, I'm a pretty big guy, but I'm getting kind of old. In case you haven't noticed those are little gray hairs on the side of my head." Paul turned his head to the side pointing to his graying temple. "I don't think I will be able to single handedly prevent a riot."

Alan reached in his pocket for his keys. When they got in the car Alan began to explain everything to Jackson. By the time they negotiated the traffic back into the agency's parking lot, Alan had Paul Jackson up to speed on the last two days.

"Hmmm, I knew you guys were working some serious issues but I had no idea..."

Alan cut him off. "I'm telling you, things are going to go to hell fast if I'm right and we don't find these guys. We've got a ton of leads that end in St. Louis. Not sure why, but it's what we have to work with, so we need to run with it."

They pulled through the security gate and headed for Paul Jackson's car. Alan got back to the subject of the trip to St. Louis. He glanced at the security uniform that Paul was wearing. "You'll need to change into something a little less conspicuous. That is, if you're going to be working with me. If not, then I'm going to have to shoot you because I just told you secrets of national security. Your choice."

Paul Jackson got out of the car and pulled on the leg of his trousers. "What, you got a problem with blue pants with a red stripe on each leg? I know some Marines that would kick your ass if they heard you talking like that." He continued, "I got a feeling we're gonna be needin' all the Marines we can get, so try not to piss them off, ok?"

Alan looked at his watch. "You got about an hour and a half to tell your wife about your new job, pack your stuff and kiss the family goodbye before I pull up in front of your house and honk my horn. I'll let Gabe know that I briefed you, so we can drive straight to the airport."

"Gabe? Is that the big boss?"

"Yes, Gabe Anderson is my boss. The Director is his boss, then there's the Secretary of State and then the President. Oh, do you own your own sidearm, chest holster and vest?"

"Hold it, Hold it, Hold it. You can't just nonchalantly say that my new job is just three levels away from the President and then change to another subject." Jackson was shocked at the level of government that Alan Ramsey was working within.

"Four, not three, four. What am I, chopped liver?" Alan smiled, and then explained further. "First there's me, then Gabe, then Patterson, Secretary Erickson, then President Carlton." Alan stated, still rather casually for Jackson.

Paul Jackson replied, "Got it, I have a chest holster, a leg holster, pistols for both, and my Capitol Security Assigned revolver. I also have a shotgun, a twenty-two hunting rifle that I got when I was a kid, an AR-15 short stock assault weapon, and I'm wearing the vest under this shirt right now." He backed away from the car so he could shut the door.

Alan rolled the window down as Jackson closed the door. "What are you, Rambo? Leave the revolver, the shotgun and the rifles but bring the pistols. I'll get us through security. See you in ninety minutes."

Paul Jackson gave Alan a thumb up. "See you then, Alan."

Alan Ramsey was too involved in his thoughts to realize that Paul Jackson had finally called him by his first name. About two blocks later it occurred to him, while sitting at a red light. He quietly muttered to himself after laughing out loud, "See ya, Mr. Jackson."

CHAPTER 27

RELOCATION

AHMED ZUQAWRI closed his phone and walked toward the entrance of the E.R. Through the doors he could see the amount of activity going on inside. People lay wounded and dying, and although it was his doing, he still felt an ironic obligation as a doctor to help. He had been a doctor before he'd been recruited by al-Muhajeer to be a soldier for Allah. His faith was of the utmost importance to him and demanded that he perform in such a manner as to please Allah first. He knew he must do as he was told by Leaja bin Masri, but had to figure out how to get away from his duties without raising suspicion from the others, especially Dr. Taylor who already seemed suspicious.

Zuqawri entered the building and checked on the first patient and the attending intern. "Let me see your chart." The intern, a young woman, reported all she knew about her charge and waited for a reply from Dr. Zuqawri.

Zuqawri was looking around the E.R. He needed to get to his office without notice, but that would be near impossible given that he was needed in the E.R. Leaving would look strange when there were so many wounded that needed urgent care. "Where is Dr. Taylor?" he asked the intern. She'd been awaiting a reply concerning her patient and was surprised that Dr. Zuqawri had ignored her information about the patient on the gurney in front of them.

"He was here a minute ago. Said he was going to check in with Hope Children's to check the status of the students that were brought there." She retrieved the clipboard from the doctor. "It's really sad to think that someone could do such a thing to children. It's bad enough that it happens to adults."

It never occurred to Zuqawri that the wounded children would be taken to a hospital that was over two miles away from the zoo. He just assumed they would be sent to his hospital across the street. He supposed it was possible that there were very few wounded children that needed care. He calculated that anyone that was within twenty-five meters of the blast would have been severely injured or dead.

The woman on the gurney moaned and squirmed a little. Overall she was not badly injured. She was conscious and looking around. "You must not move much. Please lie still until we can get you into the operating room." She looked to be about twenty years old. Zuqawri asked, "Are you a teacher?"

The young black woman winced in pain. "No, but I will be. I am a student teacher. This is my first year."

"We will get you back on your feet soon." Zuqawri directed the nurse to give her patient the required dosage of pain medication to keep her comfortable while she waited for surgery.

The girl asked about the attack. "Where are the children? How many were hurt?" Zuqawri answered her, but with little information. "They were all sent to Hope Children's Hospital. We do not know exactly how many have been injured. One of our doctors is trying to find out." He thought about asking about Joshi then decided against it. He needed to get moving. Zuqawri looked at the intern's nametag. "Carol is doing a fine job caring for you. She will answer any other questions you may have."

By now police and FBI investigators were beginning to arrive to question those who had survived and there was no sign of Dr. Taylor for the moment. If Ahmed were to leave, now was the time. He headed for the elevators and waited for the car to arrive. The elevator seemed to move slowly as it made its way to its destination. The doors opened and Zuqawri nearly broke into a jog moving down the hall to his office.

He opened his office door and, stepping inside, scanned the room trying to decide what to take. He was emptying his desk when the phone in his pocket started to vibrate. He reached in, lifted the phone and looked at the display. It was Bedalla calling again. Ahmed flipped open the phone and hit the talk button.

"Hello, Bedalla. Please be brief. There is much happening here and time is in demand." Ahmed emptied the contents of a cardboard box to put it to a new use. He began to shovel the personal items from his top drawer into the box as his wife spoke.

"Tell me what has happened, Ahmed." Bedalla said in a flat expressionless voice.

"Surely you have seen the reports. There has been an attack at the zoo. We have many injured and are very busy here." He thought of removing the declarations of his doctorate from the walls, but thought it would be too obvious to anyone who came looking for him.

Bedalla continued, "And our son, Ahmed, have you heard anything about our son?"

Ahmed stopped packing and concentrated on his answer. His son had to be dead. There was no use pretending otherwise. "Joshi is dead. He was killed in the explosion. I am sorry I did not call to tell you, but I was not sure what to say, how to tell you this."

Ahmed Zuqawri tried his best to sound concerned for his wife's feelings.

"Are you sure of this, Ahmed? Are you sure he is among those killed today? I have only received word to go to the Children's Hospital and wait. No one has told me that he is dead." Bedalla began to cry, thinking about losing her child to such an attack.

Ahmed thought about what to say. Surely his son was dead. Ahmed had felt the explosion in his office a quarter of a mile away and Joshi was holding the bomb. There was no sense denying it. He began, seemingly without feeling, to tell Bedalla about their son. "Woman, he had to be killed by the explosion. I have gotten no word otherwise. This can only mean that he was very close to the explosion. Do you not remember the attacks in our own country? Some bodies were never recovered because the damage was too great." Ahmed paused for a second. "I'm sorry to have to tell you this news, Bedalla."

There was only sobbing from the phone. Ahmed selected the speaker option on his cell and placed it on his desk. He moved throughout his office grabbing his belongings. He found his gym bag in the closet. It had a change of clothes as well as a sweat suit and running shoes, neither of which he had ever worn, but had been bought by his wife in hopes that he would heed his own advice and begin exercising.

"Liar!" Bedalla, who could not hold back any longer, suddenly shattered the silence.

Ahmed stopped in his tracks and spoke back in disbelief. "What did you say?" He walked back toward the phone.

"I said you are a liar. Joshi is alive. He is resting in his own bedroom after you tried to kill him! How could you do such a thing to your own son, Ahmed? How?"

Ahmed quickly picked up his phone. "Joshi is alive? Praise Allah! That is…"

"Stop it Ahmed!" Bedalla cut him off. "You are the one who tried to kill him. You were using him to blow up the others. That is why you drove him to school. That is why you would not let me in on your "surprise". You did not want the bomb to blow up too early. You do not care about him or me, only your beloved Allah!"

"Are you insane, woman? How can you accuse me of such a thing? I am a doctor. I help people..."

An angry Bedalla cut off Ahmed again. "Liar! Do not lie to me! I found your phones and your bomb making equipment. I found the other lunchbox, so do not patronize me with your stories and lies." She thought for a second. "You are a terrorist. Nothing more. You are no better than those who destroyed our mosques and our cities in Iraq, the people we loved and cared about. Or did you orchestrate those attacks as well?"

"They were helping the Americans. That made them traitors. I gave the cleric some names. That is all. I did not kill them." Ahmed defended his actions. "Allah requires us to be helpful, to assist with the jihad against those who interfere, those that support the infidels. It is our duty!"

"You Bastard! You killed them just the same as if you pulled the trigger yourself. You killed them with your assistance to the extremists. You destroyed our country. You and others like you that cannot see past the illusions of the radicals and their twisted translation of the Quran."

Ahmed shouted back into the phone, "The Americans destroyed our country! The Christian infidels, with their forced democracy! They are to blame for the changes that have left our country in such chaos."

The Americans came to help us! Do not forget that our families died in Saddam's gas attack. We were lucky to be in college, away from home. Do you not remember coming home to find your parents, your grandmother, and sisters all dead? Well I do. I buried my only sister next to my parents. Why, retaliation for wanting to be free of a madman's rule? Saddam was a bastard tyrant then, and is burning in hell now for his crimes. Or, do you now consider him a martyr as well?"

"Stop it woman! It is Allah's bidding to follow our clerics. It is Allah's will not mine!" Ahmed's voice seemed to calm down as he began to recite the five holy guidelines of the Rahs Allah Shrine and Mosque where he now practiced his faith.

"We are soldiers of the Jihad. We are required to obey the guidance of our clerics. The Imam of the Shrine of Rahs Allah demands that we do our part to battle the infidels. We must preserve the rights of our people to praise and cherish Allah. We must remove the threat of Christianity so that Allah will be the supreme guidance for the world."

Bedalla could see that her husband was totally lost to his beliefs and, although she was Muslim, she was not an extremist. She was reasonable and forgiving of others. That, she was sure, was Allah's true intention and the true interpretation of the Quran.

She stood quietly outside Joshi's room listening as Ahmed spoke quietly into the phone, "Bedalla, I know that you see what I did today as a terrible thing. Believe me when I say that I am relieved that our son is alive. The mission that was set upon me was still a success and our son was protected. It is Allah's will that he was saved. That is how I know I am right. Joshi was to be sacrificed for the Jihad, but Allah saw that I, no, that we were willing to sacrifice him for the good of the Quran and Allah gave him back to us as a reward for our unwavering loyalty. It was Allah who saved Joshi for doing what was required of him. I am sure of this. You must trust in Allah. Do you understand?"

Bedalla thought about what Ahmed was saying. How did Joshi survive such an attack when he carried the bomb? Was it simply luck that he had held the snake and then had to wash his hands? Could it be only coincidence that the bathroom was made of reinforced thick concrete to keep him safe from the explosion? Although she did not agree with the methods of the Jihad, she could not understand how Allah could let it happen if it was not the right thing. Allah saved the life of her son who should have been destroyed in the blast. She was confused about how she felt.

Ahmed explained what he had to do next. "I must leave to meet Leaja bin Masri at the warehouse. He is one of the Brotherhood."

His wife interrupted, "The Brotherhood? Here, in America? How could they..."

Ahmed continued, "Do not worry about that, I will be home soon to gather my things. I don't know when I will be returning, so I will be packing my clothes. It would be very helpful if you would assist me with this. I will be home within the next thirty minutes. Do not touch the items in the basement. I will collect those things. I will see you then." Ahmed closed the phone ending the conversation. He continued to clear out his desk drawers when there was a knock on his door and the door opened. Jason Taylor stood in the doorway.

"I have some very good news for you Dr. Zuqawri. It's about your son." Taylor noticed the box on his desk and the gym bag on the floor by the door. "What are you doing? Are you planning on leaving?"

"Yes, I have cleared my absence with Dr. Manchen. He will be taking over my duties immediately. I just found out from my wife that Joshi, my son, is alive and unharmed. I am going to take some time off to be with him." He stopped packing and faced Dr. Taylor. "That is what you were going to tell me, isn't it? That my son is not dead."

"So you are clearing out your desk to take a few days off?" Jason Taylor looked skeptical of Zuqawri. "And your locker?"

Ahmed answered quickly, "I'm not clearing out my desk, what I am taking is none of your business. I need to get home."

Taylor, understood he was stepping out of bounds, but there was something about Dr. Zuqawri that triggered his wariness.

"You're right, Dr. Zuqawri. Sorry about that. Just seems to me that we are really in need of someone with your background right now."

"Yes, well I am needed at home as well."

Dr. Taylor didn't let the conversation drop. "I understand that you feel that you should go home, but your son is alive and unharmed. His needs can wait. It's not every day that a crime like this happens causing war type injuries. I would think, that, more than anyone, you would see that your specific past experience is in short supply. Dr. Manchen is a great surgeon, but he does not have your experience with this type of trauma."

Ahmed Zuqawri was tiring of Taylor's insistence. "It is also not everyday that my son is a victim of such an attack and requires consoling by his parents."

Taylor shot back, "There are some children whose parents are downstairs right now needing immediate medical attention. Who is going to console those children when their parents die because you are at home watching your child sleep?"

"I must be with my family. If there is something that cannot be resolved I can be reached on my cell phone," Ahmed lied. "Now, if you will excuse me I must get finished here."

Dr. Taylor could not stop the man from leaving and he knew it was of no use to continue the argument. Zuqawri was right; it was none of his business.

"Look, I understand that you have had a tough day, but I don't agree with what you are doing and I intend to report the way you interacted with the E.R. patients to Dr. Manchen. It will be up to him to pursue this any further."

Taylor backed through the open office door closing it behind him. He stood in the corridor trying to make sense of what was happening. He still could not get past the uneasy feeling he had about Dr. Zuqawri. Taylor always followed his instincts. This time he wasn't sure what it was, but something was wrong, and it had to do with Ahmed Zuqawri and the bombing at the zoo. He just couldn't put his finger on it, but somehow the two were connected. Maybe he was wrong, but the feeling was there and it wouldn't go away. He decided to at least discus it with Dr. Manchen. Taylor headed down the hall, breaking into a run towards the open elevator.

Back in his office Ahmed Zuqawri sped up the process of finalizing his departure. He now threw everything he could, quickly, into the box. He slipped off his black loafers and tossed them into the gym bag. He retrieved the athletic shoes and put them on in case he had to escape on foot. He closed the box, overlapping the flaps to keep it from coming open and grabbed his gym bag, then headed out into the hall.

He locked his office door and made his way toward the main elevators that would take him as far as the first floor lobby and the main entrance of the hospital. He could see the helicopter landing-pad from the windows adjacent to the elevator and the parking area beyond it where several other similar contraptions were now parked. Not all of them were medical birds. Two had the FBI markings on the side doors and the small brown St. Louis county police helicopters were there as well. The FBI and local police had command and control vans on the lot at the hospital and across the highway at the zoo. As Ahmed stepped into the elevator he stopped as he caught a glimpse of yet another helicopter descending into the zoo parking lot across the highway. He recognized it as an American Black Hawk helicopter, but without any designating letters and only gloss black paint. He was not sure what agency it belonged to. He stepped fully into the elevator letting the doors close and the elevator shot to the first floor without stopping. When the doors opened Zuqawri hurriedly walked toward the main entrance of the hospital and out the automatic doors. There were no news crews at the main entrance, no police or other investigating officials to bump into. They would not be suspecting anything anyway, at least not yet.

Ahmed made it to his Nissan Maxima and threw his items in the back seat. He pulled out of his parking place and into the early evening traffic that was compounded by the closing of several roads leading through Forest Park. He decided to take Oakland, a secondary road that ran adjacent to the highway instead of jumping onto the interstate for the short ride home.

CHAPTER 28

CRIME SCENE

THE flight from Washington's Reagan International to Lambert International Airport in St. Louis took a little over two and a half hours. Alan and Paul Jackson were escorted to the awaiting Black Hawk and transported to the crime scene in about fifteen minutes. It had been more than fifteen years since Jackson had been in a Black Hawk.

The rotation of the rotors and the reverberating noise caused an adrenalin rush as he remembered several missions with his Eighth Airborne Rangers. At forty-eight years old he was still young enough and in good enough shape to get back into extreme training. It was possible that he could take the young Special Forces Soldier turned operative that sat across from him, on a good day.

Alan noticed that Paul was looking at him and was going to ask why, but knew that he would have to yell for him to hear. Besides, he seemed as if he were deep in thought and he would hate to ruin that. They would have plenty of time to talk in the hotel later.

The co-pilot tapped Alan and gave him the two-minute sign. Alan looked down at the highway below. He spotted the park, recognizing it from the map search he had done to get familiar with the area. They would be landing just north of the highway at the zoo's south entrance.

The aircraft lowered itself to the pavement. The suspension of the landing gear absorbed the contact with the parking lot with little or no discomfort to the passengers, not like the rides to which both Ramsey and Jackson were accustomed. Most of the time those birds didn't land at all, but instead released the passengers to repel to their destiny with terra firma.

The two men exited the aircraft and headed in the direction of the FBI step van set up near the entrance. They stopped in to show their credentials. Before the door to the van could close fully, FBI agent Mark Alexander greeted them. "Well, well. It's about time forensics sent someone over. Must be nice. We get the place all set up for you and all you gotta do is pick up a map and go."

Ramsey looked at Jackson and then at the tall heavyweight behind the counter. "Not exactly..." Ramsey looked at the man's identification badge hanging from a neck that was easily twenty inches in diameter. "...Agent Alexander. I'm Alan Ramsey and this is Paul Jackson. We are special investigators from Langley. We work in the Antiterrorism Division."

Alexander straightened up some and extended a hand in Ramsey's direction. "Sorry about the chiding fellas. We've been waiting for the forensic folks to get here. Thought maybe you were them."

Ramsey was surprised. "How long have you guys been set up? And you don't have any forensic teams on site?"

Alexander quickly corrected Ramsey's statement. "Not us, we got people here. Started in right after the explosion with photos of victims, survivor interviews and such. We even got the big forensic trailer on site, but we were told the city and county cops would be heading up the investigation. We're waiting on them." He talked as he struggled to tuck in his shirt that tended to pull out with nearly every move he made.

Ramsey thought that at least the different divisions and departments were trying to work together. "Well, we are going to start working now. Have your people report to me when they get here. No need to do everything twice."

"Absolutely agree." Alexander turned around and reached up to grab a stack of brochures from a shelf above him, undoing any success he may have had with his shirt tail and revealing a pistol tucked into a holster, that up to that point had been all but hidden from view by the girth of the man's arms.

Paul noted the sidearm and chest harness and wondered where a person the size of the man in front of him could find a harness to fit. It had to be custom made, he thought.

The agent saw Jackson looking. "It's a Glock twenty-three." He set down the stack of brochures and motioned to his pistol as if he were going to remove it and show it to Paul. "I like it because it's very light weight."

Paul waved off the offer and Alexander turned back to the business at hand. He gave them a quick briefing with basic information such as time of detonation, casualty count and type of explosives used. Ramsey thanked the man, signed in and then asked the agent for directions to the scene.

Special Agent Alexander pulled a slimly folded brochure from the stack, placed a number on the front and annotated the same number in the sign in book, then slid the brochure across the counter to Ramsey. The brochure, a full color threefold document, was handed out to zoo visitors all over the park. The illustrated map seemed a bit out of place given the circumstances surrounding its necessity. Agent Alexander opened the brochure and with a pen pointed to the area that represented the crime scene.

"Go through this entrance, the south entrance, and walk to the right, past Ben and Jerry's, past the welcome center and the seal pens. Keep following it around and you will come to the food court next to the lake. There are bathrooms here and a fence here. The bomb was detonated here." The agent placed an X to mark the location of the central point of the explosion's radius, otherwise known as ground zero, just to the right of center of the food court. "Will you be needing an escort?"

"Thanks, but no," Ramsey said as he folded the brochure in such a manner that the map side was facing out. The agent gave a strange look and said, "Ok, then gentlemen, enjoy your visit to the St. Louis Zoo." Paul Jackson thought that was funny, but since Alan did not show that he was amused in the least Jackson made sure to hide his mirth.

Ramsey and Jackson arrived at the scene within a few minutes. The area was cordoned off with miles of police tape. The outermost ring of tape was a triple level. The next ring had a double row of tape and the innermost ring was just a single band of bright yellow plastic tape. Each successive ring from center was indicative of the crime scene investigation level. The first ring was roped off at the inner edge of the immediate area of the most damage. Originally it had been placed around the casualties and the detonation point to preserve the scene as much as possible. The bodies had since been removed, but either an outline or paper silhouette indicated their locations. Some areas needed no additional markings other than the blood staining the asphalt.

For an hour or so the two men scoured the site taking notes and photographs. They stopped at each of the orange marking cones that were scattered throughout the area to determine the direction from which the projectiles traveled. The cones were typically reserved to mark bullet casings but were put to use this time to mark the location of any of the hundreds of stainless steel ball bearings now on the ground. In some areas, such as around the concrete structure of the bathroom, it was hard to negotiate a walk through due to the amount of ball bearings that had gathered there after ricocheting off the concrete.

Ramsey noted that the bench at ground zero was merely two steel legs and a cross brace with a piece of tape in the form of an X to mark the absolute center of the attack. Standing there looking around Ramsey could see the blast radius from the bomb's perspective. Paul watched as Ramsey placed himself as near center as possible turning slowly, stopping to scan every degree of the three hundred and sixty degree rotation.

The ground and fencing near the manmade lake were littered with lunch bags and lunch boxes, baseball caps and dead swans and ducks. There were even sparrows lying dead along the fence. The fencing acted as a four foot tall net, catching the debris from the explosion and depositing it on the ground.

Paul Jackson had seen his share of explosions and the damage they could cause, but not in the context of what he was looking at now. His experience was different in that there was always a gaping hole in the ground or the mechanized infantry vehicle and only a few casualties, depending upon the type of fighting vehicle involved in the attack. Here though, he could see the belongings of many people. He couldn't imagine being the first on the scene to find the bodies of dead children and adults in civilian attire.

"Alan, is this the kind of stuff you saw during your tour in Iraq? The stuff I did wasn't like this. There weren't any kids or civilians involved. We were strictly one on one with known insurgents."

Alan continued his sweep, writing notes and drawing pictures of the site. "I was attached to a Spec Ops Ranger Battalion. Some of my guys didn't wear uniforms. They blended with the populace to gather info. Our tasking was mostly urban infiltration and support. We painted targets, we observed, and that put us in situations much worse than this."

Ramsey scribbled a few more notes about trajectory and force and placed his notebook and pen in his pocket. "There were times that my own men were victims of the insurgent bombings because they were part of the community and just happened to be in the wrong place at the wrong time. We would have to move in to collect the bodies of the soldiers that were killed. Sometimes you would lift up one body only to find the lifeless body of a child looking up at you." He took out his camera and began to photograph the site.

"That had to be the hardest part, finding children dead. But even there, in some of the most active insurgent attacks, they never specifically targeted children."

Ramsey paused to focus on some of the items against the fence. He could plainly see the pockmarked holes from the passage of the steel balls. Even the paper lunch bags and drink containers were perforated in such a way that you could easily make out each individual hole. He focused on a pink plastic lunch box about twenty meters away. The holes were so perfectly punched through that it looked as if someone had taken a drill to the box to punish the colorfully illustrated pony on the cover. In one corner a shard of plastic was embedded in the box from front to back.

Alan put down his camera and walked over to the pink lunch box. He turned the box to get a better view of the projectile that was embedded through the plastic. He photographed what he saw before disturbing it then carefully removed the six-inch plastic spear.

Alan held up the plastic and studied it. There were tiny sand-size pieces of glass embedded on the concave side of the projectile. On the opposite side, on the convex surface were the letters S-P-A and what appeared to be an illustration of the left booster rocket and a portion of the external fuel tank of a space shuttle. Under the first three letters were two others offset by one character, the letters S-H. He looked again at the pink lunchbox. It was distorted and full of holes, but for the most part it was intact. He stared at the plastic shard. It looked as if it had been part of a cylinder that had peeled open. It had to be a thermos bottle, Ramsey thought. That would explain the shape and the pulverized embedded particles of glass. Still, it looked as though it had been blown apart from the inside out, and, to be moving with such force...

Alan suddenly stood up. "Paul, look for more of this! Look for anything that has a picture of the shuttle or a rocket or anything to do with space, Star Wars, or even E.T. I think the explosives were packed in this thermos or possibly a lunch box."

Paul Jackson stood upright. "Wouldn't that have been completely destroyed? I mean if the explosives were inside a thermos. Wouldn't it have... evaporated or something like that?"

Ramsey got up and held the shard out and tried to quickly explain his theory. "Did you ever put an M-80 in a soda can? Remember how the can blew open? It didn't disintegrate; it just opened up from the force of the expanding gasses. Well, it's the same for bigger bombs. The initial blast forces the container open, but the explosion has only just started to expand. Some materials such as concrete and glass can be reduced to mere molecules but steel and plastic have properties that keep the pieces together." Ramsey held up the spear of plastic before continuing, "Plastic molecules overlap, weaving together during the manufacturing process. They tear and peel instead of shattering, and then they ride the shock wave like a surfer. Unless the pieces are heavy or they meet resistance, such as another object, they're the first out of the gate so they're moving faster than everything else and just keep on going." He tapped the piece against his free hand. "Frankly, this was a lucky find. But then, I'd rather be lucky than good any day."

"Thank you, Dr. Ramsey. So, these pieces would have been ahead of any of the projectiles, so no holes or damage from them?" Paul asked.

"Exactly! They would all be traveling at the same speed away from center, well, until wind resistance and weight came into play, but yeah, no damage from the projectiles."

Paul turned and looked back in the direction of the explosion. If Ramsey were right the pieces of the thermos would be spread in a three hundred and sixty degree radius from the center. He began to scour along the fence-line and the curbing along the pathways. He found several smaller pieces that appeared to have the same pattern as the first. Then he found what appeared to be a mangled piece of metal with the same color scheme and the words NASA and the NASA emblem on one corner of the crumbled piece of tin. Along the folded edge were two pieces of metal that appeared to be the remnants of a pressed metal hinge. It was the lid of a metal lunchbox.

"Alan! I got something over here. Looks like the lunchbox lid to me. Same color scheme, no holes, just crumpled up!" Ramsey ran to where Paul was stooped. On his way he motioned for one of the FBI guys to join them.

The agent arrived just as Ramsey completed photographing. Ramsey introduced himself and explained what was going on. "I believe we may have found the delivery system for the bomb. It looks like it was in a lunchbox. Spread your men out and look for anything that has to do with NASA or the space shuttle."

The agent pulled up his radio. "Agent Matthews, come to my location over by the lake fence." He turned back to face Ramsey. "You got it. Sounds like a good lead."

Ramsey pressed for more assistance. "I need to use your forensics van to look for prints and explosive signatures. I'd like to start with what I've got and go from there as the pieces come in."

"No problem, I'll let them know you're on your way."

Ramsey lightly slapped the agent's shoulder. "Thanks Agent..." He leaned over to get a look at the badge for the agent's name. The agent pushed out a hand. "Sorry, Mr. Ramsey, I'm agent Darin Martin, Forensics Division Team Leader. I should have introduced myself."

"No problem. Things are moving pretty fast here. He pointed to Paul. That is Agent Jackson, Paul Jackson."

Paul picked up the piece of metal carefully and placed it in a plastic bag. He turned and shook Martin's hand then turned to face

Ramsey. He pointed to the barely visible inner side of the metal lid. "Alan, looks like there is something written on the other side. We'll have to bend it open to see what."

Alan thought about the condition of the painted metal lid. "If the bomb was inside the lunchbox you would think that the lid would be folded inside out. Residue test will explain it I guess. Let's get it to the van. We'll let the forensic teams get a good look."

Before the two could get out of the secondary perimeter Agent Mathews was calling in. "Martin, this is Matthews. Over."

Agent Martin keyed his mike. "Go ahead, Matthews."

The agent keyed back, "Sir, looks like we've got the rest of the lunch box. It's pretty mangled, but pretty sure it's the box. Still has the latch intact. I'm sending one of the juniors over with it."

Martin responded, looking at Ramsey, "Good job. Tell your guys to keep looking for other pieces though. We need to keep this moving forward."

Matthews ended the transmission. "Roger that, good copy, Matthews out."

Ramsey yelled back to Martin. "Have your man bring it to the van. Anything else you find related to the bomb, bring it up immediately."

Martin responded with a thumbs up and turned toward two of his people. Ramsey and Jackson walked out of the zoo to the vans in the parking lot and entered the mobile forensic unit.

"You Ramsey?" The words came from a middle-aged doctor who was going through hundreds of digital photos of the crime scene. "Used to be we spent hours developing the film before we could look at anything. Had to have a film processing lab on wheels just for that. Now I complain that it takes too long to download the images if it takes more than five minutes." He looked at the evidence the two were holding. "What have you got for me?"

Ramsey explained what he suspected the items in the bags meant and handed them over to the bespectacled man still sitting by the large flat screen full of photos. Ramsey saw the images on the monitor and motioned to Paul to take a look. The doctor saw Alan's gesturing and began to narrate the grisly images. "I've been doing this for eighteen years or so. This has to be the toughest group of photos to label and organize I've ever had to do." A photo of three of the dead children sprawled against the rough concrete of the bathroom in a mangled heap was in the forefront of the images.

Paul Jackson turned away, disturbed by the graphic image and concentrated on removing the items from the bags for the doctor. The man started to describe his findings. "I believe that boy, there, was holding the device that caused all this damage." The doctor pointed at the monitor with the end of the pen he had been chewing on. The subject had no arms and was missing, as best Ramsey could tell, his jaw, most of his face and an abundance of the rib cage and torso flesh. "Looks like his legs are intact. He was probably standing by a picnic bench and was protected somewhat. The calf structure is damaged pretty badly indicating he was standing between the bench seat and the table part of the bench. If the bench had been made of concrete instead of recycled plastic he probably wouldn't have any legs either."

Ramsey looked closely. He agreed with the doctor based on the photo that this was the person who was nearest to, if not holding, the bomb. "Has he been identified?"

"By process of elimination only. No pun intended." The doctor held up his list of checked names. "The parents have identified all the other bodies at the hospital including the other two bodies in this photo." He used his to point to the two bodies on the left side of the monitor. "Out of the twenty four students on the field trip there were only three kids who survived the attack, and we know who they are, so that leaves this one." He circled a name on a list to his right that had been circled several times before and showed it to Ramsey. The name was Demarcus Johnson.

"His parents can't identify him? Shouldn't there be a positive ID by now?" Ramsey sounded skeptical that the boy wouldn't have been identified since the explosion happened over five hours before.

The forensic doctor looked over his glasses at Ramsey. "I don't think they know where the mother is and, supposedly, he doesn't have a father. "Who knows, maybe she's pullin' a double somewhere to make ends meet and hasn't heard about the explosion." He ended his photo tour by switching programs to a viewer that was hooked to a microscope. "I try not to get too involved with the details. Makes it too personal. It's bad enough it was kids that were targeted. I don't need all them specifics, you know?" He pushed the objects around on the desk some and then moved the plastic shard to the microscope.

"First we gotta dust for prints. Need to see if anybody other than this Johnson boy had their hands on this bottle." He turned to Ramsey. "You can watch if you want, but this stuff takes a while."

Ramsey stated, "I'm going to stay until we unfold this metal lid to see what is written inside. I can wait."

The doctor looked at Ramsey and then at Paul Jackson. "Why don't we look at what you want to look at first? I can discount your fingerprints and your partner's when I dust. Otherwise I'm going to be looking for explosive trace residue and proximity clues to verify these pieces are from the same component."

Ramsey knew that the chemicals used in the trace testing could damage the writing if not remove it completely. "We just want to see what is written on it in case it could give us a lead to follow while other things are going on."

The forensic specialist picked up the wadded piece of metal and sniffed it, then placed it back on the counter. "It has the same odor as the plastic. It's going to be part of the same component. Smells like nitro glycerin. Not the normal amount that is in C-4.

May have had an enhancement of nitro glycerin to increase the bomb's strength. As far as the straightening of the metal you need a blacksmith, not forensics, for that." He smiled.

Ramsey picked up the twisted piece of metal and placed it on the floor so that the opening was facing the steel floor of the van. He eyed it carefully then stepped down on it as if he were smashing a soda can.

The metal made popping and clicking noises, but when Alan Ramsey lifted his foot up it was fairly straight. He could now make out the entire picture of the space theme on the lid. He reached down to retrieve it.

Paul Jackson looked on as Alan turned the lid over. Alan looked around the lab, and then asked the doctor, "Do you have communications with Agent Martin?"

The doctor pulled up a radio from the shelf under the counter and turned it on. "I keep it off so I can work in peace, otherwise it's hard to concentrate on one thing without getting sidetracked by someone who thinks one piece of evidence is more important than another." He handed the radio to Ramsey.

Alan Ramsey keyed the mike, "Agent Martin, this is Alan Ramsey. Come in. Over."

"This is Agent Martin, go ahead. Over."

"Agent Martin I have a lead I want your guys to follow up on. One of the victims of the bombing. I've got an address and a phone number."

Martin acknowledged Ramsey, "You got it. I'm ready to copy. Over."

Ok, name, Joshi Zuqawri." Ramsey spelled the name out using the phonetic alphabet used by the military. He paused for a couple seconds to give Martin a chance to catch up and then continued. "The address is 18201 West Park, St. Louis, Missouri. How copy? Over."

Martin read back the address and waited as Ramsey dictated the phone number. "522-0463, good copy. Over."

Ramsey finalized the communication. "Get your guys on that. Put it on first priority. That info should lead us to our bomb maker. If not it will get us real close."

"Roger. We're on it. Martin out."

"Ramsey, out." Alan started to return the radio to the doctor and scribbled his phone number on a piece of paper. "Call me if they call you back. I'd like to hang on to your radio for a while if that's OK. I'll be just outside the van."

The doctor looked up from his microscope, nodded his agreement on the use of the radio, then stabbed a finger at three of the names on his list. "That kid you just named, Joshi Zuqawri, he's one of the survivors."

Ramsey stared at the man as he handed him the slip of paper and thinking about what he just said, motioned to Paul to head outside. They stepped out of the van as the junior agent walked up with the remaining section of the lunchbox. "You looking for this?"

Paul Jackson answered, "Yeah, put it inside with the good doctor. He'll take it from there. Thanks."

The young agent slipped inside the van and closed the door. He was back out in a few seconds and headed back in the direction from which he'd come.

Paul broke the silence. "Zuqawri don't sound like the name of a Klan member to me. Not unless the KKK is accepting Muslims into their clique. If that's the case I'm gonna feel really left out as a black man."

The radio in Alan Ramsey's hand suddenly came back to life.

"Ramsey, this is Martin. Over." Ramsey keyed in. "Go ahead, Martin."

"That kid, Joshi, survived the attack. He was in the bathroom when the bomb went off."

Ramsey acknowledged the information. "Yeah, I just found that out."

Martin continued, "Yeah, well that's not all. Get this, his dad works at the Best Health Hospital just on the other side of Oakland."

"Oakland? Is that a town close by?"

Martin apologized, "Sorry, Sir. Oakland is a street. If you look from your location across the highway, Oakland is just on the other side."

Ramsey and Jackson turned to face the noise of the speeding traffic and spotted the name of the hospital near the top of the tan, brick building just opposite of their position across the interstate. "Got it. That's convenient. We're going to need a vehicle."

"I'm already on my way with our ride." Martin pulled through the gate at the north end of the parking area in a black Chevrolet Yukon, pulled up alongside Ramsey and Jackson and lowered the window on Ramsey's side.

Alan dropped the radio to his side and called through the open window, "I take it you're interested in going across the street with us."

"You got it. My team wouldn't give up the keys unless they could come along."

Alan pulled open the door of the forensic van and called to the doctor, "Here you go," as he tossed the radio to the man. "Call me when you get trace signatures that are proof positive that the lunchbox was the source of the explosion. I'll need all the numbers for a team that will be paying a visit to either Dr. Zuqawri at work or will be setting up in his driveway at home. Ramsey pulled his phone out and flipped it open as he got into the Yukon.

Gabe Anderson was just getting ready to call it a day. He had gotten his first call at two-thirty that morning and hadn't stopped working except to eat lunch. It was his twenty second wedding anniversary and he had promised his wife that he would be able to have dinner with her at Morgan's Point, her favorite seafood restaurant. It was already after six and she would be worrying that something had come up to change their plans. He made sure that his calls would be forwarded to his secure home line, set his computer for remote access and then closed the door.

He felt the familiar buzz of his cell phone and juggled his laptop bag with his jacket as he reached into his pocket. He saw that it was Ramsey and slid the cover of his phone open to answer. "Hello, Alan."

"Gabe, we have the source of the explosion. It was a lunchbox and a thermos bottle. Forensics is verifying, but it looks like it was carried in by one of the students. We found his address and phone number on the inside of the lid. His name is Joshi Zuqawri. His father is Ahmed Zuqawri who works across the highway at a local hospital. We're on our way there now."

Gabe Anderson contemplated for a few seconds. "You think his father has something to do with it? He killed his own son?"

"We don't know whether Zuqawri had anything to do with this yet, but his son, Joshi, isn't dead. He was in the bathroom and wasn't hurt. Gabe, it's possible his son is involved if it was a timed device or maybe his father detonated it remotely from across the street. It's too early to tell until forensics has figured out the make up of the bomb." Ramsey looked back from where they had come and then at the hospital. He thought it was too far for radio control, but it could have been detonated by cell phone, unless the boy had set it off somehow.

"Anyway, we are going to question Zuqawri and see what we can find out. I may need subpoena support if we want to search the hospital or his house." The Yukon pulled into a limited parking area close to the E.R. entrance. "I'll keep you posted."

Gabe looked at his watch. "Ok, I'll get legal to start working on it. They'll need all the info though, addresses, local jurisdiction statements, the works. Make sure all the t's are crossed and the i's are dotted. You know how they are."

Ramsey always found it painful to work with the legal department. "I'll get with Jennifer. She's a wizard with that stuff. I may need her to get me some other information anyway."

Gabe Anderson was relieved for the moment. "Call me after you speak with Zuqawri...good luck."

Gabe Anderson waited for Ramsey to hang up and then closed his cell. He selected the silent mode and hoped that it would stay that way at least through dinner. He could already see the look that he was going to get from his wife when he told her he would be heading back to the office after dinner. She would understand. She always did.

CHAPTER 29

HOMECOMING

ZUQAWRI stopped at a traffic signal and nervously looked around. He opened his cell and called Leaja bin Masri. The phone was picked up on the first ring. "What is it? What do you want?" came the greeting from the other end.

"I have just left the hospital. I need more time. One of the doctors there was asking me questions as I was packing."

"Does he suspect anything? Surely he has no way to connect you with the attack."

"He has suspicions of me, but they are only that. He cannot know that I was involved. I am a victim like the others. My son was targeted in an attack."

Zuqawri contemplated his next sentence. "My wife called me. Joshi is not dead. Somehow, praise Allah, his life was spared."

"What? How can that be? The triggering mechanism was mechanical, was it not?" bin Masri asked.

"Yes, a pressure sensitive detonator." Zuqawri explained all that he knew thus far. "I do not know the specifics yet. Bedalla called me ranting about how I tried to kill our son. She was very angry. I tried to deny it, but she told me she found the explosives and other components."

Bin Masri cut him off. "She knows that you are responsible for the explosion?"

"Yes. But she understands that the cause is a just one, that we are acting for Allah," Ahmed reasoned.

"The plan to use your son was foolish, Ahmed. Do not underestimate a woman's love for her child. You cannot trust that she is so understanding of our cause as to allow you to sacrifice her only son."

"So then, Leaja, you are saying it was foolish for God to ask Abraham to sacrifice his only son, Ishmael," Ahmed shot back.

Leaja bin Masri responded curtly, "Do not question God's Will! Allah did not allow Ishmael to die for His desire to test Abraham." Leaja thought for a moment. "Tell me Ahmed, did Allah come to you and tell you to sacrifice your son?"

"No, but Allah spared my son just as he sent the angel that spared the life of Ishmael. It was Allah's will. You will not convince me otherwise."

Bin Masri thought of the risk to their mission. This was the plan of Hamza al-Muhajeer whose lifeless body he had left in the desert not more than twenty hours before, giving everything for the cause of all Muslims. He was not willing to take a chance that the poor decision of a mere worker-ant would cause it to come apart now, not after all the months of planning.

"Ahmed, you must remove all proof of your involvement in the attack. If it is discovered that the attack today was done by the Brotherhood our entire mission will be at risk."

Zuqawri thought that bin Masri saw him as a buffoon. "Why do you speak to me as if I were a child? I told you I was going to my home to collect all of the remaining components and explosives. I will leave no trace of the materials."

He tried again to convince himself that he was just another victim. "The police have no reason to suspect me and as far as the hospital knows I am leaving to be with my family after the attack that nearly claimed the life of my son."

Bin Masri retorted, "And when you don't show up at the hospital they will eventually come looking for you. What do you suppose your wife will tell them when they threaten to take your child away and her into custody? What if she is interrogated? What will she reveal? We cannot trust that your woman will be true to our goals. She and your son are both risks that cannot be afforded."

Ahmed slowed his car and pulled to a stop along the curb to concentrate on what bin Masri was telling him. "What are you saying Leaja?" he asked warily. "Am I to bring Joshi and Bedalla to the warehouse?"

Leaja bin Masri took a deep breath. "Ahmed, we can not take the chance that all that we have sacrificed for this mission will be for nothing. I am sorry to say that you are going to have to kill them both. It is too bad that the bomb did not claim the life of at least one of them as you were expecting."

Ahmed Zuqawri felt the blood rush from his face. He nearly dropped the phone as he began to tremble thinking about what he had been told to do. He broke into a cold sweat and stammered out his reply. "I...am not sure...I can do what you are telling me to do."

"You do not have much choice, Ahmed."

"Send someone else to do this. I cannot. I will not!"

"There is no one else. It is your responsibility!"

"I can not kill them without purpose! True, Joshi was to die today. But, it was to deliver the will of God to the infidels. A martyr's death, not murdered at the hands of his own father for no reason."

"Ahmed, you yourself spoke of Ishmael and Abraham. Maybe this is the true test. If it is not to be then it is Allah's will, but you have to draw the blade and make the sacrifice. Do this Ahmed. There is no ram in the thicket to sacrifice in place of them. Allahu Akbar min kulli shay!"

Ahmed heard the words that bin Masri spoke. "God is Greater than everything," he said to himself in a low voice, then to bin Masri he asked, "It will be hard. What if I fail?"

Bin Masri continued to convince his soldier that what was required of him was the right thing to do. "Ahmed, the Caliphs have spoken of the Jihad for over fourteen hundred years. It has culminated in this war, this mission, at this time, and we are the key to the success of the end result. The Muslim Empire will be as it once was. We have defeated the Byzantines, the Syrians, Egypt, Spain and Northern Africa and now, America will fall. Muhammad's legacy has been to take what is rightfully ours. The land bequeathed to the sons of Abraham. We must show the infidels that it is not their place to stand in our way. It is at our fingertips, brother; we must not let it slip through our grasp. You can do this, Ahmed. You will be strong and persevere. Remember that Allah is with you."

Ahmed leaned over and unlocked the glove box of his Nissan. He removed a towel and unfolded it to expose the black leather of the holster wrapped inside. He snapped the holster open and pulled the weapon from its sheath. The nine-millimeter pistol was cool to the touch. He held it by the grip and inspected it closely. He could feel the power that it possessed giving him strength. He snapped the cartridge release dropping it out onto the seat next to him, and racked the weapon to clear the chamber. He released the safety and dry fired the pistol to check its action.

"I will have to bring the bodies with me for disposal," he said to bin Masri callously. "Do you think you can have someone take care of that or do I have to bury them myself as well?"

Leaja bin Masri was sure that Zuqawri was committed to the Jihad and would do what was expected of him. "You must make sure that you have removed every shred of evidence. Everything. I will have someone waiting here to help you with the bodies. I will let them decide on the method of disposal. You will not have to be involved with that."

Ahmed reloaded the weapon and placed the selector lever on safe. He shoved the pistol down between the console and the seat and pulled back into traffic. "I should be home in five minutes or so. I will call you when it is done."

Zuqawri slid the cover over his phone and tossed it on the seat next to him and picked up the pistol again. He was no longer trembling and felt a confidence he had not felt since he left Iraq. He had told Bedalla that he was not responsible for the deaths of the members of the council. He had lied. He had pulled the trigger that sent nine of them to their fates with Allah, his own brother among them.

He had tried to convince his brother, Omar, to join the Brotherhood, but Omar had insisted that the Sunni's should act as leaders and show others that the way to peace and stability was through the new constitution and working with the council and the Shiite Prime Minister Nori al-Makim. They should embrace the change, he'd said.

Ahmed warned his brother several times to stay away from the council, that supporting Makim's planned government and its illegal constitution would only bring him to harm. All sympathizers with the new government were considered traitors. Their cooperation warranted an immediate death sentence, but Omar would not listen to reason.

Ahmed's heart began pounding in his chest. His mind flashed through memories from the days before the massive American surge. He suddenly felt detached from reality. His palms began to sweat as he gripped the steering wheel hard trying to shake off the sounds and images from his wartime experiences that were suddenly and vividly flooding his mind.

Again he was back in Mosul, standing in the government building staring at his brother. Ahmed was breathing hard, his warm breath filling the knitted fabric of his mask. He had not given the others, whose bodies lay contorted and lifeless against the wall, a chance to pray, but he paused momentarily to allow his brother the time to do what he needed to do to prepare himself for his life with Allah. The two men faced each other. Ahmed held the pistol to his brother's forehead, waiting, chanting in a low voice, "Allah Akbar, Allah Akbar..."

One of the others told him to hurry. "Now! We must go!" Ahmed glanced down to see the urine run off of Omar's shoe and puddle on the floor. He looked into the eyes of his brother and saw the fear. Ahmed knew that he was finished with his prayer and was now thinking only of self-preservation. Omar began to speak. "Please..."

Zuqawri's mind raced backward in time to the childhood he shared with his two brothers. The older disappeared after the war with Iran, only making contact with him once or twice after the war ended and then Ahmed never saw him again. His younger brother now stood before him, pissing his pants and begging forgiveness and mercy. He was a traitor to his country and worse, a traitor to Allah. That thought gave him the strength he needed. He closed his eyes as he squeezed the trigger and, in that fraction of a second, ended the life of his brother.

The sound of the gunshot, and the smell of the just fired weapon filled his senses. His eyes stung from the smoke. Every second of that scene came back to him, including the image of his brother sliding down the pockmarked, bullet riddled, marble trimmed wall to the floor.

He had spun around in slow motion as the rest of the group turned to run out the front of the building only to be greeted by American forces and Iraqi Police. The sound of the American soldiers yelling for the men to drop their weapons filled the hallways of the large building. Ahmed looked for another exit and turned toward the staircase that led to the lower level. His heart was pounding in his chest. He watched the others engage the enemy with their assault rifles. One of his men fell backward into the hall as bullets ripped through his body, exploding from the man's back and striking the carved stones that made up the "Wall of Freedom", a mural etched in stone that represented and was dedicated to the new democracy of Iraq.

The horrible flash and explosion of a concussion grenade was all Ahmed needed to decide that if he stayed and fought he would surely die. His was a war of stealth and secrecy, not of open engagement.

He pulled off his mask as he ran down a flight of stairs, then slipped through the door and crossed through the adjoining courtyard. He packed his weapon away and blended in with others as they ran from the American attack. Ahmed's heart was racing. His lungs burned from breathing so hard. He darted between two parked cars and ran directly in front of a moving vehicle. The driver slammed on the brakes and laid on the horn. The blast from the horn snapped Ahmed back to the present.

Ahmed looked up into his rearview mirror. He could see the infidel behind him impatiently flailing his arms about in a frustrated gesture, then again blaring the horn. Ahmed tried to figure out what he was doing wrong as he came back fully to reality. He felt groggy, almost drugged.

He realized he was barely moving. The driver behind him honked again. This time Ahmed sat up and stepped down on the accelerator, speeding ahead. He reached the next traffic light as it turned yellow and matted the accelerator down to ensure he would not have to stop.

He suddenly realized he was holding the pistol and noticed the expended shell casing on the seat. He looked around the car quickly. No glass was broken. He found the point of impact near the floor at the right kick panel. The bullet had gone through the thin plastic cover and into the metal framework of the car right where the carpet and the plastic met.

The flashbacks were becoming more frequent now, affecting him when he was fully awake. He thanked Allah that he had not shot himself or someone else and that he had not gotten stopped by the police. He had his orders and did not need another setback. Fighting to clear his mind as he reached the safety of the opposite side of the intersection he slowed down to the legal limit, turned down the next street and was about a block away from home when he thought about his bank account.

If he were going to withdraw all his money he may be required to bring some documents to the bank that only Bedalla would know where to find. No, he could not kill her until he had the money in hand. He would stop at the bank first to see what was required to remove the money from his account. Ahmed pulled into a driveway and then backed out to change his direction. The bank would be closing at five o'clock, but with luck he should get there just in time.

CHAPTER 30

MEDICAL STAFF

ALAN RAMSEY entered the emergency department followed by Paul Jackson and Agent Darin Martin. Paul Jackson walked past Ramsey, stepped up to the desk, flashed his old security badge, then held out a picture of Ahmed Zuqawri.

The nurse at the desk looked at the picture. Paul stated, "We would like to speak with this man. Is he around?"

"We are very busy at the moment. Give me a few minutes and I'll see if I can locate him...um...Agent Jackson." She read his badge slowly to make sure his credentials were real, then picked up the phone, but instead of calling for Zuqawri, she called for Jason Taylor. Taylor called back on speaker letting the nurse know that he was heading her direction.

About the time the intercom clicked off the doors to the E.R. from the main hospital hallway opened and the young looking doctor walked in.

"Good afternoon, gentlemen. How can I help you?"

Alan Ramsey stepped up and read the nametag on the doctor's white jacket. "Dr. Taylor, I'm Alan Ramsey and this is Paul Jackson and Agent Martin. We are looking for Dr. Ahmed Zuqawri. Do you have any idea where he is?"

"He left here about fifteen minutes ago. His son was at the zoo when the explosion occurred and was pretty shaken up. He wasn't hurt, but it's traumatic even for someone who lived through that kind of stuff day after day."

"I'm not sure I'm following you."

"Oh, sorry. Dr. Zuqawri is from Iraq. Used to live in Mosul, in the Anbar Province, I believe. He said it was pretty bad. Still, you probably get numb to that kind of thing when it happens all the time."

Ramsey excused himself from the conversation, pulled his cell phone out of his pocket and called his page back in Langley. She answered immediately. "Jennifer, I need you to do a search of our database for a guy named Ahmed Zuqawri. He's from Mosul, married and has at least one son named Joshi."

"The same Joshi that's all over the news? The kid who survived the explosion?"

"That's the one. We believe he was carrying the explosive device. He may have been involved and may have even detonated it. I've got an FBI team heading to his house now." Ramsey thought for a moment. "Jennifer, this guy Zuqawri may be the same guy we tracked a couple years ago. He's a doctor, so you might want to check with the hospitals in Iraq also. See if you can get some background on him."

Jennifer Wilkins was already starting the search process. "I'll call your cell when I complete the search."

Jason Taylor overheard the conversation between Alan Ramsey and his page. "Mr. Ramsey, I was getting an uneasy feeling about Dr. Zuqawri this morning. He was acting defensive and nervous, talking about his son being killed when in fact he didn't even have any information about his condition. At first we thought his wife called him to tell him, but we found out later that she hadn't."

Ramsey turned to Paul. "Paul, find out where the FBI is. If they get to Zuqawri's house before he does, I want his wife and son in custody. If he's the one who set the bomb in his son's lunchbox I wouldn't put it past him to go take care of any evidence in the house including his wife and kid." Without taking a breath Alan turned back to Taylor, "Dr. Taylor, what kind of car does Zuqawri drive?" Jason Taylor thought for a second.

"It's a white Nissan. A Sentra or Maxima. I don't know what year, late nineties I think." Alan managed a quick thank you before his phone rang. He looked at the display, then at Paul.

Jackson could read his mind. "Late nineties white Nissan Maxima. Got it. I'll let the Feds and local police in on it." He smiled as he lifted his cell to dial. Ramsey turned back to his own phone still ringing in his hand. It was Jennifer Wilkins.

"Alan, I found something right off the bat. This Zuqawri guy was involved with the group Ansar al-Islam, and had direct contact with Hamza al-Muhajeer. Muhajeer was one of the people killed yesterday morning at the Texas border."

"Yeah, I got that. Involved how?" Ramsey asked.

Jennifer read some of the information she had on the screen in front of her. "Involved, like, he was the guy who ratted out the people who helped the government of the Shiite Prime Minister. No criminal record. This says he was a suspect, picked up and questioned for several attacks that occurred in Mosul, Iraq. Evidently, he was open about his support for Ansar al-Islam, a very radical extremist group.

He had two accounts in his name and one in his name and Leaja bin Masri's. All three accounts had high deposit and withdrawal activity found to be linked to Ansar al-Islam."

Alan asked, "What happened to the money?"

"Well, two of the accounts were closed and the Iraqi police confiscated the money. Where that went nobody knows, I'm sure.

The other account was transferred overseas. Looks like to Frankfurt maybe. At least, I think that is what the identifier means. I'll have to look up the code and get back with you."

"Get a trace on the money. Let me know what you find out. If we can find out where that cash is, we might be able to slow them down. Have Gabe get a lock down on Ahmed Zuqawri's local bank account. The money could be tied to it." He finished up his conversation with, "Good work, Jennifer."

"You think Dr. Zuqawri is responsible for the explosion at the zoo?" Jason Taylor asked.

"I don't know if he is or not, but I don't want to take any chances." Alan pulled the piece of paper from his pocket on which he had written the information from the lunchbox lid and flipped open his phone to key in the number for Zuqawri's house.

Bedalla had just checked on her sleeping son when the phone began ringing. "Damn!" Bedalla thought. The phone hadn't stopped ringing since she had walked in the door, bringing Joshi home from the hospital. Bedalla assumed it was one of the reporters calling to ask questions about her son and his miraculous survival of the explosion. She let it ring until the answering machine picked up. Soon there would be no more room for messages. She peeked out the curtains at the reporters and news trucks camped in front of the house as the answering machine came to life.

"Mrs. Zuqawri, this is Alan Ramsey of the CIA. We need to speak with you. It is urgent."

Bedalla ran to the phone and picked it up. "Hello, this is Bedalla Zuqawri."

"Mrs. Zuqawri, my name is Alan Ramsey. I'm an investigating agent for the CIA. We have reason to believe that you may be in danger and also reason to believe that your husband may be a threat to you. To ensure your safety I am sending a tactical team and an agent..." Ramsey looked towards Martin. "I need a name. Who are you sending?"

Martin didn't hesitate. "Mirso Kojic as lead and..."

Ramsey didn't wait for the rest of the information. He turned back to the phone. "...An agent named Kojic. Mirso Kojic, will arrive momentarily for you and your son."

Bedalla was surprisingly calm. "There are news people out front. They have been calling all morning and are waiting for me to go outside." Bedalla peeked through the edge of the blinds. "They will see me leave with you and report it. I cannot be seen helping you." She began to feel as if she were back in Mosul.

Ramsey asked, "Is there a back way out? A way to escape the reporters?" Ramsey motioned to get Dan Martin's attention again. "Martin, call the TAC team, and tell them not to pull down Zuqawri's street."

Ramsey turned his attention back to what Bedalla was saying. "Yes, there is a back door and an alley behind our garage. They can enter the alley from Forest or McCausland Avenue."

Alan looked at Dan Martin who was listening closely to the conversation. Martin gave Ramsey the thumbs up sign and turned away to call in to update his team.

"Mrs. Zuqawri, stay put for now, but pack a few things for a couple days. Keep the phone close. We'll call you back soon to tell you when to move. Do you understand?"

Bedalla was getting anxious. "Yes, but please, hurry. I don't know what Ahmed will do when he gets here. I found explosives in the basement and he knows it. He tried to kill our son..." She was beginning to feel panicky.

"Mrs. Zuqawri, I have men on the way. Fifteen minutes at the most. The police and the FBI are looking for Ahmed's car. You and your son are safe. Just do as I said and wait for my call."

Bedalla shook off her anxiety, "Ok, yes, we will be ready when your men arrive. Thank you." Ramsey could hear the click of Bedalla hanging up as he folded his phone and placed it back in his pocket.

CHAPTER 31

BANKERS HOURS

"GOODNIGHT, Mr. Harrison." Blanch Hargrove, the bank's drive up teller, tossed on her jacket and lifted her purse from the floor by the counter. "I've got to go pick up my kids from my sister's house. She's had them since after school." She walked past the bank guard giving him a smile and a quiet goodnight. The guard opened the door for her, smiling and nodding as she passed through the doorway.

Greg Harrison smiled and gave a quick wave. "I'm right behind you. Have a nice evening." He turned back to the man sitting across from him. Harrison's smile faded as he stared at the nine-millimeter pistol pointed at him from the opposite side of his desk.

Ahmed Zuqawri had waited for about twenty minutes for service only to be told that he would need his wife's signature to remove the amount of money he was trying to take from his account. He remembered the conversation with his wife the day she had opened the account. She'd called him for his input and he'd told her to handle it. That decision was now hampering his efforts as Bedalla had made herself the primary account holder. Harrison explained even if he could oblige the request, it would take twenty-four hours to process because the satellite branch just didn't have three hundred and thirty thousand dollars to give him.

Ahmed had been stalling, waiting for everyone else to leave before he could act. Now it was only he, the guard and Mr. Harrison. "Well then, Mr. Harrison, if there is nothing more you can do." His words trailed off as he stood. He glanced outside to see that nobody was in the parking lot and then looked through the teller window for anybody who may be looking for service.

The guard, Andrew Gibbs, was just beginning to feel uneasy about this last customer and when Zuqawri stood up Gibbs locked the deadbolt and dropped his right hand down to place the keys in his pocket, but first reached back to his holster, unsnapping the fastener.

Zuqawri could hear the click of the snap as it was being undone. He looked back, over his right shoulder at the guard who suddenly looked tense. Andrew Gibbs slid his hand under the leather strap and began to grab the stock of the pistol as the first shot from Zuqawri's nine-millimeter pistol slammed into his chest. The guard tried to recover from being hit. He was wearing Kevlar under his shirt and, at the moment, the vest was performing as it was designed. Although he was knocked backward, was having difficulty breathing, and was in serious pain, Gibbs managed to regain his footing.

He looked up to see Zuqawri with the pistol still aimed in his direction. Frantically, he reached for his service revolver. Zuqawri immediately fired a second shot, correcting his aim by moving the pistol upward. The second round shattered the skull of Andrew Gibbs after first passing through his right cheekbone under his right eye. The guard fell backward with a thud on the hard marble floor of the lobby, unmoving.

Zuqawri turned back to face Harrison. "I believe our transaction is not complete." He motioned for the banker to get up, but Harrison just sat there, stunned from what he had just witnessed.

"Move!" Zuqawri leaned across the table and shoved the pistol against the man's forehead. "Now!" he screamed.

"Move where? What do you want me to do?" Harrison yelled back, hands raised as if to surrender.

"Open the vault and get my money. That is what," Zuqawri said sternly.

Harrison laughed bitterly, "Even if we had three hundred and thirty grand here today, I can't touch it until tomorrow. The vault is timed and won't accept my password to open the lock until tomorrow morning at nine o'clock. Harrison felt a bit more courageous at the thought of Zuqawri's failure. "So, unless you plan on camping out here until nine tomorrow, you're out of luck."

Zuqawri pushed Harrison in the direction of the vault. He was not about to give up that easily. He scanned along the vault door, keeping the pistol against the bank manager's back. Zuqawri grabbed one of the waiting room chairs and pushed it against the wall. He stepped up and pushed one of the ceiling panels up and away. He repeated this twice more before he found what he was looking for.

Ahmed jumped down from the chair. "There, those conduits. Where do they lead?" Zuqawri pointed up at the grey steel piping that was fastened to the wall just above the drop ceiling.

Greg Harrison really had no idea, but guessed that they were the steel conduits that carried the power to and away from the vault. "I don't know."

Zuqawri was getting impatient. He pushed Harrison with the pistol to force him forward. "Move!" he ordered.

They followed the path of the wiring conduits, turned a corner, and stopped at a locked access door. The piping traveled down from the ceiling above and disappeared through the wall. Their trail ended at the door.

"Do you have the key for that door?" Zuqawri asked.

Greg Harrison was not a good liar. He nervously answered Zuqawri with an unconvincing voice, "No, I am not authorized access to that room."

Zuqawri hit the man hard with the weapon. "I do not believe you. You are the manager of this facility. You must have access to everything in here. Now, open this door."

Zuqawri shoved the pistol against the back of Harrison's ribs. "If you do not do as I say, not only will I kill you, but I will kill your wife and your beautiful daughters." He forced Harrison to look toward his desk. The silver framed photo of his wife and two daughters was easily seen from where they stood.

"Now, you can protect them and possibly save yourself much pain and trouble, if you just open this door. If you do not, then I will begin by shooting you where it will not kill you. I am a doctor. I will keep you alive only to hurt you more."

Harrison's head was pounding from the blow.

"How do I know you won't kill me anyway?" Harrison asked Zuqawri over his shoulder.

"I will make a deal with you. If you open this door and reset the timer so that the door can be opened I will not kill you or harm your family. I will lock you in the vault, and leave you for the police to find tomorrow. If you fail, or I believe that you are deceiving me, I will shoot you. You have everything to gain if you do as I say, and everything to lose if you do not."

Harrison didn't have much choice. He could die now or worse, suffer the unimaginable pain of being shot, or do what he was told and possibly live. He pulled away from Zuqawri's hold and reluctantly swiped his identification card across the magnetic reader. He keyed in his password on the pad to the left of the door resulting in a metallic click and the buzz of an electric solenoid that emanated from somewhere inside the door casing. He opened the door and put down the doorstop.

Zuqawri shoved him inside the room. There were electronic screens and panels to one side, and the routers, phone and alarm lines on the other. Zuqawri followed the conduits to their perspective panel boxes. He chose the smaller of the electrical boxes and opened it.

"There, change the time to read nine a.m. and you can then open the safe." Zuqawri pointed with his free finger and tapped on the timer's glass cover.

"It's not that simple. This is a mechanical timer; you can't just move the numbers to where you want them to be. The timer has to run its course in a kind of fast forward mode. It will take about six minutes to complete each hour's rotation. It is five-fifty two p.m. now. The bank's safe controls go active at seven a.m., which means it will take a little more than an hour to make this work. About seventy minutes or so."

Zuqawri looked at the analog clock face on the timer and snarled, "I have already given you too much time. You have one hour. I suggest you get started."

Harrison stood fully upright and moved toward Zuqawri. "Look, you want your money? Then, you need me. I'll get in when the system lets me in. If you can't wait, then kill me now, but you will leave empty handed."

Zuqawri pushed the man away. "Do not push your luck, or I will give you the time and then I will kill you. Get started, now."

The two men stared at each other. Harrison was sweating, nervous, and breathing hard while Zuqawri seemed very relaxed. Harrison turned away from his captor's glare and toward the timer. He moved to a small console and placed his thumb on the scanner. The red glass flashed briefly then placed a matrix of green points connected by a series of green lines, superimposed over a scanned image of a Greg Harrison's thumbprint on a small LCD screen.

After a few seconds an electronic tone announced that the thumbprint had been recognized and the word "match" appeared over the picture on the LCD. A second later, the screen prompted him for a password. Greg Harrison typed in his code and selected the "SET CLOCK" prompt then selected "MOVE TIME AHEAD" from a drop down sub menu. Lastly he selected a reason for the time change by highlighting "RESTORE AFTER SERVICE OUTAGE". Upon completion of the final selection the timer began a loud clicking and the mechanical hands of the analog clock under the timer's glass began to click and tick in a fast forward motion. Harrison stood up and turned to face Zuqawri. "Now we wait." He was sweating and nervous and suddenly realized how much. He wiped his palms across his shirt, leaned back against a tall thin table and looking warily at his captor, crossed his arms to begin the wait.

The sound of the gearing inside the clock was incredibly loud. Harrison had never paid attention to it before, but that would be all that he would hear for the next seventy minutes.

CHAPTER 32

WITNESS RELOCATION

BEDALLA hurriedly located a small rolling suitcase and a black and white gym bag. She was nearly running as she made her way to the basement. There was still no light in the laundry room. The discovery of the explosives and the thermos had caused her to abandon her search for a new bulb. It had been five hours since then, but to Bedalla, it seemed forever ago.

She fumbled around getting what would be sufficient for "a few days" as Alan Ramsey put it. She thought it best to take more than he suggested and decidedly stacked Joshi's clothes-basket onto hers and headed back upstairs with both where she could actually see what she was doing. Bedalla thought once again about the explosives in Ahmed's workroom. She paused for a moment, suddenly having the urge to gather all of Ahmed's terrorist paraphernalia to give to the tactical team that was coming to get her.

She briskly moved over to the workroom and opened the first cabinet. She grabbed the elongated containers of the C-4 explosives and laid them in the basket with her clothes then opened the second cabinet and pulled down the box of detonator cord and blasting caps. She looked at the cell phones and wondered whether she should take them as well. The cell phones were evidence for sure, but Bedalla thought more about the explosives. She didn't want to see anyone else hurt or killed. She was less concerned about providing the evidence that the American government would use to prosecute her husband. Although, he deserved what punishment would come to him.

Ahmed had admitted his involvement when she had confronted him. He had asked her to gather his things, because he would be leaving, but instead she would pack her own things, as well as the explosives.

She wondered where he was. Why was he not home yet? Her mind was reeling with all the information she was trying to process as she reached across the shelf attempting to slide the phones off the shelf and into the basket. One of them hit the rolled plastic edge of the clothes basket and bounced away and down to the concrete floor. The damaged phone came to rest under the shelves, the case split apart exposing electronics and the modified battery pack that Ahmed had made to replace the three-cell battery with a more compact nine-volt battery, a detonator cap and approximately two ounces of C-4 explosive paste. The phone itself was a small explosive detonator that could be used to set off larger amounts of explosives remotely. Unaware of the phone's modification and assuming that it was broken, Bedalla did not bother to retrieve it.

She tossed the remaining phone into the basket with the explosives and ran upstairs. She stopped short nearly running into her son who was walking towards the bathroom.

"Joshi, you startled me. I wasn't expecting you to be there. I thought you would still be sleeping." She walked into her bedroom and began folding the clothes she was planning to pack when she realized that the explosives were in plain view. She quickly covered the C-4 and the other items with the bedclothes.

Joshi asked groggily, "How long have I been sleeping?" He rubbed his eyes and stretched. "Why am I dressed for school?"

Bedalla looked sympathetically at her son who seemed very confused. "Today was a very long day, little man. Do you not remember?"

Joshi looked upward as if reviewing an image in his mind, "Yes, I remember now. There was an explosion..." His words tapered off.

Bedalla knelt down to hug her son when there came a knock on the back door. She jumped up, raced through the kitchen and looked out the small window above her sink, straining to see who it was. When she didn't see a camera crew she knew it had to be the team sent by Mr. Ramsey. She threw the lock back and opened the door.

"Mrs. Zuqawri?" The agent asked. He flashed his credentials. "I am Agent Kojic, Alan Ramsey sent us to pick up you and your son. Are you ready? Is there something I can do to help?" Agent Kojic looked past Bedalla at Joshi.

Bedalla turned to face her son. "Come, Joshi. Help me get some things packed for you to wear. We are going on a trip for a couple days. Take this gym bag and fill it with your socks and underwear and any small toys that you would like to have with you while we are gone. But you must hurry, we have to leave right away."

"Where are we going?" Joshi asked as he grabbed the strap of the empty bag and threw it over his shoulder, the whole time looking at the agent.

"I will explain on the way, just do as I asked and hurry." Bedalla turned back to the agent standing in front of the kitchen door he had quietly closed behind him.

"Please come in. I was almost ready when my son woke up and started asking questions."

The agent raised his hand to his face and appeared to talk into his fist. "We'll be out in five minutes." An acknowledging "Roger" came through his headset as Bedalla hurried back to her bedroom.

Bedalla dumped the clothes from the basket into the wheeled travel bag. She looked at the explosives and began to have second thoughts about taking them. She held the blocks of C4 in her hands as if weighing them then laid the C4, the detonators and the phone on top of the clothes she had just packed. She would give the explosives and the supporting paraphernalia to the investigators eventually.

Joshi walked past her door lugging his bag of who knows what up the hallway. She saw that he was wearing his jacket and had put on his shoes. Between what he'd packed and what she'd thrown in her bag for him he should have plenty to wear, she thought.

She stopped at the bathroom and grabbed a few personal hygiene items and headed toward the kitchen. She looked toward the basement door and stopped, thinking about the remaining items in the basement.

Agent Kojic began to prompt Bedalla to move faster. "Mrs. Zuqawri, we really need to get moving. Is something wrong?" Bedalla thought about the evidence that she had and then about the lunchbox and thermos in the workroom. "There are some things you may need in the basement. There is evidence that will help you with this case. I already have some of it, but..."

Agent Kojic cut her off. "Where is it? I'll get it, but please, hurry to the black Chevy Yukon waiting in the alley." He opened the door and prompted her to move, handing her off to another agent who would take her to the SUV.

"Under the workbench you will find a lunch box and thermos. It is identical to the one that was used at the zoo to deliver the bomb." The agent stared briefly at her, then turned and ran down to the basement. He found the workroom and the bench easily. He could smell the explosives. C-4 had a significant odor and Kojic could always tell when it was around. He found the thermos and threw it into the lunchbox. He also noted a few scraps of C-4 paste and a wrapper from the block of explosives and threw them in there as well. If Bedalla Zuqawri was authorizing him to get the evidence then, he thought, he would grab what he could. He saw a few cans of paint thinner on the floor under the shelves, but didn't see the broken phone that Bedalla had dropped between the two containers. Kojic ran up the steps and out the door. He sprinted through the yard and out to the alley to the awaiting SUV. He noted that Bedalla and her son were both in the truck then got in the seat next to them and told the driver to go.

Joshi stared in disbelief at the object in the man's arms. He tugged at his mother's shirt. "Mom, that guy has my lunchbox." Bedalla knew that she eventually would have to tell Joshi the truth, or at least what appeared to be the truth. She decided that now was not a good time to do so. She looked at her son and smiling, gave him a kiss on the side of his forehead. "When we get to where we are going, we will have to have a long talk. Can you wait until then?"

"I guess so," Joshi said, as he stared at the man holding his lunchbox and tried to figure out what was going on.

CHAPTER 33

SECOND DISTRICT STATION

THE investigation into the St. Louis Zoo bombing was being conducted through the Operations Division at the Second District Station. The station was the headquarters for all districts in the Southwest part of the city. The facility was fairly new and the equipment was current. The Terrorist Tracking Teams set up shop in the FBI headquarters within the station.

Paul Jackson splayed out his maps of the zoo and the park on an oversized table in the center of the room. On one of the wall mounted plasma screens information about Ahmed Zuqawri, his wife and his son was falling into place. A live feed was streaming into a small viewer within the border of the monitor. The feed was set up at the entrances and exits of the hospital. The electronic guard would keep watch using facial recognition software and alert the anti-terrorist staff if a person matching Zuqawri's height, weight and features entered or left the building.

As Alan Ramsey looked over the information in front of him his phone buzzed in his pocket. "Ramsey, go ahead."

"Sir, this is Kojic. We've got Mrs. Zuqawri and her son. They're safe."

"Good. Bring them to Second District. Any sign of Zuqawri? Has she had any contact?"

Agent Kojic looked towards Bedalla repeating the question. She shook her head and mouthed the word no. "That would be a negative, Sir. There are news crews camped out in front of their house. I doubt he will show up there now."

Ramsey asked, "Were you stopped by any reporters?"

Kojic quickly replied. "No, Sir. We slipped in, got the Zuqawris and left undetected. I even had time to collect some evidence that will give a direct link between the delivery system and Zuqawri."

"Then don't be too surprised if Zuqawri manages to get past them as well. Apparently Ahmed Zuqawri has more than enough experience in subversion and espionage. We've got information that puts him on location in Mosul during the assassination of the Prime Minister's council."

"Roger that, Sir. Point taken. We should probably get some officers to pull surveillance on the house," Kojic noted.

Ramsey turned his attention to Paul Jackson and motioned. "You just get them here as soon as you can. I will get a couple agents out to the house. See you when you get here. Ramsey, out."

Joshi looked out the window and saw the bank that his family visited on occasion. He could have sworn he saw his father's car in the parking lot. He looked around the vehicle at the agents. Then he looked at his mother. She looked sad and scared. He wasn't sure what was going on, but he was pretty sure that his father was involved, and he was positive that it had something to do with the explosion at the zoo that nearly killed him.

He looked back over the seat twisting hard to look in the direction of the bank. He could no longer see the car. Maybe it wasn't his father's. "What is it? What is the matter?" Bedalla saw her son squirming. Joshi thought for a second and noted again how sad his mother looked. He wondered if she had seen the car and just not said anything.

"Nothing," he replied, "Just looking."

CHAPTER 34

THE VAULT

GREG HARRISON looked at Ahmed as the timer neared the final minute before it would allow the safe to be opened. He pressed the illuminated "Real time" button to stop the advancing of the mechanism then mentally counted down the last few seconds. Five, four, three, two...

An electric fan on the PC console hummed to life and the monitor went from a sleep mode to the start up window. The hard drive clicked away as the system came back on line. A single word flashed on the otherwise blank LED screen: INITIATING. The cursor flashed repeatedly for several seconds and the welcome screen took its place.

"There. The system is on line now." Greg Harrison wanted to get through this with his life intact.

The two men walked to the vault door. Harrison noted that the stainless steel covering the door reflected the image of Ahmed behind him holding a pistol within inches of his head. He suddenly had the urge to make a move to disarm the man behind him. He rolled the knob of the combination lock as he contemplated how he would achieve surprise and overpower Ahmed. His heart pounded in his chest from the anxiety. He spun the dial to the right and looked up again at the reflection in front of him. Ahmed was staring straight at Harrison through the reflection of the steel. His eyes were wide and attentive and easy to see due to his dark complexion. Harrison continued to move the dial counter-clockwise slowly, buying time, while he contemplated his options.

Ahmed shifted his weight to his left foot. Harrison saw him look to his left towards the dead guard on the floor. Now was his chance. He tensed for an attack that would spin him hard so that all of his two hundred and ten pound body mass would slam his elbow into Ahmed's right rib cage. As Ahmed lost his footing Harrison would get behind him and force him hard into the large steel bolt release mechanism and disarm him. Harrison's heart was beating furiously. He thought surely that his attacker could hear it. Sweat began to form over his brow. Ahmed still was not looking at him. "Do it! Do it!" he told himself. He braced his left hand on the cold surface of the vault door and clenched his right fist.

The sudden sound of a cell phone ring-tone punctured the silence. Ahmed pushed against Harrison forcing him forward against the door and pushed the pistol against his head. "Do not move," Ahmed nearly spat. He backed away from the banker and moved toward the sound, and stopping at the dead guard's body, kicked him over on his side. A second later the phone fell silent.

"I'm sure that was his wife. She's probably getting worried. He was supposed to be home over an hour ago."

Ahmed raised the pistol in Harrison's direction. "Your wife will be calling for you soon as well. Hurry, or you will not able to answer your phone when she does."

Harrison spun the dial back to the right realizing that he had lost his chance to prevent this man from succeeding to get what he wanted.

"You will still let me live once I open this door, right?"

Ahmed made a face that reflected dismay. "That is what I told you. Now, hurry."

Harrison stopped on the last number. He placed his thumb on the scan mechanism at the control pad. The LED lit indicating the match and the release mechanism for the vault door began to move. Finally the word "OPEN" appeared on the console.

Regrettably, Greg Harrison pulled the door open revealing the contents of the vault. Ahmed shoved him in and Harrison walked to the cage that housed the money. A secondary lock secured the cage. Harrison reached into his pocket under the careful scrutiny of Ahmed and removed the key. There was no sense resisting at this point. He unlocked the thick padlock and let it fall into his right hand. Inside the cage was another stainless steel cabinet that housed, for all practical purposes, an automatic teller. Greg Harrison flipped the final switch to activate the money machine.

"There. Take what you want."

Ahmed stepped over to the cabinet. Ahmed forced Harrison to stand where he could see him. Ahmed reached in his jacket pocket and removed his account information. He read from the documents and typed three hundred thirty-six thousand two hundred and forty on the numeric touch-pad.

Greg Harrison began to laugh. "After all this, all you are getting out is your own money?" He couldn't help but find it funny that Ahmed was only interested in what was his.

"I am not a thief, Mr. Harrison, I came only for what was rightfully mine. If you would have given it to me earlier, I would have left long ago and your friend would not be in the condition he is in." Ahmed waited for the machine to count out his money.

The machine clicked and whirred as it calculated and counted. Eventually the small door opened and the bills began to count out into the tray.

Ahmed stared at the bank manager and pondered his fate. Greg Harrison stood quietly, waiting for what was going to happen next. He didn't think he would get out of the bank alive. He probably wouldn't see his wife and daughter again. Nervously, Harrison broke the silence.

"Well, you got what you came for. Now, lock me in the vault and leave. That will give you about eight hours to get away from here. If you stick to your word, I will hold off as long as possible before I acknowledge that it was you."

Ahmed walked towards him with the gun raised.

Harrison backed away some, stumbling. "You gave me your word. You said you were a man of your word that you wouldn't kill me!"

"I know what it was that I told you, but if I let you live..."

Harrison cut him off. "They have you on video! They have all of your information! Killing me will not stop them from finding you! For Christ's sake, they can check the withdrawal history and figure out what happened. If you kill me, and they catch you that will only make things worse for you... and your family," Harrison added.

"I am afraid that I do not have a choice. Letting you live only complicates matters for me. I am sorry, Mr. Harrison. It has been a pleasure doing business with you." Ahmed aimed his pistol, holding it steady.

Harrison noted that the man's hand did not shake at all. He looked past the pistol and into Ahmed's eyes. Harrison suddenly felt the weight of the padlock that he still held in his right hand. Without thinking he swung the lock hard at Ahmed, planting it firmly against the side of Zuqawri's head with a resounding crack.

Ahmed fired the pistol, but missed his target, stumbling, then falling on the weapon. Harrison was already running from the vault towards the bank's exit.

Ahmed's ears were ringing and he was struggling to regain his balance. He jumped to his feet and, with an unsteady aim, fired again at Harrison, but missed, hitting a tall office chair. Harrison was weaving through the desks and around cubical walls. Ahmed shook his head side to side to clear it, then sprinted to the first desk and leaped on top. From his vantage point he could see Harrison closing on the front door.

Harrison was moving quickly. As he neared the door he reached for his keys only to realize that he had left them in the vault. Without thinking he threw the padlock at the door to break the glass. The lock hit the window hard and bounced back coming to rest near the dead guard. In exasperation, Harrison ducked down beside a low wall that was just inside the doors of the bank.

"It's no use, Mr. Harrison." Ahmed scanned the bank with his pistol raised. He would not take another chance with this man.

Greg Harrison listened for Ahmed's voice and noted that he could see the man's reflection in the tinted glass on the door in front of him. He was standing on one of the desks waiting for him to step into view. Harrison was in a darkened corner, not visible from Ahmed's vantage point on the desk. He looked at the lifeless body of Andrew Gibbs. He did not want to end up the same way. He decided to go for the dead guard's gun when he saw the door keys still in the man's left hand.

Ahmed was losing patience. He jumped down from the desk and began walking slowly through the cubicles, scanning either side for any signs of his fugitive bank manager. Harrison heard him contact the floor and glanced back at the door glass to confirm that his attacker was no longer standing on the desk. He reached out and grabbed the keys, wrapping his hand around them all before pulling them free from the hand of the corpse so Ahmed would not hear them jingle.

Ahmed was closing in on him. He didn't have any time left to think and surely had nothing to lose. He had to act now. Harrison leaned over the guard, grabbed his belt and pulled hard to roll the lifeless figure over on to his left side exposing the unfastened holster and the revolver. He yanked the pistol from the holster and pulled the lever back to cock it. The sound of a car pulling up outside caught his attention. He looked up, nearly blinded by the headlights of a minivan. It was his wife, Diane.

Zuqawri saw the vehicle pull to a stop just outside the door. Ahmed glanced over at the picture of Harrison's wife and daughters and realized who the woman was.

Diane Harrison began to open her car door, the whole time looking at the man who was crouching inside the darkened foyer. That was Greg, but why was he down on the floor? What was he doing she wondered as she slowly stepped from the car. The body of the bank guard became visible when the reflections of the light on the glass changed as she walked toward the doors.

Harrison was truly afraid now, afraid for his wife. His heart was racing, and he was breathing hard and sweating. He backed towards the door and banged on the glass with the butt of the pistol getting both his wife's and Zuqawri's attention. He motioned for his wife to get back in the car and yelled for her to leave.

Harrison's wife stopped and backed away when she saw her husband with the pistol. She could barely hear his voice through the doors, but could easily see the fear on his face and read what his lips were saying. She looked up, seeing another man appear suddenly from around the corner.

Her husband's face was illuminated suddenly from the muzzle flashes of the pistol he was holding. She jumped when she heard the two muffled shots and saw the flashes. She couldn't run, paralyzed by what she was witnessing. Suddenly the tempered glass of the door shattered. Bits of glass cascaded to the ground as bullets raced to their unseen destination, howling a high pitched zinging sound that she had only ever heard in movies and on television. Instantly, the sounds of the gunfight became extremely loud. Her husband scrambled through the shattered door, glass crunching and falling around him, firing another haphazard shot in Ahmed Zuqawri's direction.

"Go! Go! Go! Get in the car!" He screamed as a shot from inside the bank shattered the glass of the adjacent door and whizzed by his ear. Harrison fired two more shots as he ran around the passenger side of the van and opened the door. His wife, already behind the wheel, started the van and pulled the selector lever hard into reverse, and slammed the accelerator to the floor, sending the vehicle careening backwards.

The van's window would not lower fast enough. Harrison tried to shatter the glass with the pistol, but failed. He maneuvered his hand and the pistol through the still lowering glass and fired again into the bank as Zuqawri fired consecutive rounds through the van door and down the side of the van as it passed by.

Harrison heard the rounds as they struck the steel and plastic of the van and then felt the burn of a hot round as it imbedded into his side. He yelled for his wife to go. "I've been shot! Get to the hospital! Hurry! Hurry!" Greg Harrison winced in pain and grabbed his wife's cell phone from the cup holder in front of him. He flipped it open and dialed 9-1-1.

Zuqawri watched as the van disappeared out of the lot and around the corner. Ahmed turned back and ran into the vault to retrieve his money. He dumped the small trashcan near the door and pulled the white plastic bag from the can, stuffed the money into the bag and ran to his car. He would have to get rid of his Nissan. It would be on the bank's video. He was out of time. He had to go home and collect his wife and child and the explosives. Then, once he got to the warehouse, he could figure out what to do about the car and about Bedalla and Joshi. He hurriedly placed the car into reverse and drove out of the lot and down Oakland to Forest. As he sped down Forest he could look ahead to West Park and could see that there was a news van in front of his house. The van was parked under the only streetlight on his block, which happened to be directly in front of his house.

Zuqawri looked at his watch. It was nearly seven thirty and was beginning to get dark. He wondered why his wife had not called. She would be wondering what to do, he thought. He considered the fact that she may have been taken into custody. He drove past his street and could only see the one news van. Zuqawri thought it was odd, considering there were at least four news teams at the hospital. He pulled down the narrow alley that went the length of his block and parked near the corner on a slab of concrete that once supported the walls of a garage. This was one of the older neighborhoods that once made up the suburbs of St. Louis. Up and down the length of the alley were concrete pits that used to be used for the burning of leaves and garbage. Ahmed used the deteriorating structures to move closer to his house. The sound of footsteps caught his attention. He peered through the cracks in the concrete ash pit and spotted a man in a dark tee shirt and dark glasses. Ahmed studied the man for a moment and noted the near transparent earpiece and the wire leading to it in the man's right ear. The agent spoke into his hand that it was clear at the back and turned toward the opposite end of the alley.

Zuqawri waited for the man to round the corner and disappear behind his neighbor's privacy fence. He noted the illumination of a lighter and saw cigarette smoke drift around the corner of the fence. Carefully, he moved towards his garage, turned the handle of the bay door and slowly raised the door enough to slide under it and into the darkened structure. He lowered the door behind him, taking care to be quiet. Ducking low, he walked to the window of the garage and peered through the darkness of his yard. The only light he could see in his house was through the basement workshop window. Bedalla had to be gone and, along with her, his son. The authorities must have picked them up. He wondered about the explosives.

Silently, Ahmed opened the side entry door and, crouching low, moved up the sidewalk to his house. He rushed over to where the light streamed onto the grass surrounding the basement window and looked inside. He could see the empty, open cabinets. The explosives, the detonator phones, all of it was gone.

Ahmed moved away from the window and toward the garage. He was getting angry and frustrated with the day's events. He carefully lifted the garage door and peered through the opening at the bottom. It was clear. He lifted the door just enough to squeeze under and slipped into the darkness of the alley to his car.

He must call Leaja bin Masri. This was not good at all. Ahmed fumbled for his phone. He was trembling, trying to think how to tell Leaja that he had failed him, how he had failed Allah and the mission. He flipped the phone open and pressed the contacts button. The list of names and numbers came up. Ahmed scrolled through the first five entries, then stopped. He stared at the phone in his hand as the answer to his problem appeared in front of him. The words PHONE 6 and PHONE 7 looked back at him from the display.

Ahmed praised his God and without hesitating pulled up the entry "PHONE 6." He was about to press the call button when he was startled by a voice behind him.

"PUT YOUR HANDS WHERE I CAN SEE THEM, SIR, AND TURN AROUND!"

At first Ahmed was going to ignore the man behind him, but the FBI agent grabbed him and pulled him around. Ahmed spun to face the man's pistol. The agent, Curt Morgan, saw that Ahmed was not armed, but had something in his right hand. Zuqawri moved the phone a little back and forth for his captor to see.

"Place the phone on the roof of the car behind you and then place your hands behind your back."

Ahmed stood staring at the man. He was sweating. He could tell that this man before him had never been in such a situation with a real person. Training sometimes just did not do justice for

241

real life scenarios. Ahmed stared at the man then pressed the "call" button on the phone as he placed it down on the roof of his car.

The cell signal found the nearest tower. That tower relayed the signal to a satellite that ironically sent the signal back to the same tower. For a split second the electronic chime of the ring-tone of the cell phone that Bedalla had left on the basement floor pronounced itself, but was suddenly silenced as the detonator and two ounces of C4 exploded. The ensuing blast detonated both of the one gallon steel containers of paint thinner and several aerosol paint cans that were on the shelves above the thinner. The expansion of the explosion blew the wall between the laundry room and workroom sideways blowing the gas dryer away from the wall and against the washer. Once disconnected the natural gas spewed into the basement creating a third reactive explosion that leveled the kitchen and bathroom above creating additional fuel as the stove and gas line separated from the wall.

The agent turned briefly towards Zuqawri's house and the sound of the explosion. Zuqawri was surprised by the explosion of his home, expecting instead that the explosives were with Bedalla, wherever she was. For a brief moment he saw the huge fireball as it lifted a section of the roof from the structure and lit up the neighborhood.

Ahmed turned, catching the agent off guard, and grabbed his weapon. He kicked the man's leg sideways at the knee, breaking it, causing the agent to collapse in agony, but before Morgan hit the ground Ahmed trained the agent's own weapon on him and placed one round in his left temple.

Zuqawri recovered his phone and ran around the car. He jumped in and sped away down the alley. He could hear the sirens as he ran the stoplight at the first intersection and slammed the accelerator to the floor.

CHAPTER 35

SUDDEN REALIZATIONS

ABOUT ten miles away Alan Ramsey had just poured a fresh cup of coffee when the first sounds of chaos came over the radio.

"Dispatch, this is Peterson. There has just been a major explosion at the Zuqawri house. Fire crews are en route. We have one agent KIA from a gunshot wound. It's Morgan. He's gone."

The sudden silence after the call was amazing. The dispatcher answered. "Roger, one man down, emergency crews en route, ambulance en route."

Ramsey stepped over to the dispatcher's desk. "Ask him for a report," Ramsey barked. The dispatcher relayed Ramsey's request as Paul Jackson stared at the radio as if waiting for an image to appear.

"Not clear what happened. Morgan must have confronted someone in the alley behind Zuqawri's garage. My guess is he was here."

"Who was there?" Ramsey asked.

"Well, I don't know, but the garage door is lifted some and the entry door was left open. I figure Zuqawri must have come back and made it back into the house to set some explosives. Morgan must have confronted him on his way out."

"How the hell did he get in the house?" Ramsey asked looking at Paul who was thinking the same thing. "You had the front and back entrances covered, right?"

Before Peterson could answer one of the communications specialists called to Paul Jackson, "Hey, Sir, I think I might have a trace on one of the cell phones that we were tracking for you. The call was made at about the same time the explosion occurred." Jackson walked over to the young man and stood next to his tall, thin frame as he manipulated the data in front of him. He placed his hands on a multi-touch table and several images appeared. "This is the signal location of the caller." He made some gestures on the glass tabletop and the graphic representation of the cell signal target suddenly changed into a satellite image showing the streets of Zuqawri's neighborhood.

Paul Jackson watched in amazement as the communications specialist moved his hands around causing the satellite image to zoom within a thousand feet of the road surface. "That's the alley behind Zuqawri's house. That's where the call was made." He pointed to a spot on the glass.

Jackson looked hard at the table. "Where's Zuqawri then? How come we see the signal origin, but not the person who made it?" Jackson was amazed at the level of technology in front of him.

Jay smiled, but explained, "It's not live feed, sir." These are just Google maps that are tied into a search database. It works together to give us a visual image of the signal location. Like triangulating on a regular map. Just reference is all it is."

Jackson suddenly felt a little foolish for the question. "Ok, ok, I get that. How about the phone that he called, can you trace that signal as well?"

"That's the interesting part. The same tower relayed the call back from the satellite. That meant the call was in the same location within about twenty miles. From here it looks like the exact same point." The specialist referred back to the signal and the map showing the target area from a thousand feet up. "Now look what happens when we get a close up." Paul Jackson looked at the kid in front of him incredulously. "That ain't a close-up already?"

Again the techie smiled and placed his hands on the glass causing the image to get even more detailed. As the area on the ground got closer the signal graphic split and became two separate locations. Eventually Paul could make out the roof of Zuqawri's house.

"Wait a minute. You telling me he called his house phone?" Paul was following but it didn't make sense.

"Sir, he didn't call his house phone, he called another cell phone that was in the house. The call only lasted long enough to connect.

"Shit!" Paul Jackson turned to face Ramsey. "Alan, he blew up the house. He called it in. It was an RCD." Ramsey recognized the term. Remote Cellular Detonator, basically a cell phone initiated detonating device that could be called from anywhere. "He must have had the house rigged to explode," Jackson said out loud. It was very fortunate that none of the agents were inside.

Ramsey thought for a second. "Wait a minute. Why would he come back to the house to blow it up, if he had a cell phone initiator? That doesn't make any sense." He walked over to the table. "Look, the man stood right here and set off the explosion, and I will bet you he knew the house was being watched otherwise he would have walked in the front door."

"Maybe he couldn't get in so he blew it up to get rid of the evidence." Jackson offered.

Ramsey suddenly had a strange look on his face. "His wife told me that Zuqawri knew that she had stumbled onto the explosives in the house. She said there were phones and explosives in a cabinet. Maybe he was trying to kill her by blowing up the house."

Jackson looked confused. "He had to know she wasn't there. He probably saw the agents and figured his wife and kid were both gone. Still doesn't make sense."

"Unless, he realized that she took it all with her. Maybe he was trying to set off the explosives that she took with her."

Ramsey thought about the possibility of Zuqawri setting off explosives in the agent's vehicle that was heading toward Second District station.

"Shit!"

Ramsey ran to the communications desk. "Get Kojic on the line and tell them there may be explosives in the truck that could be remotely detonated! Tell him do not come to the station and to get out of the truck. Try to pull over somewhere away from people, but tell him to do it quickly!"

The young man was already calling.

"This is Kojic, go ahead."

The police SUV was about two blocks from the station. McCarthy was moving a little too fast down the tree lined road for Bedalla's liking. He didn't have any lights on and there was no siren, yet the man driving acted as if people should know to get out of his way. She was going to say something to Kojic when she saw the agent reach for his headset, then turn, look at her, and then yell at the driver.

"PULL OVER! GET OFF THE STREET NOW!"

McCarthy looked in the rearview mirror at Kojic. "What are you..."

Kojic cut him off pointing ahead at a park and yelling, "THERE, GO OVER THERE! DRIVE INTO THE PARK AWAY FROM PEOPLE AS BEST YOU CAN! DOWN TO THE BALL FIELDS!"

McCarthy didn't know what was going on, but knew it couldn't be good. The Suburban slammed over the granite curb and bounced across the sidewalk. McCarthy accelerated and steered around large oak trees to the open ball field.

Back at Second District Station everyone turned toward the Coms Specialist as a high pitch tone blasted out of his speakers, Jay jumped up from his seat. "There! Look! I've got it again!" The techie yelled excitedly, pointing at the imaging table. "He's placing a call right now!"

"STOP! STOP! Everybody get out and get away from the truck as far as possible!" McCarthy slammed the brakes on hard, engaging the antilock brakes. Joshi had just unfastened his seat belt and he slammed forward against the seat in front and fell to the floor of the truck.

Kojic had his door open before the vehicle could stop and was running around the back of the truck to the side where Joshi Zuqawri sat when the earth suddenly shuddered under his feet and the eruption of the massive explosion blew the armored rear hatch from the vehicle, sending it and Kojic over a hundred feet across the field where he tumbled to a stop intact, but broken under the heavy door.

The pain was incredible, but the agent knew that if he was in pain he was still alive as he struggled to move from under the weight of the back hatch. He was able to maneuver himself enough to see that the vehicle had been totally destroyed. The eight thousand pound heavily fortified Suburban was designed to prevent small arms and some rocket propelled grenade attacks from outside the vehicle, not an explosion from within the truck. What was left of the body of the truck was strewn thirty feet in all directions from where it stopped. All the doors and outer sheet metal were gone leaving a skeleton of steel and plastic burning in its place.

Kojic scanned the field and burning wreckage for any sign of the passengers or the driver and found none. He was sure they could not have made it out of the truck before the explosion. He heard voices and could see several people running to the scene to see what was going on. Kojic was bleeding badly from a large gash on his forehead and feeling disoriented. He attempted to move the door one last time only to be met with the most severe pain he had ever felt in his life. He looked as best he could through the blood running down his face and could see that although his legs were there, one of them was bent at an angle that was normally not possible.

A siren could be heard in the distance as the pain and the effects of the explosion took effect and he began to lose consciousness. The last thing Kojic felt aside from the tremendous throbbing pain was the touch of a hand on his shoulder and the sound of somebody's voice telling him that he would be ok and not to move. He wanted to respond with a smart-ass answer about his options at the moment, but found that he didn't have the energy. The pain seemed to diminish suddenly as he closed his eyes for a moment to rest.

Ramsey was moving to the multi-touch display table when the "HARUMPH" sound and the thud of an explosion could be heard and felt. Windows and coffee cups rattled throughout the building. Some of the technicians and officers in the room looked at each other with dismay, some asking, "What was that?" But Ramsey and Paul Jackson both knew the sound of large amounts of explosives detonating.

"Signal's gone," Jay said in disgust as the signal dropped from the imaging table. Ramsey looked at the audio tech who appeared to understand what just happened. "I just lost communications with Kojic."

"Shit! Shit! Shit!" Ramsey cursed as he ran out the door with Jackson and some others behind him. He ran through the doors to find a few officers running to their cars and the fire department across the street mobilizing their vehicles out of the building onto the street. The wail of the siren kicked in loudly as the traffic stopped to let the emergency vehicles out of the lot and onto the main thoroughfare.

He spotted the first plume of smoke wisp above some trees in the distance and followed that back to a large pall of thick black smoke that appeared to be only a few blocks away. "What's over there?" Ramsey, pointing, asked one of the men from the area.

"Not much really. A park and some athletic fields," he replied.

Ahmed Zuqawri also heard the sound of the explosion as he sat in his car staring at the phone in his hand. The detonation had sounded close. But then, it was amazing how far away a bomb could go off and still be felt. "Hopefully that will end it," he thought. Though, he wouldn't know for sure until the news reports that were sure to be aired within the next few minutes.

He thought about calling Bin-Masri to let him know all that had happened, but decided it unwise to use his phone again. He had to ditch his car as well. By now it would be a major target for the police.

Zuqawri assumed that Bedalla and Joshi were probably being held at the local police station. If that were the case, that meant that the Second District Station would be involved with the aftermath of an intense explosion.

Now was the time to run, while the police were busy with their own mess. He grabbed the few things that he needed and stuffed everything into the bag with the money. Anything else left in the car would be destroyed.

Ahmed opened the door and stood, placing his belongings on the roof of the car. He opened the glove box and fumbled around for a moment and extracted a thin wire from the contents. Next he reached under the seat and pulled out what appeared to be the male end of a seat belt and snapped it in place on the seatbelt receiver near the middle of the car seat. He untangled the electrical leads that were attached to the pressure initiated remote detonator mounted on the seatbelt bracket and stuffed them between the seats, then ducked down low and plugged the two wire connectors together arming the explosives that were packed under the front and rear seats of his Nissan Maxima. Finally, he unwound the trigger wire attaching it to the detonator and, after setting the door locks to the locked position and partially closing the door; he attached the trigger wire to the pre-positioned screw just inside the doorjamb on the door. Then, he closed the door.

Grabbing his stuff from the roof of the car he looked at his watch. There should be a bus coming by soon, he thought. He could take it all the way downtown and from there walk to the warehouse. He walked across the street to the bus stop dropping his cell phone and his keys in the nearest trash can along the way and sat to wait for the next bus. He was tired. It had been a long day. He was sure the night would not bring him any rest.

Ramsey and Jackson walked back into the op center looking beat. Ramsey looked around the room knowing that these people had probably just lost two of their own. That was never easy. Darin Martin, the agent that had driven them, walked up to Ramsey. Paul stepped in closer to hear what the man had to say.

"First reports from the scene aren't good. It was our vehicle that exploded. You tried hard guys. I would have never put that together like that, and it's possible they would have driven right up to this building and more people would be hurt or dead." Ramsey didn't feel like a hero knowing what had just happened.

Martin continued, "The good news is that Kojic survived. He's pretty beat up with a compound fracture and probably a major concussion. Evidently he got out and ran to help the Zuqawris but didn't get past the back of the truck when it exploded. There were people close by that called 911. He's on his way to St. Mary's."

Paul Jackson asked for more. "What about the others? Anybody else make it? How about the kid?"

Martin responded with a sorrowful look on his face. "Nobody else survived. McCarthy and the Zuqawris died in the explosion according to the info we just got."

Jackson was pissed and it showed. He wanted to punch a wall or a desk, but everything around him was electronic equipment and very expensive at that. He turned and walked toward Jay who saw the look on the man's face and put himself between his multi-touch imaging table and the angry man. Jackson stopped short of Jay and looked at him strangely. "What?"

Jay didn't say anything; he just stood fast, thinking about protecting his equipment.

"Look, thin man, I ain't gonna break your table. Not unless you don't sit your ass down there and get me the location of that phone so we can go kick some terrorist ass." When Jay didn't move Paul stepped a little closer. "I need to be messin' something up pretty soon, so I suggest you hurry." With that Jay hurriedly sat down and started moving his hands around the screen manipulating all the information he could get his hands on.

Paul Jackson walked around behind Jay and stood with his arms crossed, leaning on the console behind him. He looked up and around the room. Everybody including Ramsey and Agent Martin were staring at him. Jackson unfolded his arms and stood up straight. "What, am I the only guy in here that wants to find this guy?" He turned his body from side to side as he looked around the room.

"Does anybody in here think that this Zuqawri guy *is not* responsible for the zoo field trip bombing?" He paused, waiting for someone to speak. "This man tried to blow up his son and did kill a whole lot of students, parents and teachers, and now not only did he finish the job on his son, but he took out his wife, Agent McCarthy and just about killed Agent Kojic. Let's go people, get on track and find this guy before he does something else."

"Looks like there's one more." Tony Rebello, the Second District Captain stepped into the room from his office. "Earlier tonight there was a robbery at the Southwest Bank. First District took the call. They report that the bank manager was held at gunpoint. The bank guard was shot and killed and the manager was shot, but ended up getting away after shooting it out using the dead guard's gun. There's a lot more to the story, but it was definitely Ahmed Zuqawri. The bank manager, Greg Harrison, identified Zuqawri. The guy robbed the bank, but only took his own money. He used his account information and is all over the monitors and video. They even got the shoot-out in the parking lot and afterward Zuqawri getting into his car. The plates match. There's no question it's our guy."

Paul Jackson motioned with his hands and his body an I-told-you-so look, then crossed his arms and leaned back on the console. He listened as the sound of police work picked up pace. He looked over at Ramsey who was giving him a look of amused approval, yet shaking his head.

Paul Jackson mouthed the word "What?" and unfolded his arms and turned his hands upward like he had done nothing.

Ramsey had known that his pick for a partner would work out well and tonight proved that Paul Jackson was off to a great start.

CHAPTER 36

THE WAREHOUSE

THE noise of the diesel powered forklift drowned out the sound of the television, but Leaja bin Masri didn't need words to see what was going on.

He turned his attention to the driver of the forklift who was moving a section of the concrete "clean" room that would be constructed and used for the final assembly of the bomb.

"What is taking you so long? This room should have been done yesterday. Mctelov is proceeding ahead of schedule and needs this room completed to finish the device. Now hurry!"

The driver spun the forklift around and headed swiftly to the far end of the warehouse building. As the vehicle pulled out of the way, ahead of Bin-Masri, he could see the silhouette of Dr. Metelov on the plastic sheeting of the makeshift disassembly and inspection room. He was busy interpreting the electronic signature of the device. Due to the lack of soviet era quality controls and many different assembly plants, each warhead was slightly different.

Leaja walked to the enclosure, pushed aside the plastic curtain and was met with the cool air that kept the room a constant temperature and maintained a positive pressure to keep contaminates away from the sensitive equipment inside the tent.

"Good afternoon, Doctor. I trust that you have found everything in line with your requirements."

Dr. Metelov looked up at bin Masri as the entrance curtain fell back into place. "Yes, everything is fine. Is there anything else or did you come here to make small talk and distract me from my task for absolutely no good reason?" He looked back at the oscilloscope and checked off the readings on his laptop.

Leaja found that the small, balding man grated on his nerves. "I only come for a progress report. I, like you, would like to see you complete this ahead of schedule so that your little vacation will be over and you can be reunited with your family. And, I might add, much, much richer."

The physicist raised his head above the device. "Yes, that would be nice, if I actually thought that you were not going to kill me when I have given you what you desire."

He made one more electrical measurement, noting the color and location of a short wire harness connector that was buried under a small removable panel. "Kiev," he said suddenly.

Leaja moved closer, interested to see what the physicist was looking at so intently.

The doctor tugged on the connector to examine the colors of the wire, moved slightly to the side to let his captor see, then let the plastic connecter fall back into its position in the jumble of wires and small tubes.

"This one was produced in the factory at Kiev." Dr. Metelov turned to his laptop and began poking at the keys. "Now the assembly process can begin. I will review the schematics and will be ready to assemble the device in a few hours, maybe sooner."

"And when will it be ready to transport?" bin Masri asked.

Metelov looked at his watch. "Be prepared to release my family and pay me what you owe me by tomorrow morning, early." He looked one more time at the wiring, then the schematics before continuing, "Maybe even tonight, if that is what you really intend to do."

Leaja bin Masri turned to leave. This was good news, he thought. Yes, he would release the man back to his family and pay him as he had told him he would. The doctor's diligence had proved very helpful. However, if the bomb was a failure, bin Masri would have the physicist and his family hunted down and killed.

CHAPTER 37

GOOD SAMARITAN

THE bus driver looked in the rearview mirror as he slowed for the next stop. The woman at the very back of the bus did not look at all happy. When she'd gotten on the bus the good looking redhead had smiled pleasantly enough, but now, she looked, well, angry.

Cheryl Blake looked up and saw the driver looking at her. She gave the driver a look of disapproval and the man quickly averted his eyes.

"This is ridiculous," she thought, "Why anyone would want to take a bus everyday is beyond me." The only reason she was on it herself was because her Toyota Four-Runner would not start and had left her stranded. Well, at least she was wearing casual clothes. Because of her day's busy schedule, she had decided to wear her running shoes and jeans rather than a dress and heels, which was the norm.

The doors hissed open as the bus stopped. A dark featured man stepped onto the bus. The woman watched as the new rider trudged to his seat. She thought, "Can this guy walk any slower?" She was aggravated and it showed as she rolled her eyes in disgust. The man looked familiar. She stared at him trying to remember where she had met him or had seen him before as he found a seat and slid in next to the window. As the bus moved forward Cheryl couldn't shake the feeling that she recognized him from somewhere. She was good with faces and normally didn't forget a name.

The bus rounded the next corner and slowed for some emergency vehicle. That was it! The man who sat just ahead of her looked like the one who was all over the news. Yes, she was sure he was the doctor that the police were looking for. She checked herself to be sure she wasn't profiling. No, she was sure she was right. He was definitely the man in the clip that had been playing over and over throughout the day.

She pulled her cell phone from her pocket and checked it for service. She moved to the front of the bus and asked the driver about the next stop. She knew that the next stop was not hers, but wanted to get far enough away so that the man she knew was the terrorist from the news didn't hear her talking.

She pressed 911 on her phone and waited. "My name is Cheryl Blake. I am an Army Reserve Engineer Major and am on a bus heading downtown. I believe the man you are looking for is on this bus." She spoke quietly and hoped the operator could hear her well enough.

The driver overheard what the woman was saying and glanced in the mirror to look back at the rest of the passengers. The Middle Eastern man stuck out like a sore thumb. She was right, that was the man from the news.

The emergency operator asked for the bus GPS identification and Major Blake relayed the question to the driver. The driver turned on the emergency beacon and also gave her the answer to relay back, Bi-State 702.

"The driver has turned some kind of GPS signal on so you can find his vehicle. I will keep my cell on and you can track it. If he gets off the bus, I will get off, too and try to follow him if it's not too obvious." Cheryl Blake was not afraid. She was ready to help if needed.

The operator disagreed. "Ma'am, please just stay on the bus where it is safe. Let the police deal with the situation. They should be there any second."

Zuqawri noted that the bus driver had looked at him several times. The woman with the red hair had also made eye contact with him. He was sure that they recognized him. The fact that she was on her phone now could be trouble. He needed to get off the bus.

The driver stopped at the next bus stop and opened the doors. As the new passengers stepped up into the bus Zuqawri shot toward the rear door. The doors closed leaving Zuqawri on the curb. As the bus pulled away the driver looked again into his mirror and didn't see the Middle Eastern man. "He's gone. He just got off the bus." Blake stood up and looked to the rear of the bus, then turned to look in the right rear view mirror. She could see the distorted image of Zuqawri walking away from the stop at the edge of the convex mirror. "Shit!" she muttered. "Stop up here." She pointed at the next corner. "Let me out." She spoke into her phone as the bus slowed to a stop. "He just got off the bus at Market Street and Grand. I'm going to follow him."

The Major, although not on duty today, still had a pistol she carried for protection. It was in her sling-bag along with her laptop. She spun the bag down and fumbled for a second, then pulled out the nine-millimeter and one full magazine. She locked and loaded the weapon and replaced the pack on her back. She was not going to lose this guy, but she didn't intend to die playing the part of the hero either. She looked up the street, but didn't see him. She knew he hadn't crossed the street, so she figured he must have moved over one street or turned down an alley.

She ran south on Jefferson Street, away from Market Street and looked for any sign of the terrorist. As she got to the next intersection, she saw him. He was walking quickly in her direction, but on the opposite side of the street. Cheryl hid in the shadows of the building and waited for the man to pass before falling in behind him about a half of a block back so as not to be easily seen. She walked swiftly holding her pistol at the side of her hip hoping nobody would see her and freak out.

The emergency dispatcher was still tracking the phone that Cheryl had purposely left on. The call was being streamed to the First District station downtown and from there to all the surrounding stations. The dispatcher at Second District monitoring the system heard what was going on. He pressed the record button on the console and ran across the room to where Ramsey was standing.

"Sir, we just got a report that Zuqawri was on a bus heading downtown." The dispatcher motioned to the touch-screen and pointed out that the network was streaming live audio, but that there was nothing going on at the moment. All the same, he was recording it.

They stopped at the touch-screen table, and Ramsey looked at the situation board and saw the red dot flashing. "That the last spot the bus was located?" Ramsey asked.

"Uh...actually, that is the cell phone we are tracking. The police should be there any minute. They were just getting ready to fall in behind the bus when the subject got off."

"I can't believe that Zuqawri would have such an obvious cell trace signal. I figured him to be smarter than that," Ramsey noted.

Jay looked up from setting an electronic marker on the tracking table. He had been watching the scenario unfold from the start and interjected, "That's not Zuqawri's phone that they're tracking. It belongs to an Army Reserve Major. This woman recognized our subject and called in. She left the phone on for the GPS marker.

That was pretty smart. She's been following him since he got off the bus."

The dispatcher spoke up. "The emergency dispatcher told her to leave it to the police, but had she followed their directions, we wouldn't have a track on Zuqawri right now."

Ramsey thought for a moment, "Tell the units to stay way back. We don't want to spook him. They can rush in once he stops moving. Maybe he will lead us to bin Masri or the bomb."

"That may be sooner than later," Jay joined the conversation again. "She stopped moving. That either means she lost him or he got to where he was going."

Zuqawri ducked in between two buildings and waited for the woman. He wondered who she was and whether or not she was a member of the police department, FBI or CIA.

Cheryl Blake looked around for the man she was following, but couldn't see him. He may have gone into one of the buildings, but she couldn't be sure. She could feel her heart beating now and her adrenalin was causing her to feel on edge. She walked forward cautiously and wondered where the police were. They should have been here by now.

Ahmed leaned close to the brick wall of the restaurant and reached for his pistol. After releasing the safety, he pulled the magazine and noted there were only three rounds remaining. He needed ammunition. Just as he snapped the magazine back into place the woman walked into view at the edge of the building.

The Major heard the click of Zuqawri's magazine and turned to face him as he raised his pistol to fire. She instinctively dove behind the trash dumpster as the first projectile pinged against the steel of the container and ricocheted. She dropped her phone and could hear the emergency dispatcher faintly, asking if everything was all right. Her heart was racing and she realized she was holding the pistol grip too tightly. Though she'd had both military and civilian classes on the handling of weapons, she had never been shot at before. Blake looked down and saw that the dumpster had wheels which raised it about six inches off the asphalt. She threw herself down flat on the ground.

Suddenly Zuqawri's right ankle exploded in pain as the round from Major Blake's pistol found its target. Ahmed fell to the ground on his right side with his pistol extended and fired off another round when his pistol hand hit the ground. The round smashed into the pavement and a parked car.

Zuqawri tried to get to his feet, but found he couldn't stand. He was fighting just to get onto his knees when he heard the woman's voice from the other side of the dumpster.

"Look asshole, you just need to give up, or I can kill you if that's what you want." She continued to speak, yelling at him, "You hear me? I might just shoot you for the hell of it. You know you deserve it. I can't believe you tried to kill your own kid." Cheryl Blake was quietly climbing on top of the dumpster. Zuqawri pulled himself over and leaned against the dumpster.

For some reason he felt the urge to answer her. "He would have been a martyr for causing the deaths of your infidel brothers and sisters. Allah will bless him regardless, just for carrying the bomb."

"You are so damned stupid. You think you can impose your religion on everybody else. Think you can kill innocent Americans? You are in the wrong country for that and your Allah isn't here to save your stupid ass." Ahmed knew the voice was coming from above him now. He was trapped. He should take his own life with the last round, but this woman made him so angry and he wanted to kill her now more than anything else. Pulling his bleeding, shattered ankle up against himself and mustering all his strength, he stood up quickly, bringing his pistol up above the dumpster lid in an attempt to kill the infidel.

Cheryl Blake saw the pistol and instinctively grabbed it with her left hand and pulled hard toward the front of the dumpster, yanking Zuqawri's face against the steel lifting lug. Zuqawri fired his last round, striking only the wall of the adjacent building, then fell to the ground unable to stand the pain any longer.

Cheryl looked back to see the police cruiser pulling up. She jumped down from the dumpster, set both weapons on top of the receptacle then placed her hands up for the police to see that she was not armed. Still the first officer that approached her told her to kneel, putting her in close proximity to Zuqawri. She looked intently at him as the police called for an ambulance.

"Ma'am, which of these weapons is yours?" asked the officer standing behind her. He reached down and picked up her phone and closed it.

"Mine is that one," Cheryl said as she pointed awkwardly with her hands over her head. "The one with the braided leather strap."

"Ma'am we are going to have to take you in to get your account of the incident," the officer told her as she got to her feet.

She looked hard at the man still lying on the ground wincing in pain as the officer held pressure on the wound. "You are such an asshole. I hope it hurts, bitch!"

CHAPTER 38

REASSURANCE

THIS was agonizing, Alan thought as he listened to his boss trying to reason with him about his responsibilities. "Look, Alan, I know you don't like the attention, but you represent the highest investigative level. Yes, you will need to answer questions, but most importantly you need to be the one who reads the prepared statement." Gabe Anderson stopped for a second. This gave Ramsey his opening to interject.

"Gabe, we haven't finished with the interrogations. We don't have all the information we were hoping for yet. The guy is still in surgery at the hospital."

Gabe started in again, "Look, all you are going to be telling people is that we have, in custody, the man responsible for the recent local attacks. He admitted that, didn't he?"

Ramsey began to explain that he had admitted it, but that the confession had been made to the woman who'd shot him, recorded by the emergency dispatch office and not made in such a way that it could be considered a true confession. It was yet to be proven beyond a reasonable doubt and should not be disclosed to the public given the fact that the investigation was only just beginning.

"Have you even read the prepared statement?" Gabe asked. "I don't think there is anything in there that will risk the investigation. Just put yourself in front of the camera and read it to the people. It's only a little reassurance to let them know that we are on the job."

"Roger," Ramsey said in quick acknowledgement that he would do as he was told, then he was quiet.

"Thank you, Alan, I know you'll do fine." He heard the phone disconnect.

"Well?" This time it was Paul Jackson.

"Well, it looks like I need to freshen up a bit seeing as I have to speak to America," Alan said as he walked towards the restroom.

"What time is the news conference? I think I'm good, but I just like to know our schedule," Paul said nonchalantly.

Ramsey stopped walking and turned to look at Paul, who was pruning himself in the mirror near the front door of the station. "Our schedule?" he asked.

Paul looked at Ramsey behind him in the reflection. "Oh, you're going to be the one talking. I'm just going to be behind you looking all badass for the camera. It comes with the new job."

Alan smiled and shook his head as he continued toward the rest room. "I guess I missed that in the contract," he said as he walked away.

Leaja bin Masri stopped short on his way to see Dr. Metelov for an update. He had been told that the assembly had progressed well over the last few hours and was hoping to see for himself the final phase of the assembly, but the television caught his attention.

Again the photo of Ahmed Zuqawri flashed on the screen. This time, the words "Breaking News" was superimposed over the photo. The words "Terrorist Suspect Caught!" rolled across the banner at the bottom of the screen.

He could not believe what he was seeing on the news. Zuqawri caught by local authorities? This was not good news. He quickly found the remote and yelled to the operator of the forklift to stop the vehicle as he turned the volume up so he could hear. The operator of the fork-truck dismounted and walked to where bin Masri was standing.

"In what police are describing as the ultimate help from a local citizen, we have just learned that the suspect, whom police and federal agents have been seeking, was captured in a bizarre exchange of gunfire with a local off duty Army Reserve Soldier." The image behind the reporter changed to a photo of a woman in a military dress uniform. "Major Cheryl Blake, an Army Reserve Engineer Officer, recognized this man." The graphics changed to show the picture of Ahmed Zuqawri taken from his hospital badge. The reporter continued to tell the story of what had happened a little more than two hours earlier. Cut scenes of the alley, police tape and officers at the St. Louis City Hospital Emergency Room appeared in the background showing Zuqawri being wheeled in under police escort as the story unfolded for the public to see. An attractive redhead was shown talking to police investigators as she was walked into the precinct.

Leaja bin Masri was outraged. "How could this happen? He wondered. "Imbeciles!" The thought of Zuqawri being caught by this woman was sickening. He had taken so many precautions. He had sacrificed everything.

Leaja could not allow Ahmed to remain in custody. One way or another he would eventually talk. Somehow he would have to be silenced.

The anchor brought the story back to the desk and then announced that the police were getting ready make a statement. The scene moved to the Second District's Special Investigative Unit Headquarters, where a podium had been set up in front of the entrance. The Chief of Police made a statement about the zoo attack and the explosions that had occurred over the last couple of hours, and then turned the podium over to the lead investigator, introducing him as Alan Ramsey.

Alan stepped up and settled in behind the podium and a slew of news microphones. He laid his notes down and looked into the camera. "At approximately six forty this evening a suspect in the case of the bombing at the St. Louis Zoo was apprehended after being identified by one of our local citizens. This man, known as Ahmed Zuqawri, an Iraqi National on a work visa to the United States, is also being held for questioning as a suspect in the arson and explosion of his home in the 18000 block of West Park and for the death of his wife and son as well as the deaths of two Special Investigation Officers and one local Police Detective. Another incident, which took place at a local bank is also under investigation and appears to be strongly linked to Mr. Zuqawri."

Alan continued to give some of the details of the investigation that led to the capture of Zuqawri. His voice faded as Leaja bin Masri stared in amazement at the television. Everything around him blurred as memories came rushing back. Suddenly he was transported back in time, to the al-Ban apartment complex near Baghdad.

Leaja relived the moment of the first hail of gunfire, the door exploding as his men emptied their magazines into the hallway.

His adrenalin began to build, and he could feel his blood pulsing through his body. He remembered looking for his wife and finding her in the doorway, his son at her leg screaming. Suddenly, a blinding flash, an explosion, the sound of automatic weapons, and they were gone.

Leaja had been startled by the sudden appearance of the face of Captain Alan Ramsey in front of him that day. The sound of the AK-47 rounds bursting from the muzzle and the flashes of the gunfire came back to him, and he could feel the machine in his arms as the clack of the bolt mechanism ejected the shell casings in a dramatic slow motion fountain of brass. He could hear each casing as it pinged against the wall next to him and then the agonizing sounds of the man in front of him as the bullets tore through his flesh nearly killing him.

He stumbled backward against the table behind him and watched as the images in his mind melded with reality. Turning toward the light streaming through a broken window of the warehouse, his memories reacted to this new stimulus, adding the light and the broken glass to the replay of images in his mind.

He was sweating. His heart was pounding in his chest as he reached into his pocket for the nametag he'd carried with him since that day. He held it in front of him and stared at the name, then back at the image on the television in front of him.

Allah was delivering his salvation to him by giving him the means to end his nightmares. He had vowed revenge on Ramsey, and now he would have it. Here was his reward for his dedication to the Jihad. He had maintained his faith through it all. Finally, he could destroy the man who had taken everything from him.

Still, the mission had to take precedence. To do that he must eliminate the possibility that Ahmed Zuqawri would compromise all that they had worked for. He had to be silenced. Zuqawri himself would expect it.

Leaja turned off the television and called to his recently promoted number two man. "Majid, call the men together. We have a distraction that threatens the mission. We must contend with it immediately. Gather them in my office so that we can review and make new plans. I am afraid some changes are in order to increase our chances of success." Majid Saeed nodded and quickly went to find the others. Leaja called after him.

"Majid, stop at the assembly station and tell the doctor that he needs to hurry as well. Time is not on our side."

Ramsey wrapped up the press briefing and disappeared into the hallway where he found Darin Martin waiting. "Nice job, Alan. Not a bit nervous. At least I couldn't tell if you were."

"Yeah, well my palms were sweating so bad that the ink on my notes began to smear. You can bet your ass I was not comfortable."

Darin Martin looked around. "Where's your buddy, signing autographs?" The comment got a laugh out of Ramsey.

"He was supposed to be calling the hospital about Zuqawri. We're heading that way directly. You might want to pull your vehicle around so we can make a run for it," Ramsey said, not really joking.

Martin turned to look down the hall. "Speak of the devil..."

Paul Jackson walked out of an office and into the hall catching the tail end of Martin's comment. "What about the devil?"

Martin chuckled. "Never mind," he said then turned back to Ramsey smiling. "The guy does look good, I'll give him that. I'll meet you two out front." With that he turned and jogged away.

Jackson watched him move out then turned his attention to Alan Ramsey, "Did I miss something?"

Ramsey smiled and motioned for him to continue, "No, not really. What did you find out?"

Jackson pulled out his notepad. "Ok, I talked to one of the officers at the city hospital. Got what info I could over the phone. He said someone will meet us there and give us a briefing once we hit the ground."

Ramsey looked around the corner to see that the conference room had cleared out. "Let's go. We can go over it in the car."

The black Chevrolet Tahoe pulled up in front of the precinct amid the numerous reporters who were waiting for more information.

Paul Jackson maneuvered through the crowd of reporters repeating the same words over and over, "Make a hole" and "No comment." Ramsey followed closely behind. Agent Matthews would be driving them to the City Hospital. This was his first real case, and he was not about to be left behind. Ramsey saw Matthews as he entered the vehicle. "Anything new at the zoo?" Ramsey asked.

"Not that I am aware of, Sir. I haven't been involved on that end since we came over here. I asked to stay with you guys and it was approved."

Ramsey gave a nod of approval. "Glad to have you on board, Bob." They closed the doors, languishing for the moment in the quiet inside the vehicle before they pulled away.

"Who do we have guarding the hospital? If Bin-Masri is involved with this, you can bet he will attempt to eliminate Zuqawri."

Paul Jackson pulled up his notebook and began to give the names of the people involved in the hospital security detail. Ramsey cut him off. "I don't need names, just the agency responsible."

Jackson caught the edge in his boss' tone, but ignored it. They had been up for about thirty hours. "Second District is in command, but has mostly people from First District detailed out for the security."

Ramsey thought for a second. "Isn't Second District pushing it a little? I understand the zoo is in their jurisdiction, but they have to be pushing their limits."

Paul rechecked his notes. "Yeah, well, the City Hospital neighborhood belongs to First District. Evidently they don't have enough cops. Second district is providing the manpower and the command and control. They can tap the County Police if they need more bodies."

Alan looked skeptical. "Well, I don't think they can have enough security on this. Call back and see who we can take away from the other locations to give them a hand."

"You got it, Boss." With that Paul Jackson switched gears and began making the calls.

Kenneth Wash

CHAPTER 39

SPECIAL FREIGHT

JOEL FRANKLIN rolled to a stop on the eastbound lanes of the Blanchette Bridge. The traffic coming from St. Charles over the Missouri River was always bad here. He crept forward a few feet and then stopped again. Highway 70 snaked its way around St. Louis in a wide arc and then turned abruptly east over the Mississippi River into Illinois. He looked at his freight dispatch while he had the opportunity and figured he would end up in the middle of the downtown St. Louis area just in time for the rush hour traffic that would be heading across the river.

He looked at his navigation system and read the destination again. He had been in that area before to drop off some heavy equipment. The warehouses were close to the river and negotiating on some of the cobblestone streets could be difficult. Most of the streets were steep and ended at the historic riverfront.

The delivery would be easy enough. One crate was all. And, given the items he usually hauled, this one was light at about eight hundred pounds. He wondered about the company receiving the freight. It must be an auto parts warehouse or a supplier. He couldn't remember any auto or truck repair shops in that area, at least not one that would install an Allison MT643 truck transmission.

Whatever, he thought. Once he dropped his load he would stop somewhere for dinner. Maybe call his wife and see what she was doing. Thinking of that he fumbled around for his phone and called the number on his dispatch order.

Majid Saeed heard his phone ring and quickly flipped it open. It was Parcel Freight. "Marconi Industries, how can I help you?" he said in near perfect English.

"Hello, this is Joel with Parcel Freight and Dispatch. I just wanted to let you know that your delivery is about twenty minutes out. That is, if the traffic clears up in the next few minutes." He was actually moving at about 40 miles per hour now, so it was looking rather promising. "I just wanted to confirm that someone from your office would be there to receive the delivery."

"Yes, this is good news. We are working late tonight so we will be here when you arrive. Thank you for calling ahead." Majid hung up the phone. This was indeed good news he thought. He might be able to begin shipment late tonight or very early in the morning. He would know once the two components were assembled. He hoped his engineers were correct and that the bomb would fit within the confines of the aluminum transmission case. He was neither an engineer, nor a mechanic and did not know anything about either occupation. He knew from the meetings he had attended that the test of the detonation system could only occur with the device fully assembled. "Oh well," he thought, "that is their problem, not mine to think about."

Majid ran to the office where Leaja bin Masri was going over the aspects of the new mission with Nasir al-Din, a stocky man who had been a bodyguard to Hamza al-Muhajeer in Iraq.

Majid waited for the men to stop their discussion before approaching bin Masri. "I have some good news, Leaja. The transport truck with the enclosure will be here soon, fifteen minutes or so. I just got off the phone with the driver."

Leaja looked excited. "Yes, that is very good news. Perhaps our luck is changing. Majid, I will be leaving with Nasir in less than that time, so you must follow through when the delivery arrives. Are you sure Fadil will be able to drive the truck?"

Majid assured Leaja that the replacement driver would be acceptable. "Fadil has been practicing with similar vehicles. They are a bit smaller, but nearly the same otherwise."

Leaja still looked concerned. "It is a long drive to the East coast. He must not make mistakes that would jeopardize the mission. You must be sure, Majid."

Majid felt comfortable with his part of the plan. "Leaja, it will be fine. Now hurry. Go. Take care of our loose end. We are almost ready."

Leaja pulled Majid to his shoulder. "You are a strong soldier Majid. Allah Akubar." With that, he turned to Nasir al-Din. "Let's go Nasir. We must hurry before they move Ahmed."

CHAPTER 40

LUCKY DAY

ACROSS town Arnold Montgomery stopped his cart under the canopy of the bus stop. He would rest there for a while, but not until he went through the nearby trashcan. He always found plenty of cans there owing to the fact that there was a vending machine located just outside the fire station.

"Hello, Arnold." The voice came from behind him. He turned to see a fireman, whose name he didn't know. He wondered how people knew who he was. He smiled a snaggletooth grin at the man in suspenders, gave a slight wave with the can, and returned to what he was doing.

He carefully piled the overflowing trash out of the way and extracted each can, setting it aside. He moved some paper and fumbled around, feeling more so than looking, for the next can. His fingertips touched something, but it wasn't metal. He dug through the debris and pulled Zuqawri's discarded phone from the rubbish.

He flipped open the phone and fumbled around with the buttons until the screen lit up. This was great, he thought. He had never owned a cell phone, but he had used them on occasion. The only number that he knew by heart was his mother's. He punched in the numbers and hit the CALL button, smiling again as the phone began to ring.

The high-pitched signal began to chirp loudly on Jay's desktop speakers. The noise snapped Jay from his transient thoughts and brought him to the sudden reality that the signal for Zuqawri's phone had been reestablished. He looked around for Ramsey or Jackson, but remembered both were gone, heading toward the hospital. He set the trace settings to lock onto the phone and ran to get his boss who had stepped into the break room for dinner.

Arnold's mother picked up on the other end and said hello questioningly, not knowing who was calling her. Arnold spoke quickly and relayed the story of how he had found the phone. He and his mother continued to talk as he went about his foraging. Within a few moments he stopped rummaging through the trash and stood upright holding Ahmed's keys in front of him. There were a couple of house keys and a key for a Nissan. He didn't know what model Nissan, but the silver double-sided key, as well as the remote entry control fob had the word Nissan emblazoned on them.

His sudden silence worried his mother. "Arnold... Arnold, what's the matter, Baby?" Arnold heard his mother, but was busy examining the keys in his hand. "Arnold Montgomery, are you there, Son?"

He pressed the unlock button on the key fob and heard a slight car horn chirp, but couldn't make out where it was coming from. He found the alert button, poised his thumb over the button, and then scanned up and down the length of the street for a car to match the key. There were three of them spaced fairly far apart. At least, he thought they were all Nissans. He pressed the red button and immediately the white Nissan Maxima across the street began blaring its horn and flashing its lights.

He pulled the phone back to his ear. "I'll call you back, Momma." He pushed the lock button on the remote to quiet the blaring horn. With the noise stopped, Arnold looked around to see who was watching. Only the firefighter appeared to take note of the alarm going off on the car, but returned to what he was doing when it stopped. Arnold collected his things so he could go investigate further. He had plans to move on, start a new life somewhere else. His luck was changing and now he had two more tools to help him survive. Hell, he thought, worse case, he at least had someplace out of the wind and rain to sleep. He smiled to himself and crossed the street.

Jay spun around the corner and flung the break room door open. "I have the signal. Zuqawri's phone is back on the grid!"

His boss stopped eating and looked up. "What are you talking about? That guy's been captured." He wiped his hands and began moving away from the table. He didn't understand what he was talking about, but if Jay said something was up he knew better than to ignore him.

Jay was out of breath. "I've set the tracking. It should have gathered some info on past calls and I should have a GPS lock by now." He rambled excitedly, "We need to call those two CIA guys. They will want to know." They entered the op center with Jay still talking loud and fast. His boss called to the dispatcher to have a squad car sent to the GPS location on the grid. He patted his pockets to find his phone and touched Jackson's name from his contact list.

"Look! Shit! Man, that's weird." Jay was nearly shaking with excitement. "The signal is nearly in the same spot as when we lost it... within feet." He didn't know what that meant, but found it odd.

"OK, we got officers on the way and I'm calling your buddy, Jackson, now, so just relax and keep an eye on it."

"Don't worry, I won't even blink this time."

Mark Manson, the driver of the squad car turned right onto Jaimeson Street and saw the man pushing the cart, but really didn't think anything about it. His partner scoffed as they passed him by. "What?" Manson asked, "What's so funny?"

"A bum with a cell phone, that's what. How many soda cans does it take to pay a phone bill?" Terrance Moore laughed out loud at his own joke.

Manson joined in. "Yeah, uh, sorry sir, but you're over your minutes. That will be an extra Coke can, please." The officers found themselves funny.

When they didn't see anything out of the ordinary Mark Manson called in. "This is Manny. We're here. What the hell are we supposed to be looking for, Jack?"

"Says here you're looking for a cell phone." He explained how the police and the FBI were tracking the signal. "According to what they sent me, it just popped up right there on the South corner of Jaimeson and Fyler, by the firehouse. Evidently pretty important."

The two officers looked at each other. "Shit," Terrance said out loud. "You gotta be kidding me."

Manny Manson spun the cruiser around and headed back with the lights on and the siren chirping.

Arnold had just popped the driver's door when he heard the siren and saw the police moving in his direction. He had no reason to believe that they were coming for him. He decided that it would be best to get out of the way of the squad car, so he opened the door fully to get in.

The trip wire attached to the door pulled tight joining the contacts together within the detonator, allowing twelve volts from the car's battery to pass through the switch, triggering the explosive caps embedded in the C4 explosive blocks mounted under the seat.

The squad car was about to stop just behind the Nissan when there came a blinding flash and the noise of the explosion. The windshield of the cruiser suddenly shattered, impacted by the flying rear door of the Nissan Maxima and both the side windows on the cruiser blew inward from the blast's concussion. The homeless man, his cart and the front door of the Nissan Maxima all lay motionless in the driveway of the fire station across the street. Car alarms were blaring up and down the street and the neighbors who lived close by were beginning to emerge from their homes, some needing medical attention due to flying glass from their shattered windows. It took the two officers a moment to come to their senses and get out of the car to survey the effects of the explosion.

Manny stepped out of the driver's side, leaned over the door holding the microphone and called in a report. Terrance Moore ran around the car to the driver side and then across the street where the firefighter was kneeling down examining the body of the homeless man. He would have to be moved to get the truck out and across the street to put the fire out on what remained of the Nissan. The two men lifted Arnold Montgomery and moved his body so the emergency equipment could squeeze by.

As the truck moved past him, Terrance bent down to collect what was left of the phone. Manny joined him, looking somewhat bewildered, then asked, "What the hell just happened?"

CHAPTER 41

FAMILY VISIT

JOEL FRANKLIN was maneuvering his truck close to the warehouse dock when the large garage door opened next to it and one of the men inside motioned for him to turn his truck around and back it in the door. He could see the forklift inside the building, an operator in the seat.

He started to back up when he saw two vehicles approach and stop. Joel motioned for them to pass, but they didn't move. They would just have to wait for him to dock before they could get by now.

Within minutes Franklin had the back of the trailer inside the building. The ground guide motioned for him to keep moving and didn't stop him until Franklin's rig was completely inside the building. The veteran truck driver was surprised, and thought it odd when the huge bay door rattled to life, grinding and squeaking as it closed.

Joel placed the truck in neutral and set the brake. The dust from the concrete below the truck blasted into the air as the truck driver stepped down out of the truck. He grabbed his clipboard to review the manifest and, looking in the direction of the lowering door, saw the two sedans pass slowly. Franklin turned toward the back of his truck and stopped short when he noticed that the building was nearly empty. He began to speak to whoever would listen.

"Ok then, I got one crate in the back for you guys," he said, as he smiled at the man in front of him and walked past him toward the back of the truck.

As he rounded the rear of the trailer, he saw that one of the men was releasing the latch on the doors. "Hey, you need to step back, son. I'll get that." He sat the clipboard on the forklift and reached for the rear door latch when his forehead suddenly exploded. The gunshot was deafening and echoed through the warehouse as Joel Franklin fell to the concrete floor motionless.

Majid lowered the pistol and barked to the others in Arabic. "Get rid of the body. Hurry! We have work to do." The forklift rolled forward as the body of the truck driver was moved out of the way. "Get the crate and bring it to the doctor. Send the mechanics with the tool boxes." He pulled up his phone to call his boss. "Do not damage the crate. I want the bomb assembled in the case and back in the crate in less than one hour." We leave here immediately following the assembly."

The opening of the service door next to the large doorway captured Majid's attention. He squinted, trying to see clearly the four men silhouetted against the evening sunlight. Majid tucked his weapon away behind his back as the last of the men stepped fully through the doorway, pulling the door closed behind him. "Can I help you?" Majid asked routinely.

The tallest of the men moved forward of the group and stopped near Majid. He was wearing sunglasses, something Majid did not trust. He didn't like that he couldn't see the man's eyes. When he spoke, Majid detected a European accent immediately.

"I am looking for Leaja bin Masri. Is he here now?"

The hair on Majid's neck was bristling. "I'm afraid we do not have anyone working for us with that name. You might try one of the other warehouses."

The large figure stepped closer and picked up the clipboard from the forklift and glanced at the bill of lading. The paper was spattered with blood and bits of bone fragments. He glanced down to see a pool of blood and the unmistakable trail heading away into the shadows. The man showed no emotion. He read the name of the company on the clipboard before setting it back down.

"This is Marconi Industries, is it not?" He held up his hands to punctuate his sarcastically pronounced words with the finger gestures for quotation marks. "Where is Leaja bin Masri? I know that he runs this, ah, business. I need to speak with him on behalf of one of his suppliers. Perhaps you will recognize the name. Dmitri Gregorov." With that the man reached for the pistol that was tucked into his chest holster.

Majid yanked his weapon up at the same time and spun to put this man between him and the three men standing just inside the doorway. He was at a disadvantage with the evening sunlight streaming through the four glass panels of the service door. He needed to act first or he would not have another chance. Before the Russian mobster could raise his pistol, Majid fired into his chest, dropping him to the concrete, leaving himself exposed to the three other armed Russians.

The men in the warehouse ducked for cover or to retrieve their own weapons as Majid dove over the dead Russian to land under the truck just behind the rear dual wheels. He scrambled to the other side as the first volley of gunfire reverberated through the steel structure.

Majid jumped to his feet and ran around the right rear of the trailer toward the forklift. One of the mobsters appeared to the right front of the truck firing at Majid. The rounds were not well aimed, striking the truck and the floor. Majid fired back hitting the

Russian in the throat and chest. The man dropped his pistol and grabbed at his throat.

Majid rounded the back of the truck to find the forklift operator slumped in the seat, his pistol near his feet. The sound of automatic machine gun fire came from behind him. Majid looked over his shoulder to see one of his men firing in the direction of their new enemies. He reached over and grabbed the weapon from the forklift and sprinted hard toward the front of the warehouse. As he reached the front of the truck, he turned sideways and brought his pistols up to fire on the mobsters. He was greeted with the muzzle flash from one of the Russian weapons and instinctively dove to the floor. Majid watched as both of the mobsters reacted to the fire of the AK-47. Majid fell to the floor, sliding against the steel wall of the building and fired wildly in their direction. The rounds from the AK-47 slammed into both men knocking them backward. The one closest to Majid attempted to get back up only to be met with more rounds from the automatic weapon.

Majid stood in the sudden silence of the warehouse. He thought about the two vehicles parked outside. Raising his weapon, he slammed the service door open and sprinted along the front of the building to the first of the parked sedans. He spun around the corner of the building and placed two rounds through the windshield of the closest sedan killing the driver. Before he could fire on the second vehicle, that driver accelerated hard, pulling away from the building, spinning rocks and gravel against the car and building next to it. Majid fired into the back of the vehicle, but could not stop it from speeding away.

Chapter 42

Reprisal

THE Corrections Medical Facility was a sprawling complex of old and new buildings, the oldest being the old city hospital complex. City Cor-Med, as it was known, was the most secure due to the thick stone construction used over a hundred years before. Dentists, physical therapists, psychologists and surgeons all pulled special duty at the hospital. It didn't matter what other hospital or private office you were associated with, if you held a medical license in the St. Louis or the surrounding area, and if you had earned your licenses with the aid of any government grants or tuition, you had to give time to the Cor-Med Facility. And it was just as hard to get out of as jury duty when your name came up.

The rules were initiated with the introduction of the new National Health Care Program. For interns and new physicians, it was just more practice, and for them, the duty seemed to come around far too often.

The young doctor looked at the information in his hand and could not believe he was reporting again, the second time in as many months. Jason Taylor settled his bag into his locker and sat on the bench. He was tired. It had been a long day already with the explosion at the zoo and then the situation with Dr. Zuqawri. It was hard for him to believe that his Medical Chief had been directly involved in such a hideous attack.

But, it didn't stop there. Dr. Zuqawri was a prisoner in this hospital. Taylor wanted to see him, now that he knew the man for what he really was. The two doctors hadn't always seen eye to eye, and they had had their share of political arguments, but Taylor would never have thought that the man could have such deep rooted hatred for America.

He turned his attention back to his schedule and pulled out his smart phone to review the charts on the first two patients for whom he would be caring. Luckily, Zuqawri was not on his list of things to do today. He picked up his things and moved to go begin his shift.

The utility van pulled up at the rear of the hospital close to the laundry dock. Leaja bin Masri and Nasir al-Din stepped out into the alley behind the building and moved around to the back of the van. Nasir removed a cart with tools and an electronic test oscilloscope. Leaja handed him a clip on badge and secured a folder containing a work order for the inspection and repair of a Magnetic Resonance Imaging scanner. The documents looked legitimate enough. Leaja bin Masri was amazed at what information could be found in only a few minutes while perusing the Internet. The security guard at the rear entrance did not seem the least bit interested in looking at the paperwork and only briefly glanced at their badges. Leaja noted that the guard's glasses were on the desk near the daily paper. The thought that the guard probably couldn't see the badges clearly crossed his mind. "Incredible," he thought.

The guard opened and held the door for Nasir who was burdened by the cart. The contents of the cart rattled and bounced as the wheels contacted the threshold. Nasir al-Din was relieved at the ease of their entry into the hospital. The two silenced pistols located inside the plastic toolbox would have been easy to get to had they been needed. Leaja thanked the guard for his help and caught up with the MRI technician. The two men moved into the brightly lit main floor hallway and headed toward the elevators.

Leaja bin Masri knew that the sixth floor of the old hospital was the high security ward. They would have to go up two floors, and then move to the secure service elevator. That would hopefully circumvent any real police officers. Leaja bin Masri would much rather take his chances with the security staff. Worst case would be that any guard they confronted would call down to the desk to verify who they were. Too easy, he thought.

The elevator doors opened as the chime indicating an available elevator sounded. Bin Masri stepped in taking note of the position of the two city police officers at the front doors of the hospital. The doors closed and the elevator shuddered slightly as it began the ascent to the third floor.

Ramsey's vehicle sat at the light waiting for it to change. The City Hospital was about two blocks away. Jackson suddenly shuffled in his seat, pulled his phone from his pocket and stuck it against his ear. Ramsey could hear the voice, but could not make out what it was saying. Jackson looked surprised.

"What? How? Are you sure?" Jackson looked at Ramsey for a moment with a look of disbelief on his face and hung up. "That was Jay. He got another lock on Zuqawri's phone signal. Evidently he dumped his phone and his car keys in a trash bin and a local homeless guy found the phone and decided to make a call home."

"Did they pick him up?" Ramsey asked

Jackson rolled his eyes. "Oh yeah, they picked him up all right, with a shovel. It would appear that Zuqawri rigged his car to explode when the door was opened. This homeless guy found the keys and the car. Poor bastard, probably thought it was his lucky day."

"So they have the phone?" Ramsey asked trying to get Paul Jackson to cut to the chase.

"The phone is damaged, but Jay is trying to scrub the SIM card to see what might show up. From what I understand, they have some history of the calls made to the dead terrorists in Texas. He says that could be all he's going to get as it's pretty badly damaged."

Ramsey suddenly reached for his own phone. Jackson could hear his phone vibrating as he fished it from his pocket. It was Captain Rebello. Ramsey put the phone on speaker. "This is Ramsey, go ahead."

Mr. Ramsey, this is Rebello. We have a satellite call for you from overseas. A guy named Dmitri. He says he needs to speak with you."

Ramsey looked at Jackson. "Overseas, where?" he asked.

Captain Rebello sounded skeptical. "He says he's calling from Moscow, as in, Moscow, Russia. Needs to talk to you. Says he saw you on CNN and knows you are looking for a bomb. I'm patching him into the system. It's a little fuzzy, but you should be able to hear him." With that there came a series of clicks and then a steady hissing sound.

"Hello, is this Mr. Alan Ramsey?"

"This is Alan Ramsey. Who is this?" Jackson and Martin leaned in to listen.

"I am Dmitri Gregorov. I am, what you might call, a small businessman. I have information that might help you find what you are looking for."

Ramsey motioned for Agent Matthews to pull over out of traffic. Ramsey looked around the vehicle then back at his phone. "Mr. Gregorov, why would I trust that you know anything about what is going on here or what we are looking for?"

"Please, call me Dmitri." The Russian exhaled loudly. "Look, Mr. Ramsey, this man you are looking for is a client of mine, a man who stole from me. I sent some of my associates to...talk...to him and they were killed. As much as I dislike your government, I dislike the Muslim Fascist Extremists even more. We had a deal. They did not hold up their end of the bargain. So, due to this recent development, I feel compelled to offer you some...assistance."

Ramsey thought about what to say next. "Look, Dmitri, you could have gotten this information from watching what is happening on the news. You need to give me some information that was not reported. Something only you and I might know."

Dmitri smiled to himself. This man was new at the game of espionage. He remembered how that felt. "Perhaps, if I told you a love story about a beautiful, sexy, Russian girl and a handsome, young, U.S. Airman named Mark Beirman. Is that the kind of information you are looking for, Mr. Ramsey?"

Ramsey sat upright. He knew that information had not yet been made public. "What can I do for you, Dmitri?"

"Actually, Mr. Ramsey, the question is, what can I do to help you? But first you must promise me that any information linking my organization to this terrible situation is only investigated by you, since, as I said earlier, I am willing to help you." Dmitri Gregorov was all about who owed who what favor. He hoped that Ramsey understood how such favors worked.

Ramsey knew that he could not promise what he was being asked to do, per se. He could, however, allude to the fact that he was in a position to manage any such investigation. "I look forward to working with you, if the need arises. Now, Mr. Gregorov, as I said before, how can I help you?"

Gregorov hesitated only for the dramatic sense of what he was about to say, then said simply, "You will find what you are looking for in the Lawrence Industrial Park. Warehouse number 5, I believe."

"And, what would that be, Dmitri? What are we going to find there?" The phone clicked off without a reply.

Ramsey looked down the street. He saw several squad cars and some officers standing near the entrance of the hospital. "How far is the Lawrence Industrial Park from here?"

Darin Martin was plugging away at the information base that was similar to the military's Blue Force Tracking system. The maps and GPS information came up quickly. A flashing arrow indicating their position came up, then the image backed away, widening, to encompass all of St. Louis. Information with updated police activity scrolled across the bottom of the screen indicating that the FBI was already running with the information.

"The FBI is already heading toward the warehouse. Looks like they were privy to your phone conversation."

Martin hit the enter key and a marker was placed on the grid indicating the location of the warehouse. The marker showed up as a flashing yellow star.

"Ok, got it, the warehouse is roughly six miles away. Downtown near the Arch. We could jump over to Arsenal Street and run it all the way to I55. That would put us there in about ten minutes."

Ramsey didn't like that the FBI, and probably every other law enforcement agency on the ground, was listening in on his conversation. It was all part of the information awareness push brought on by the attacks of 9/11. With it came the ability to track each agency's movements, the reason for the update banner, so that each agency knew what the other was doing. The system had its merits, but Ramsey couldn't help but think of it as eavesdropping.

He glanced at the map and back at the police gathered in front of the hospital. "Darin, you and I will go see our friend Ahmed. Jackson and Matthews, you two head to the warehouse. I want you to be there when the FBI gets there. I will meet you there as soon as I talk to Zuqawri."

Bob Matthews maneuvered into the covered emergency parking and stopped. Ramsey unbuckled his belt and stepped out. Paul Jackson had come around the car to get in the front seat, meeting Ramsey at the door. Jackson smiled broadly, "Shotgun!" he said loudly as he took control of the open passenger door.

Alan Ramsey started to close his door and stopped. "Paul, try not to shoot anybody. You don't really have a license to carry that thing. Keep him in check for me, Bob."

Matthews gave Ramsey the thumbs up sign and placed the vehicle in gear. "Don't worry, I'll keep him from hurting anybody, especially me."

Ramsey watched as the Tahoe pulled away, turned and headed into the hospital, catching up with Agent Martin at the door. The two men approached the desk sergeant. Ramsey flashed his credentials followed by Martin and Ramsey read the name badge on the man in front of him. "Good evening, Sergeant Avery, I'm Alan Ramsey, and this is agent Darin Martin. We're here to speak with Zuqawri."

Avery eyed the two men, giving them a once over, matching the credentials to the men displaying them. He stood, stepped around the desk and then extended a hand to each in succession. "Good evening. I was told you would be coming. I'll call for an escort to take you up."

Ramsey thanked him and asked, "How's your security set up here? He looked around taking note that there were no other officers or agents in the large lobby.

"I've got ten uniformed patrols in the building, two guarding Zuqawri at all times and an additional four plainclothes cops wandering the halls. A couple of them are dressed like doctors." Avery responded.

Alan contemplated the odds and considered them in his favor. "The hospital has their own security as well don't they?" he asked.

The answer came from Dr. Taylor, who had stepped from the doorway a few feet away. "Yes, there is a hospital security staff, but don't leave anything of value laying around. It might not be there when you go back for it."

Ramsey turned to face the voice. "Dr. Taylor, you work here too?" He extended his hand in greeting.

"Well, let's just say I'm performing my civic duty. Although, it is good training for when I become a successful family physician. I will more than likely have to be in three or four places at once." Taylor smiled and shook Ramsey's hand.

Ramsey introduced the doctor to the agent standing next to him and told Taylor that he was there to question Dr. Zuqawri.

Taylor was not planning on being involved in anything here, but knew that eventually he would be spending a lot of time with investigators and then in court giving testimony. That is, if it came down to a trial. With the new anti-terrorism laws a suspected terrorist could be held indefinitely, though this case seemed pretty cut and dried to him. "I haven't seen him yet, but I understand that the first surgery on his injury was not so successful. Evidently, there are bones that are completely destroyed. There is a chance he will lose his foot."

Ramsey replied sarcastically, "Hardly an eye for an eye, but then again he hasn't gone to trial. If he doesn't get the death sentence, then I don't know who should."

A uniformed officer appeared in the lobby and headed in Ramsey's direction. "Well, Dr. Taylor it would appear our tour guide has arrived. I'm sure we'll be talking again. Have an uneventful day." As the doctor turned away, Ramsey held out his identification. Darin Martin did the same.

Sergeant Conrad scanned them both. "Ok, good, one CIA and one FBI. Good to see you two talking." The officer chuckled at his own joke and asked about weapons. "Both of you have side arms?"

Ramsey and Martin both pulled back their jackets to reveal shoulder holsters and nine-millimeter pistols.

"Ok, do either of you have additional weapons? I know how you agency folks like to carry extra firepower."

"Does a Gerber count?" Darin Martin replied jokingly.

Sergeant Conrad gave him a disdainful look, then continued. "There are fourteen officers here today. So far, nothing unusual has happened. There are several construction guys on the books today. Most of them can easily be recognized. They will be wearing hardhats and tool belts. You should not see any of them above the third floor."

He glanced at his notes before continuing, "There are also a few maintenance folks that you might see that have been cleared already. They might be seen anywhere on any floor. All of them should have a badge like this one." Conrad held his badge out for them to examine. "They should have paperwork or a job order sheet as well, so if something doesn't seem right ask to see their paperwork."

Conrad looked at them intently reinforcing his message. "This is the city's correctional medical hospital. It's a jail as much as it is a medical facility. Everybody has to have a badge. The only people who don't are the families who visit the folks on floors one and two and they have to have a security escort. So, the first place we need to go is down the hall here. I will log each of you in and you will receive a badge like mine. Once you are logged in and tagged you will be free to move through the hospital unchecked. Be sure that the badge is visible at all times."

He took a second to write their names and agencies in his personal note pad. He asked each for contact numbers and after writing that information down as well, closed the book and slipped it back into his pocket. As he buttoned his shirt pocket he looked back up at them. "Are there any questions, gentlemen?"

Martin had none and shook his head. Ramsey put his identification away and answered, "No, I believe you covered everything. Thank you."

"Ok, then if you will follow me, we can get your day started."

CHAPTER 43

MOVING OUT

"*CAREFUL* with that. Do not let the wiring get caught on the casting." Dr. Metelov winced as the warhead and all of the attached components were fitted into the case of the Allison transmission.

The aluminum transmission housing was nearly the perfect case for the reworked warhead. Once inside the case the transmission's front pump assembly would be bolted back in place sealing the warhead inside. The front pump housing had to be modified to accommodate the new components. The rear of the mechanism would be too deep to accommodate the device and secure it with the original bolts. The pump's rear housing, impeller and shafts were removed and discarded, thrown into the pile of internal shafts, gears, clutch disks and other parts that had made up the internal components of the Allison MT643 transmission.

The scientist routed the wires to the external control box through the hole in the side of the aluminum housing that once held the transmission control module's wiring harness and plugged the connector into the detonator. The electronic control box of the TCM was the perfect housing to contain the new control boards and the components of the wireless detonator. The only thing that looked out of place was the flexible plastic wiring conduit for the manual control box that would be mounted inside the Volvo tractor's cab in the event that the remote detonator didn't function correctly and the controls had to be manually configured. The wired remote could be used to program the timer within the detonator case mounted inside the transmission.

The preferred method of setting off the bomb was the wireless detonator. This was a mechanical contact switch controlled by a cell phone. The phone could be called from anywhere in the world, provided that there was cellular service. Metelov combined the use of electromechanical force with a chemical reaction to provide the initial explosion that would trigger the warhead's primary explosives. The only downside to using the nitro-glycerin and RDX explosives was the possibility, although slight, that the nuclear fission could be triggered prematurely. Dr. Metelov warned Leaja bin Masri that one strike from a Rocket Propelled Grenade or any other shoulder-fired missile such as the stinger could begin the fission process. More than likely, in the event of a direct strike, the components would separate and the device would be rendered inoperative. It was a possibility just the same, therefore, he warned, great care should be taken to protect the weapon.

Once the front pump was secured, the torque converter was installed and the shipping straps were reinstalled on the bell housing to keep the converter from falling out during shipment. The best part was that the crate weighed nearly the same as it had originally with all of the guts removed and the bomb inside. Unless someone knew to look for it, there was no discerning it from the transmission as it had originally shipped from California.

Metelov watched as the crate was reassembled and the forklift moved to the trailer. His job was now complete. The defining moment for him and his family was upon him. He would either be killed, and likely so would his family, or he would be a half million dollars richer. Either way, soon he would be guilty of the deaths of thousands of innocent people.

Metelov was no friend of the U.S. government. If the plan succeeded much could change in America, and, when America changed, the world tended to change. Hopefully, this would end the constant meddling for which this country was so well known. Had it not been for America, his own homeland, Bosnia would not have been thrust into a war of false hope, thousands of people dead and missing due mainly to the collapse of the Soviet Union. That collapse was triggered by the West's constant provoking. Freedom and democracy, he thought, there was too much of both. The thought disgusted him and it showed by the scowl on his face.

Majid saw his look. "Dr. Metelov, cheer up. Today is the day that you will be reunited with your family." He walked past the man, disappearing into an adjoining room and continued to talk from beyond the door.

"Leaja sends his congratulations. I spoke with him minutes ago to tell him of the progress. You are a hero, Doctor." The sounds of scuffling and desk drawers opening and closing piqued his curiosity. Dr. Metelov walked to the open doorway, stopping short, leery of what awaited him on the other side.

Majid saw the man and called him inside. "Come in. I am not going to kill you, if that's what you are thinking." He pulled his pistol out and set it on the desk. "Not that I agree with releasing you." He continued, "If it were up to me you would not go free. Too many loose ends to contend with." He patted a pack of cigarettes and removed one. Lighting it and taking the first drag, he shook out the flame on the match and spoke after exhaling the smoke through his nostrils. "How will you convince your wife and daughters not to say anything about their captivity? They wait for you in a hotel in Moscow. They have been locked in for over two weeks. What will you tell them to keep them quiet? They will be angry, don't you think?"

Metelov began to answer, but Majid held up a hand. "What about you? Is having your family and your life back enough to keep you from running to the Americans?"

The question was rhetorical, but Metelov answered, "I am no friend of the Americans."

Majid quietly studied the genius that stood before him, then suddenly broke the silence. "Dr. Metelov, you are free to go. Here are your bags already packed for you. Majid motioned to the two luggage cases on the floor near his desk. "In one you will find your personal belongings. Even your toothbrush is there." He smiled a crooked smile and continued after another pull on his cigarette. "In the other, is over a million dollars. More than double what was agreed to." Metelov's eyes grew wide, but Majid still would not let him speak.

"However, if you decide that the burden of your guilt is too much to bear, and you feel the need to report what you know to the police, or if the bomb that you are being paid for building fails to detonate, we will come find you." Majid slid the two cases toward the man.

Metelov wasn't sure what to say. He stood silently, contemplating. Finally, he said quietly, "I understand. I will make my wife and children understand as well."

"Then you should go. There is a plane ticket to Moscow in your bag. Also, you will find the name of a man who can help you...invest your money. The plane leaves tomorrow morning, so you do not have much time."

Dr. Metelov picked up the two bags and walked out of the office and through the warehouse to the closed bay door by the truck. The trailer doors were latched shut. The blue Trailblazer that Bin-Masri had driven from Texas was parked in a corner of the warehouse, a lone soldier behind the wheel. Metelov was nearly at the exit of the warehouse when he stopped and looked around at what had been his home for the past few weeks. It was empty now, the mechanics released to report back to their fictitious lives as sleeper agents until needed again. The only other person in the warehouse now was the one who would be driving the truck. The man was going over the mechanicals of the truck making sure it would make it to the East Coast. It was fully fueled and ready to go. The doctor noted the new wire harness exiting the truck trailer and snaking into the cab of the truck. "They are really going to do this," he thought as he opened the steel service door and stepped out onto the dock. The sunlight was low over the city. He squinted and turned to his left and began walking the length of the concrete dock to the stairs.

He could see the gleaming stainless steel of the Gateway Arch in the near distance. The sun reflected brightly on the far leg catching the light from the evening sun. The sounds of the city were overwhelming. He had no car, but he knew there was always a bus stop close by. He would get a hotel room and spend one last night here.

He was rich, he thought. He would be able to make a great life for his family even better. All they had to do was put behind them the memories of the last few weeks. Metelov, however, would have to forget what was about to happen and the knowledge that he would be largely responsible, but for a million U.S. dollars he could heal.

Majid watched as the doctor walked out, closing the door behind him. He tossed his cigarette down crushing it under his foot as he walked towards the truck. The driver, Fadil al-Din, was closing the hood.

"How much longer, Fadil?" The man bore a striking resemblance to the dead truck driver. His only qualification to drive the truck was that uncanny resemblance to the man whose identification and licenses were now in his possession.

"Give me another minute to adjust the mirrors and we can leave." He latched the hood fasteners and climbed into the truck.

"I put your bags inside the sleeping compartment along with my own." He closed the door and lowered the door glass to make his adjustments and repeated the process for the passenger side.

"I am sending Mahmud to fuel the Trailblazer and pick up supplies for the trip. He will catch up with us on the road."

Majid didn't like the idea of using the stolen Trailblazer, but all the vehicles arranged for the mission had not made it back from the pick-up point in Texas. They did not have time to secure a new vehicle. It was good they would be traveling separately. He raised the door as the truck rumbled to life behind him. The exhaust filled the bay with smoke as the steel door clanked and rattled. The bright red and white Volvo pulled out into the diminishing daylight. Majid pushed the button to lower the bay door and stepped outside as the door began to close.

They would head east out of the city and stop at the first rest stop to wait for Bin-Masri and Nasir al-Din. That would be in Illinois about an hour away. Getting to the highway would be a task. The warehouse area was located in an area not easily accessible to the highway. They would have to jockey around to get onto the highway by driving several blocks on well-traveled truck routes. The next obstacle would be getting over the Poplar Street Bridge. Traffic would be bumper to bumper on the aged expanse of highway that merged four major highways and funneled them across the Mississippi River into Illinois.

Majid jumped up on the step and opened the door. He sat down in his seat and was buckling his safety belt when the first indication of trouble rounded the corner of an adjacent warehouse. The first of the FBI's black Crown Victoria sedans turned onto the warehouse road.

Jack Murray and his team saw the door closing on the warehouse and the truck sitting in the roadway. "That's the building! Looks like we won't be having to go in after them."

His driver turned on his flashing lights and sped up to block the truck, but was forced into the side of another warehouse as the semi lurched forward and closed the gap between the building and Murray's car. The truck maneuvered forward then hard left to pull down the street. "Go Fadil, move! Do not stop!"

Fadil was glad that the truck had an automatic transmission. He still had to shift, but only to gain power ranges for heavy loads and hills. He yanked the gear selector into the hill setting and pressed the accelerator hard. The huge Volvo Turbo Diesel roared as the power was transferred through the drive train of the all wheel drive chassis. The trailer, having delivered most of its cargo before getting to St. Louis, was light. The truck's power was more than adequate to move the vehicle and accelerate quickly.

Jack Murray called to the other teams warning them so one of them could head off the truck. An agent from the third vehicle called back, "I got it. I'm moving to the west end of the street to block it in."

The black sedan pulled in front of the truck just as the huge Volvo made it to the end of the street. There was no way to stop the truck. Fadil instinctively slammed on the brakes. Before the tires could protest the action, Majid screamed for him to go.

Fadil released the brake and accelerated, slamming into the side of the sedan. The massive truck pushed the car out and across the intersection. The left rear quarter of the car caught a power pole at the corner of the next row of warehouses. The sedan spun away from the truck, but only enough for the bumper of the semi to rip and smash the right side of the vehicle and wrap it around the pole rendering it non drivable.

Jack Murray's car was damaged, but still in the chase and was moving up behind the semi trailer. Team two was now on the road behind the warehouses hoping to get in front of the semi. The four men in the sedan unbuckled and were readying their weapons, wishing they had heavier firepower. That equipment was with the

FBI Heavy Teams who had yet to arrive on the scene. They would have to make due with only their pistols.

Majid could see between the structures that the black sedan was speeding down the row of buildings to get ahead of them. He looked for a way to maneuver out of this direction of travel and saw an opening to the right. "Fadil, go through there, through that parking lot!" Fadil was not reacting fast enough. Majid grabbed the steering wheel and directed the truck through a chain link fence and into the parking lot. The tires protested the sudden maneuver as the huge truck leaned hard to the left. Fadil looked terrified, but regained control of the truck.

Majid screamed at Fadil, "Keep this truck moving! We cannot get stopped here. Keep moving to the highway. If you cannot then I will!" Fadil looked at Majid who had his pistol pointed at him and understood that he did not have a choice. Majid could see that Fadil was nervous, shaking and sweating profusely.

Murray followed the rig, but couldn't make it across the downed fence. The chain link hung up under his vehicle, stopping the sedan. He placed the car in reverse, but couldn't move backward either. The men in the car couldn't get out and began firing at the truck through the windows as they tried to push the doors open over the tangled fencing.

Fadil was beginning to break down. His foot was shaking on the accelerator, and he wasn't thinking clearly. Sweat was dripping from his nose and chin. His hands could barely grip the steering wheel, and now, he had a pistol pointing at him. Without thinking, he stepped on the brakes to stop the truck. "I cannot do this, I cannot do this," he said in Arabic over and over. He held tightly to the steering wheel and began sobbing the words while rocking back and forth.

"Move, Fadil! Move now! We do not have time!" Majid screamed at him. He heard gunshots and looked out his window. The agents were climbing from the car through the windows and over the chain link fencing.

Majid turned again to Fadil. "Move! Get out now. Out of the truck. Move!" Fadil continued to sob and pray as if he were in a trance. To Majid he was useless.

The last sedan turned the corner. Ken Schryver, a ten-year veteran of the Special Ops team, spotted the truck. He accelerated, moving down the row of warehouses. Suddenly the left door glass of the semi blew outward in a reddish blast of glass and blood. The door opened and Fadil's lifeless body fell to the ground. Schryver yelled back to his men, "Holy shit! I think they just killed themselves."

Majid jumped into the driver's seat and watched as Schryver's vehicle quickly moved up behind him. He placed the transmission selector in reverse and waited. He watched and waited for the vehicle to get closer and then suddenly slammed the accelerator down. The tractor lurched under the trailer. The weight of the trailer would not allow the tires to slip and the torque of the 600 horsepower turbo diesel engine propelled the rig backward toward the sedan.

Agent Schryver couldn't react fast enough to the sudden movement of the truck. He was hit with the sudden realization that the distance between the two vehicles was closing faster than he intended. He released the accelerator, but did not have enough time to apply the brakes before the two vehicles collided.

Agent Dickson, the front passenger, planted his hands on the dash in an effort to stop his forward momentum. The force of the impact shoved the sedan backward. Schryver slammed against the steering wheel as the airbag deployed. The force of the deploying airbag propelled him rearward causing the back of his skull to collide hard with agent Don Jeffries' face and forehead. Agent Jeffries' neck snapped at the base of his skull as his body tried to keep moving forward at the equivalent of more than sixty miles an hour.

The semi continued moving backward forcing the deck of the trailer over the sedan's hood. The sedan impacted the left rear dual tires causing the vehicle to slide under the trailer at a forty-five degree angle. The lowered bumper of the trailer chassis folded upward as the base of the rear deck sliced through the right windshield pillar smashing through the windshield at dashboard height.

Dickson's arms shattered. Without his seatbelt to restrain him, he smashed against the airbag and dashboard putting him in the way of the moving trailer as the rear deck cut through the car.

Majid felt a sudden burn and extreme pain in his right thigh as he heard more gunshots to his right. Someone had shot through the door and the round was now embedded in his leg.

Nick Chalk was the first agent out of Murray's entangled sedan. He ran toward the truck, weapon raised and firing. He managed to get off several rounds, shattering the passenger side door glass and piercing the light metal and fiberglass door. As he got to the truck, the semi began moving forward again. He grabbed the handle of the door as several rounds from Majid's pistol burst through the fiberglass side panel of the sleeper compartment. One of the rounds struck the agent's arm and another round slammed hard into his Kevlar chest plate. The impact stopped him in his tracks, knocking the wind out of him.

The vest he was wearing prevented the round from penetrating his chest, but it did nothing to protect his extremities. The agent's arm was damaged badly. A severe wave of pain swept over him. He could now feel the blood as it oozed from the wound. His arm and hand quickly went numb. His knees buckled, and he could not hold out his pistol to fire another shot. The truck was getting away.

The Volvo picked up speed and drove away down the road. The other agents held their fire knowing that it would be no use and instead concentrated their efforts on first aid for the men in the Team Three sedan and for Agent Chalk.

Jack Murray quickly called in a request for air medevac and then called in his report while he walked toward the warehouse. He motioned to one of his men to cover him as he carefully opened the service door. When there was no resistance from within the building, he and his colleague stepped through the door and into the warehouse.

The light from a single light fixture cascaded across the concrete floor illuminating the face of the dead truck driver. Murray found the light switch. The ceiling mounted tungsten lamps buzzed to life exposing several dead bodies on the floor near the wall. At first Murray thought that they had fallen where they'd been executed, but as the lighting turned from dull blue to a flickering bright white, he could see the telltale mopping of blood left behind from the bodies being dragged across the floor.

He wondered who the men were. They did not appear to be Middle Eastern. Well, except for the one shot in the back of the head, Murray thought. Other than that guy, they all looked European. One, he was sure, had to be the driver of the car parked outside. The hole in the windshield, the matching damage to the person's face and the sparkling bits of glass confirmed it for him, but this would have to wait. For now, he had too much going on to worry about it.

Paul Jackson was just getting to the scene when the radio barked the information about the truck and what had just happened.

Bob Matthews spun the Tahoe around the turn and down the row of warehouses to find Jack Murray exiting the warehouse and holstering his weapon. Blood had streamed down his face and dried from a gash on his forehead. Jackson could see sparkling bits of glass in the man's hair and on his shirt.

"You look like shit," was Paul Jackson's greeting.

Murray didn't necessarily find it amusing. "Yeah, well some of us ain't as lucky as me." He looked past Bob Matthews to focus on Jackson. "Maybe you'll want to go tell that to Dickson and Jeffries. Actually you can tell it to their widows and kids, Asshole."

Murray recovered his composure and continued with a quick report. "The inside of the warehouse looks like a slaughterhouse with blood and shell casings everywhere. We've got six dead bodies in there. Five have some identification. One guy may be one of the bad guys. Not sure. No identification. Looks like he was executed. Shot at close range through the back of the head." He looked through his notes.

"You can see the sedan there." The FBI agent pointed to the car parked next to the building. "That's not one of ours. I'm not sure which one of the dead guys it belongs to, but my guess is it's the guy with glass all over him who's been shot in the face. We got one dead terrorist. We think he was driving the truck, but for some reason he was shot and pushed from the vehicle. Last thing, there's some sort of "clean" room in the warehouse. It looks like a bomb factory to me. We found some sort of a casing, might be an artillery shell opened up, only it looks bigger. Lots of small parts and wires. We aren't going back in until somebody checks that thing out. I told everyone to stay out in case of radiation or something. You never know. Anyway, there's no bomb here. It's got to be on that damn truck. We called in air support to trail it, so they won't be getting far."

Jackson knew he had made a mistake earlier, but was glad the agent had gotten over it. "Which way did the truck go?"

Murray pointed and explained that the truck must have been pulling out as Matthews' SUV was coming in one street over. "You had to just miss it. But look, there's only one way you can go to get to the highway from here. They gotta take the frontage road west for about a mile or so then cross over the highway to jump on Highway Seventy, east-bound."

Jackson saw a police helicopter fly overhead as the medical chopper was landing in the field by Murray's vehicle. He quickly thanked Murray, and got on the radio. "This is Special Agent Jackson from the Anti-Terrorism Task Force, Washington Bureau.

I want to know where that police helicopter is at all times. Can somebody patch me in?"

The voice of the dispatcher came back quickly, "You're already patched in. Their call sign is Raven Four-Four."

Jackson answered, "Roger, good copy thanks. Break, Raven Four-Four this is T2T agent Jackson. How do you copy? Over."

The radio crackled for a second then the sound of a helicopter and a man speaking over the noise of the rotor wash came on. "This is Raven, I copy Lima Charlie. Over. How 'bout you?"

Jackson had the familiar feeling of being back in the military. "Roger, Raven, I have you loud and clear also. Need the location of the truck. You have a description?"

"Roger, red and white truck. Aluminum trailer. Matter of fact it's on the frontage road heading west. I'm right over it now."

Jackson sat up in his seat. "Good copy, we're on our way. Fast moving black Tahoe. Just got on the frontage road out of the warehouse park."

The Lieutenant in Raven Four-Four turned to look for Jackson and Matthews' vehicle. "I see you guys. You better hurry. Your semi just turned onto the overpass. Looks like he's going to get on Highway 70 East."

"Roger, thanks. Are there any other units in pursuit?"

"There are units heading this way that should be here soon. Not on site yet." Raven Four-Four paused for a second. "Do we need to get the bomb squad in on this? I heard rumor the truck is rigged to explode or something"

Jackson looked at Matthews. "Better get them involved. Not sure what they can do until we stop the truck."

Matthews shrugged like it didn't matter. "Let's just hope the guy doesn't set it off before we stop him."

"Raven Four-Four, be advised this isn't a typical bomb. Not sure what the protocol is on this. I suppose you can call them and have them stand by." Jackson didn't know what to do other than secure the bomb. What if it went off? Shouldn't there be an evacuation now? Who do you evacuate? He decided he had better call Ramsey. "Raven Four-Four, I will have to get back to you on that question."

"Roger, but you better hurry, your truck just hit the entrance ramp to 70." Four-four looked back and could see the black SUV several blocks back, but coming up on the overpass. He looked further down the highway and saw the flashing lights of the police heading their direction also. "Looks like you got a whole squad of mobiles coming this way."

Matthews turned on his warning sirens as he came up on the bridge. He looked to his left and could see the semi moving fast maneuvering into the traffic lanes. He floored the accelerator and took the next turn sliding around the corner onto the overpass. Jackson looked down onto the highway. The patrol cars were nearly at the overpass, lights flashing and sirens wailing. Matthews' Tahoe spun sideways as he moved onto the entrance ramp of the highway. Vehicles on the highway were moving out of the way for the patrol cruisers as they gained on Majid's truck, but as the traffic yielded to the cruisers they moved directly into Matthew's way.

Jackson held fast to the door as Matthews maneuvered down the shoulder, picking up enough speed to overtake the group of police cruisers. He swerved around slowing vehicles and then pulled into the traffic lanes just ahead of the police cruisers, accelerating again to catch up to the semi truck.

Jackson readied his pistol while eyeing the shotgun that was locked in place between the seats. Matthews glanced over as Jackson removed the latches that secured the riot gun. Jackson looked up in time to see Matthews looking at him.

"Hey, this is my first mission with the T2T. I'm just making sure it won't be my last."

CHAPTER 44

FOCUS

RAMSEY and Martin followed Sergeant Conrad as he led them down the corridor. He stopped short of the high security ward and pointed out the set-up. "We have two men stationed here at all times. One at this end of the hall and the other down there." He motioned to the end of the hallway. "I give them a break if we have FBI or CIA here. Since you are the first to come visit, I am going to let them out of here for a bit."

He pulled the handset from his shoulder. "You guys can take a break. I'll cover. Keep your radios on in case I need you, but go get a coffee or something. Bring me one when you come back up." Turning to Ramsey and Martin he asked, "You guys want anything?"

Ramsey was ready to get started. "No thanks." Martin's answer was the same.

Conrad's radio crackled. "Roger, I'll be taking a smoke break. Black on the coffee, right?"

"Roger, thanks." They moved to the center of the hallway and down an adjacent corridor. Conrad stopped just short of Zuqawri's room and pointed to the door. "That's your man's room, gentlemen. I'll be down there if you need me." He pointed to the end of the hall to the door where they had entered.

Leaja bin Masri placed two syringes on the cart. One filled with Pavulon, also known as Pancurium Bromide, the second contained Potassium Chloride. If Zuqawri were unable to walk, he would be of no further use to the Brotherhood and bin Masri would administer the two drugs. Normally death row inmates are given a third drug, Pentothal, and put into a comforting deep sleep before the other two drugs were administered. Bin Masri, however, was not concerned for Zuqawri's comfort.

Nasir al-Din pulled the pistols from the toolbox, inspected the cartridges and installed the silencers. He pulled the upper carriage back and chambered a round in his weapon, did the same for the other one, then placed them and the two syringes in the toolbox and closed the lid. All that was left was to get to the service elevator. This would put them into the restricted area, supposedly bypassing the guards completely.

The only obstacle came in the form of an override key that was required to open the doors on the secure floor. Thanks to the recent code changes in the North American Elevator Code a common key used by firefighters and other emergency crews was readily available. Information about the key and instructions on how to bypass the electronic code panel were also easily obtainable online. Leaja bin Masri thought again about how the Internet would be the undoing of America.

The two men left the maintenance room and walked down the hall to the secure service elevator. As they rounded the corner and entered the elevator lobby, they found it was being guarded by a hospital security guard. The guard was in conversation with another man and both of them were laughing about something using very animated gestures. Both were black and speaking to each other in the slang that bin Masri found very hard to understand. The two men might as well have been speaking Chinese.

The guard, Lawrence Campbell, a bespectacled man with a broad smile, stopped laughing and turned to the two terrorists as if they were interrupting an important meeting. Campbell looked at their badges. "Can I help you?"

Bin Masri moved in front of the cart, noting the other man looking at the oscilloscope and test meters. "No, we are good to go. We need to get up to the sixth floor to look at some equipment."

The taller of the two men reached toward the cart and grabbed the work order folder and opened it, but did not appear to look at its contents. "I was just up there. Nobody said nothing to me about any problems." Leaja saw that he had several teeth missing. The man reeked of tobacco.

Nasir removed the folder from the man's hand. "Do you work on the medical equipment or the facility's? We are here to fix the MRI table, not to change a light bulb in the restroom."

Campbell looked at bin Masri and then at Nasir skeptically. The guard held out his hand and motioned for the folder to be handed over. "I need to take a look at that work order."

Leaja bin Masri gave Nasir a glance of concern. He turned his attention to the guard as Nasir began to comply with his request.

"I have the repair part and the diagnostic equipment. Here, let me show you." Nasir opened the toolbox while holding the file out with his left hand. The lid of the toolbox flopped open as Nasir reached in and grabbed one of the two pistols.

The guard reacted quickly to the threat. He shoved the cart back and reached for his sidearm. The cart slammed against Nasir, knocking him slightly off balance, but still he pulled his weapon first, firing a shot that hit Campbell in his neck. Blood sprayed from the wound. The second man looked terrified as Nasir swung his weapon to the left firing a shot that found its mark dead center of the man's head. The round caused the back of his skull to explode spattering the stainless steel elevator doors with blood. He stood for several seconds before falling to the floor.

Campbell had managed to put enough pressure on his neck with his left hand to recover somewhat. He was going to die in this hallway and all for twelve dollars an hour. That pissed him off. In his last remaining seconds, he fell to his knees and pulled the service revolver from its holster. As he brought the weapon up to aim he saw his friend's head explode. He pulled the trigger firing the first round low into Nasir's stomach.

Nasir felt the impact of the round and the sudden pain as he turned to face the guard. Campbell fired once more shooting Nasir in the face. Nasir fell away from the cart and slid down the wall behind him. The guard next attempted to target bin Masri, but Leaja kicked him full force in the head knocking him to the concrete floor. Campbell was too weak from the loss of blood to recover. Leaja bin Masri looked at the mess around him. He looked at Nasir and Campbell, who was not yet dead, but would be soon.

The blood from the wound on Campbell's neck was no longer gushing, but simply oozing out of the wound. Bin Masri knelt down to pick up Nasir's weapon and noticed the dying black man's eyes following his movements. "You are a brave man," he paused to read the name on the man's nametag, "...Mr. Campbell. May Allah be with you." He turned his attention back to the cart and removed the two syringes and the pistol from the toolbox. Kneeling again, he searched the guard for any keys and found the elevator override key he would need now that Nasir was dead. Leaja bin Masri stepped into the elevator and inserted the key into the override control box and selected the button for the sixth floor.

Alan Ramsey entered Ahmed Zuqawri's room followed by Darin Martin. He stepped up to where Zuqawri was sitting, more than lying, on his bed. Ramsey flashed his credentials and introduced himself. "Dr. Zuqawri, my name is Alan Ramsey and this is agent Martin of the FBI. We need to talk to you about your associations with Hamza Al-Muhajeer and Leaja bin Masri as well as your role in the bombings at the zoo and the attack that we know is about to take place."

Ahmed scowled at the man and quietly spoke, "Why do you wish to confront me about things that are under control of Allah?"

"Dr. Zuqawri, I am not here to present a theological argument or listen to you ranting about your beliefs. Your religious convictions are of no concern to me. My interest is the actions that occur because of them, and right now, I want to talk about what you know about the two men I mentioned and whether or not there is a nuclear weapon in their possession."

"Hamza al-Muhajeer is dead. You do not know what you are talking about."

"Hamza al-Muhajeer was killed by our border patrol agents. He threw away his life for no reason."

Zuqawri spit in Ramsey's direction, "You know nothing of him. He was a hero who martyred himself in a hero's death."

Ramsey did not have the patience to banter. "Tell me about the bomb. What type is it? Where did you get it? Where is the target?"

Zuqawri smiled, "I do not know what you are talking about."

Ramsey slammed his hand down on Zuqawri's injured leg. Zuqawri recoiled and winced in pain as Ramsey put pressure just above the terrorist's damaged ankle. "I'm not here to play games Ahmed! We know you're working with bin Masri and the others. Tell me about the damned bomb!" Ramsey applied a bit more pressure.

Zuqawri grimaced and gurgled a loud moan. "I have not seen a bomb. I haven't even met the man you claim that I am working for." He was not lying.

"Bullshit! You've been in constant contact with him. We've traced your calls. We have your cell phone."

Zuqawri looked up at Ramsey. "You are full of lies."

Ramsey began to unfasten Zuqawri's restraints. "Let's go, get up!"

"What?" Zuqawri resisted. "I can not walk. Can't you see that?"

"I said get up!" Ramsey pulled his pistol and pointed it at Zuqawri's head. "Or would you rather I blow off your other ankle?" He pointed the pistol at the terrorist's left ankle.

Darin Martin saw the look in Ramsey's eyes. He could tell he was not kidding around. He pushed off the wall and stood upright. "Alan, what are you doing?"

"We are going for a walk, is all." Alan hit Zuqawri's bad leg with the pistol causing him to scream in agony. "We're going to walk and talk." He tapped again on the man's leg causing a shooting pain. "Now, get up!"

Zuqawri stumbled off the bed and hobbled on his left foot trying not to put any pressure on his right. "Where is my lawyer? I have rights. I am a citizen of the United States," Zuqawri nearly yelled out, afraid for what was about to happen.

Ramsey pointed to the door. "Sorry, haven't you heard? Terrorists don't have rights. Besides that, you're not a citizen. You're here on visa."

Ramsey shoved Ahmed forward trying to make him move. Zuqawri hopped, desperately trying to avoid any more pain. Ramsey grabbed Zuqawri from behind at the shoulder and placed the pistol at the back of his head. He looked over at Martin. He could see that the agent didn't approve of what he was doing.

Ramsey turned his attention back to Zuqawri. He pushed the pistol against his skull. "Where is Leaja bin Masri?"

Zuqawri looked over his shoulder at Ramsey. "I told you I never met him."

Ramsey pushed him forward, off balance, causing him to place weight on his damaged leg. He wailed and nearly collapsed from the pain as Ramsey pulled him up by his collar allowing him the opportunity to shuffle back to his left foot. The pain was incredible. He felt the flushing flow of blood to his head and tried to hold back his obvious discomfort. He was breathing rapidly as if out of breath. "He...he called me from a warehouse downtown. He said he got my number from al-Muhajeer."

"What kind of bomb is it? Where is the target?" Ramsey pushed forward again. Zuqawri leaned back against the pressure. "I don't know about a bomb!"

"You are lying, Zuqawri. Tell me what kind of device it is and where the target is." He kicked the man's ankle causing him to groan loudly and pull his foot up away from the floor. Zuqawri tried to hop forward to break Ramsey's hold, but Ramsey had control. He shoved the pistol against his skull and yelled again, "What kind of bomb is it?" Ramsey shoved him forward making him take another step onto his bad leg.

The man screamed in agony, "It is nuclear! I do not know how big!"

Ramsey pulled Zuqawri up again, as he managed to get his good leg under him. He hopped in place trying to regain his balance, shaking and breathing hard in unbearable pain. He wasn't sure how much more he could take.

Zuqawri turned towards the hallway, hopping in place and wincing in pain. He saw movement in the hallway through the glass in the door. There was someone standing in the dimly lit corridor. Although they had never met, he recognized the man from a photograph. It was Leaja bin Masri. He must have come to kill him, to send him to Allah and protect him from the infidels.

Zuqawri suddenly felt the strength of his God growing inside him. A sudden of serenity came over him as the pain in his leg disappeared. He spun to face Ramsey grabbing at him to keep balance.

Martin drew his weapon, training it on the terrorist' forehead. Zuqawri saw Martin's weapon come up and held up his left hand.

Ramsey quickly regained his hold and placed the muzzle of his weapon on the terrorist's cheek. "Tell me about the bomb."

Zuqawri spoke calmly. "It is not a dirty bomb. It is designed to have the maximum effect of a nuclear explosion. It will destroy one of your cities and all of the infidels in it."

Before Ramsey could form another word Zuqawri thrust his free hand forward and grabbed Ramsey's pistol hand squeezing it tight. Ramsey tried to pull away, but Zuqawri wrapped his other hand around the top of the pistol, placed his thumb on Ramsey's trigger finger and pulled the nine mil harder into his cheek.

Darin Martin saw what was about to happen and moved forward to stop it, but was not fast enough.

Zuqawri looked at Martin and screamed, "Allah Akbar!" He squeezed Ramsey's finger against the trigger causing the pistol to fire the round through his cheekbone and upward into his brain. The back of his head exploded spattering across the door glass.

As Zuqawri's body fell to the floor Ramsey saw the muzzle blast from the hallway. The glass on the door shattered as Darin Martin spun and hit the ground having just been shot in the shoulder. Ramsey's first thought was that Sergeant Conrad was responding to the shot fired, and was trying to protect the two men, but as the glass fell away to the floor he saw the shooter was Leaja bin Masri.

Leaja's gaze locked on Ramsey and his anger flared. Ramsey brought his weapon up and fired. Bin Masri moved to find cover while firing successive shots at Ramsey.

The bloodied glass shattered inward. Ramsey could see the direction that his new adversary was moving based on the location of the impact of the rounds through the glass. Ramsey returned fire through the shower of flying glass. Neither could see the actual position of the other and fired on reflex through the glass and thin wall panels.

Ramsey slid to a position among the bits of glass at the bottom of the thick wooden door and took an opportunity to reload. He heard bin Masri moving through the broken glass in the hallway. Ramsey settled in at the end of the room's long wall behind the door. He was breathing hard contemplating what to do next.

At the end of the hall Sergeant Conrad pushed the door open slightly and peered through the opening. He could see bin Masri crouched in the hall armed with a pistol. Conrad popped the door open and yelled down the hall, "Police! Drop your weapon and move to the middle of the hallway!"

The answer came in the form of a burst of fire in his direction. The rounds hammered the steel door and framework. Leaja bin Masri expended the rounds in Nasir's pistol and tossed it down. He pulled out his own pistol as he looked at the discarded weapon and thought about his current situation. He had completed what he had come here to do. Ahmed was dead. Whether it was by his hand or Ahmed's own it did not matter. Leaja bin Masri wanted to kill Ramsey more than anything else, but he knew that he must not jeopardize the mission. He had to meet up with the others. He must leave now while he was able.

Conrad took a deep breath and kicked the door open only to see the man running toward the stairwell. He yelled for him to stop and pulled his pistol up to fire only to draw down when Ramsey suddenly yanked open the door to Zuqawri's room and ran down the hall after bin Masri.

Bin Masri slammed through the exit door and down the stairwell nearly jumping down the first full flight of stairs. He careened off the wall and down the second set to the next floor. He heard the door above him clatter against the wall and knew that Ramsey was behind him. Bin Masri used the moment to catch his breath. He needed Ramsey to challenge him. He needed him to be out in the open so he could kill him. He stopped, pointed his pistol back up the stairs and waited.

Ramsey looked over the stair rail carefully only to be greeted with a bullet ricocheting from the steel railing. He moved against the outside wall as he reached the first landing. He could see the light fixture and the exit sign, but was not close enough to the edge of the stairs to see much lower. The door above him opened suddenly. It was Sergeant Conrad. Ramsey motioned for the officer to stop and told him in a few gestures that bin Masri was below him on the next landing.

Leaja bin Masri moved back to the ascending steps and looked for the man a half story above. He saw Ramsey's hand moving and followed the gestures. He was talking to someone, probably the police officer from the hall. Ramsey moved forward a bit too far and bin Masri fired a round in his direction. Ramsey instinctively dove to the floor attempting to take cover on the concrete landing, but instead placed himself in a more vulnerable position, facing the man who had just tried to shoot him. He rolled to his side and scrambled to his feet quickly while firing off his last two rounds. The first nearly hit bin Masri, the second round penetrated the fiberglass light fixture directly over him, shattering the huge tungsten bulb, causing an explosive shower of electrical sparks, hot glass and porcelain. The debris from the light rained down on bin Masri and, for a brief moment, Leaja's concentration was broken. He maneuvered to escape the burning pieces of the tungsten light, wiggling and shaking to dislodge the pieces. Ramsey recovered his footing, tossed his empty pistol aside and, without thinking, jumped to the next level, landing nearly on top of the fugitive terrorist.

Ramsey grabbed the pistol and tried to wrench it from bin Masri's grasp. Bin Masri spun Ramsey around and slammed him hard against the metal railing of the staircase. Ramsey pulled bin Masri's arm over and down, bending it across the railing to force his hand open. The pistol plummeted to the bottom of the stairwell careening from rail to rail. Alan slammed his forehead onto the bridge of bin Masri's nose, smashing the cartilage, and forcing the man to fall back a bit. He got his leg up and pushed the terrorist against the concrete wall.

Leaja bin Masri was bleeding profusely now as he moved toward the stairs. Ramsey kicked his feet out from under him causing him to tumble down several steps. Ramsey lunged at bin Masri, again landing on top of him. He tried to pull bin Masri's arms behind him to secure him, but bin Masri rolled quickly causing them both to fall further down the stairs. Bin Masri's bloody face stared down at Ramsey as his hands closed around Ramsey's throat. Ramsey was on his back with his head against the stair railing, his left arm pinned underneath him. He pushed up with his right hand, found bin Masri's face and grabbed on as if to rip out the man's eye and cheek. Bin Masri growled through clenched teeth and leaned forward, putting most of his weight on Ramsey's throat. Alan could not breathe now and was beginning to feel the frantic need to get free at all cost or die.

He arched up with a quick thrust, but could not break free of bin Masri's grip. Bin Masri's eyes were wide with crazed anger. He spoke, almost growling through the grip that Ramsey still had on his face. "You killed my family. My wife and my sons."

Ramsey could not respond. He flailed his body upward again as his face turned purple. He was afraid he was going to pass out. He felt something under his hand as he moved it a little more trying to free it from the weight of both of them. He could not make out what it was but grabbed it anyway, thinking if he could just free himself, he might be able to use whatever it was as a weapon.

Bin Masri seethed, "You came to my country and you killed my sons. You and your army took them from me, Captain Ramsey." He leaned harder against Alan's neck. "Do you have a wife? Do you have any children, Captain Ramsey? I would kill them as well. First, I will kill you and then I will kill your family!" He was almost smiling, staring into Ramsey's eyes and squeezing Ramsey's neck as hard as he could.

Sergeant Conrad suddenly landed on the platform above the two men with a thud. He pointed his pistol at bin Masri, but didn't shoot. If he fired from his position he risked hitting Ramsey. Conrad yelled to the terrorist, "Hey! Get up, Asshole!"

Bin Masri was startled by the sudden interruption. He pulled away from Ramsey's weakening grip on his face and looked up to see the officer with his pistol drawn. He was almost there. He needed to kill the man below him. No, he would not stop, he thought to himself.

Ramsey used the distraction for one last attempt at freeing himself from bin Masri's grip. He pulled his hand out from under his back and looked at what he was holding. It was a syringe, filled with what he didn't know or care; all he knew was that he had something he could use as a weapon. Ramsey managed to pop off the protective cover and spin the syringe around to hold it tight in his fist.

Conrad screamed, "I said move or I'm going to shoot. Get up, NOW! Last chance!"

Alan Ramsey plunged the needle of the syringe into bin Masri's neck and through his jugular, shoving in the plunger. He yanked it out and with his remaining strength, repeatedly stabbed bin Masri in the neck. He let go, leaving the empty syringe sticking out of the terrorist's neck.

The potassium chloride shot through bin Masri's body. The pain was overwhelming. At first, bin Masri thought he had been stabbed with a knife. Then he felt the burning sensation move through his arm. He released his grip on Ramsey, sat upright and made a sound like a roar. He jumped to his feet and screamed as the pain increased throughout his body. He struggled to control his arms as they began to convulse in muscle spasms. Bin Masri managed to pull the syringe from his neck. He looked at the syringe and then at Ramsey who was gulping in air, then doubled over, grabbing at his arm. He stared at Ramsey as the crushing sensation in his chest enveloped him. Ramsey scrambled to get to his feet.

Alan Ramsey watched as bin Masri fell onto his knees, leaned back and screamed something that neither of the Americans could understand, and then fell, rolling down the stairs to the concrete landing.

Ramsey, beat to hell and looking the part, got shakily to his feet, rubbing his neck. He looked up at Conrad who was relaxing his position at the top of the steps.

Conrad ran down the stairs with his gun still drawn, stopping at the man sprawled on the concrete. He knelt cautiously and pulled bin Masri's eyelids back, then felt for a pulse, "He's dead," he said, holstering his sidearm. Conrad looked at bin Masri and then back at Ramsey with a slightly bewildered look on his face.

Ramsey watched Conrad reach down and pick up the nametag that was sticking half out of bin Masri's shirt pocket. He stood back up and held it out, offering it to Ramsey.

"Here, I think this belongs to you."

Kenneth Wash

CHAPTER 45

THE CHASE

MATTHEWS' Tahoe swung left around the last two cars between his vehicle and Majid's semi. Jackson was trying not to drive from the passenger seat, but found it hard not to press on the imaginary brake and accelerator pedals. Matthews floored the accelerator and moved up and to the left of the semi-trailer.

Majid saw the police vehicles in his mirrors. All of them now lined up directly behind him. The Tahoe was maneuvering to the left in an attempt to pull up beside his vehicle.

Majid veered to the left forcing Matthews to fall back and rethink his maneuver. The semi swung hard, leaning from the sudden change of direction. The rear dual wheels of Majid's Volvo tractor clipped a small sedan causing it to spinout in front of Matthews.

"Watch out!" Jackson couldn't help but yell as he braced for the impact that didn't come. The Tahoe moved right just enough to miss the sedan. The first of the fast moving police cruisers was not as lucky, smashing hard into the spinning vehicle.

Jackson spun back around. "Shit! Man, you need to stay right behind him. Get on his ass, he won't be able to see you then. It's safer there anyway."

Matthews took the suggestion and pulled behind the truck. The Tahoe bucked against the turbulence as it moved closer to the trailer. Suddenly the Tahoe lurched forward as it was locked into the semi-truck's draft. Matthews' SUV came within a foot of the back of the trailer as Jackson slammed his foot down again on the imaginary brake. "Damn, I didn't mean that close!"

Majid saw the truck disappear behind him. He looked in his right mirror then back to the left and saw only the police cruisers. Above him was a police helicopter. The exit for Highway 70 that would take him across the river into Illinois was just on the other side of the next overpass. He had to make a decision. Given his current circumstances there was no way he would make it to Washington, D.C. with the bomb. He searched the cab for his cell phone and found it on the floor near the control box for the bomb.

He would just have to detonate the bomb here, in this city. It wouldn't destroy the infidel government, but it surely would have a profound effect on the population of the country.

He saw the huge Gateway Arch on his left and decided this was the spot. Although it wasn't as well known as the monuments and buildings of Washington, D.C., it was recognized nationally. He wasn't sure what it represented, but it was a sufficient enough target, in a sufficient enough city, to kill a sufficient amount of infidels, he thought. He slammed on the brakes and pulled the wheel hard to the left. The 18 wheels of the truck stopped turning, dragging the protesting tires in a long skidding stop on the pavement leaving the truck suddenly blocking three lanes of traffic.

The SUV with Paul Jackson and Matthews was directly behind the truck when its brakes locked up. The howl of the tortured rubber against the pavement echoed loudly under the overpass. Matthews' eyes went wide at the sight of the semi slowing so suddenly. Jackson barely had time to react when Matthews instinctively slammed his brakes to the floor. He was flung against the restraint of the seatbelt and could feel the Tahoe's antilock brakes grind and chatter as the brakes worked against the momentum of the 6,000-pound truck.

The semi-trailer swung out of its position directly in front of Matthews and the Tahoe moved past it as Matthews tried to regain control of the situation. The Tahoe impacted the left rear outer tire on the semi-trailer, smashing the bumper and fender into the tire, and did what the anti-lock brakes were trying to do, only much faster. Paul Jackson felt the truck lift into the air and begin to spin. For the briefest of seconds, he wondered why his airbag had not deployed as the SUV spun around backward and slammed against the still moving trailer.

Gary Johnson was in the lead police cruiser coming up fast on the two trucks when he saw what was happening and also tried to stop. He could not react fast enough to keep from hitting the Tahoe.

Paul Jackson was disoriented. He now found himself facing the opposite direction. He looked over at Matthews who was bleeding, and hopefully only unconscious, and then turned back to see the flashing lights and the front of Gary Johnson's cruiser smash against his vehicle. The explosion of the airbag and the sudden pressure of the seatbelt told Jackson that he had just been nailed hard. The airbag deflated nearly as fast as it inflated and in just enough time for Jackson to see the third and last cruiser skid to a stop behind the first.

As Alan Ramsey emerged from the stairwell his cell phone buzzed. He was amazed that it still worked after his tumble down the stairs and subsequent thrashing. He was still breathing somewhat irregularly as he answered. Ramsey set the phone on speaker. He was just too tired to even hold the phone to his ear at the moment.

"What's your status, Alan?" Gabe Anderson said without any greeting.

"Zuqawri is dead, bin Masri just tried to kill me and now he's dead and Jackson and some of the local CIA and police are on their way to locate the bomb. We have the location at a warehouse down in the riverfront district here. I haven't had any updates for about an hour."

Anderson sounded tired. "Well, evidently the bomb is on a truck trying to head out of the city. Your man Jackson has been in contact with one of the helicopter patrols and is very involved in the chase."

Sergeant Conrad interrupted, "I just had a call about that. They have the truck stopped on the highway downtown. There's been quite a pile-up. Your agent's vehicle is involved. I don't have a status on injuries yet, but told them to keep me posted."

Ramsey looked worried for the first time since this whole thing began.

Gabe Anderson continued, "Look Alan, the Governor of Missouri has just asked for permission to order an air strike on that truck in the event that we can't get hold of the bomb and secure it. He figures it would be better to have a dirty bomb to clean up after than a destroyed city. I can't say that I disagree."

Ramsey thought about that. "I would do the same thing. What kind of time have we got?"

"Well, I don't know. The President will have to approve this one. That could take some time." Anderson looked at his notes. "According to the request they are in the process of arming the Air National Guard's F22s out of Whiteman Air Force Base. Sounds like they are putting two in the air just in case. Those planes are supposed to be fast as hell. My guess is they are there in twenty to thirty minutes once they get the go."

Ramsey looked at Sergeant Conrad and Dan Martin, standing next to him, bandaged, but alive. He leaned back on the table. "Ok, Gabe, I'm heading that way to see what I can do to help. I'll report to you when I get there."

"Alright then, call me when you get on site. Good luck, and be careful." Gabe Anderson didn't wait for a reply. Ramsey couldn't help but laugh at what his boss had said. Conrad and Martin looked at him strangely.

"What? You don't find it a bit humorous that we are getting ready to go to the location of a possible nuclear bomb and my boss just told me to be careful?"

The remark got a chuckle out of Conrad. Martin, however, didn't smile. "I won't be going with you. I can't do anything with this busted up shoulder."

Ramsey patted the man's good shoulder. "That's ok, Darin. You were a tremendous help. Thanks for everything."

Ramsey turned to Conrad. "You got a car with a siren and lights?"

"I do. It's parked out back."

Ramsey tucked in his shirt and scraped a hand through his hair trying to look somewhat professional. "Good, I need a ride to that truck and I don't have much time."

Gary Johnson shook off the accident and stepped out of his vehicle taking cover behind the door. The officer in the last cruiser did the same. Johnson assessed their situation and quickly called in his status.

Jackson watched the two men move into position. He worked to open his door and managed with some pressure to force the door open past the smashed fender. He saw Matthews move and hoped he was going to be ok. There was nothing he could do at the moment. He stepped from the vehicle turning to look at the cab of the truck through the vapors of the steaming radiator.

Majid saw Jackson in his rear view mirror. Jackson's pistol hung at his side. He had to work fast. He pulled open the phone and began to chant to his God as he pressed the numbers on the keypad. "Alluha Akubar, Alluha Akubar." With each button, he called to Allah for help for what he was about to do.

Jackson, still reeling, saw Majid in the mirror of the truck. Majid looked up. He was sweating and speaking words that Jackson could not hear, but watching him Jackson made out the word "ALLAH" and couldn't help but feel frightened. He yelled back to Gary Johnson, "Damn! I think he's going to set off the bomb!" With that Jackson pulled his weapon up and fired.

Majid heard the shot and winced as the round sped through the door glass opening and then the windshield. Jackson fired twice more causing Majid to throw himself down to the floor.

Jackson moved closer, yelling at the man inside, "Get the hell out the truck!" Majid couldn't concentrate and had to start over with the numbers. He pulled his weapon up and fired back at Jackson without aiming. Jackson ducked as the rounds flew wildly into the asphalt and the back of his truck. Majid looked at the phone and back to the mirror when the mirror suddenly shattered.

Gary Johnson moved wide around the side of Jackson's SUV near the sedan that was stuck between the tractor and the guardrail. Jackson cursed at the loss of the mirror. He couldn't see Majid at all now.

Johnson burned off a few more rounds through the door of the truck. The first of the volley managed to penetrate the door skin and strike the terrorist's left hand, shattering the bones and causing the phone to fall to the floor in two pieces.

In terrible pain Majid screamed Allah's name and cursed the Americans. Pulling up his pistol and resting his shaking bloody left hand under his right, Majid got up from the floor of the truck and took aim at the police officer that had just tried to kill him.

Gary Johnson had only a brief instant to see the truck driver. Majid fired several rounds with a dead aim. Jackson saw Johnson's chest explode in a spray of blood and flesh as the officer tumbled backward and fell across the hood of a sedan. The driver of the sedan was screaming, but could not be heard through the closed windows of her vehicle as the officer slid off the hood and down to the ground.

Jackson holstered his weapon and jumped up on the rear bumper of his SUV and then onto the roof. He mustered all of his energy and threw himself upward toward the top of the semi-trailer. He managed to pull himself up and stood, crouching between the top of the trailer and the underside of the overpass and ran toward the cab of the truck, drawing his weapon as he ran. He jumped from the trailer to the sleeper cab then onto the roof of the tractor. Jackson emptied his magazine, firing through the roof of the cab. When his magazine was empty he jumped back to the sleeper and reloaded.

Majid had just opened the control box for the manual over-ride when the nine-Millimeter rounds from Jackson's pistol burst through the roof of the tractor. Majid felt the burn in his back then his neck and shoulder. Blood from his wounds sprayed across the control box. He could barely move his right arm. Wiping the screen with his bloody left hand he tried to set the control to manual so he could enter the code to set the timer. He flipped the cover on the override switch. The six-inch LED touch screen came to life. The cursor began flashing, prompting Majid to place the first number of the code in place.

Jackson was shaking as he locked the last of his magazines into the butt of the pistol. Majid was praying loudly now, sobbing, gasping for breath, asking Allah to give him the strength to complete his task. Jackson moved back to the cab roof. He had to finish this. He grabbed the truck's air horns and swung himself over the side of the cab, firing blindly into the cab as he slid off the roof, then ducked below the open door window, after landing on the fuel tank step.

Jackson pressed himself against the cowl of the truck and assessed his present situation. Suddenly the sound of the traffic and the city itself seemed incredibly loud. Traffic was backed up far as he could see. The westbound lanes of traffic were slowing as drivers rubbernecked the scene. Horns honked and people yelled at each other. Many drivers had gotten out of their vehicles and were walking toward the semi, cell phones to their ears. A few stopped as they noticed Jackson crouched on the fuel tank with his weapon drawn. Others continued to move cautiously forward, curious about what was happening.

Jackson didn't hear any sounds from inside the truck. He peered through the window opening and saw the terrorist lying face down between the seats. He saw no movement and assumed the man was dead. Jackson noted the number of holes in the ceiling of the truck. There was no way the terrorist had survived that. Blood was pooled on the floorboard.

Jackson reached over, grabbed the door handle and opened the door, slowly entering the cab. He leaned over the driver's seat and pushed the man with his pistol. When there was no movement he rolled him against the seat and reached down to feel for a pulse at his neck. Jackson felt a large open wound as he fumbled around for the pulse that he would not find.

The flashing lights of an LED screen caught Jackson's attention. He holstered his weapon and pulled the control box toward himself wiping at it with his fingers. The image cleared enough for the words on the screen to become legible. A single word flashed in red LED script: ACTIVATED. Jackson rolled the box around trying to figure out if there was a way to stop it. In the corner of the screen a small timer ticked. The clock read four hours, forty-four minutes and ten seconds. Jackson watched as the seconds ticked down and the timer changed to four hours and forty-three minutes.

The only thing he could think to do was call Alan Ramsey.

CHAPTER 46

GETTING THE HELL OUT OF DODGE

ALAN RAMSEY'S phone buzzed in his pocket. He saw it was Paul Jackson as he flipped up the cover, relieved to hear from his new partner.

"Yeah, Paul. What have you got?"

Paul Jackson looked around before speaking. "What have I got? Well, I got a highway that is completely shut down, one dead cop, one dead terrorist, and a nuclear bomb in a jack-knifed rig that is activated and currently ticking away the last five hours of my life, and probably yours too, depending where you are and how big this thing is. How 'bout you? Things as good as this at your end?"

Ramsey decided that he might as well break a bit more bad news. "You may not have to worry about the nuke," he said rather nonchalantly.

Jackson could hardly hear Ramsey over the sound of the traffic and sirens. "I'm sorry, did you say don't worry about the nuke? How's that?"

"Because there is probably going to be an air strike on the truck. You'll be killed by conventional weapons."

Jackson made a face that Ramsey couldn't see. "Oh, well, that is good news then. What are we doing here, Mr. Ramsey? What's the next move?"

Ramsey asked, "Are you sure it's armed?"

Paul described the control box and what was happening. "It looks just like in the movies. Just missing the soundtrack to set the mood. I'm pretty sure it's going to blow up in less than five hours."

Ramsey thought for a moment. "Paul, do you know how to drive a truck like that?"

"Ain't no different than an M920. Maybe the shifting is different, but yeah, I can drive it." Paul looked at the truck and began to figure out how to get it out of its jack-knifed condition.

"If I can get it unstuck, I can drive it, but I'm leaving the dead guy here. I ain't driving with a dead terrorist laying on the floorboard."

Now it was Alan's turn to make a face. "Whatever, just get in the truck and move it away from there. Head away from the city, find some open area where the EOD teams can get in there and shut that thing down."

Conrad was listening to the conversation. "Tell him to get across the river. Stay on Highway 64 East. There is farmland about forty minutes to an hour away. More if he drives farther. Scott Air Force Base is out there too. They'll have EOD teams there."

Ramsey repeated the directions nearly verbatim to Paul. He heard the truck fire up on the other end. Paul spoke loudly to compensate for the noise of the diesel engine, "Got it, 64 East." For a few seconds there was only the sound of the diesel truck.

"Alan, you think that the EOD teams can disable this thing?" He picked up the control box and rolled it in his hands again. Suddenly the display went blank.

"Oh shit!"

"What's going on, Paul?"

Paul shook the box. "I think I just broke the timer thing. It just went blank. Nothing on it now except a power light or something. Other than that it's just a dark screen." He turned the mechanism over and looked at the wires going into the metal box. There was a scar in the metal case near the opening. Two of the wires in the loom were nearly cut in two. The strands of wire were touching. Jackson pulled the two wires apart and could see a faint spark indicating the current flowing through it. The screen came back to life.

"Got it back on. Must have gotten hit by one of the bullets. Oh, hell no!"

Ramsey heard Paul Jackson's exclamation. "What is it, Paul. What's wrong?"

Paul couldn't believe this. Somehow the timer had lost two hours. "We got a problem here. This thing says we have less than three hours now. It's reading two-twenty five and still counting down."

"Look Paul, you have to get that truck moving. Get to Scott Air Base. We will get the EOD teams to you possibly before you get there. Otherwise they will be waiting at the Base." Ramsey looked at the map. "There is a rest stop about midway. We will try to link up with you there."

Jackson was working on straightening the truck out of its jack-knifed position. He looked at the shattered mirror and saw movement back at the SUV. He had forgotten about Agent Matthews who appeared to be conscious now and was being helped from the SUV.

"Hey, Alan, just want you to know, Matthews really did a great job today. Make sure somebody knows. He got beat up pretty bad in the accident, but it looks like he's going to be OK."

Ramsey listened to the sound of the truck shifting gears. "I'll let them know, Paul. Sounds like you're on your way. Good luck. See you soon."

"Yeah, hopefully not for the last time." Paul hung up his phone.

Ramsey closed his phone as the Black Hawk helicopter came into view. The aircraft slowed to a hover then moved to Ramsey's right to land in an open area in the cloverleaf entrance of the highway.

"Sergeant Conrad, I can't thank you enough. Call me if you want to do something in the CIA or FBI. I'll write you a good reference," Ramsey said as he turned to shake the officer's hand.

Conrad smiled, "Thank you sir, I might just do that." Ramsey ran across two lanes of slow moving traffic now slowing even more to get a view of the helicopter.

The side door opened and a man grabbed Ramsey's hand and pulled him into the aircraft. "You Ramsey?" the man yelled as he handed him a headset. Ramsey shook his head yes as he placed the headset on, effectively stopping the noise around him.

"Alan Ramsey. You guys the EOD team?"

The man settled back in his seat, adjusting his microphone. "Yeah, that's us. I'm Captain Wright and these are the two nuke specialists, Master Sergeant Gordon and Captain Wagner."

Ramsey nodded to the two men. The larger of the two leaned forward thrusting his huge hand toward Ramsey. He took the hand and shook it marveling at the huge appendage.

"You know bombs are much smaller these days. You actually work on them with these?"

Jody Gordon found the remarks about the size of his hands funny and laughed, "I just hold them, sir, the Captains do all the work. I think they just bring me along as a human shield." He laughed again and sat back against the seat. Ramsey realized the man must be fifty years old and had to be at least six foot four with very relaxed mannerisms. Alan liked that. The man to his right, Captain Wagner, just smiled and rolled his eyes.

The helicopter lifted and headed east toward downtown St. Louis. Ramsey saw the skyline of the city from a much different angle than he had coming in. The city of St. Louis was a sprawling metropolis. The Arch was a magnificent structure, taller than any other building. The sun was lowering to the horizon and the deep yellow glow had begun to paint the glistening stainless steel.

As far as Alan could see there were businesses and homes spreading from the center for miles in every direction. If this bomb went off thousands of lives could be in jeopardy. Directly below them was the highway. Ramsey could see the effect that Paul had had on the local traffic situation. He looked in the direction of the Arch and realized that all eastbound traffic lanes were at a standstill. The chopper climbed to about two thousand feet and moved toward the river, following the highway.

It appeared that there were only a few bridges that allowed traffic to cross the Mississippi River into Illinois. The older bridges appeared to have too few lanes to move traffic effectively. On the newest span at least three highways merged to share the corridor and almost all of the traffic was moving east at the moment. Or, at least the vehicles were pointed that direction. Implying that the traffic was moving at all would be lying, Ramsey thought.

Suddenly the intercom crackled and came to life. "Sir, I believe that's your truck down there." The Captain pointed down and to his right.

Ramsey looked down to see the bullet-riddled top of a red and white semi and its trailer moving along the shoulder. Creeping along the entrance ramp and up onto the bridge, Paul was moving, sort of.

Paul Jackson maneuvered the truck close to the concrete median wall. He could hear the tires dragging against the concrete even over the blaring of the horns coming from the vehicles around him that were trying to move out of his way.

He pulled the lanyard to blare the air horns at the person whose car he was about to push out of his way. "Get the hell over!" he yelled, but not loud enough to compete with the horns. A Toyota squeezed over and Jackson moved carefully past, looking in his mirror and dragging tires against the median.

His phone rang. Paul pushed the answer button on his headset and immediately began complaining about his situation.

"These people are pissing me off. I'm thinking I could park this truck right now and just blow them up for spite."

"Paul, stay calm. There's not a lot of room to maneuver on that bridge. Once you get across you'll be fine. We've got plenty of time." Ramsey tried to be positive.

"Officers from Illinois and Missouri are trying to get to you to help clear the path. The Illinois State Patrol is diverting cars from the highway to get you off the bridge, but the first exit is a single lane and a mile away." Ramsey could see the flashing lights in the distance.

Paul moved forward laying on the horn. He contacted the bumper of a pick up truck that did not want to give him any room. He could see the driver's face in the mirror and gestured for him to move over. The driver stared back, but didn't move.

Jackson butted the bumper of the truck again and blared the horn. The man in the pick up threw the vehicle in park and got out yelling at Paul. "What the hell is wrong with you, Asshole?"

Jackson wanted to show the man some sort of official badge, but didn't yet have one. "I just need you to get out of the way. Trust me when I say it's important for all of us. So please, just move to the left."

The man, who was easily over six feet tall and well built, flipped his hands over, raised both middle fingers and thrust them upward to give Jackson his answer.

Jackson put some pressure on the bumper of the pick-up. "Sir, if you don't move your truck I will have no recourse other than to move it for you. This is a matter of national security. You have to believe me."

"What, are you the President or something? Kiss my ass!" He moved toward the truck and began to climb onto the step when Jackson popped the door open hard striking the man and knocking him backward.

The man recovered quickly and began to charge. Jackson pointed his pistol at him and barked, "Now look, Jerk, get your piece of shit out of my way! I don't have time for this crap!"

The helicopter hovered over the bridge. Ramsey could see that Paul was in trouble. Ramsey keyed his mike, "Get us down there, next to the bridge as close as you can."

Paul kept his weapon pointed at the driver of the pick-up. He pushed the truck a little.

"Move the truck or I'll move it for you, and it won't be pretty!"

The driver stared upward as the helicopter fell to the height of the bridge. He stood, jaw agape. The pilot spoke over the loudspeaker startling the man and Paul Jackson as well.

"Please move your vehicles to allow the semi to pass on your right."

The pilot repeated the same words. The driver of the pick-up looked at the helicopter and then around him. He could see other vehicles trying to comply and moving to the left. He looked up at Jackson.

Paul Jackson had a broad smile and a relaxed look on his face. He motioned to the truck with his weapon. "Well, you gonna move that thing or am I?" He nudged it a bit more, this time breaking the tail light lens.

"Asshole." With that the man stormed back to his truck and accelerated out of Jackson's way. As the semi rolled by he flipped Jackson off again.

Jackson wanted to fire one round into the guy's radiator, but knew better. He waved with the pistol instead. He got back on his phone. "You still there?"

"Yeah. You OK?" Ramsey asked.

"Yes. Thanks for coming down and helping out." Paul looked to his right. He could see Ramsey through the helicopter's open door. "It's good to see you, Mr. Ramsey." Alan gave him a look and Jackson smiled. "Who you got with you in there?"

"EOD guys. They're ready to get to work. Waiting on you to get somewhere so they can get started."

"Yeah, well they could have jumped over here a few minutes ago when I was stopped." Paul thought about what he had just said. "Hey, do they have the highway clear up ahead yet?"

Ramsey looked ahead. "Think so. Why?"

Paul Jackson thought for a second. "I'm thinking we could get them an early start if they don't mind riding in the back of a moving truck."

Ramsey looked past the bridge and down the highway a short distance. "There is a rest stop about a mile past the bridge."

"I'll meet you there, and we'll get the back opened up."

"Sounds like a plan, Paul. Is it locked?"

Paul looked at the keys in the ignition and then around the blood spattered cabin.

"If it is, I don't have a key. I'm guessing that the only way they were going to let the bomb out of the truck was under its own power. That or the dead guy has them. I left him back at the overpass."

"That's OK, we can get it open. I'll meet you in about five minutes."

Paul thought about what Ramsey had just said. Yesterday five minutes was nothing. Now, though, five minutes was everything. He decided he should call his wife and selected Ming-Lee's number from his list.

The phone rang once before she picked up. "Hello, Baby, I be missing you much."

A sudden wave of comfort enveloped him. His wife's voice, with her broken English, was distinct. The sound of it struck home like an arrow finding its mark.

"Hello, Ming. I miss you, too." He didn't have to worry about her thinking anything was wrong. He was very relaxed now.

"You work too hard. You go away too much time. When you coming home?" Ming-Lee was never very comfortable being left by herself.

Paul remembered thinking that it was good there were no cell phones when he'd been in Korea or he would have been getting calls from her every five minutes during training exercises. "Soon. I'll be home soon. We are about to wrap this up. We caught all the bad guys and now we..." he stopped to think, "...We have to do a lot of paperwork. Probably another day or two, then I'll be home. Ming, I love you. Just want you to know that. I love you and I miss you."

"I know you do. You tell me all a time. I love you, too. You come home now."

Jackson looked ahead to see the helicopter landing on the roadway. He only had about a minute to talk. Again the thought of time entered his mind. He chuckled at what she said. "I can't come home right now, but soon..."

She interrupted. "St. Louis is not safe. Those bad guys are there. You come home now."

Jackson cringed. She must have seen the news reports. He hadn't thought about that. "Baby, I can't. Give me a couple more days. Besides I'm not in St. Louis any more. I'm in Illinois. It's much safer in Illinois," he lied.

"Good. No St. Louis. Illinois okay. You stay two days more, then you come home. I don't think I like this new job of yours. You too far away too long." She was smiling, but Paul didn't see it.

"We'll talk about it when I get home. Love you, girl." A state patrol officer was motioning for him to pull out of traffic and straight toward the helicopter. He had to get off the phone.

"I have to go. Miss you. See you soon."

"Okay. Can't wait. See you. Love you, too. Bye." Paul wondered if that was the last time he would hear her voice.

Ramsey unbuckled and stepped down to the asphalt below. Captain Wright jumped down next to him. He was a burly man with a large head and a smile that matched in scale. "It always feels good to get out of one of those things and back on the ground."

Ramsey acknowledged his dislike of the birds. "Too noisy for me." He looked up to see the semi pulling into the parking lot. The area was roped off. His would be the only rig on the lot.

Master Sergeant Gordon stepped down with a tool bag and squeezed between the two men. "Sc'uze me, gentlemen," he said in a deep voice loud enough to be heard over the helicopter. Jodie Gordon looked around at the traffic circling through the road of the rest stop.

Captain Wagner bumped the man into motion. "C'mon, let's see what we got in that truck."

Paul Jackson stepped down, stretched and walked to the rear of the trailer. It was locked. The keys were probably in the pocket of the dead driver back on the other side of the Mississippi. He lifted the lock and let it fall back again.

"Sc'uze me, sir."

Paul turned to see Master Sergeant Gordon with a pair of bolt cutters and sidestepped out of his way. "Ah, I see you brought the master key."

Gordon rolled his eyes. "Gee, never heard that before." The large man stepped forward, placed the jaws in place and with what looked like an effortless move, snapped the lock's bale on the first attempt. He removed the lock and carefully rolled the locking lever over to the right. Slowly he inched up the door inspecting for trip wires or switches that might have been set as a booby trap. When he was sure it was safe, he let the spring-loaded door lift itself to full height controlling the speed with the strap. Sunlight blasted through the opaque fiberglass top of the semi trailer illuminating the contents.

Less than half of the trailer was filled with cargo. "Ok, I guess I'll get up in there and see what I can find. You fellas want to check out that controller and see what you think?" He paused for a second and then continued as the two captains began to walk away. "Uh...remember that I'm back here, in case you feel like pushing a bunch of buttons or something." He began to weave through the boxes examining them for any signs of wiring or antennae that would indicate the ability to receive a signal.

Gordon moved to the front of the trailer. He had climbed over several crates and moved a few boxes when he felt something under his foot. Looking down he found a wiring conduit and saw that it went through the forward wall of the trailer. He turned towards a large crate and followed the corrugated plastic conduit to a skid against the far left of the trailer. He examined the item on the skid and at first was not exactly sure he was looking at the bomb. He had installed a few transmissions in his day so he knew that was what he was looking at, but had never seen one quite that large. He knelt down to examine the metal tag that was riveted to the aluminum housing. The General Motors logo and the words Allison confirmed his thoughts. He lifted the small walkie-talkie from his belt.

"I think I found it. You're not going to believe it, but it looks like they stuffed it into a transmission case. A big transmission for a truck, I guess. If it wasn't for the wiring loom I would have never found it."

Captain Wagner answered, "We are looking at the controller here. Is there a plug or a connector at your end?"

The radio crackled for a second then the Master Sergeant came back. "Nope. Looks like it goes into an electrical box mounted on the transmission case. Going to have to open it up to see what we got."

Ramsey and Paul Jackson stood on the ground outside the driver's door. Ramsey checked his watch. "We have to keep the truck moving."

As if the two men had heard what he said, Captains Wright and Wagner began backing out of the truck cab. Wright jumped down from the top step and turned to Jackson and Ramsey.

"We're ready to go. Everything has to be done from inside the trailer. Once we get back there you can close the door and move out." He pulled a small two-way radio from his side and held it out to Ramsey.

"Give this to your driver. It's the only frequency that will be allowed through our signal jammer, so that's the only way we can talk to the driver of the truck."

Captain Wagner followed. He looked toward Paul Jackson. "Drive safely," was all he said as he moved toward the back of the truck with the tool bag in hand.

Paul Jackson looked at his watch. "We have about two hours left. How far is it to the Air Force Base?" He pulled the walkie-talkie from Ramsey's hand.

"Hey! What are you doing? I can get someone else to drive that truck. You don't have to do it."

"Are they here right now? Cause, I don't see nobody looking like a truck driver." Jackson replied as he got up into the Volvo tractor.

Ramsey looked around. "No, but I can get someone here in a couple minutes."

Paul immediately shot back, "We don't have a couple minutes to waste. Besides, why should this be someone else's job? I killed the driver. It's my truck. I can handle it."

Ramsey stared up at Jackson as he closed the door and pulled the seatbelt over his shoulder to latch it. Somehow wearing a seatbelt in this situation seemed pointless.

"OK, then. Scott Air Base is about forty minutes east of here. Stay on 64. The Illinois State Patrol is trying to get a lockdown on the highway. There's still going to be some traffic, but you'll have an escort so you can haul ass. I'll be waiting for you there."

CHAPTER 47

GOING HOT

COLONEL JECKLIN read through the Operations Order again not really believing what he was reading. As he scanned through the information he picked up the phone and pressed the programmed speed dial for his Commander.

General Atkinson picked up on the first ring. "I was just about to call you, Pete."

Peter Jecklin put down the OPORDER. "This is for real then? Not a training exercise?"

Atkinson sighed, "Yeah Pete, I'm afraid so. We just got confirmation that the bomb is on the truck. EOD teams confirmed it and are working on disarming it now."

"Do they think they can stop it? I mean, anybody give any odds, good or bad?"

"Your guess is as good as mine. We have to be ready regardless. Scramble two of your fighters, armed with whatever missiles they need to get the job done and send them in hot. Looks like we may not have a choice but to destroy the truck and the bomb together."

Jecklin had already gotten the weapons teams together and the pilots had been notified. "It's all in play as we speak, sir. As soon as we get the missiles mounted, we should be ready to go."

"Have you briefed the pilots yet?"

"No sir, I'm heading there now. They aren't going to like the mission. Can't say that I wouldn't feel the same," Jecklin offered.

"Look Pete, in a little over two hours that bomb is going to detonate. If it does there will be thousands of deaths. We just don't have time for any massive evacuation. The best we can hope to accomplish is to get people off the airbase. That's being done as we speak. Hopefully they will be clear before you have to call it. We are evacuating families first."

The General had been a pilot and knew what it meant to drop ordnance on your own people. "Pete, your pilots have to understand that there is no good choice here. It's a lesser of the two evils issue. If EOD can't disable it it's our job to destroy it. Better to have a dirty bomb to clean up after than a full nuke detonation. Now, get your pilots up to speed. If they can't handle it get someone who can. Just get those birds in the air."

"Roger, Sir."

With that the General hung up the phone and Jecklin looked out the window to the building across the road where he could see the two pilots waiting for him. He wouldn't have any problems once they knew the specifics. Spence and Isom were two of the best airmen he had ever met. They worked great together and could always be counted on to come through in a pinch.

He looked up at the cloudless sky. There was no getting out of this one. The weather was perfect.

CHAPTER 48

WILD RIDE

CAPTAIN WAGNER pried off the rectangular cover and pulled the group of wires loose from within the three by five inch plastic box. A small circuit board with a single light emitting diode pulled free from a Velcro mounting.

Captain Wright looked over his shoulder. "What do you suppose that does?"

Wagner flipped the board over, peeled away the self sticking Velcro pad and read the information printed on the back. "Well, it has a frequency and an FCC stamp. I believe it's a cell phone signal receiver. These guys weren't messing around. A timer in the cab, a cell receiver in the trailer, looks like they were prepared for any possible scenario to set it off."

Derrick Wright looked up at the hulking figure of the Master Sergeant. "You got the DUKE turned on, right?"

He was referring to the Guardian, a signal-jamming device that Gordon was wearing. The name DUKE was a just a common catchword that included any IED defeating electronic counter-measure equipment. Unlike the vehicle mounted systems that proved so successful in Iraq and Afghanistan, Gordon's device looked like a backpack radio, but sent multiple channel broadcast to kill any cell or radio signal that was not authorized by its processor, thus rendering Improvised Explosive Device detonators inoperative.

"Sir, it's been on since we got off the helicopter. I don't take any chances. You should know that by now." Gordon wasn't smiling this time.

"Roger. Just checking. Thanks," Wright replied.

With that information Captain Wagner pulled his Gerber from its pouch on his belt, configured the pliers, and reached into the center of the electronics soldered to the board, yanking a small component from the green, printed surface. He peered closely at the quarter inch device. The number stamping on it told him the origin of the part. Although he would look it up to be sure, it appeared to be a Chinese copy of a Motorola component. Without that part the board would not be capable of receiving any signal.

"Hopefully that just disabled the cell phone initiator, but I need to be sure they haven't added a redundant system to this. We'll know that once we get in the case." He moved the remaining wires around the box and clipped the wires leading to the circuit board.

"Bad news. The control box in the truck's cab isn't the detonator. It's just a programming unit." He lifted the disconnected end of a CAT-5E cable and showed it to Wright.

"I pulled the feed coming from the cab, but the timer is still counting down. The detonator has to be inside the transmission case."

"Shit. That means we can't stop it without getting in the case." He made a face. "Let's drill it and take a sample. Make sure it's not leaking before we pop it open." He reached for the toolbox to pick up the drill when the truck suddenly swerved hard to one side.

The blue Chevrolet Trail-Blazer came up fast on the tail of the police escort. There hadn't been sufficient time to close all access ramps to the highway and Mamud-Hassan found his way to an unguarded entrance by following State Street, the main thoroughfare through downtown East St. Louis, Illinois, a small blighted city on the opposite banks of the river from St. Louis, Missouri.

Barry Mitchell, the driver of the Missouri State Patrol police cruiser saw the vehicle closing in, but thought it was one of their vehicles. He turned to his partner. "Who the hell is that?" His partner turned to look at the SUV as it pulled alongside.

Mahmud lowered the tinted passenger window, lifted the AK-47 from the seat next to him and aimed it at the cruiser. The rounds from the AK-47 blasted through the door glass and then through flesh and bone.

Jackson saw what had just happened and watched in his rear view mirror as the Crown Victoria careened across the highway, went airborne and slammed into the low rise bluffs along the outer road, flipping over to rest on its crushed roof.

The SUV again picked up speed and moved toward the semi-trailer. Jackson had no idea who was driving the SUV and didn't care. He waited, and then veered sharply to the left when the SUV was about even with the trailer's rear wheels. The sudden maneuver caused Mahmud to steer the Trailblazer away from the trailer into the grass median. The Trailblazer slid sideways, fishtailing back and forth, as the driver frantically tried to maintain control so as not to get tangled in the cables that made up the highway's crossover prevention system.

The two-way at Jackson's side suddenly came to life. It was Captain Wright. "What the hell is going on up there?"

Paul grabbed the radio keeping both eyes on his mirror, but glancing toward the Illinois State Patrol car that was too far ahead. "We got company!" Jackson screamed into the radio. "Some son of a bitch just shot up our tail security and is moving up on my ass fast!"

Mahmud maneuvered the SUV back onto the roadway and was closing in again. He was the only hope for the completion of the mission and was determined not to fail in either recovering the bomb, or detonating it. Too many had died to get this far. With traffic at a minimum and only a police escort for security, this was his chance. He slammed down on the accelerator and moved toward the back of the truck.

Jackson swerved suddenly into the terrorist's path to block the SUV. Mahmud reacted, moving to the right, in an attempt to come up the passenger side of the truck. Jackson accelerated and shot to his right. He clipped the front of the Trailblazer forcing it against the brown painted guardrail. Sparks and pieces of plastic and metal flew into the air as the right front fender of the SUV disintegrated. Mahmud-Hassan tried to regain control, but spun out on the roadway.

Jackson keyed the radio and yelled into the truck's handset, "We are under attack! I say again, we are being shot at and chased by a blue Chevy Truck! Our tail security is out of commission! Ramsey, where the hell are you?"

Sergeant Jacobs was in the lead police cruiser. He had made several attempts to call in his mile marker report, but got no response. He tried to reach Jackson and the St. Louis County police rear escort, also with no luck. He threw the handset down to the floor. "Piece of shit," he said in disgust. He wrestled his cell phone from the holder on his belt, pressed the contact number, held the phone to his ear and looked back at Jackson's truck. He saw the blue Trailblazer attempt to pass Jackson's rig when the Volvo tractor suddenly lurched to the left causing the SUV to nearly crash into the crossover cables. "What the hell...?" he said out loud as he began to decelerate, falling back toward the semi.

Jacobs glanced at his cell as he pulled it away from his ear. There was no signal. The hair began to bristle on the back of his neck. He was too far ahead of the semi and cursed himself for not paying attention. As Jackson engaged in the second bout with the SUV behind him, Jacobs realized that there was no longer a rear escort. He yanked his pistol from its holster and hit the brakes hard. Jacobs decelerated, dropping back in front of Jackson's rig that was still moving at full speed.

Paul Jackson waved for him to move out of his way and blared the horn. The State Trooper moved to the right narrowly escaping contact with the tractor. Jackson tensed for an impact that didn't come and flew past the cruiser as the SUV recovered and continued pursuit.

Paul tried again to reach Ramsey, but got no answer on the truck's radio. He picked up the two-way and called back to the EOD team. "Wright, can you get anybody on your radio? I can't get shit!" Jackson yelled into his handset.

Wright called back, "It's the DUKE. We can't broadcast out. Just our local frequency, our network."

Jackson's foot was shaking on the accelerator as he gained speed in an effort to put as much distance between him and the SUV as possible. "Well, can you turn it off so I can get through to Ramsey and the others?"

Wright looked at Captain Wagner who shook his head no. "What if the guy has a detonator? We don't know that it's defeated yet," Wagner said as he worked to drill through the case.

Jackson's two-way crackled, "Can't do it. The guy could set off the bomb. Just hope that those cops managed to call it in and keep moving to get us to the Air Base."

The State Patrol car and the SUV were visible in Jackson's rear view mirror. The SUV slammed into the cruiser pushing it to the right, then the cruiser paid back in kind. A fierce battle raged behind him as both vehicles became smaller before dropping from his sight.

Jackson concentrated on the road ahead. A sign for the Air Base told him he was about eight miles away. If he maintained his present speed he would be there in five or six minutes. An eternity, he thought.

Captain Wagner drilled through the case of the transmission and inserted a halogen detector that would read for contaminates. The reading was nominal. "Looks good. Let's get this thing opened up."

He adapted the drill for removing bolts and set about disassembling the front of the transmission, removing the torque converter retainer and sliding the converter out of the front pump. He then began the task of removing the sixteen bolts that held the pump in place.

Jackson braced himself for another round with the SUV. The truck was heading his direction and he could only guess the status of the State Trooper. He grabbed the walkie-talkie, "You guys better hold on. Crazy Man is back!"

Ninety-five seemed to be the max for the Volvo tractor pulling a load even on flat ground and at the moment they were ascending a slight grade. Paul pulled his nine-millimeter up and removed the safety as he watched the SUV close in.

Mahmud-Hasan pulled to the back of the semi and closed the gap between them. Jackson could no longer see the truck. He wanted the truck to pull up next to him, as that would be his only way to get a shot. As if the driver of the SUV heard his thoughts, he suddenly appeared in Jackson's left mirror and moved quickly up the side of the trailer. Mahmud was intent on stopping Jackson and began firing at the trailer's tires.

Jackson cursed as the front left trailer tire exploded from the impact of the AK-47 rounds. The truck swerved and leaned to the left. The shredded tire's tread tore away from the wheel and slapped the underside of the trailer before flinging outward onto the pavement. Another tire blew out, but was still on the rim, wobbling and flapping like a worn flag in the wind. The trailer shook violently, smoking as the tire disintegrated from the high speed and the friction from rubbing against the inner tire.

Gordon saw a large crate sliding toward the bomb and threw himself between it and the transmission. Captain Wright was already moving another crate out of his way when Gordon leapt over them both to stop the shifting load. The weight of the box was too heavy to stop and Gordon took the load full to the chest ending up pinned between it and another large box. The pain was incredible, and he suddenly found he was unable to breathe.

Wright and Wagner heard Gordon's ribs snap and knew he was in trouble. They jumped up and began pushing the crate back the direction from which it had come. Gordon fell to the floor gasping for air. Captain Wagner pulled him out of the way of the crates and leaned him against the side of the truck.

"Don't mess with me. Do what you were doing. I'll be alright." Gordon had to force the words out in gasping breaths. He leaned back against the wall and closed his eyes. He would be no more help to them.

Wagner removed the last of the bolts and removed the pump. There were no other transmission components inside. The only thing in the case was the bomb. He was removing the brackets that fastened it to the case when the trailer suddenly leaned hard to the left. Captain Wright fell back as the large crate he was trying to secure suddenly slid back against the far wall of the trailer.

Jackson was too busy trying to evade the SUV to notice that the exit to the Air Base was just seconds away. At the last moment he threw the truck to the right, nearly slamming the guardrail, maneuvering onto the exit. Weakened from the friction and heat from the destroyed outer tire, the trailing inner dual tire exploded as the weight of the trailer suddenly shifted.

Mahmud had to react quickly to avoid the trailer that was listing heavily to the left. He accelerated hard to get out from under the trailer in case it rolled over.

Jackson saw sparks from the bare steel rim as it made contact with the concrete curbing of the exit. He thought for sure he was going to loose the trailer. The exit narrowed and then suddenly straightened. The weight of the trailer shifted back toward center and settled on the remaining tire.

As Paul fought to gain control Mahmud Hassan sped past him. Jackson watched as the terrorist slid to a stop about a mile ahead of him. Mahmud Hassan stopped the vehicle, blocking both lanes of the two lane rural highway.

Mahmud got out of the truck and raised his AK-47. He was out of breath and out of time. He began firing wildly in Jackson's direction, correcting his aim as the rounds sparked and ricocheted off the bent and twisted steel of the truck's front bumper.

Jackson heard the rounds buzzing and whistling as they careened off steel. The sound changed as Mahmud corrected his aim, walking the rounds up the front of the truck, through the glass of the headlights, the radiator, and then the windshield. Jackson instinctively ducked down as the rounds slammed into the front of the truck.

Jackson knew he could not stop. He downshifted and glanced above the dash to see the terrorist struggling to reload. Jackson slammed the accelerator down, aiming his truck directly at the terrorist. One way or another, he was going to kill the bastard who was shooting at him.

Mahmud locked in the magazine and raised his weapon. He could now see the black man whose eyes were wide with intent and anger. Jackson had his pistol raised trying to aim. The first round jumped from the muzzle of his nine-millimeter as Mahmud squeezed the trigger of his own weapon, sending more rounds from his assault rifle rocketing in Jackson's direction.

Jackson saw the flash from the muzzle and fired as many rounds as he had remaining in his own magazine, blasting a huge hole in the tempered safety glass of his windshield.

Mahmud lunged to the right to avoid both the bullets and the oncoming truck, but something else caught his eye. He recognized it as the trail of vapor and smoke from an incoming missile. There was not enough time to pray to his God before the air to surface missile from Dan Isom's F-22 Raptor honed in on its target.

The SUV exploded in a brilliant white ball of flame that engulfed Mahmud. Jackson flinched, raising his right arm instinctively to shield his face. The last round from Mahmud's AK crashed through the truck's already fractured windshield and slammed into Jackson's chest just under his arm. The round tore through skin and muscle, glanced off ribs, and peeled his skin open. Jackson felt the sudden searing pain, but at that moment was only concentrating on what was happening ahead of him.

Jackson turned, trying to avoid the burning wreckage, but the Volvo careened forward, slamming into the flaming, not yet dead, Mahmud, and into the right rear side of the burning Trailblazer. Jackson pushed forward until the hulk of the destroyed vehicle was forced to one side. What was left of the burning truck scraped and banged down the side of the tractor, glancing off the support legs and rear tires of the trailer, to burn on the roadway with the mangled, burning body of the last remaining terrorist laying motionless next to it.

As the path ahead of him cleared, Jackson saw the first of the two F-22's flying low overhead. He considered himself lucky. He was bleeding...but alive, the terrorist was dead, and they still had an hour or better before the bomb was supposed to detonate. For the moment life was good.

The tractor shuddered and jerked as the loss of coolant from the destroyed radiator caused the engine to overheat. The semi had been through hell. Jackson backed off the accelerator dropping his speed by more than half as the engine and transmission protested the loss of oil, coolant and transmission fluid. Jackson began to wonder if the Volvo could hold together the quarter of a mile or so to the gates of the air base. He could see emergency vehicles heading his direction as he chugged over the last hill between him and Scott.

Jackson picked up the walkie-talkie and spoke to the EOD team. "Ok fellas, a lot has just happened. As long as the tires hold out, the engine continues to run and we don't run completely out of transmission fluid, we should be on the airfield in about ten minutes. Other than that, the rest of the ride should be smooth sailing. You having any luck back there?"

Captain Wright was sitting near Master Sergeant Gordon when Jackson's voice came over the handheld. "What's the immediate situation?"

"No more bad guys, if that's what you mean," Jackson replied.

"We need to call ahead for an ambulance for Gordon. I think he's got a few broken ribs and is having difficulty breathing. We're going to shut down the DUKE so we can transmit out. We still have to figure out the internal timer and shut it down, but the remotes are all disabled."

With that Captain Wright reached over to the man-pack that Gordon was wearing and switched off the system. Immediately Jackson's phone rattled to life in his pocket. Jackson dropped the two-way to pick up the call from Ramsey.

"Hey, Mr. Ramsey. Glad to hear your voice again." Ramsey would never know exactly how much. "We sure could have used a little of your help a while ago."

Ramsey was relieved to hear Jackson's voice. "We got the report from the pilots. They're circling like vultures waiting for final orders. How are you doing?"

"Me personally or the bomb?"

Ramsey loved the way Paul made everything about him. "The bomb, then you."

"Well, from what I understand they have one more thing to do before it's totally disabled. But you can ask them yourself in a couple minutes. Now, about me, you guys have an ambulance there?"

"Yes, you hurt?" Ramsey asked, sounding worried.

"Yeah, not too bad though, just about a half a quart low on blood," he laughed. "Seriously, I been hit, but that big ass Master Sergeant in the trailer is hurt pretty bad they said. Not sure what's wrong."

Ramsey looked around the mobile command post and heard someone say the words "ambulance" and "doctor". "I believe they know about the status of their guy. He'll be taken care of. Just get here. We have orders to move out in a half hour if they can't shut that thing down. We'll put the bomb on the runway and let the pilots do their thing. We've got aircraft on standby to get us out of here."

"Holy Shit! That doesn't give them much time!" Jackson was following the Base Police to the Air Force runway. They made the final turn past a hanger and headed toward the command post. The post, a series of tents and expandable trailers was in the middle of the airstrip. A trail of orange warning cones was set up a few hundred yards away. Jackson figured that was his spot.

"I guess you want me to parallel park this thing. Don't knock off any points if I run one of the cones over." With that Jackson steered the truck so it would run right along the line of bright orange markers, flattening most of the traffic cones.

Alan watched the truck pull to a stop. "Very nice, Paul. You didn't even miss one."

The vehicle was beat to hell. The last tire on the left side of the trailer was nearly flat under its weight. A team ran to the back of the truck and an ambulance backed up to the door.

Ramsey ran to the driver's door as Jackson opened it to step down. He was a bit woozy from the loss of blood and nearly lost his footing.

"You look like crap," Ramsey offered. He tried to raise Paul Jackson's arm to look at the wound.

Jackson pulled his arm in tight. "Are you a doctor? No, I don't think so." With that he collapsed to the surface of the runway.

"Medic! This man's been shot. Right side!"

The medic stared into the cab saw the blood on the floor and headliner of the Volvo tractor and assumed it was all Jackson's. "Damn! How's he still alive?" He yelled back to the ambulance where Gordon was already being loaded. "Marty, bring a gurney and some plasma!"

His partner rushed over with the requested items and the two EMTs and Ramsey lifted Jackson to the gurney. The technician began probing for a vein to insert the I.V.

Ramsey saw that Jackson was still conscious. "I'm getting you out of here, Paul."

Jackson didn't like the idea of getting this far and then not being present for the conclusion. "But that's like leaving before the movie's over."

Alan liked that Jackson could hold onto his sense of humor no matter what. "You've done your part Paul, more than enough for a first mission. Let me get you home before you hurt yourself some more."

Jackson held out his right hand and grimaced in pain. "It's been a pleasure working with you, Mr. Ramsey," he said, smiling his toothy grin.

Ramsey took his hand and shook it. "The name's Alan. Mr. Ramsey is my dad."

The technicians slid the gurney up into the deck of the ambulance and secured it there before closing the door. Ramsey turned to head over to where the EOD teams were working, but stopped when he heard Jackson call to him. The ambulance attendant had the door open again and Paul Jackson was looking out over his own feet.

"Don't forget my overtime, Mr. Ramsey. Gotta get that O.T. Makes the little lady happy, remember." He leaned back as the medic closed the door. Ramsey could see the man smiling to himself through the door window after once again having gotten the last word.

Ramsey turned his attention back to the bomb and looked at his watch. Twenty minutes before the evacuation. He ran to the back of the trailer where a forklift was extracting the load trying to gain access to the pallet with the bomb and the two EOD Captains. Ramsey stopped the forklift operator long enough to use the forks and the load on them as a means to get into the trailer.

At the front the two men were leaning over the device. Extracted from the transmission case it now perched on top of one of the crates. Ramsey appeared in front of Wright and Wagner. Wright's brow was dripping with sweat. Wagner had removed his ACU shirt and was soaked from the neck down.

Wright looked up. "This one is tough. It's pretty damned tamper proof."

Wagner suddenly spoke up, "He means booby-trapped."

"Can you stop it?" Ramsey asked.

Wagner wiped the sweat from his nose and upper lip.

"I just have to get past this circuit. If I clip it, looks like the controller will recognize the loss of the reference voltage, about five volts DC, and go into default. We just don't know what default is. Could be that it will disarm or that it will start the countdown over or that it will detonate."

Wright looked up at Ramsey again. "Not one of the wires you want to just cut and hope for the best."

Ramsey simply stared, noticing for the first time the L.E.D counter that was attached to the circuitry. It was taped over with masking tape so that the numbers could not be seen. He could tell the numbers were changing based on the glow under the tape, but the digits were not recognizable. Wagner noticed the quizzical look on his face.

"I taped it up. Nothing more aggravating than watching a countdown timer tick away the seconds while you're trying to disarm a nuclear bomb."

Ramsey shuffled his feet a bit. "Yeah, I hate it when that happens," he said sarcastically.

Wright looked at Ramsey. "Why are you still hanging around? You need to get out of here. We got this."

"Can't leave before the show's over. I might miss something," Ramsey countered.

"Trust me, you'll know the outcome one way or the other." Wright stood. "Seriously, there's no reason for you to be here. We'll deal with this. Go on, get outa here while you can."

"I know I don't have to say this, but be careful. If you can't kill it in twenty minutes kick it out onto the runway. The F22s will give you enough time to fly out. Let them handle it."

Wright looked back at him. "You don't have to worry, Sir. He may have taped up the timer, but I do wear a watch. Now, go." Wright pointed to the raised door of the trailer.

Ramsey hesitantly turned and walked toward the back of the trailer when he heard Captain Wagner's voice.

"You don't happen to know how to read Arabic, do you?" Wagner pulled the circuit board up and flipped it over. He held the board for the other Captain to see. "I believe they wrote the names of the circuits on here." Wagner was talking to Captain Wright, but Ramsey couldn't help but overhear.

Ramsey stopped short of the door and turned back. He could see the scribble from where he was standing. He walked back to the two soldiers.

Wright looked up. "I thought you were leaving."

"Does either of you know how to read that?" Ramsey pointed at the board.

Wagner spoke next, "There are no pictures, so I'm out."

Wright followed, "That makes two of us. Gordon was our linguist, but he's gone. You wouldn't have an Arabic dictionary with you, would you?" he asked jokingly.

"Actually I do." The answer surprised Captain Wright. Ramsey continued, "But it's right up here," he said, pointing to his temple and kneeling down between the two.

Wagner didn't waste any time. "Look for the word "power" or something."

Ramsey scanned the symbols from right to left. "Stop me if you hear something you like." He began reading the words out loud. "Timer marker, switch...or solenoid A, timer marker...switch B, external controller, reaction mixer..."

Wagner suddenly spoke up, "Wait! Which circuit is that one, the reaction mixer?"

Ramsey pointed to the board. Captain Wagner traced the circuit board electronics as if he were following a trail. The row of components ended at a solder joint at the far end of the board where a group of wires led from the board along a series of plastic tubes and disappeared behind a junction box cover. Wagner removed the screws that held the protective cover on the box then removed foam padding that was secured with duct tape. Captain Wright looked at the glass vials and the solenoid that was now exposed. "Shit, yeah! Jackpot!"

Ramsey watched as the two EOD specialists carefully separated the components. Captain Wagner probed further inside the case with a long pair of needle nose pliers to remove a small clear tube from a point beyond the box. He repositioned the tube and let it hang outside of the case. He then inspected the wiring closely and followed it to a small automotive type electronic solenoid. He cut four of the wires and carefully lifted the solenoid away and dropped it onto the top of the makeshift workbench.

Captain Wright probed through the remaining components as if he were looking through a filing cabinet. He rattled off a few words, reciting some learned set of EOD rules of disarmament techniques.

"That should do it," he stated somewhat nonchalantly. "We need to get a containment unit in here to box this up and get it to the Los Alamos labs, where it can be fully disassembled and studied for component origin and such."

Ramsey looked at the men incredulously. "That's it? It's disarmed?"

Wagner was packing up the equipment, but stopped when Ramsey spoke. "Yeah, pretty non-dramatic wasn't it? They can't all be like in the movies."

Derrick Wright added, "What we need is a foreboding soundtrack to spruce it up a little. You know, make it a little more exciting."

"So you're sure it's disarmed?" Ramsey looked over the few parts that had been removed.

Captain Wagner lifted the plastic tubing and waved it around for Ramsey's benefit. "Really, it was dead when I pulled the mixing tube. That would have fed one of the two ignition chemicals to a mixing chamber inside the device. No chemicals, no chemical reaction to set off the bomb." He let the hose fall back against the bomb, then picked up the solenoid. "I pulled this just to be on the safe side."

Ramsey looked at the tape-covered timer that continued to count down. "So that doesn't mean anything?" he asked.

Wagner looked at the timer readout, reached over with a pair of wire cutters and snipped the wires. The L.E.D display went dark behind the masking tape. "Feel better now?"

"Much better," Alan said as he pulled out his phone. Gabe Anderson picked up on the first ring.

"Alan, how's it going?"

Ramsey looked back at the bomb and the two men who were about leaving the truck. "It's over, Sir. The bomb has been disarmed. The EOD guys are ordering a container to ship it out of here."

Ramsey could hear the F-22 again as it flew over. He looked at his watch. Two minutes to go, he thought. "You can have them recall the missile strike and get the jets out of here. They are making me really nervous."

"Tell me you're not still on site," Anderson ordered.

"Can't do that, Sir or I'd be lying," Ramsey replied. "Jackson is out, though. We sent him to the hospital. He should be fine, but he did take a bullet to the chest."

Gabe Anderson thought about that. "Great, I guess I'll have to backdate his paperwork to make his employment with us permanent as of a few days ago just to cover my ass. Tell him congratulations for me. He has just been accepted for full time duty with the CIA."

Epilogue

Moscow, Three Months Later

RAMSEY scanned the array of flat-screen monitors that lined the wall of the temporary operations center, tapping impatiently on one of them. "Rick, why don't I have a video feed from inside the restaurant?"

"Working on it, sir. It's not at this end. Something's wrong with the equipment there. I don't get it, I verified all the connections. I guess we could have a bad cable." He moved to the control panel and switched feed cables then threw a couple switches. The center video monitor suddenly flickered to life. Ramsey looked at his monitor and could see their subject. He spoke into his headset, "Vee, you and Marks getting this?"

Approximately one half kilometer away in a hotel room overlooking the Merinsk Street Café, Agents Villacruze and Marks had set up shop. Vee put down his binoculars, glanced at the satellite-fed monitors placed around the room then keyed his headset. "Got it, Sir. That would be General Dmitri Gregorov. Looks like he's got his usual entourage of Russian Special Service or prior KGB operative bodyguards with him." Vee, still new to the CIA's T2T, used every opportunity to show off his skills.

Marks moved the joystick left to pan through the restaurant. It was dark in the corner where Gregorov liked to sit, but thanks to the technological advances of the new equipment it looked as if he were in bright daylight. Marks suddenly stopped the camera settling on the figure of Nikki Sidorova. "There's our girl."

Ramsey leaned back a bit, looking at the Nikki. "Ok, in case you all haven't bothered to read the information that was dug up on her, here is a bit of info." Ramsey read from the report generated by his page at Langley and sent securely to his tablet.

"Nikki Sidorova, Bosnian born multi-geographical operative. Muslim, Sunni most probably based on the region. She is 33 years old, has been involved with many different groups within the Russian Mafia Syndicate and, we believe, early on, the Muslim Brotherhood, since she was seventeen or eighteen. We're still putting a file together on her, but most recently she has been involved with Dmitri Gregorov. She tends to follow the person with the most power. You can bet if she is involved, there is a major player involved."

Agent Villacruze suddenly spoke up, interrupting Ramsey's report, "Heads up, folks, the doctor is in the house."

The monitor showed the image of Dr. Metelov making his way toward the entrance of the restaurant. The man looked nervously towards the building that housed the agents. "Damn, man, don't be looking around like that," Vee said to no one in particular.

Ramsey watched the feed and reiterated the goals for the mission. "Alright guys, here's the deal. When Metelov engages with Gregorov make sure that you are getting the audio. Metelov will be talking about any new jobs that require his expertise as a bomb builder. Stay awake. We need something to hang Dmitri, but more importantly listen for anything that could indicate any upcoming events. Dr. Metelov is putting a lot on the line to help us with this."

The video feed switched to a different viewing angle as Metelov walked through the restaurant and then stopped in front of Dmitri Gregorov's table. Nikki moved around the man and yanked off his jacket searching for any sign of a wire or weapon, found his Motorola phone, opened it and saw that it was not powered on. She removed the battery case cover and removed the battery. Satisfied that it was not bugged she tossed the phone in its disassembled condition onto the table.

"We lost Metelov's microphone. She yanked the battery," Rick White said over his coms set. "I still got her phone though, and the restaurant bugs."

One of the bodyguards stepped in and frisked Metelov. He was about to pronounce him "clean" when the doctor offered the info himself. "I am not armed, I assure you."

He turned his attention fully to Gregorov. "Hello, Dmitri. How have you been?"

Dmitri Gregorov smiled and gestured for the doctor to sit. "Please, have a seat. We have much to talk about. How is your family? Are they enjoying your newfound wealth?" Gregorov lit a cigarette and inhaled deeply. "I am concerned that one day they will say something about what happened. What do you think Doctor? Am I worried for no reason?"

Nikki moved around the table to sit next to Gregorov and directly across from the physicist. She placed her weapon on the table and played with it, spinning it slowly and eyeing up Metelov.

Metelov found himself staring at the woman. She looked familiar and he wondered had he ever met her before. He shook away his thoughts and returned his gaze to Dmitri, concentrating instead on what Dmitri had just said. Metelov thought it ironic that

Gregorov would express his concern for his family's disloyalty when in fact he was the one helping the Americans with their investigation. Though, again, he did not have a choice. Spending life in a Russian prison was not an option for him. He would not be able to survive there. No, his only choice was to help the Russian Investigators. He was to work with the Americans under the supervision of the Russians to help implicate Dmitry or be tried for treason.

"You do not have to worry. They still believe that they were abducted and held for ransom. My wife does not know about the money yet. She thinks that I had to pay to free them. I am a modest man and my wife a modest woman. She does not need more than the love of her family to be happy."

Gregorov leaned against the back of his booth, smiling. "Ah, a love story. I think I feel a tear welling up." He laughed heartily at his own joke, striking the table with his hand and then became serious again. "Speaking of money, Doctor, you are aware that your friend, Ahmed, stole from me? He did not pay me the final payment of one million dollars. That was the deal I made with his boss, Leaja, you know. One million after delivery."

Metelov wondered where the conversation was going. "Zuqawri was not a friend. He was a kidnapper and a murderer. Besides, it is of no matter now that he is dead, I would imagine."

Dmitri took another long draw on his smoke. "After he was captured I sent a...liaison to meet with Leaja to discuss the matter. They never got to meet with him. Ahmed's murderous Muslim Brotherhood killed all but one of my men."

He downed the last of his drink, set the glass down on the table, and gave it a spin. He waited for the glass to settle before continuing, "I tried to negotiate with them and all I got was their treachery. They stabbed me in the back." Gregorov smacked his left palm with the side of his fist as if he were plunging an imaginary knife through it. "Therefore, I was determined for them to fail, so I gave the Americans a little push in the right direction."

The doctor looked inquisitively at Gregorov. "Then it was you who led them to the warehouse?"

Gregorov moved the meeting along, "Why are you here, Doctor? Why did you arrange this meeting? Is one and a half million American dollars not enough money for you to live your...modest life?" He smashed out his cigarette as if punctuating his sentence.

Metelov answered without hesitation, "On the contrary. I was paid more than agreed. I feel that my obligation for the money is not settled. I come to you to offer my services."

Agent Marks was checking the audio feed on the external camera when he noticed the first of the two black UAZ Hunter S.U.Vs pull down the street. "Heads up. We got company. Looks like two RSS vehicles heading this way."

Ramsey turned to face the three Russian Security Service agents in the room. "What's going on here? This is our investigation. You gave us full authority to run this operation and capture Gregorov, if possible."

"I assure you we do not know anything about this." The Russian pulled out his cell phone to make a call to his superior when Marks came back on the speaker.

"Look at your monitors, folks. There's some bad shit going down here."

Both vehicles were stopped and two groups of masked Russian Special Service Police formed up at the curb and entered the building.

Nikki was the first to react. She pulled up her weapon pointing it in the direction of the intruders. Then suddenly, she turned and shot both of Dmitri's bodyguards before they could pull out their own weapons.

Dr. Metelov jumped up and began to plead, "Please do not kill me. I am not one of his men. I am only here because I am working

371

with the police and the Americans!"

Nikki stepped from behind the table staring at Dmitri as she made her way to the doctor. She held her finger to his lips and told him to be quiet. Metelov dropped his arms down to his sides and stood, shaking.

Nikki suddenly stepped up to him and placed her pistol on his forehead. Metelov closed his eyes tightly and cringed.

"Are you afraid, Doctor? Is that why you help the Americans? Because, you are afraid of what they might find out about you...Jovan Kovicevic?"

Metelov opened one eye slightly. He glanced at Gregorov and back at Nikki. "I don't know what you are talking about," he stammered in a low voice.

Nikki hit him hard with the pistol causing him to fall to his knees. "You are Dr. Jovan Kovicevic. You are from Bosnia and you are a traitor to the Muslim people," Nikki yelled at him as she walked around his kneeling figure.

"I am Vladimir Metelov. I don't know what you are talking about." Metelov would not look up for fear of being struck again.

Nikki screamed at him, "You are a traitor and a murderer!" She reached in her jacket pocket, removed some photos and tossed them down on the floor in front of Metelov. One of the photos showed at least a hundred lifeless bodies or more correctly, pieces of bodies, laid out on tarps next to one another, excavated from a mass grave near the town of Srebrenica. Others showed rows of green fabric-covered coffins on a hillside, each waiting next to a freshly dug grave.

Metelov recognized the subjects in the photos as the remains of some of the eight thousand men and boys killed by General Ratko Mladic's Serbian army, remains that had been identified recently, making national headlines. He began to sob uncontrollably.

"Yes, Yes. I am Jovan Kovicevic," he said through his sobbing. "Mladic's men forced me to help them. I had access to the names and birth records of all of Srebrenica." He looked up at Nikki, tears welling in his eyes. He wiped away his tears and glared at her. "I recognize you now. You were there, at the busses, before the massacre, when the Serbian soldiers came to take the Muslims away."

He suddenly remembered the moment he told the Serb officer the true age of Nikki's brother. She had lied to them to get him on the bus with her, the bus reserved for the women and children. He could see the image of Nikki screaming at the Serbian soldiers to let go of her brother as they pulled him from her grasp and pushed her aside. Now, he stood in front of her once again. He had to make her understand. "They were going to kill me if I didn't help them."

"You sold out your own people. My father and my brother were taken from me. For fifteen years I waited for word that they had been found alive, then, as the years passed, I hoped only that their bodies might be found at last."

Nikki picked up the photos and looked at the rows of coffins. "Five hundred more bodies were recovered. The last of over seven thousand that were tortured and murdered, identified and laid to rest on that hillside. And now, they have stopped looking for any more. My father's own countrymen, the government that he stood with to help secure the freedom of the people of Bosnia, have stopped searching. And still, they have not found my father or my brother."

In the apartment, a half a kilometer away, the Russian agents were screaming into their headsets that something had gone wrong. Ramsey was asking for information, but the Russians ignored him as they walked out into the hallway.

Nikki stood over the man, contemplating the photos in her hand. She took a deep breath and shoved the pictures back into her pocket. "But now, Jovan Kovicevic, I have found you." Without hesitating further, she pulled the trigger, sending the man backward to the floor.

Everyone in both apartments stopped when the sound of the gunshot punctured the tense atmosphere. Villacruze's voice came over the speakers next, "Metelov is down. He's been shot."

Ramsey turned to face the lead agent. "What the hell are you waiting for? Get your men down there and stop her before she kills Gregorov."

The Russian looked stunned. "We have people on the way."

Ramsey wanted to go to the inn and capture Nikki and Gregorov, but he had no jurisdiction, no weapons and no vehicle to get there. He was fuming over losing Metelov.

"You've got three men right there. He motioned beyond the closed door into the hallway. You could walk there faster than your response team can be on site!"

He threw up his hands in exasperation. There was nothing he could do. Next time, he thought, their operation would be secret. No approval and just Americans.

Gregorov stared at Nikki not believing what he'd just witnessed, then raised his hands and stood at the table. He turned toward Nikki. "What is going on here?"

The sounds of emergency vehicles and the wail of police sirens could be heard in the distance. Nikki Sidorova studied the man in front of her before speaking, "How is it that you know Jovan Kovicevic, eh, Dmitri?" Nikki walked around the table closer to Gregorov.

"I only know of him because of Zuqawri." Gregorov waved his hand through the air dismissively. "Ahmed needed someone who had knowledge of our warheads. I am a businessman. I get people what they need."

Nikki motioned for two of her masked accomplices to move forward. They grabbed Gregorov and forced him to sit. Nikki moved to the corner of the table to retrieve Dmitri's satchel. She pulled his laptop from the bag and set it in front of her. Nikki looked upward with a feigned look of contemplation. "Now, let me see, what was that password?" After a few keystrokes she turned it to face him. Dmitri displayed a genuine look of surprise at her ability to defeat his password security.

"I want you to see something, Dmitri. Look at your account information. What do you see?"

Gregorov saw that he had no money in his safe account. He touched his fingers to the touchpad and scrolled through the document. Millions of dollars were gone.

"You whore bitch. You stole my money."

Nikki leaned across the desk, closed the laptop and then slid it to the side. "Money that you earned selling the rifles and the bullets to General Mladic for his assault on Srebrenica." She began to walk toward him, "Money that you earned by becoming partners to a war criminal and kissing the ass of Slobodan Milosevic!"

"I do not know what you are talking about," Dmitri lied, regretting that he did not have a sidearm.

Nikki stepped forward and shoved the pistol against Gregorov's forehead. "You do not remember the chants of the Serb Nationalist? Slobo, Slobo, Slobo! You were there, Dmitri, chanting with them all, thinking about how rich you would become selling the weapons of the defunct Soviet Union to a mob of Christian madmen."

Gregorov winced from the pressure of the steel barrel against his skin. "General Mladic killed those people. He was to blame and was hung for it."

"Wrong, Dmitri. Mladic is still a fugitive. He has never paid for his crimes. The Americans had him, but let him go. You know where he is, don't you, Dmitri?"

Gregorov was sweating now. He pulled a cigarette from his pack and lit it, inhaling deeply and exhaled quickly.

"I have not seen him in years. I have no clue as to his whereabouts." Gregorov leaned his head to the side and waved his cigarette around as he spoke as if to dismiss the whole idea. He looked over his glasses, scowling at Nikki.

"Now, take the money you stole from me and leave...consider it...reparation."

Nikki pushed hard on the pistol. "Where is Mladic? Tell me!"

The sirens were very close. The taller of the two men holding Dmitri spoke, "We must hurry. Let's go."

Dmitri recognized the voice and turned suddenly to look into the eyes of the man wearing the mask. He noted the fear, the flitting back and forth of the eyes recessed within the opening of the knitted fabric. He smiled nervously as he motioned towards Nikki with a sideways nod of his head, then turned back to face her.

"You must keep your eye on this one, Anatoly. She is a pathetic bitch and will surely throw you to the wolves when it benefits her."

With that Nikki Sidorova fired the shot to end Dmitri's life. She cursed for not getting the information she wanted and then yelled for her people to move. Anatoly hesitated, stunned by what he had just witnessed.

Nikki pushed him toward the door with the side of her pistol. "Move!" she yelled as she followed them out the door to the awaiting vehicles.

The sound of screeching tires and gunned engines filled Ramsey's headset. He pulled off his headphones. "Get that feed cleaned up! I want to know what just happened there."

Agent Villacruze was calling, "We need the Ruskies to get someone on their asses! We need to stop them! They are heading toward the city."

The three Russian agents were also trying to figure out what had just happened. Ramsey was furious.

"We must go now," one of the Russians stated. "I will contact you with any information about what has happened here." He started out of the apartment when Ramsey stepped in front of him. "Hold on a second. Who the hell is Mladic? What was Nikki talking about?"

The Russian rolled his eyes and sighed as if it was hard to muster an answer. "General Ratko Mladic was a Serbian General in charge of Slobodan Milosevic's Serbian forces. The Bosnians believe he is responsible for the genocidal attacks on the Bosnian Muslims, and the destruction of nearly all of Bosnia."

Ramsey knew little of the Balkan wars or the American efforts to end them. He only knew it had been a mess of failed diplomacy. He guessed that he would be getting a crash course on the topic.

The Agent turned toward the door. "We will contact you with any information that arises from this. Meanwhile, you may want to look to your own government for some answers." With that he turned on his heel and left.

Ramsey picked up a microphone and keyed the transmit button. "Vee, Marks, shut it down. There's nothing more we can do. No Gregorov, no weapons. At least not for now."

The sounds of emergency vehicles filled the streets below Vee and Mark's position in the hotel. The two agents packed up their gear as the Russian police moved into the building across the street to assess the situation.

Ramsey looked around the room. "Let's pack it up and get it back home so we can scrub through the audio and video. Paul, we need to get some flights arranged. Looks like we got our work cut out for us when we get back home."

"You got it," Jackson said as he stacked one of the components on a two-wheeled cart. "I know one thing," he began as he removed his phone from his pocket to call the international ticketing agent. "I sure as hell wouldn't want to be anybody that had anything to do with that whole Bosnian shit. That woman is on a mission."

Ramsey was still going over what had transpired not ten minutes before.

"That's what worries me. That she *is* on a mission."

He looked at his watch noting the time and did the math to figure what time he might be back home.

"I hope you can sleep on a plane, because in about fifteen hours we're going to be back in full swing trying to determine what role our government had in Bosnia and whether or not we should be worried about Nikki Sidorova."

OTHER BOOKS BY KENNETH WASH

FLAGS OF VENGEANCE
SECRETS OF STATE

IN Washington, D.C. the curtain surrounding a decades-old conspiracy begins to unravel revealing information regarding a failed multi-national political plot: an attempt to topple Serbian President Slobodan Milosevic, from power and end the war in Bosnia. The U.S. brokered mission backfires, allowing Milosevic's bloodthirsty generals to advance his genocidal plans.

Code-named Directive Seven, the plan produces deadly results: the killing and disappearance of over eight thousand Muslim men and boys during the final months of the Bosnian conflict and a cover-up of the locations of mass graves scattered across the country.

Bosnian-born Nikki Sidorova, a sexy and deadly operative for a post Soviet arms dealer, is on a mission to hunt down those responsible for the atrocities known as the Srebrenica Massacre when she stumbles across information that leads her on a quest across Europe in search of a cache of Soviet era weaponry and information regarding the whereabouts of her father and brother who were abducted by Serbian forces during the conflict.

Alan Ramsey and his team have to stop Sidorova before she finds the weapons and discovers that America's involvement may have only placed more Bosnian lives in jeopardy, but Ramsey's investigation six thousand miles away uncovers more U.S. political secrets, placing Ramsey in a position that could affect the balance of power in America and make him and his team targets.

ABOUT THE AUTHOR

KEN WASH lives in St. Louis, Mo. He is an Army Reserve soldier who has served over 32 years in Active Army and Army Reserve enjoying a career in the Ordnance branch as a 915E Senior Automotive Technician, having attained the rank of Chief Warrant Officer Five.

Mr. Wash has worked in the civilian automotive repair industry for over 25 years as an ASE Certified Master Technician, publishing numerous technical investigative reports as a professional technical writer, subject matter expert and mechanical claims witness for major insurance companies in the areas of automotive forensic investigations of fraud and theft.

Mr. Wash has been writing as a hobby on and off for about fifteen years. He has written several short stories, edited and produced documents for military publications and directed, produced and edited military videos and keynote presentations for high visibility military staff functions.

WASHBOARD PRODUCTIONS

Copyright © 2010 Kenneth Wash

www.ingramcontent.com/pod-product-compliance
Lightning Source LLC
Chambersburg PA
CBHW061922170626
46813CB00006B/2270